Praise for Ben Bova

"Fast and exciting and keeps you turning pages all the way. Mysterious and awe-inspiring."

—*Science Fiction Review* on *Voyagers*

"The alien within Stoner serves Bova as a splendid device. . . . The very best, however, is the plausibility of detail that makes his work a sort of poetry of the near future."

—*Chicago Tribune* on *Voyagers II: The Alien Within*

"Fast-paced action for fans of hard-core SF adventure."

—*Library Journal* on *Voyagers III: Star Brothers*

"Bova's excellence with combining science with believable characters and attention-grabbing plot makes him one of our most accessible and entertaining storytellers."

—*Library Journal*

TOR BOOKS BY BEN BOVA

Able One
The Aftermath
As on a Darkling Plain
The Astral Mirror
Battle Station
The Best of the Nebulas (editor)
Challenges
City of Darkness
Colony
Cyberbooks
Empire Builders
Escape Plus
The Green Trap
Gremlins Go Home (with Gordon R. Dickson)
The Hittite
The Immortality Factor
Jupiter
The Kinsman Saga
Mars Life
Mercury
The Multiple Man
Orion
Orion Among the Stars
Orion and the Conqueror
Orion in the Dying Time
Out of the Sun
The Peacekeepers
Powersat
The Precipice
Privateers
The Prometheans
The Rock Rats
The Sam Gunn Omnibus
Saturn
The Silent War
Star Peace: Assured Survival
The Starcrossed
Tales of the Grand Tour
Test of Fire
Titan
To Fear the Light (with A. J. Austin)
To Save the Sun (with A. J. Austin)
The Trikon Deception (with Bill Pogue)
Triumph
Vengeance of Orion
Venus
Voyagers
Voyagers II: The Alien Within
Voyagers III: Star Brothers
The Return: Book IV of Voyagers
The Winds of Altair

BOOK IV OF VOYAGERS

THE RETURN

BEN BOVA

A TOM DOHERTY ASSOCIATES BOOK • NEW YORK

This is a work of fiction. All of the characters, organizations, and events portrayed in this novel are either products of the author's imagination or are used fictitiously.

THE RETURN: BOOK IV OF VOYAGERS

A Tor Book
Published by Tom Doherty Associates, LLC
175 Fifth Avenue
New York, NY 10010

www.tor-forge.com

Tor® is a registered trademark of Tom Doherty Associates, LLC.

ISBN 978-0-7653-4815-9

First Edition: August 2009
First Mass Market Edition: August 2010

Printed in the United States of America

0 9 8 7 6 5 4 3 2 1

TO BARBARA,

who fell in love with Keith Stoner

Forget the myths you've heard about the White House. The truth is, they're not very bright guys.

Carl Bernstein and Bob Woodward
All the President's Men

THE RETURN

PROLOGUE

The starship had come from beyond the beyond, ending its pilgrimage through space and time back at the place where its journey had begun.

Keith Stoner came back to his home world, but it was not the Earth he had left. The coastlines were noticeably altered; the north polar sea was almost entirely clear of ice. It looked so tantalizingly similar, but it was a different world. Most disturbing of all, its history was subtly different.

Worse still, the people of Earth were ignoring him. Politicians, world leaders, even the scientists did not answer his greeting. He had known from the outset that he would have to approach them carefully, gently. He did not want to alarm them and rouse their deeply rooted xenophobic fears. But his messages were ignored. They were doing their best to pretend that he did not exist.

And there lay the danger. They were all in peril, both the star voyagers and all those who lived on the crowded, brawling surface of the planet.

Life itself was at stake. The brief candle was already flickering, failing.

Puzzled, frustrated, Stoner decided to try a different kind of message. They won't be able to ignore this, he thought. But he wondered if that would be right.

BOOK I

RAOUL TAVALERA

The greatest dangers to liberty lurk in insidious encroachment by men of zeal, well meaning but without understanding.

Louis D. Brandeis,
Olmstead v. United States,
1928

CHAPTER 1

"You've changed."

"*I've* changed?" Raoul Tavalera cast a surprised look at Evelyn Delmore, sitting on the sofa next to him.

The party had pretty much drifted away from the living room. The old-fashioned, overfurnished room was almost empty, except for a few of his mother's white-haired friends and Evelyn, who'd been at Tavalera's side since the instant the party started, just about.

His former neighbors and old schoolmates had gathered in his mother's house to celebrate his returning home after nearly six years in space. But it was a strangely quiet, subdued sort of party. Hardly any alcohol, for one thing. When Tavalera had asked for a drink his mother had handed him fruit punch. He had to get one of his old college buddies to spike his glass with a dollop of tequila. The guy poured the booze surreptitiously out of a pocket flask, eyeing the tiny red light of the security camera up in the corner of the ceiling.

And not all of his classmates and former buddies had shown up. When he asked where Vince Tiorlini was, Tavalera got shifty looks and embarrassed mumbles about work camps in the flooded Pacific Northwest. Zeke Berkowitz, too: re-education center for him. They said he'd be out in another few months, maybe. Even Ellen O'Reilly. Her flaming temper had gotten her sent away somewhere, nobody seemed to know where.

Six years, Tavalera thought. A lot had changed in six years. Or maybe, he thought, it's just that I'm looking at everything through different eyes, after being away for so long.

There had been dancing, of sorts. Very subdued shuffling around the floor of the dining room, which had been emptied of furniture for the evening. Dull, old-fashioned music from individual phones that each dancer clipped to his or her ear. So that the noise won't disturb any of the older people, Tavalera's mother had explained. He had tried to tune the phone to something livelier but got only a god-awful shriek in his ear; the phones were restricted to one single channel, bland and boring. Finally Tavalera had given up in numbed disgust and returned to the living room. That wasn't dancing, he told himself. He'd had more fun in kindergarten when the teachers made them all march in time to patriotic songs.

Looking around the hushed living room, Tavalera found that most of the partygoers his own age had crowded into the kitchen, but even there they were a pretty quiet crowd, he thought. He remembered impromptu parties aboard the *Goddard* habitat, all the way out by the planet Saturn, where'd he'd spent a couple of involuntary years and fallen in love. They were noisy, cheerful bashes, fueled by home-brewed booze everybody called rocket juice. People danced to music that made the walls vibrate, for crying out loud. This homecoming gig was more like a wake than a party.

I've known these people since I was a little kid, he mused. We all went to school together, right through college. But they're different now. Strangers. Maybe it *is* me, he repeated to himself. They haven't changed. I guess I have.

Tavalera was a compactly built middleweight, exactly

one hundred and eighty-two centimeters tall. He had a long-jawed, melancholy face with a set of teeth that made him look, he knew, like a caricature of a horse. Not handsome, but not entirely unattractive, either. Somber brown eyes, dark hair that he kept cropped short after years of living and working aboard spacecraft.

"Yes, you've changed," said Evelyn Delmore, peering nearsightedly at him as she sat beside him on the sofa. The crumbs of his homecoming cake were scattered over the big tray on the coffee table, the table itself, much of the floor, and Tavalera's travel-weary slacks. He realized how old-fashioned the living room was, with its fake fireplace, overstuffed furniture, and the wall-sized TV screen that was never off. There were only a few of the older neighbors in the living room now, all of them placidly watching the TV news.

The big wall screen over the mantlepiece was showing bulky, ungainly robotic soldiers clanking through some village in a jungle. Might's well be the same newscasts they were running before I left, Tavalera thought. The info bar running along the top of the screen read: **Medellín, Colombia.**

That red unblinking eye of the security camera bothered him, up there in the corner of the ceiling, by the old-fashioned crown molding that his mother loved so well. It seemed to be staring at him. Why does Ma need a security camera? Tavalera wondered as he sat on the sofa. She's got one in every room, for chrissake, even the kitchen.

He heard somebody yowl with laughter, back in the kitchen, where almost everyone had moved to. Except for Evelyn, all the people of his own age had squeezed in there. That's where the food is, he thought. The laughter quickly cut off, as if some teacher or librarian had hissed out a warning shush.

He got up and headed toward the back of the house, Evelyn half a step behind him. Tavalera felt almost annoyed. I don't need her hanging on me! He thought of Holly, back at the *Goddard* habitat. I wonder what Holly's doing right now.

The kitchen was jammed: people were sitting on the counters, crowding into the mudroom, couples sitting on the back steps that led up to the bedrooms. But their talk was subdued, low-key. They were almost whispering, as if they were in church, or afraid to let anyone hear what they were saying. It unnerved Tavalera.

His brother, Andy, was entertaining them all with an impromptu display of juggling. Impromptu and inept, Tavalera thought. Andy had a big grin on his face as he tossed pieces of fruit in the air. The floor around his feet was littered with oranges, apples, and something that had splattered and made a pulpy mess.

It didn't bother his mother at all, Raoul saw. She seemed dazedly pleased at all the friendly faces crammed in around her. She was standing by the stove, looking kind of dumpy and round and as white as bread dough, smiling vacantly, hardly changed at all in the years Tavalera had been away. Except that now her white hair was dyed ash-blond.

Why in hell did she dye her hair? he wondered.

He realized that Evelyn was staring intently at him, as if trying to read his thoughts.

Embarrassed at her attention, he asked, "I've changed, huh?"

"Yes. Definitely." She kept her voice low, just like all the others.

"How? For the better?"

"I don't know yet." She was about Tavalera's age, pretty in a pale blond way, even though she was decidedly on the bony side. Holly was lean, too, but vivacious, always full of energy, full of color and fun.

"You're . . . quieter, I guess," Evelyn continued. "More reserved."

He shrugged. He'd been off-Earth for nearly six whole years. He'd seen massive Jupiter, giant of the solar system, up close; he'd repaired scoopships that dove into that planet's swirling, multihued clouds. He'd nearly been killed out there. He'd lived in a huge space habitat that carried him unwillingly to Saturn, with its bright gleaming rings. He'd left Holly in that habitat that was now orbiting Saturn. He'd promised her he'd return. But the government had refused to allow him to leave Earth again, wouldn't even let him send messages to her.

He'd received no messages from her, either. Was the government blocking them, or had Holly already forgotten about him?

Messages. He'd expected the local news media to make at least a little fuss over him. Back home after traveling halfway across the solar system. None of his old buddies had ever gone into space. But nothing, not a peep in the news nets, even though his brother worked for the local TV center. Just like I've never been away. Nothing. Everything here's the same, even the friggin' never-ending war against terrorists and drug cartels. Except for Mom. She's a blonde now, for chrissake.

But it's not the same, he told himself. Or I'm not the same. Evvie's right. I've changed. Six years off-Earth changes you. Has to. What I took for granted before I left looks . . . strange now. Stifling. It's like coming back to kindergarten after six years of being on my own.

"Before you left," Evelyn was saying, "you were sort of a wise mouth. Now you're . . . well, quieter. Guarded, sort of."

"I'm older," he said with a cheerless smile.

"Aren't we all?" she replied.

Tavalera gestured toward his brother, still juggling, with a silly grin pasted on his face. "Andy's exactly the same as he was the last time I saw him."

"Oh, Andy!" said Evelyn. "He'll never grow up."

Somehow the quiet buzz and restrained laughter seemed almost desperate. It's like everybody's afraid of making any noise. Like we're all back in Sunday school. It became too much for Tavalera. He pushed his way toward the back door.

"Where're you going?" Evelyn asked, right beside him.

"Outside. I need some fresh air." I need to get away from these zombies, he added silently. And I don't need a clinging vine smothering me. He wanted to tell Evelyn to go away and leave him alone, but he didn't have the nerve, didn't want to hurt her feelings.

She came with him as he shouldered his way through the well-wishers who pretty much ignored him in their determination to have a well-behaved good time. Except for his mother, whose eyes followed him every step of the way, looking—not worried, exactly. Concerned. Maybe she's hurt 'cause I'm not enjoying the party, he thought.

Outside it was twilight. The sun had just set; the sky was deepening into violet. Not a cloud in sight, Tavalera saw. The sky fascinated him, after years in spacecraft and artificial habitats. Everybody here took it for granted, that big blue bowl that turned red and gold and deepened gradually into black, dotted with stars that twinkled at you. It isn't that way aboard spacecraft. Even the *Goddard* habitat, big enough to house ten thousand people, didn't have a sky or even a horizon.

It was warm enough outdoors to be comfortable in

just his shirtsleeves, even though spring didn't officially start for another month or so.

The neighborhood looked subtly different from the last time he'd seen it. The backyard seemed smaller than he remembered it, the stubbly grass worn down in spots where Tavalera recalled playing ball with his buddies. But now there was a tall aluminum pole in the far corner of the yard, anodized olive green, with another one of those red-eyed security cameras atop it. That was new. The camera turned slowly, slowly, then stopped for a moment when it aimed at Tavalera and Evelyn. He grimaced; then the camera resumed its slow sweep of the area.

Rows of houses stood along the wide, slightly curving street, equally spaced. Just like before I left, Tavalera thought. Maybe a little more crowded, new houses where there'd been open lots and playgrounds before. Or maybe they've shortened the backyards so they could squeeze in some extra houses. Otherwise nothing seemed changed. Except for the poles and the cameras every third house. Who are they watching? he wondered. Who's doing the watching?

Most of the lawns looked half dead, a sickly brown caused by the warming. The new high-rises poked above the screening line of struggling young trees out behind the houses, where the park used to be. Tavalera had played baseball in that park and pedaled his old bicycle until it fell apart. Now the area was a refugee center, housing for people driven from their cities by the greenhouse floods. Hispanics, mostly. And some Arabs or Armenians or something like that. They didn't like to be called refugees, he'd been told: they preferred to be known as flood fugitives.

I guess the world has changed in six years, Tavalera thought, even though most people are doing their best to ignore the changes.

He walked around the house and down the driveway in silence, Evelyn step-by-step beside him. She made him feel nervous, edgy. No cars in the driveway. All the partygoers had either walked to his house or taken public transportation. Driving individual autos wasn't forbidden, exactly, he had learned since his return. But the city frowned on unnecessary driving. And the fuel rationing kept people afoot, as well. Rationing hydrogen, Tavalera thought. They get the stuff from water, for chrissake. Why should they have to ration it?

Something flickered in the corner of his eye. He looked up, and his breath caught in his throat.

"Jesus H. Christ! Look at that!"

Evelyn looked shocked. "You shouldn't take the Lord's name in vain! They might hear you."

"But look!" Tavalera lifted her chin to the heavens.

Long ribbons of shimmering light danced across the sky: soft green, pale blue, white, and coral pink. Like trembling curtains they moved and shifted while Tavalera stared, goggle-eyed.

"What is it?" Evelyn asked in an awed whisper.

"The Northern Lights, I think."

She broke into a nervous laughter. "Not the end of the world, then?"

Shaking his head, his eyes still turned skyward, Tavalera murmured, "Aurora Borealis."

"But why's it showing this far south?" Evelyn asked. "We never get the Northern Lights in Little Rock."

"Must be a really big flare on the Sun," he replied. "Or something."

APOLOGIA PRO VITA SUA
BY YOLANDA VASQUEZ

As they say, the road to hell is paved with good intentions. All I wanted to do was to teach children. I had a vocation to teach, but they eventually drilled that out of me. I adored working with kids, watching their eyes light up when they discovered something new. But I ended up doing little more than going through the motions, just like everybody else.

Now I am an old, old woman and I have seen us all—all of us—fecklessly strolling down that gradual, inevitable slope toward hell, good intentions on every side, the best of intentions, I assure you. But the path slopes downward, nevertheless.

You may think I am bitter. I don't believe that I am. They tell me I'm too old to receive the replacement heart that would save my life. So be it. They say that my time is up and it would be against God's will to artificially extend my years beyond my natural span. God is calling me, they tell me, and I should not seek to evade His call. The truth is, I'm too tired to fight it.

Of course, up in Selene—on the Moon—they would use stem cells or nanomachines or some other form of secularist science to rebuild my failing heart. On the Moon a woman of one hundred and seven years isn't regarded as a lost cause waiting for death to claim her. People have lived to be a hundred and fifty or more on the Moon, or so I've heard. Maybe the low gravity helps them.

No, I am not bitter. But if they're going to do nothing but pray over me while my heart slowly gives out, at least I'm going to tell the truth about them. About me. About us all.

I'm writing this in pencil, a stumpy old-fashioned pencil that I smuggled into this hospital's death ward along with my little bag of clothes and personal items like my favorite toothpaste. The toothpaste they give you here tastes like gritty wet cement. They don't call it the death ward, of course; it's the All Saints Hospice for Terminal Patients. That's the official name. It's a whole separate wing of the enormous hospital here in the New Morality's headquarters complex in Atlanta.

I hope I have enough paper to get all my thoughts down. I hope I live long enough to say everything I want to say. Need to say. Somebody's got to say it. I'm scribbling these thoughts onto the backs of old-fashioned photographs, menus I've saved for donkey's years, letters and invitations and even some of the evaluation reports I received back when I was teaching. Nothing electronic. Nothing they can trace.

Even so, I have to be careful because they have cameras in every room, every hallway, watching us all the time. But the cameras are only as good as the people who monitor them and most of the monitors are either lazy or stupid or both. Or maybe they're just bored with watching old people shuffling through the last days of their lives.

They think I'm working on my scrapbook, pasting all my fading memorabilia into an old-fashioned book with microfiber pages that they'll send to my nearest living relation once I've given up the ghost. My great-grandniece. She lives way out in the Asteroid Belt, at an asteroid called Ceres. Far enough away from the New Morality and all their holier-than-thou jail guards.

That's how I think of them: jail guards. They call themselves doctors and nurses and even pastors and ministers of the Lord. They're nice as pie when they sweetly disconnect your pacemaker or pump you intravenously full of tranquilizers so you won't bother them with cries of pain in the night. But they're really guards in a jail that's as big as this country, from sea to shining sea. Or maybe they're more like orderlies in a great big nationwide insane asylum.

I can remember the old days, back when I had just started teaching. Back then the kids were free to play punchball in the schoolyard, and sometimes to punch one of the other kids if they got into a scrap. I remember when they could roll in the dirt and tussle with one another to settle their argument, and then be pals afterward.

But then I saw on TV that some cartoonist in Holland was put in jail because the government there was afraid his cartoons would offend Muslims. Freedom of expression? Forget it. You had to be nice to everybody. Don't give offense to any person or group. Especially those who might blow up your apartment building.

The schools were invaded by social workers and psychologists. They came to do good, to help the children avoid violence and shun evil thoughts. They *organized* all the sports activities; kids shouldn't be allowed to just go out and play on their own. They've got to be controlled, for their own good. They've got to have organized leagues and official statistics. And no name-calling!

Nowadays even if a kid raises her voice in the hallways she's sent to the school psychologist to learn how to control her anger. And they bottle it up inside themselves all their lives until sometimes it bursts out and people get killed.

Like I said, the road to hell is paved with good intentions. Nobody set out to create this dictatorship. Yes, that's what this is, a dictatorship. Benign, for the most part, but still a dictatorship. Not a police state, not exactly. They're much too clever for that, much too subtle.

We still have elections, sure. Vote for the candidate of your choice: tweedledum or tweedle dumber.

And it took me so long to realize what was happening! I've got nobody to blame but myself. Nobody sat down and deliberately planned all this. It just happened, step-by-step, one good intention after another.

Yes, I know, the country was in an awful mess before the New Morality brought us to true Christian righteousness. Students walked into schools with guns and killed people. Thirteen-year-olds had babies. Drug gangs had more firepower on the streets than the police and felt perfectly free to shoot up their neighborhoods. More often than not the police were part of the problem.

So the people turned to God. To religion. The New Morality led the way. There were lots of other religious groups, too, but over the years the New Morality sort of absorbed them all.

Little by little. Incrementally. Local associations tried to clean up their neighborhoods, make the streets safe and livable. Good people, earnest people. The local churches were natural focal points for them, meeting places, centers where they could make their plans and recruit others. New Morality ministers showed up to help them, give them pointers and even funding, lead them on the path of righteousness.

Knowing they were doing good, they could be stern, even ruthless. But it was all for the good of the community, after all. So a few bad apples got sent away. And one or two others were permanently tranquilized with deep brain stimulators. It was all for the best. We were doing God's work and we knew it.

CHAPTER 2

He dreamed of the space habitat again that night, and of Holly, the warmth of her, the joy of her. He had promised to return to her at the habitat in orbit around Saturn.

But the next morning the bureaucrats of the Office of Employment Allocation had other ideas.

The forty-something woman behind the desk had a patently phony smile pasted on her chubby face. Relentlessly cheerful, she was plump, with dimples in her face and her elbows. I wonder where else? Tavalera thought as he watched her sitting at her desk, humming to herself while she studied her desktop screen.

She worked in an actual office, a real room and not a cubicle. It was a small room, but it had a window that looked out on the new housing tracts that had been put up where the sports arena used to be. She wore a dark blue one-piece suit that almost looked like coveralls. On her left breast was the palm-ring emblem of the New Morality. A larger version of the emblem hung on the wall behind her desk chair: a pair of palm boughs bent into a circle.

"I did my two years of public service," Tavalera said, hoping to get her to pay attention to him instead of whatever data she'd pulled up on her screen.

Without taking her eyes from the screen she singsonged, "Yes, but you owe your community two more years, don't you."

"When I'm fifty."

Finally she looked at him. Her eyes were deep blue, almost violet, Tavalera saw.

Her smile stayed fixed on her round face while she spoke to him as if he were a kindergarten pupil. "Mr. Tavalera, you need to understand that the rules have changed since you left Earth. The greenhouse floods and the other climate shifts have forced us to require your public-service commitment immediately. Your community needs you now, not twenty years in the future."

"But I want to go back—" He stopped himself, but not in time.

The woman's smile faltered momentarily, then flicked back on. But her voice hardened. "Back to Saturn? Back to that colony of misfit unbelievers and humanists? For shame, Mr. Tavalera! You're needed here."

"You got no right to force me to stay."

She sighed heavily. "I'm afraid that's an old-fashioned attitude, Mr. Tavalera. We have a perfect right to require that you stay where you can do the most good for your fellow citizens. After all, it's God's work that you'll be doing."

Tavalera said nothing, but he wondered who decided what was God's work and what was not.

"And even if we should grant you a travel permit," the woman went on, back to her patronizing schoolteacher tone, "how would you pay for your transportation all the way out to Saturn?"

"I'll work my way, on one of the supply ships."

"And how will you get a work permit?"

Tavalera saw where she was heading. Work permits were issued by the Office of Employment Allocation.

Before he could think of anything to say, the woman put her smile on again and said sweetly, "You have been assigned to the New Orleans Restoration Project. Nine doors down the hall, on your right."

Restoration project? he wondered. New Orleans had been underwater since before Tavalera had been in grammar school.

"Nine doors down the hall, on your right," the woman repeated. "They're expecting you."

Numbly Tavalera got up from the chair and went to the door, then hesitated and turned back slightly.

"Count your blessings, Mr. Tavalera. With your technical background, you could have been assigned to repairing infantry robots in Latin America."

Tavalera felt his insides go hollow. The army? They could assign me to the army?

Still smiling, the woman said, "The Lord loves a cheerful giver, Mr. Tavalera. Give your services cheerfully, and all will be well."

He nodded at her, but he was thinking, Two years of mandatory service. Two more friggin' years. I've gotta figure a way out of this.

He trudged unhappily down the corridor to the door labeled: NEW ORLEANS RESTORATION PROJECT. He rapped his knuckles on it once. No answer. He banged harder, and when there was still no reply, he pushed the door open and stepped into a large room filled with two rows of desks. All of them empty. There were blank computer screens on each totally bare desk, comfortable-looking swivel chairs, even trash baskets on the floor. All of them empty.

A door at the far end of the room popped open and a bright-eyed redheaded young woman called, "This way, Mr. Tavalera."

Yep, they're expecting me, all right.

Tavalera walked briskly along the aisle between the empty desks while the redhead held the door and smiled at him. "Nice weather for February, isn't it?" she said as if they'd known each other for years. "No twisters yet."

Tavalera nodded. The redhead pointed at still another door, this one labeled: T. R. BEAUREGARD, DIRECTOR.

"He's waiting for you," said the redhead, still smiling.

T. R. Beauregard's office was big enough to land a

rocket jumper in it, Tavalera thought. The director's desk was wide, gleaming, impressive. Beauregard himself was standing behind it, hands clasped behind his back, giving Tavalera an imitation of a steely gaze. He wore a dark gray tunic over a white turtleneck shirt. It made him look almost like a minister, Tavalera thought. The man was chunky: his face looked soft, like children's putty, although he was doing his best to make his dark eyes seem piercing.

A holographic display hovered over one corner of Beauregard's desk. From where Tavalera was standing it looked like a list or a printed form hanging there in midair a few centimeters above the desk's gleaming surface.

Gesturing to the display, Beauregard said, "Says here in your file that you've got a degree in electro . . . elec . . ."

"Electromechanical engineering," Tavalera prompted.

"Yeah. Whatever. Elec-tro-mechanical," Beauregard said.

Standing before the desk, Tavalera explained, "It means I'm qualified to work on electromechanical systems, like the actuators that control a spacecraft's life-support systems."

"Spent some time out in space, didja?"

Tavalera nodded.

"Well, the work you'll be doin' here won't be spacey, that's fer sure." Gesturing impatiently, Beauregard said, "Siddown, siddown."

Tavalera sat in one of the two handsome armchairs in front of the desk. They were covered in smooth deep burgundy leather. Real leather, from the feel of it, Tavalera thought.

Beauregard sank into his high-backed swivel chair and regarded Tavalera unsmilingly for several moments. At last he said, "What we're doin' heah is God's own work, my boy. You oughtta be proud to be allowed to take part in it."

God's work again, Tavalera thought. He bit back the reply that leaped into his mind.

Beauregard turned slightly in his chair and the wall on Tavalera's right began to glow. "Look at this," the project director said grandly.

The wall screen showed a wide expanse of water. No land in sight. Soft blue waves surging across the sea beneath a pastel blue sky dotted with fat white clumps of clouds.

"That's the Gulf of Mexico," Beauregard said. "Some people are callin' it the *Sea* of Mexico, it's got so big."

The camera seemed to be moving swiftly across the wide sweep of water. Off in the distance Tavalera saw something jutting up from the water. The camera zoomed in on a single slim tower standing in the midst of the sea, bright silvery metal glinting in the sunlight.

"That's the N'Orleens Monument," said the project director. "Memorializin' all those pore souls that got themselves drowned in the flooding."

"I was just a kid when it happened," Tavalera said.

"Yeah, yeah. Now watch this."

The camera sank beneath the waves. The ruins of the city sprawled across the sea bottom, shimmering in the shallow sunlit water. Rows of buildings, most of them roofless, street after street. Then, before Tavalera's eyes, a huge dome began to take form, a dome of glass. Computer graphics, he realized. The camera moved through the glass shell, and inside it grew new buildings and walkways, hotels and parks, thronging crowds of people strolling along from one garishly lit building to another. Children ran by, laughing. People stood along the curving transparent shell and looked out at the remains of New Orleans.

"That's what we're gonna build," said T. R. Beauregard. "And you're gonna be part of mah team."

CHAPTER 3

"Me?" Tavalera blurted.

"Yup. You and about a thousand other bright young men and women. We're gonna build an underwater center right smack in the middle of old N'Orleens."

"That's the restoration project?"

"That's it. Kinda grand, ain't it? Hotels, amusement parks . . . That shell's gonna be made outta glassteel. We're importin' it from Selene, on the Moon! Had to get special permits from th' Archbishop's office."

"How does that restore New Orleans?" Tavalera wondered.

"It'll attract tourists! It'll show the survivors of the tragedy that God hasn't forgotten them. It'll bring money into the region!"

And who gets the money? Tavalera asked silently. He knew better than to say it aloud.

"We're gonna have a big exhibit down there showin' how man's evil ways brought on the floods. God's wrath, y'know. Rampant sex, crime in th' streets, child abuse, and all that. The New Morality's puttin' up half the money for the dome."

"And the other half?"

"Federal government. And the State of Louisiana."

"But there isn't any State of Louisiana anymore," Tavalera said. "It's all underwater, isn't it?"

"Most of it," Beauregard admitted cheerfully. "There's

a li'l bitty corner left. Enough to qualify for two seats in the U.S. Senate and one in the House of Representatives."

"And federal handouts."

"Don't call 'em handouts, boy!" Beauregard waved a warning finger. "They're entitlements."

"So you want me to work on this . . . project."

"That's right. You been in space, you worked in spacesuits. I figgered workin' underwater won't be all that different. You're used to it, ain'tcha?"

Tavalera had to swallow hard. Underwater? For the first time since he'd been a child, he wanted to cry.

Beauregard wasn't one to waste time. He walked Tavalera down the corridor to a big room filled with mostly empty workstations and handed him over to a quartet of engineers huddled over a wide display table in one corner. They immediately began briefing him on details of the project.

"You're going to be our point man," said one of them, a thin-faced, balding man with a big silver crucifix dangling around his neck. Tavalera thought it looked pretty heavy.

"You'll have a lot of responsibility," said another, younger, his face round and pouchy eyed.

It took some time before Tavalera tumbled to the fact that what they meant was that he was going down into the water to supervise the dome's construction while they would be directing his work from the dry safety of a big dredging barge.

He felt totally depressed by the time the day ended and he rode the nearly silent maglev commuter train back to the suburb where his mother's house stood. I'll have to get my own apartment downtown, Tavalera told himself. And some life insurance.

He scrolled through the channels on the TV screen set into the train's seat back. The newscasts showed mostly scenes of devastation: a firefight in some dust-blown village, cruise missiles being launched from a warship, twisted burnt bodies of people that the voice-over identified as terrorists. Some of them looked like children to Tavalera. The nets had no listing for the Northern Lights he'd seen the previous night. Guess they don't think it's news, Tavalera said to himself. But hell, seeing the Lights down here this far south is really something different. It oughtta be on the news someplace.

Still, he could find no mention of it on any news show. Not even the science channel mentioned it. They were doing a docudrama about the search for Noah's Ark.

Switching to the entertainment channels, Tavalera flicked from one stupefyingly banal show to another. Family comedies, cartoons, historical dramas about saints and sinners, a horror vid about scientists using cloned slaves and nanomachines to destroy the world.

Nothing about the Northern Lights.

It was twilight by the time he got off the train and hailed an autocab to drive him home from the station. My credit account's getting thin, he realized. I'll *have to* go to work for them, get some money coming in.

The cab's automated guidance system left him precisely at the driveway of his mother's modest vinyl-paneled Dutch Colonial–style house. He stood on the sidewalk for a moment as the taxi purred away into the lengthening shadows. The street was silent except for the dry rustling of the trees in the warm evening breeze. Not a soul in sight. No kids playing. Nobody walking a dog, even. The neighborhood looked sterile, as if none of the houses were occupied.

A police car glided by, then stopped a few meters up the street. A black-uniformed police officer stepped out of the car and walked slowly toward Tavalera. Despite her white plastic helmet, he recognized that the officer was a woman, almost petite in stature. But she carried a pistol at her hip, its holster flap unbuttoned.

"Sir, can I help you?" she asked. Her voice was slightly muffled by the clear plastic face screen of her helmet.

"I just got home," Tavalera said.

The police officer glanced at the house. "You live here, sir?"

"Yeah. Tem—"

"We have no record of a person fitting your description in residence at this address, sir."

"I just came back a couple of days ago."

"That would be entered into our files, sir."

"I'm not a permanent resident. I'm visiting."

"Your name, sir?"

"Raoul Tavalera."

The police officer pulled a slim palmcomp from her shirt pocket.

"Spell it, please."

Tavalera spelled both his names. "This is my mother's house. I'm visiting her. I've been—"

"Raoul Tavalera," the officer said. "Yes, you're a registered visitor." She looked up at him. "You should be indoors at this time, Mr. Tavalera. There's an emergency alert in effect."

"An emergency? What?"

She almost smiled at him. "They didn't give us any details. The orders are to keep everybody indoors from six P.M. until dawn tomorrow."

"But why?"

"Just go into your house like a good citizen, Mr. Tavalera. Don't make trouble for either one of us."

Tavalera stood there for an uncertain moment. The officer's hand slid to the butt of her gun. He'd heard that they used nonlethal tranquilizer darts instead of bullets, but Tavalera decided he didn't want to test the officer's patience any further.

"Okay," he said, feeling defeated. "I'm going in."

"Thank you, Mr. Tavalera. Thanks for being a cooperative citizen. Have a pleasant evening."

As he started up the walk to the house's front door, Tavalera glanced back over his shoulder. The policewoman hadn't moved. She was entering something into her palmcomp, he realized.

Then he looked up and saw that the darkening sky was gleaming with the Northern Lights again: long shimmering ribbons of ethereal color, dancing silently across the bowl of the heavens.

Two nights in a row.

The police officer took no notice of the Lights. She watched Tavalera until he opened his front door and stepped into the house.

STARSHIP

It wasn't a spacecraft in the sense that any engineer of Earth would recognize. Part organic, part pure energy, the starship had entered the solar system more than twenty years earlier, carrying Keith Stoner, his wife, Jo, and their two grown children. Humans, born of Earth, but more than human now.

"They've got to reply," Stoner told his wife. "They've got to answer me."

Jo gazed at the blue sphere of Earth, flecked with clouds of purist white, and pictured in her mind an ant heap teeming with scurrying mindless fools.

If any of them realize we've returned, she thought, they're doing their best to ignore our presence among them.

Jo understood the frustration that her husband felt. His son and daughter, though, wondered why their father was bothering with these primitives.

CHAPTER 4

Tavalera opened the front door of his house and stepped inside. He closed the door and peered through its window until the police officer returned to her car and drove away. Then he went back toward the kitchen, where he knew his mother would be.

She was a sweet-faced woman, round and snowy white. She seemed almost totally unchanged in the years he'd been away, except for dyeing her hair. That bothered Tavalera, but he didn't know why. Now that he looked at her more closely, he saw lines in her face that he didn't remember from earlier. And her eyes looked . . . guarded. He didn't see the warmth he remembered from childhood.

She was sitting at the kitchen table, watching the news on the wall screen over the microwave oven. Something about a celebration in some big church. Up in the corner above the screen was that damned red eye of the security camera, watching him.

A row of medication bottles was lined up in perfect order to one side of the microwave, each blue- and red-lettered label facing outward. That was different, Tavalera realized. Ma didn't take any pills when I left for my public service duty. Aspirin, maybe, now and then.

At the end of the row of pill bottles was a tiny gray electronics box, with what looked like a pair of headphones connected to it by a hair-thin fiber-optic wire.

Tavalera went to the headphones and picked them up. "What's this, Ma? You into music now?"

"Put them down!" she said sharply, jumping up from her chair. She looked almost frightened.

Holding them in his hand, he asked, "What are these, anyway?"

"They're not for you. Put them down. You might damage them."

"Damage them? What're you talking about?"

Impatiently his mother snatched the headphones from his hand and placed them back on the shelf alongside the row of pill bottles.

"They're for treating my depression," she said almost sullenly.

"Depression?"

"It's just a mild case. I use the headphones to make me feel better."

Tavalera stared at her. "A doctor prescribed this?"

"Of course. Lots of people use them. Brain stimulators, they're called."

"You've been diagnosed with depression?"

She cast an annoyed look at him, then changed the subject as she sat down again. "How did your job interview go?"

"Not good," he said, pulling up the chair next to hers. "They want me to work down in Louisiana."

"Louisiana?" She frowned, puzzled. "But it's all underwater."

He decided not to tell her everything; it would only worry her. Depression, he kept thinking. Ma's taking electrical stimulation for depression.

"Isn't Louisiana underwater?" she repeated.

He nodded. "I'm going to appeal the assignment. First thing tomorrow."

She looked uneasy. "Don't make trouble, Son. It's best to do what they tell you, like a good boy."

"I've got a right to appeal a work assignment, Ma. That's not making trouble for anybody."

"They'll mark it against you; don't think they won't. It's best just to accept what they give you. After all, they wouldn't give you the assignment if they didn't need you there."

Tavalera didn't want to get into an argument with his mother. Instead, he asked, "You seen anything on the news about the aurora?"

"The what?"

"The Northern Lights. They're shining in the sky again tonight. Right now." He pointed toward the curtained kitchen window.

"There's nothing in the news about it. Are you sure—"

He got up and went to the kitchen door. "Come on; I'll show you."

"Don't go outside! There's some sort of emergency and they don't want us to go outside."

"They? Who's they?"

"The police. The announcement came over the TV about an hour ago. Nobody's to go outside until dawn tomorrow."

She didn't seem afraid. Just compliant.

"Why not? What's the emergency?"

"Probably some terrorist threat," his mother said. "They're always making threats, but we always catch them."

"Ma, there hasn't been a terrorist attack since the Day of the Bridges, back before I was born."

She gave him a superior expression. "You see? The Homeland Security people know what they're doing.

And if they want us to stay indoors, that's what we've got to do."

Tavalera forced down a feeling of impatient frustration. "Well, okay, just take a look through the window, then. I think you can see—"

"Raoul, get away from the window!" She said it in the tone of voice he remembered from childhood.

"We can look out our own goddamned windows, for god's sake!"

"Don't use that kind of language in this house! I didn't bring you up to be a foulmouthed blasphemer."

He stared at her in disbelief. Blasphemer? he asked silently. What's gotten into you, Ma? Since when did you become a religious nut?

She softened. "If they want us to stay indoors it's for our own good. They know what they're doing. Just do what you're told and don't make trouble for yourself."

He sat down beside her again. "Ma, they're the ones making trouble. They want me to work in New Orleans, for Chri . . . for crying out loud."

"New Orleans?"

"Underwater. I'll be working underwater."

"You'll be safe, won't you?"

"Sure. I guess so."

"I mean, you worked in space and that was safe enough, wasn't it?"

"Sure, Ma, sure." Except for the time I damned near got killed, he added silently.

They sat side by side for several moments, neither speaking but both of their minds churning.

"You want to go back there, don't you?" His mother's voice turned dark, not quite angry, not quite hurt, but a combination of both, plus more.

He didn't answer for some while. At last he admitted, "Yeah, I do."

"Why'd you come home?" Now her tone was cold with accusation.

Tavalera was shocked at her question. He blurted, "For you, Ma. I wanted to come back home. After six years, I wanted to see my old friends, see you and Andy and everybody."

"But now you want to go back there and live in outer space."

He didn't answer. He couldn't. He couldn't tell his mother that coming back home had been a mistake. This wasn't his home anymore. Not now. His true home was a billion kilometers away, circling the ringed planet, Saturn.

"You want to leave me," his mother said, her voice low, bitter.

"I could send for you once I got back to the habitat. You'd like it there, Ma. It's big, lots of room, lots of freedom. . . ."

"And leave all my friends, all the people I've lived with all my life?"

"Most of 'em are dead, Ma."

"Like your father."

Oh Christ, he thought, she's going to throw that at me again.

"You were off in space when your father died. You should have been here. This is where I needed you."

"Ma, I couldn't leave. They wouldn't let me. They didn't even tell me that Pop had died until weeks afterward!"

"I had to deal with it all alone," his mother continued, tears filling her eyes. "You should have been here. No wonder I came down with depression. No wonder I need the brain stimulator."

And it went on that way for several hours more, while the Northern Lights weaved and glimmered in the darkening sky.

Tavalera bore his mother's tears and recriminations without reply, without argument. She's right, in her own way, he thought. I should have been here to help her when she needed me. But the bastards never even told me about Pop until it was all over, and even then they wouldn't let me go back home.

He felt anger simmering inside him. Anger at *them*, the nameless, faceless people who had been running his life since he'd graduated from school. *They* sent him all the way to Jupiter. *They* damned near got him killed out there. Now *they* were going to dunk him into the god-damned Gulf of Mexico and make a construction jock out of him.

His mother finally ran out of tears and indignation. He went with her upstairs, saw her to her bedroom, and then stepped across the hallway to the room that had been his for as long as he could remember.

He closed the door and went to the window. Outside, the Northern Lights still flickered and shimmered in the dark night sky. What's making them do that? Tavalera wondered.

Then the thought suddenly struck him: Is this why they want us indoors all night? They don't want us to see the Lights?

CHAPTER 5

The Appeals Board was in the same building as the Office of Employment Allocation, which made some sense to Tavalera, since the Board was there to straighten out problems that arose in the OEA's assignments. So instead of reporting for work the next morning, Tavalera informed Beauregard's cheerful redheaded assistant that he was putting in an appeal, then spent the morning working his way through the layers of bureaucracy that made up the Appeals Board, trying to get them to cancel his assignment to the New Orleans Restoration Project.

No dice.

"You should fall on your knees and thank the good Lord that you're being allowed to contribute to this blessed program!" That was the kindest response he got.

"The army needs men with your technical training," said one, a flinty-eyed old graybeard. "When I was your age I did three tours in the Sudan, kid."

Everyone else gave him a variation of, "That's your assignment and you're stuck with it. Be grateful we don't send you to some inner-city slum or a swamp-clearing project in Haiti."

One self-important desk jockey gave Tavalera a crafty look as he warned, "Troublemakers get troubles, young man."

Feeling frustrated and getting truculent, Tavalera grumbled, "I can handle troubles."

"Can you? I see from your file that your mother is on medical assistance. How would you like to see her prescriptions for medications canceled? Her stimulator taken away from her?"

"You can't do that!"

With a shrug and a reptilian smile, the bureaucrat replied, "Of course I can't. That would be illegal. And immoral. But . . ."

"But what?"

Another shrug. "Her file could be lost. Or her prescriptions suspended pending a complete medical review of her case."

Tavalera fought down the urge to leap over the man's desk and strangle him.

Reluctantly, grudgingly, Tavalera reported back to

the restoration project office that afternoon after lunch and began his new "career."

But night after night the skies glowed with the Northern Lights. And night after night the police declared an emergency and ordered everyone to stay indoors during the hours of darkness.

The small brass plaque by the double doors of the red-brick, four-story building modestly proclaimed:

KLRA-TV
THE EYES AND EARS
OF GREATER LITTLE ROCK

The words were encircled by the twining palm-bough symbol of the New Morality.

Tavalera remembered that before he'd left for his public-service duty in space all the TV stations in the state had been combined into a single network, under the management of the New Morality. There had been some objections at the time, soreheads and alarmists complaining about the separation of church and state and freedom of expression. But the system seemed to be working; the complaints had been silenced.

The commuter line that served the restoration project had a station stop right in front of the KLRA-TV building. As he rode home after his working day finished, Tavalera reacted to a sudden impulse and got off the maglev train at the TV station's stop. He walked toward the station's front doors while the train whisked itself away in a whisper. The Northern Lights had been flickering in the sky for four nights in a row, but he could find no mention of it on the news. And each night the police enforced the "temporary emergency" procedures that kept everyone indoors until dawn.

Maybe Andy knows something about it, he thought. His older brother was an administrator of some sort at the TV center; maybe he knew what was going on.

What bothered Tavalera most, as he strode up the walkway to the building's front entrance, was that nobody seemed to mind being forced to stay indoors night after night. True, there had been tremendous thunderstorms the past two nights, torrential downpours streaked with terrifying bolts of lightning. Electrical power had been knocked out for hours at a time, but neither his mother nor any of his new coworkers at the restoration project saw anything unusual in that.

"Springtime comes earlier now," his mother had said when he'd remarked on the storms. "We always get downpours in the spring. Be happy the good Lord hasn't sent us any tornados."

During lunch at the cafeteria in the restoration project office, he had asked about the power outages.

"Hey, don't complain. It used to be a lot worse," said one of his fellow technicians, between bites of a pathetically thin sandwich. "When they first put up the emergency housing projects for the flood fugitives, we could go without power for days. Two weeks, one time."

Everybody seemed to accept whatever was handed to them, Tavalera thought. They're like a bunch of sheep. He remembered the fierce political contests that raged in habitat *Goddard* as it orbited Saturn. Of course, *Goddard*'s people were mostly malcontents, troublemakers who'd been exiled from their homes on Earth because they were misfits. And scientists. Scientists are always ready to argue about anything, he knew.

Was it this way before I went into space? he asked himself. Thinking back more than six years, Tavalera figured that maybe it was, but he just didn't take notice of it. People's passivity seemed kind of normal back then, but now, after being really free on *Goddard*, he realized that most of the people around him were sheep. Including his mother.

People were leaving the KLRA building. It was the end of the workday for them, too. Tavalera hoped that Andy hadn't gone yet. As he came within arm's length of the smoked-glass double doors, his brother pushed through, heading out.

"Andy!"

His brother couldn't have looked more surprised if a fire-breathing dragon had suddenly materialized before him. His round, bland face went white. His soft brown eyes flashed wide for a moment, then narrowed. Frown lines creased his forehead.

"Rolly! What're you doing here?"

Making himself smile, Tavalera said, "I came to see you, pal."

Andy was dressed in a collarless pale yellow jacket and crisply creased dark brown chinos. His thinning hair was carefully combed forward over his high forehead. Tavalera felt almost shabby in his flapping tan shirt jacket and shapeless jeans.

"You can see me at my house, Rolly. Any time."

"Yeah, I know. How's Mildred? I didn't see her at the party."

"She had to stay home; one of the kids had the flu or something."

"Oh. I hope he's okay now."

"She. Yeah, she's fine. Kids can scare the devil out of you, though." Andy looked suspicious, wary. "So what're you doing here, Rolly?"

"I just thought it'd be fun to see where you work. I've never seen the inside of a TV station."

Andy glanced at the steady stream of people leaving

the building and pulled Raoul to one side of the walkway.

"You can't go inside the building," Andy said in a low, tense voice. "Security, y'know."

"Security?"

"The first thing terrorists go after is the news media," Andy said.

"But that was a long time ago, before we were even born. There hasn't been a terrorist attack—"

"Because we're always on guard against them!" Andy said forcefully. "Always on guard!"

Tavalera thought about the security cameras that had been mounted in every home. They're always on guard, all right, he said to himself. They're watching every move we make, 24-7.

"Just last month they caught a plot to blow up one of the power satellites," Andy went on. "That could've knocked out electrical power from Tennessee to Texas!"

With a shake of his head, Tavalera said, "I didn't know you'd be so uptight about security."

"We're still at war, you know," Andy retorted. "We're fighting terrorism all around the globe."

To Raoul, his brother's words sounded like a slogan that he'd memorized.

Shrugging, Raoul said, "Well, if I can't go in, I can't go in."

"You could apply for a visitor's pass," Andy suggested more reasonably. "Might take a couple of weeks to check you out, though."

Raoul nodded glumly. "Yeah, maybe I'll do that."

Brightening, his brother said, "And then I'll give you the grand tour of the place."

"Great."

They started walking toward the maglev train stop on

the elevated station. Half a dozen people were already up there on the platform, waiting, with more climbing the stairs. Raoul recognized the redhead who worked in Beauregard's office as she passed him, walking briskly toward the stairs. Wondering what she was doing at the TV station, he smiled at her. She smiled back.

Turning back to Andy, Raoul said, "I thought you had a car."

"Sure. But we're not allowed to drive to work if we're within a fifteen-minute walk of a train stop. Keeps down the pollution and greenhouse emissions."

Helluva time to worry about greenhouse warming, Raoul thought, with Florida and Louisiana and a good slice of Texas underwater. Besides, all the cars are either hydrogen fueled or electrical.

Aloud, he asked, "Cheez, whattaya do when it rains?"

Andy grinned. "Get wet. Or carry an umbrella. And watch your language, pal. They might hear you."

Tavalera had heard that line before. They might hear me. So what if they do?

"Andy, I'm curious about—"

"Curiosity killed the cat," his brother interrupted.

Screw the cat, Tavalera thought. "I wanted to ask you about the Northern Lights. Isn't it weird—"

This time Andy grabbed him by the arm and walked rapidly away from the train stop.

"Rolly, you've got to understand there are some things you don't ask about."

"Huh? The Northern Lights? I can't ask about the Northern Lights?"

Practically dragging Raoul along with him, Andy headed around the corner of the redbrick building.

"Have you seen a news report on the subject?" he asked almost belligerently.

"No. That's why I—"

"If it's not on the news then you shouldn't ask about it. That's a simple-enough rule, isn't it? You can understand that, can't you?"

"But why isn't it on the news? What's the big deal? And what's this emergency that we have to stay indoors after sundown?"

"Lord have mercy!" Andy hissed. He had broken into a sweat, beads of perspiration trickling down his round cheeks. Pointing to a security camera fixed to the building's wall, Andy said, "You're gonna get us both in trouble, Rolly! If the powers that be don't want the Northern Lights story aired, it's gotta be for a good reason. Don't—"

"What stupid kind of reason can they have for hushing up the Northern Lights?" Raoul demanded, wondering even as he spoke who *they* were supposed to be.

Wiping his brow with the back of his hand, Andy said, "How should I know? Maybe they think people might get scared if they see the Lights. Think it's the end of the world or something. They don't want to cause panic, riots . . . whatever."

"That's crazy."

"You're not in charge. They are. They see more than you do, pal. They know a lot more."

"It's still crazy," Raoul said.

Andy shook his head hard enough to make his cheeks wobble. "Look, Rolly. I'm going home. I don't know you. Not anymore."

And his older brother marched away from him, head down, fists balled at his sides. Raoul stood there, too stunned to move.

CHAPTER 6

The next morning when Tavalera showed up at the restoration project office he knew something was wrong.

The Northern Lights had glowed in the sky again the previous night. And again all the news media had warned that there was a police emergency in force and everyone was to remain indoors from sundown until dawn.

But Tavalera had sat by his bedroom window for hours, watching the delicate shimmering curtains of light dancing in the dark night sky. They're not afraid of a terrorist attack, he was convinced. They're scared of the friggin' Lights.

His train ran a bit late that morning, so Tavalera's coworkers were all at their desks when he arrived at the office. They all said their good mornings warily, as if they might be infected with something if they got too close to him. When he asked his computer for his morning's schedule the holographic display spelled out: SEE MR. BEAUREGARD IMMEDIATELY.

Uh-oh, he thought. That doesn't sound good.

The others in the office watched him silently as he got up from his workstation and walked toward Beauregard's office, holding his head high to show that he wasn't worried.

But he was. Tavalera figured his conversation the previous afternoon with his brother had brought trouble down on his head, just as Andy had warned. Either that damned camera on the building wall picked up everything we said, or Andy himself gabbled to somebody about me.

He almost grinned, though, as he approached Beauregard's door. Maybe they'll boot me out. Exile me to *Goddard*—and Holly.

Even Beauregard's redheaded assistant looked at Tavalera solemnly, worriedly. No smile on her pretty face this morning.

Beauregard was unsmiling, too, as he sat behind his desk in his usual dark tunic and white turtleneck. But this morning his tunic bore the twined palm-bough symbol of the New Morality on its breast. And a small silver crucifix hung on an almost invisible chain around his neck.

There were two grim-looking men sitting in the burgundy leather chairs in front of the desk. Both of them wore tan uniforms, like soldiers. But they were both too old to be real soldiers: one had bushy gray hair; the other was shaved bald, his face seamed with wrinkles. They turned in their chairs to glare at Tavalera as he stepped into the office.

Tavalera closed the door behind him and stood there, waiting.

Beauregard said, "These gentlemen are from the Federal Security Department. Seems you've been askin' some pretty touchy questions."

"Me?"

"You," said the bushy-haired security agent. He had narrow cold blue eyes, and his muscular body threatened to burst the seams of his uniform.

The shaved one got to his feet. He was slimmer than his partner but still looked strong enough to lift Beauregard's desk with one hand.

"Raoul Tavalera," he said, his voice a flat nasal twang. "What kind of name is Raoul? Cuban, maybe?"

Feeling his brows knit, Tavalera answered, "My grandfather was Cuban. He worked at the Cuban embassy in Washington after the Reconciliation."

"Habla español?" the security agent asked.

"Huh?"

"Do you speak Spanish?"

Tavalera shook his head. English had been the official language of the United States all his life. No one spoke or wrote or even thought in anything except English.

The bushy-haired agent stood up. "You'll have to come with us, son."

"With you? Where? What for?"

"Like Mr. Beauregard here says, you've been asking questions about a sensitive area."

"It's a crime to ask questions?" Tavalera felt his temper heating up.

"No crime," the agent said. "But you've stepped into a sensitive area and you need to be briefed."

"On security regulations," said the shaved one before Tavalera could ask.

"You'll be back before the end of the day," said the first one.

"Or tomorrow, at the latest," added his partner with a smirk.

They came up on either side of Tavalera. The shaved one opened Beauregard's door and they marched him out. They didn't grab his arms, didn't touch him at all, but Tavalera certainly felt like a prisoner being marched off to jail.

Parked in a geosynchronous orbit high above the Earth's equator, the entity that had once been Keith Stoner puzzled over the total lack of response from the billions of human beings on the planet below.

For nearly a human generation he had been trying to communicate with his former brethren. His first tentative attempts at contact had been swallowed up in fear-filled paranoia. His later electronic messages had received no response, even though the planet was awash with wireless communications. He had resorted to stimulating the planet's ionosphere, making the aurorae glow from pole to pole. Still no response, although the procedure recharged his starship's power systems.

Why don't they answer? Stoner asked himself. They've got to act on my information before it's too late for them. Before they destroy themselves.

Why bother? replied his wife, silently, in his mind. He could sense Jo's revulsion at the stubborn refusal of the people of Earth to make contact with the star voyagers.

For them, Stoner answered, mentally picturing Cathy and Rick, their children. Both of them were adults now. Rick barely remembered the Earth of his childhood; Cathy had no memory of her earlier life at all.

The two security agents walked Tavalera to the parking lot behind the building, where a gray tilt-rotor aircraft was waiting. It looked old to Tavalera, hard used, its big rotor blades drooping almost to the ground.

They climbed the dull gray beryllium ladder into the craft, the shaved agent ahead of Tavalera, the gray-haired one behind him. The ladder creaked and sagged slightly beneath their weight. Inside was a small compartment with four bucket seats. Tavalera took the seat that the agents indicated.

"Where're we going?" he asked.

The bushy-haired agent, settling his bulk into the seat next to Tavalera's, nodded ponderously. "You'll find out when we get there."

The plane's engines growled to life and its big rotor blades started turning, whooshing like giant scythes. The entire cabin rattled; the engine noise made Tavalera's ears hurt.

Before he could click his seat belt the vehicle wobbled off the ground with a lurch that made Tavalera's stomach heave. He gulped and tasted acrid bile in his mouth.

"I thought you've been in space," said gray-hair, beside him.

"I have," Tavalera replied, barely avoiding gagging.

"Hmp. You look kind of green, kid."

CHAPTER 7

Once at altitude the tilt-rotor's engines swiveled to the horizontal position and the ride smoothed out, although the cabin still rattled and creaked. Tavalera couldn't see outside, there were no windows in the cramped cabin, but the agent sitting beside him calmly reported that they were flying at nearly the speed of sound.

"Goin' where?" Tavalera asked.

"Ski country," said the agent sitting in front of him. "You like to ski, kid?"

Tavalera remembered the stuntman he'd met aboard the *Goddard* habitat: Manuel Gaeta. Manny had skied down Mt. Olympus on Mars.

"Naw, I never been on skis," he said.

"Good thing," said the agent, with a bitter laugh. "There hasn't been any snow to ski on for years."

They flew for nearly three hours, and then the tilt-rotor spiraled down to a landing. The hatch opened automatically and, again with one agent ahead of him and the other behind, Tavalera clambered down the shaky little ladder and planted his feet on solid ground once more.

They were in the mountains, he saw. Probably the Rockies, judging by the stark granite peaks. It was decidedly chillier than it had been in Little Rock; a cold, dry wind cut through his thin shirt jacket and made him shiver. He was glad when the agents quick-marched him across the windswept landing pad and into a concrete building set into the side of a bare rock cliff.

Tavalera noticed the emblem above the sliding steel doors of the building: the stylistic eagle of the federal government, surrounded by the twining palm boughs of the New Morality.

Inside, the place looked like a more-or-less ordinary office complex. No windows, but long corridors dotted with closed doors. Each door bore a coded plaque that apparently indicated who or what was inside that office, Tavalera figured. Small rectangular electronic keypads were mounted on the walls beside each door. There were plenty of men and women walking along the corridors, some of them hurrying, pinch faced, others looking relaxed, almost at leisure. Most of them wore ordinary street clothes, although a few were in uniform and several were dressed in what looked like clerical garb.

Nobody using pocket phones, he noticed. The building must be screened against wireless transmissions.

The agents guided him through the maze of corridors to a door, finally, that bore an understandable title: CONFERENCE ROOM C-120. The shaved agent opened the door, and his younger partner shooed Tavalera inside with a brusque gesture.

Then they closed the door behind Tavalera, leaving him alone in the room. It held an oval table with eight plush-looking chairs arranged around it. The walls were featureless gray. Smart screens, Tavalera guessed. He didn't see any security cameras but figured there could be all sorts of surveillance sensors behind the softly glowing ceiling panels.

Wondering if he should sit or remain standing, he stepped over to the small table at the far end of the conference room. It bore a stainless-steel pitcher and a stack of plastic cups. Tavalera took a cup and poured from the pitcher. Water.

"That's real Rocky Mountain water."

He whirled, nearly dropping the cup in his surprise. A slender young black woman stood in the doorway, smiling brightly at him. He hadn't heard the door open. Before she closed it again Tavalera glimpsed his two agents standing out in the corridor, looking bored.

"It's rather rare, you know," she said, still smiling. "Without any snowmelt in the springtime, this area is drying out, turning semiarid."

Tavalera nodded mutely.

"My name is Sister Angelique," said the young woman as she walked gracefully to the head of the table. "Please sit down and make yourself comfortable."

She was as slim as a newborn colt and almost Tavalera's height. She spoke with a faint hint of an accent that he couldn't quite place. Jamaican, maybe. Or some other Caribbean island. Sister Angelique wore a black clerical dress, nearly floor-length, its high collar edged with white. Over her slight left breast was the inevitable palm-bough symbol of the New Morality. But hers had a white cross inside the circle. Tavalera stepped up and took the chair to her right, close enough to smell the scent of fresh flowers she was wearing.

"You're probably wondering why we asked you here this morning," Sister Angelique said, her smile widening.

Tavalera had heard that old saw before but realized she was trying to put him at his ease, so he tried to smile back at her.

"Something about the Northern Lights, huh?"

Sister Angelique nodded. "Yes. About the Northern Lights."

He waited for her to continue. Her smile faded and

her face grew quite serious. Her dark brown eyes were large, almond shaped. They almost looked Oriental.

"The hierarchy has tried to downplay the Lights," she began. "I thought that was an ill-considered decision. After all, anyone can see them, can't they?"

"In Little Rock the police are making everybody stay indoors from sundown to dawn."

Sister Angelique shook her head. "Not very wise, is it? Bad for restaurants and other businesses. And even with modern surveillance systems, how can the police enforce such a measure?"

She had a habit of framing her statements as questions, Tavalera realized. Trying to get me to say something, he figured.

"You saw the Lights?" she asked.

"Night after night."

"What do you think of them?"

"They're beautiful."

"But what's causing them, do you think?"

"Damned if I know." From the sudden flare of her eyes he immediately regretted his minor vulgarity. "I mean, that's what I was asking my brother about."

"You're curious."

"Aren't you?"

"No, Mr. Tavalera. I am not curious. I'm afraid."

"Afraid? Of what?"

She hesitated. "Some people fear that the Lights signify the coming of the end of the world."

Tavalera made a face to show what he thought of that.

"But it could be just that, you know," Sister Angelique said quite seriously. "Exactly that. The end of the world—as we know it."

"I don't understand."

"You've spent the past several years in space, haven't you?"

"That's right."

"You were assigned to the Jupiter station but somehow ended in the Saturn colony?"

He almost laughed at the perplexity on her face. "I was working on the scoopships. You know, they suck up hydrogen and helium isotopes from Jupiter's atmosphere. Fuel for our fusion generators."

Sister Angelique nodded uncertainly.

"We had an accident while we were refueling a habitat vessel heading to Saturn. I got stranded, and one of the guys from the habitat came out and rescued me. Saved my life. But I had to go with their vessel all the way out to Saturn."

"And you stayed there?"

"Until I could get transportation back home," Tavalera said. Silently he added, I stayed long enough to fall in love. But not long enough to get smart enough to stay on *Goddard* with her.

CHAPTER 8

Sister Angelique said, "So you've lived in space for several years, then? You've had experience on spacecraft?"

"Yeah, right. Is that important?"

"It's . . . unusual, Mr. Tavalera," she said, almost frowning. "We don't have many people with your kind of experience among us. Most people who go to space never return to Earth."

Can you blame them? he asked silently.

"We need someone with experience in space to help us deal with the problem—"

"What problem?" he snapped. "The Northern Lights? That's a problem?"

She bit her lip, obviously struggling with a decision. At last she said, "Mr. Tavalera, I've got to ask you to sign a secrecy agreement."

"Why? What for?"

Her smile returned, fainter this time. "I'm afraid I can't answer your questions until you sign the agreement."

"And if I don't?"

She cocked her head slightly to one side. "If you refuse, you'll be returned to Little Rock." Before Tavalera could say anything, she added, "And be assigned to a different job, I'm afraid. Probably far from your home and family."

Feeling the heat of anger rising in him again, Tavalera grumbled, "Damned if I do and damned if I don't, huh?"

"I pray that you're not damned at all, Mr. Tavalera."

"You know what I mean." He waited for her to reply. When she didn't, he demanded, "Look, what's this all about? Why do I have to sign a secrecy agreement?"

"You said you were curious."

"About the Lights."

"Once you sign the agreement we can begin to satisfy your curiosity."

Tavalera gave her a skeptical look. But she simply sat there, smiling sweetly at him, with a hint of something in her eyes: expectation, maybe? They've got me royally screwed, Tavalera thought. If I don't sign the agreement they're going to send me to Alaska or Guatemala or someplace where I can't talk to my friends. Goddamn New Morality runs the government, and I'm just a speck of dust to them.

"Damn," he muttered.

Sister Angelique leaned slightly toward him. "Mr. Tavalera, the truth is that we need you. I need you."

"You?"

"There are forces within the New Morality who are

misusing the power God has granted us. Old men, for the most part. Tired, frightened old men. They don't trust the people. They fear them . . . and the Lights."

Now Tavalera felt confused. "You're saying—"

"I've already said much more than I should. Please sign the agreement. Then I can be completely frank with you."

He puffed out a defeated sigh. "Okay. Where do I sign?"

A panel of the conference table's surface lit up before him, showing a dense block of small print with a dotted line at its bottom. The panel beside it slid open, revealing a stylus in its compartment. Feeling as if he'd just been talked into buying something he really didn't want, Tavalera picked up the stylus and scribbled his signature on the dotted line.

"Thank you, Mr. Tavalera," said Sister Angelique, her smile at full wattage.

The tabletop went opaque once more. But the wall opposite Tavalera began to glow.

"Remember, Mr. Tavalera, that you have agreed to keep everything you see completely secret. You will not discuss it with anyone who is not an official of the New Morality with a documented need to know."

He nodded impatiently.

She hesitated for a moment, her dark almond eyes searching his. Then she swiveled her chair to the glowing wall screen. "Initiate," she said, like a princess giving a command to a servant.

A man's face appeared on the screen. It was an impressive face, with a patrician nose and strong high cheekbones, a thick deeply black beard matched by an equally thick and dark head of hair. Piercing gray eyes. He seemed middle-aged to Tavalera: his face wasn't wrinkled, but it didn't have any youthful softness to it.

All bone and skin tanned almost walnut brown. The fierce uncompromising face of an Old Testament prophet, Tavalera thought.

Then the man smiled warmly and seemed to become almost youthful.

"Hello. My name is Keith Stoner," he said in a deep, resonant voice. "We've just returned from the stars."

Tavalera rocked back in his chair. Sister Angelique froze the image.

"That message was received by the Arecibo radio telescope in Puerto Rico and every major astronomical facility on Earth, as well as the Farside radio facility on the Moon, slightly more than six months ago."

"From the stars?"

"There is more to the message. The important point is that we have been unable to track its origin."

"The guy's a nutcase," Tavalera said.

"Perhaps." Sister Angelique turned back to the screen and commanded, "Continue."

The image on the screen stirred to life once more. "We left Earth in the year 1985 of the Gregorian calendar. Thanks to time dilation we've been able to visit a number of stars in the Milky Way galaxy." The bearded face grew serious. "We have important discoveries to tell you about. It's vital that I meet with your best scientists and governmental leaders. Sooner or later, I'll have to speak to the general public, but I'd like to see the scientists first."

Again the image froze.

It took an effort of will for Tavalera to pull his focus away from those steel gray eyes and look at Sister Angelique again.

She said, as if reciting a report, "Twenty-two years ago, several government agencies reported observing an object that entered the solar system moving at a tenth of the speed of light. It slowed significantly as it passed the orbits of Neptune and Uranus, heading inward, toward the Sun."

"Toward us," Tavalera murmured.

"It orbited around the planet Saturn several times; then, as it neared the orbit of Jupiter," Sister Angelique went on, "it disappeared."

"Disappeared?"

"Radar reflections stopped. Optical telescopes could no longer see it. We checked with several other national governments; they all reported the same. Even Selene, on the Moon."

"It disappeared."

"Like turning off a light," she said, her voice quavering slightly. "For twenty-two years nothing more was seen or heard. The authorities could find nothing, and there were no more messages. It was decided that it was some sort of anomalous body, a comet, perhaps, that broke up from the strain of Jupiter's gravitational field."

"But it wasn't?" Tavalera asked.

"About six months ago we received the message you have just seen. We have been unable to track its source."

"A spacecraft?" Tavalera wondered. "A stealth craft?"

Ignoring his musing, Sister Angelique went on, "We checked all the files. There is no record of a crewed spacecraft leaving Earth for the stars or any other destination in 1985. Or at any other time. To this day, no one knows how to construct a spacecraft capable of reaching even the nearest stars."

"He said his name—"

"There is a record for a Dr. Keith Stoner, however. He was an astrophysicist with the National Aeronautics and Space Administration's research center in Greenbelt, Maryland, working on the Hubble Space Telescope. He died in 1985 in an automobile accident."

CHAPTER 9

"That's weird," said Tavalera.

"It's . . . unsettling," Sister Angelique replied.

Despite himself, Tavalera felt intrigued. "Astronomers saw this spacecraft enter the solar system? And then it disappeared?"

"The official explanation is that it was a comet that was observed back then and it broke up as it neared the planet Jupiter."

"Twenty-two years ago."

"Yes."

"But you don't believe the official explanation," Tavalera said.

She shook her head ever so slightly. "Calculations have shown that the object never got close enough to Jupiter to cause it to break up."

"Uh-huh."

"And now there is this message. It's too much of a coincidence to think that the two events are not connected."

"Twenty-two years apart?" Tavalera wondered.

"Even so."

"Okay," he said. "So what're you doing about it?"

Sister Angelique turned her back to the image of Keith Stoner, still frozen on the wall screen, to look directly at Tavalera. "In cooperation with the appropriate international authorities, we have kept the message secret. Even Selene is cooperating with us; they are just as concerned about this as we are, although for different reasons, of course."

Tavalera asked, "Why're you wound up about it? It's a joke. A gag. Gotta be. Some bright wiseguy's pulling your leg."

"How could this person produce optical images and

radar returns of a spacecraft moving through the outer solar system at a tenth of the speed of light?"

"Whoever rigged this message knew about the comet or whatever it was twenty-two years ago, and he's using it to yank your chain."

Angelique shook her head disbelievingly.

Tavalera insisted, "Aw hell, I knew dozens of scientists on the *Goddard* habitat who could probably fake something like that."

"Probably?"

"Well . . . maybe. They're pretty bright people, you know."

"And why would they try to hoax us?"

Suddenly Tavalera saw the deep pit of a trap ahead of him. But there was an opportunity there, too.

Carefully he replied, "Some of those bright people have been exiled from their homes on Earth. Maybe they're trying to get even by tying you up in knots."

Sister Angelique seemed to consider this for a few moments. Then she said, "But if it's *not* a hoax, if it actually is a spacecraft from the stars . . ."

"Driven by a guy who's been dead for more'n a hundred years? Get real."

"How can he make a spacecraft disappear?"

"Because it wasn't really a spacecraft, in the first place! You're falling for a joke."

"Many people in the New Morality hierarchy feel pretty much as you do."

"But not you," Tavalera realized.

Again she shook her head. "This is much too important to dismiss as a joke, Mr. Tavalera. If it's real, the technology involved in that spacecraft is far beyond our understanding."

Tavalera had to admit to himself that she could be right. If it's real, he told himself. Which it isn't. It can't be.

"I hadn't thought about the possibility that this could be a hoax conceived by the dissidents in the *Goddard* habitat," said Sister Angelique in a distant, almost wistful voice.

"Or maybe some wiseass here on Earth," Tavalera suggested.

She gave him a frosty look. "Your vocabulary needs refinement, Mr. Tavalera."

"Yeah, guess so," he said a little sheepishly. "But the point is, you could be tying yourself into a knot over nothing more than some bright guy's idea of a joke."

"I wonder," she murmured.

For several moments she sat in silence at the head of the conference table, her eyes focused far beyond Tavalera's presence. He began to feel uncomfortable, fidgety.

At last he asked, "So why've you dragged me into this? What good can I do for you?"

She stirred as if surprised that he was still in the room with her. "Why, you've already made a contribution, Mr. Tavalera. We hadn't considered the possibility that the *Goddard* dissidents might be behind this."

Is she going for it? he wondered. Keep your big mouth shut. Don't let her see—

"Perhaps we should send someone to *Goddard* to investigate the possibility," she mused, her eyes on him.

Tavalera felt his heart leap, but he forced himself to remain silent, hoping his desire didn't show on his face.

"Would you be willing to go back to Saturn, Mr. Tavalera?"

He nodded, not trusting himself to speak.

Then Sister Angelique smiled at him. "You *want* to go back to that habitat, don't you? You applied for a return flight almost the moment you touched down on Earth, didn't you?"

"Yeah," he admitted.

"So you've invented this idea of a hoax as a means of getting us to allow you to return there?"

"No! I honestly think it's a possibility. I really do."

She watched him for several long moments, still smiling, until he began to feel uneasy under her gaze.

"Look," he said. "I want to go back, sure. But I really think that some of those scientists could have rigged this thing and—"

Sister Angelique raised a long, slim finger to silence him.

"I'll make a deal with you, Mr. Tavalera. You can call *Goddard* and speak to the authorities there. Have them investigate the possibility."

His spirits sank. Then he brightened as he realized, I'll get to talk to Holly! She's the chief administrator of the habitat. I'd have to talk to her about an investigation!

But he heard himself say, "It'd be better for me to go there in person. I'd get better results, don't you think?"

Her widening smile told him that she saw right through him. "No, Mr. Tavalera, I don't agree. First, you are not a trained investigator. It would be better for you to ask *Goddard*'s security people to conduct the investigation. Second, I prefer to have you here, working with me."

"Working with you?"

"Yes. While the idea of a cabal of *Goddard*'s scientists perpetrating a hoax on us is a possible answer to our puzzle, it is only one possibility. I want you to assist me in tracking down some of the others."

"But you just said I'm not a trained investigator."

"That's all right. You'll work with me and do what I tell you."

"And my job back home?"

"That will all be taken care of. I am the personal assistant of Bishop Zebulon Craig. I can get you reassigned to my staff. No problem."

"I'll have to move here?"

"You'll move to wherever I am, Mr. Tavalera. Wherever this task takes us."

"But my home's in Little Rock. My mother's there and she expects me—"

"You will go home when this task is successfully finished, Mr. Tavalera. Not before."

"But why me? Why can't you pick on somebody else?"

"You have been chosen. The Lord quite often works in mysterious ways."

"In other words, I don't have any choice, do I?"

"No, Mr. Tavalera. I'm afraid you don't. You will work with me until we solve this puzzle."

Whether I like it or not, he groused to himself.

"Don't look so unhappy," she said with a little laugh. "Once we find the answers we're looking for, I can see to it that you are allowed to return to *Goddard*."

"You can?" he blurted.

"Once we find the answers, Mr. Tavalera. Once we find the answers."

CHAPTER 10

His mother looked distressed.

"They told me you'd been arrested," she said, nearly in tears.

Tavalera sat in a cubicle in the New Morality's Rocky Mountain base and said to the image on the desktop screen, "No, Ma. I've been drafted, that's all. Not arrested."

There was a noticeable lag before her response reached him, longer than the normal delay in the relay of a message from a commsat in geosynch orbit, Tavalera thought.

"Drafted? Into the army?"

"No, Ma. I'm on a special assignment for a branch of the New Morality."

"What do they want you for?"

Good question, he thought. "Damned if I know."

His mother blinked at him. "What did you say? I saw your lips move, but the sound didn't come through."

Keeryst, Tavalera said to himself. They must have a censoring circuit blocking out words on their disapproved list. Or maybe a live censor listening to every word we say. Probably'd block out anything I might say about this work I'm supposed to be doing, too.

"When will you come back home?" his mother asked.

"Tomorrow. I'm staying here overnight and then they'll fly me home tomorrow."

"Oh. Good."

He had to tell her. "It'll just be to pack some clothes and things, Ma. Then I go out on my new assignment."

"You'll be leaving again? For where?"

"Don't know yet."

"But they can't just pull you this way and that way! First New Orleans and now you don't even know where!"

"Yes, they can, Ma." Silently he added, They can do any goddamned thing they want to.

The next day a different pair of agents flew him back to Little Rock and caused a neighborhood sensation when they landed their rattling, roaring tilt-rotor in the middle of the street, right in front of Tavalera's house. Pedestrians walking their pets gaped; people came out of their houses and stood at their front doors, staring.

He packed his travel bag as quickly as he could while his mother wept and bombarded him with a thousand questions he couldn't answer. At last he kissed her goodbye, promised to call her every day (if he could, he told himself), and then sprinted gratefully back to the waiting tilt-rotor, its big rotor arms whooshing as they swung lazily. Once he got aboard, the ship whisked him to Atlanta and the headquarters of the New Morality.

The headquarters complex lay in the heart of the city, a sprawling congregation of buildings centered on the massive neo-Gothic cathedral that stood on the site of the modest white clapboard church where the movement had begun, nearly a century earlier. That old wood-frame church had been taken down board by board and then lovingly restored inside the gleaming geodesic dome of a new museum that stood at the edge of the complex's soaring glass and steel skyscrapers. The towers held the offices, meeting rooms, hospital, hotels, and auditoriums of what had become a supremely powerful international organization.

The tilt-rotor had touched down on a spacious grassy field off to one side of the complex of buildings. His escorts had given Tavalera a pocket phone programmed with the location of the office he was to report to and warned him that the phone was programmed only for the GPS channel. They pointed him in the right direction, then left him alone. The tilt-rotor zipped away, clattering noisily. Heading for their next victim, Tavalera said to himself.

He was alone for the first time in days, he realized. Then he figured that the pocket phone they'd given him showed exactly where he was and if he didn't follow its instructions to the office, a couple more "escorts" would show up and make certain he went where they'd told him to go. With a shrug of acquiescence, he started off.

The headquarters complex was like a big university campus, Tavalera thought as he followed the GPS directions on the tiny screen of the pocket phone. The walkways were thick with people; none of them were using pocket phones. They must be outlawed, Tavalera figured. Nearly silent electric autos glided along the gently winding streets. He hadn't seen Sister Angelique since leaving the Rockies. Now he walked through the bright morning sunshine to the office where he'd been told to report for work.

It was hot, even this early on the February morning. Tavalera felt surprisingly good, though, despite the fact that he'd been picked up and hauled around the country like a sack of potatoes, moved this way and that without any recourse or say in the matter. That didn't bother him too much, because he was thinking about the possibility that he might, he just might, be able to get back to the massive habitat *Goddard*, back to the woman he loved, back to the life he had foolishly left behind.

At last he found the building where his office was located, in the maze of glass and steel towers, and even found the office on the fourteenth floor that he was told to report to.

"We've been expecting you," said the young woman behind the reception desk. She wore her light brown hair in a stylish sweep down one side of her attractive face, even though her clothing looked more like a dark cleric's robe than the kind of fashionable dress that a good-looking young woman would wear. She spoke in a sibilant near whisper.

Tavalera followed her softly voiced instructions down a long corridor, past three cross corridors, and finally a right turn at the fourth crossing. The corridors were thickly carpeted; the soft pastel walls seemed to absorb sound. Men and women walked past him, smiled, and nodded; some even said, "Good morning." All in whispers. It began to make him feel nervous.

At last he found the room he was looking for. Its door was open. Windowless, but all four walls glowed with smart screens showing the palm-bough symbol of the New Morality. There was no desk, but a pair of comfortable-looking armchairs covered in butterscotch fabric sat in the middle of the room, with a low table between them.

Tavalera stepped in and looked around. Nothing else in sight. The door swung shut and clicked. One wall broke into a life-sized image of Sister Angelique, sitting at a desk in another office somewhere. She broke into her bright, pleased smile.

"Good morning, Mr. Tavalera. Are you ready to begin God's work?"

CHAPTER 11

Tavalera sank into one of the armchairs.

"I guess so," he said.

"Good. I'm sorry I couldn't be with you in person this morning. This interactive program will tell you all you need to know, though, and get you started."

"Interactive program, huh?" Tavalera had used them before, when he worked on scoopships at Jupiter.

"Interactive program. The program will respond to your vocal questions and commands. It will also lay out your work assignment for the day."

"So I'm talking to a digital program."

Her image froze for an eyeblink. Then she replied,

"You are speaking to a digital avatar, Mr. Tavalera. I'm sorry that I couldn't be with you in person this morning, but I am tied up on important business elsewhere."

Meaning I'm not all that important, Tavalera said to himself.

"Your first assignment is to contact the habitat *Goddard* in Saturn orbit and request that their leaders start an investigation into the possibility that our message from the alleged starship is a hoax perpetrated by a person or persons aboard the habitat."

Tavalera nodded to the image. Contact Holly, he thought, his pulse thumping faster. Contact Holly.

The planet Saturn orbits ten times farther from the Sun than Earth does, which means that it takes communications—though moving at the speed of light—more than an hour to travel from one world to the other, even when the two planets are at the closest distance. There is no way to have a conversation when there is more than a two-hour lag between sending a message and receiving its answer.

So Tavalera leaned back in the softly yielding armchair and called out, "Message to Ms. Holly Lane, chief administrator of the habitat *Goddard*."

The wall screen facing him printed out his words, white against a deep blue background. The data bar running across the bottom of the screen showed the current time lag between Earth and Saturn: one hour, forty-two minutes.

Suddenly Tavalera's throat felt dry. He hadn't seen Holly since he'd left *Goddard*, nearly five months earlier. He'd promised her that he'd call her regularly, but once he'd arrived on Earth the government's telecommunications office informed him that only authorized agencies were allowed to contact the habitat and Tavalera was not only an *un*authorized agency, he was nothing more than an individual citizen, with no access to interplanetary communications allowed.

But now it's different, he thought. Now I'm working for the bastards.

"Holly," he finally said. "It's me. Raoul. I wasn't able to call you earlier; they wouldn't let me. But now I'm working for—"

He hesitated. Who the hell am I working for? he wondered. The federal government? The New Morality? Does it make any difference? They're all tangled up together.

"I've been drafted to work for the New Morality," he said. "They're worried about a message that's been beamed to Earth from a spacecraft that's entered the solar system from interstellar space. At least, that's the way it looks. Far as I'm concerned, I'm checking on the possibility that it could be some kind of joke—a hoax that's being pulled off by some of the bright guys on *Goddard*."

Again he stopped. That's kind of impersonal, he thought. I wonder how she's doing. She said she'd wait for me to come back, but that was months ago. I thought I'd be on my way back by now, not stuck in some office in Atlanta doing God's friggin' work.

He closed his eyes and pictured Holly: her flaring cheekbones and square, stubborn jaw; her sparkling brown eyes, her light brown hair that framed her face like a soft caress. Does she still love me? he asked himself. How can I explain to her why I haven't been able to start back to her?

"Holly, I had hoped to be on my way back to *Goddard* by now, but they won't let me go. I love you, honey, and I want to be with you. But there's something weird going on here, with this message and a spacecraft supposedly from beyond the solar system. The thing just disappeared! They tracked it as far as Jupiter and then it disappeared. And then they got this message from somebody who's been dead for more'n a hundred years, claiming he's been out among the stars.

"That's what makes me think it's a hoax, Holly. Could you look into it? See if some of the scientists in the habitat are trying to have some fun by scaring the bejesus out of the authorities here. They're really worried about this, honey. I mean, whatever it is, it's making the Northern Lights flash every night, clear down to Little Rock and probably farther south, as well.

"Please return this call. Please let me see you, talk to you. I miss you, Holly. I want to be with you. I really do. They say if I help them figure out what this business is all about, then they'll let me come back to *Goddard.* That's what I'm praying for. Please answer me, Holly. Please."

Then he took a breath and told the computer, "Transmit."

Sister Angelique's face reappeared on the wall screen. "This program has an automatic editing subroutine. It's editing your message now. Please stand by."

"Editing?" Tavalera scowled at Sister Angelique's smiling image, immobile on the screen. I should have known. They won't let anything go out until they've looked at it. And I went and spilled my guts to her.

Sister Angelique's image stirred to a simulacrum of life. "Your message has been edited for security, Mr. Tavalera. You may review the edited version before transmitting it to habitat *Goddard.*"

Tavalera read the edited text. To his surprise, most of his personal remarks were included. What they took out was any mention of his being forced to remain on Earth—and his brief reference to the authorities' being frightened by the message from the starship.

"Okay," he said, licking his lips. "Transmit it."

Nervously kneading his thighs, Tavalera told himself that he had nothing to do now for a couple of hours except wait for Holly's reply. If she replies. If she gets the message. What if the same wiseasses who've pulled off this stunt intercept my message and erase it? The possibility alarmed him. Then he thought, If I can show Sister Angelique and this Bishop Craig or whoever her boss is that the message was blocked, then maybe they'll send me to *Goddard* in person to snoop around. Yeah! They'd have to! Suddenly he began to hope that the message would be intercepted.

How long will I have to wait? he wondered. Two–three hours, at least. Maybe four. If I don't get an answer in four hours I'll tell Angelique that the message's been blocked.

Four hours. Then I call Sister Angelique.

He was very surprised when the wall screen began to glow a mere seventeen minutes after he'd transmitted his message. And even more shocked when the image on the screen shaped up to be not Holly Lane or anyone in the *Goddard* habitat. Not even Sister Angelique.

It was the bearded, imposing face of Keith Stoner.

"I'm not a hoax, Mr. Tavalera," said Stoner, his voice strong and calm. "I assure you, I am very real."

CHAPTER 12

And Tavalera found himself in what looked like the bridge of a spacecraft. He gulped and felt his stomach sink within him, as if he were dropping from an enormous height. He was still seated, but now his chair was a padded recliner with a footrest. Broad panels of blinking lights stretched around him; instruments beeped softly.

Above the panels was a wide window that looked out on the dazzling blue sphere of Earth, hanging in space, flecked with marching rows of brilliant white clouds.

Standing before him was Keith Stoner, tall, broad shouldered, his measured smile showing strong white teeth.

"I'm not a hoax, Raoul," Stoner repeated. "You don't mind if I call you Raoul, do you?"

Tavalera couldn't find his voice. His heart was thundering beneath his ribs. He felt dizzy, almost sick. The compartment smelled strange, different from any spacecraft he'd ever been in.

"And it's pretty obvious that I'm not dead, either," Stoner said, his smile fading.

"Wha . . . where are we?" Tavalera gasped. "What's happening? How did you . . . ?" He tried to push himself up out of the recliner, but his arms were too weak.

Stoner leaned over Tavalera and grasped his shoulder. "There's nothing to be afraid of, Raoul. It's all right; I promise you."

Tavalera felt a wave of tranquility wash over him, like a soft blanket, like sliding into a tub of warm, relaxing water. His heartbeat slowed to normal. His breathing calmed.

After a few moments, Stoner asked, "Are you all right now?" Genuine concern was etched on his face.

Tavalera nodded shakily. "Yeah. I think so." He glanced around at the blinking, beeping panels and the huge gleaming expanse of Earth hanging outside. "Wh . . . where the hell are we, anyway?"

"We're in a high orbit around the Earth," Stoner replied. "I'm afraid this spacecraft control center that you see is something of an illusion. The starship's interior doesn't actually look this way."

Tavalera looked around himself again. The compartment certainly looked completely real. The recliner he lay on felt solid beneath him.

"I'm presenting this appearance to you because it's something you can comprehend; it's within your experience."

"Yeah. . . ."

"I don't want to upset you or confuse you. You're going to have to deal with plenty of new issues, believe me."

Tavalera couldn't think of a reply. His mind was working hard to digest all that Stoner was telling him.

At last he asked, "Then we're not in orbit?" His voice sounded weak, almost pleading, in his own ears.

"Oh, we're in orbit, all right. That's really Earth hanging out there." Stoner's bearded face contracted into a perplexed frown. "The real question is, *when* are we?"

"Huh?"

Almost as if talking to himself, Stoner said, "We left Earth in A.D. 1985. Most of the time we traveled at relativistic velocities. I know that stretches out time, but now your local calendars read 'A.D. 2098,' and that just doesn't make sense."

Blinking with confusion, Tavalera asked, "Are you really Keith Stoner?"

Stoner cocked his head slightly, as if listening to some inner voice. Then he seemed to recognize Tavalera sitting there and answered, "Yes. I am Keith Stoner."

"But the records say you died in 1985."

"So they say."

"How can . . . ?" Tavalera felt overwhelmed; he didn't know what question to ask. This is crazy, he thought. It's all crazy.

"I know it seems peculiar to you," Stoner said, as if he could read Tavalera's mind. "There's a lot here that I don't understand myself."

"How'd I get onto this spacecraft?"

"You've been in space before," said Stoner. "You've been out at that habitat orbiting Saturn."

"I wish I was there now."

Slowly, almost wearily, Stoner sat on the edge of a recliner identical to the one Tavalera was on. It hadn't been there beside him a moment before.

"I've been looking through your historical records," Stoner said, his face utterly serious. "They don't jibe with my memory. Something strange is going on."

"N . . . No kidding?" Tavalera said.

"I'm not dead. I wasn't killed in an automobile accident in 1985. That's when we left in the starship."

"We? Who else is with you?"

As if he hadn't heard the question, Stoner went on musing. "Vanguard Industries was a huge multinational corporation, yet the only mention of Vanguard Industries in your records shows it was a two-bit start-up venture that folded in the nineteen nineties."

"What's that got to do with anything?"

"And there's no record of Hubert Humphrey being President of the United States. Or of Indira Gandhi being the first woman elected Secretary-General of the United Nations."

"Who?" Tavalera asked.

His bearded face looking deeply troubled, Stoner went on, "Worst of all, there's no mention anywhere of the starship that swung through the solar system. Not even of Big Eye: all I could find was references to something called the Hubble Space Telescope."

"What starship? When?"

"It came into the solar system, passed by Jupiter, and then made a flyby of Earth. I went into space and rendezvoused with that starship. I was aboard it for years, frozen cryogenically. Jo got Vanguard Industries to retrieve me and bring me back."

"Joe?" Tavalera asked. "Who's Joe?"

Stoner almost smiled. "Sorry, I'm going too fast. Jo Camerata. She was head of Vanguard Industries, a big multinational corporation. Later on she and I got married."

"She's your wife?"

Nodding, "Yes."

"And you were frozen on the alien's starship?"

Another nod. "I was the first human being to be recovered from cryonic suspension."

Tavalera shook his head. "I never heard of that. I mean, I've heard of people being frozen and then brought back to life." He thought of Holly. "But I never heard about an alien starship or you being the first corpsicle to be revived."

"I'm not surprised. I couldn't find a word about it in any of your historical records." Stoner's face hardened. "But I see that your government is freezing people convicted of crimes. Dissidents, political opponents. It's cheaper to keep them frozen than maintain them in prison. Or transport them off-planet."

This guy must be crazy, Tavalera thought. Then he realized, But if he is, how the hell did he bring me up to this spacecraft? The whole thing is weird. It's way beyond weird; it's—

"I know it's unbelievable," Stoner said. "But we've got to get the answers. And quickly. The future of the whole human race depends on this."

Tavalera was about to ask what he meant by that, but he found himself back in his office in Atlanta, sitting in the same butterscotch armchair, staring at a blank wall screen, just as if he had never been out of that room.

CHAPTER 13

The screen chimed softly and spelled out: INCOMING MESSAGE.

Tavalera blinked. A surge of panic rushed through him. This can't be happening! I'm going crazy!

Holly Lane's young, eager face filled the wall screen, smiling, beaming at him.

"Raoul! I got your message!" She seemed bursting with joy. "It's so good to hear from you! I thought . . . well, what I thought doesn't matter now, does it? Why didn't you call me earlier? How are you?"

Her words tumbled out in a bewildering rush. With the communications lag imposed by distance, it was customary for one person to talk while the other listened, but Holly was babbling away as if she hadn't spoken to anyone in years.

Tavalera sat there, staring stupidly at her image on the screen, his mind in a whirl. One minute I'm on his spaceship and the next I'm back here. It's impossible. I must be cracking up. He started to tremble uncontrollably: his hands, his entire body, shook like a dust mote in a hurricane.

Holly kept talking, smiling, laughing happily. Dimly Tavalera saw that the digital clock readout in the lower corner of the screen indicated three and a half hours had passed since he had sent his message to her. Three and a half hours! What happened? How did it happen? What's happening to me?

"I'll check with the science people, Raoul," Holly was prattling on, "but I really don't think they would rig up a fake message to send Earthside. They're too busy studying the bugs on Titan and those nanomachines in the rings. Maybe somebody else pulled off the joke, but

I really don't think it was anybody here in *Goddard*. I'll ask Professor Wilmot to put together a little team of people to look into it. He doesn't have much to do these days and . . ."

Through the whirlwind of emotions swirling through him, Tavalera faintly understood that Holly was happy to hear from him. She's just running on and on because she thought I'd forgotten about her, but now she knows I haven't and she's happy as a kid on Christmas, and how did he get me into his spacecraft and then back here again? How? How?

"So what's it like, being back home?" Holly asked. "How's your mom and all your old friends? Is the greenhouse flooding as bad as the news nets make it look? When will you be coming back here? Or do you want me to come to Earth? My term'll be over in another seven months. I can come then, if you want me to."

Holly's uninterrupted monologue abruptly stopped. Her bright, eager expression faded a bit. Now she looked uneasy, almost worried.

"You do want to come back, don't you? I mean, I could come visit you Earthside and then we'd go back together, right? Please tell me what you want to do."

She lapsed into silence. Tavalera sat there for several long moments, his thoughts tumbling wildly. I was on his spacecraft, he kept telling himself. I talked with him. He's real. He's alive.

But so is Holly. Tavalera saw the anxious expression on her face, the hope in her eyes. With all his heart he wanted to tell her how much he wished he were with her, how much he loved her.

But he heard his own strangled voice grate, "I . . . I can't talk . . . can't . . ."

The wall screen went blank. Holly's face disappeared. Tavalera just sat there, sagging in the armchair, mouth hanging open, heart racing. Then Sister Angelique's dark, almond-eyed face appeared on the screen, frowning with concern.

"Mr. Tavalera, what's wrong? Are you all right?"

He tried to speak, tried to shake his head. But the thundering of his pulse in his ears drowned out everything. It was like hammer blows battering him.

He saw the room's ceiling slide past his glassy eyes, and then everything went black.

CHAPTER 14

Tavalera heard a soft beeping sound and for a panicked instant thought he was back in Stoner's spacecraft. He tried to open his eyes; they were gummy, but the lids slowly separated. Everything seemed blurred, misty. He was flat on his back and unable to move.

"He's coming out of it," a woman's voice said.

"Call Sister Angelique," said another voice, deeper, a man's.

Tavalera blinked several times. His eyes still felt sticky, but he could make out a soft white ceiling above him. Turning his head slightly, he saw a bank of monitoring instruments lining the wall, fuzzy, blurred. I'm in a bed, he realized. This must be a hospital.

"Stimulant?" asked the woman's voice.

"Inject."

Tavalera felt nothing, but his vision cleared. The room came into focus. Two medics in white smocks were standing by his bed.

The man gave him a professional smile. "Back among us now, eh?" He had a full beard, pepper-and-salt.

"Who . . . who're you?" Tavalera's tongue felt thick, swollen. "What happened to me?"

"You collapsed in your office this morning," said the doctor.

The woman looked up at the panel of monitors on the wall. "Life signs approaching normal," she said, sounding almost disappointed about it. She was a hefty-looking blonde, with thick arms and a hard cast to her face.

The doctor made a chuckling laugh and pointed at Tavalera with a stubby finger. "You'll be fine. Just lay there and rest. We'll keep you under observation overnight. Try to relax and get a good night's sleep."

They both started toward the door.

"Wait," he called after them weakly. "What's happening to me? What's wrong with me?"

They ignored his questions and walked out of the narrow room, leaving Tavalera alone on the bed. He tried to sit up, but his head started spinning and he plopped back on the pillows again. He saw that there was a cuff around his left biceps, with a vial of clear liquid attached to it, blinking silently. It felt warm against his skin. He tried to read the label on the dispenser, but it was medical jargon he didn't understand.

Try to relax and get a good night's sleep, he repeated silently. Yeah. Great.

Tavalera waited several minutes, then slowly, slowly tried to sit up once again. He felt woozy, but he made it to a sitting position. A monitor alarm began chiming, its light flashing red.

"Please remain in your bed," demanded a computer's synthesized voice. "Do not try to get out of your bed."

How far can I get? Tavalera asked himself. Then he realized he was wearing a flimsy pale green hospital gown, tied loosely in the back. It hung on him, several sizes too big. Where'd they put my clothes?

He pulled the bedsheet back off his hairy legs and half-slid to the floor. Leaning heavily on the bed, he tried to straighten up. The floor tiles felt pleasantly warm to his bare feet.

"Please remain in your bed," the computer repeated. "Do not try to get out of your bed."

"Bullshit," Tavalera muttered. "Where's the clothes closet?"

The beefy woman medic who'd been in the room moments earlier burst in again. "What do you think you're doing?" She was clearly angry, her heavyset face florid, her eyes ablaze.

"I'm okay," he said. "I wanna go home."

She wrapped her muscular arms around him and pushed him back against the bed. "You get in that bed and stay there! Doctor's orders!"

"I don't want—"

Sister Angelique stepped through the open doorway, her eyes widening at the sight of Tavalera struggling with the medic.

"Tell them I'm okay," Tavalera pleaded to Angelique.

She smiled coolly at him. "It would be better if you got back in bed, Mr. Tavalera. It's for your own good."

He pulled free of the woman's grasp and leaned back on the edge of the bed, puffing from the exertion. The medic glared at Tavalera and he glared back.

"He'll be all right," said Sister Angelique to the woman. "Could you kindly give us some privacy? I need to talk with him."

Still glowering at Tavalera, the medic said gruffly, "He's supposed to stay in bed. Doctor's orders."

"He will," Angelique said softly. To Tavalera she added, "Won't you, Raoul? For me?"

Feeling outmaneuvered, Tavalera hoisted himself back onto the bed and sat with his back barely touching the pillows. The bed rose with a soft whirring sound and adjusted itself to his position. The medic made a single curt nod, then left the room and shut the door behind her.

There was no chair in the narrow room, so Sister Angelique remained standing. "You gave us quite a fright this morning," she said.

"Scared myself," Tavalera admitted.

"What happened, Raoul? You don't mind me being so familiar, do you?"

"It's okay."

"So what happened? What made you collapse that way?"

"I'm not sure I know," he said.

Angelique studied him with her cool dark eyes for a long moment. Then she said, "You transmitted your message to the chief administrator of the *Goddard* habitat, which is all to the good."

"Holly Lane," Tavalera murmured.

Frowning slightly, Angelique continued, "The security cameras show that you sat in your chair for three hours, not moving, hardly breathing. As if you were catatonic, almost. Then the return message came in from *Goddard* and you collapsed."

"I saw Stoner," he blurted.

Angelique's eyes flashed wide. "Keith Stoner? The man who claims he's been to the stars?"

"I was on his spacecraft . . . somehow."

"You never left your office. The cameras show you were there the whole time."

"I was on his spacecraft. He's alive. He talked to me, told me he was puzzled, that our history records don't match what he remembers from his earlier life."

"That's not possible, Raoul."

"I know it's not!" he wailed. "But it happened to me. I was *there*! And then I was back again."

"A hallucination," she said almost in a whisper. "But why? What's happened to you, Raoul?"

"I don't know! It was all so real, but . . . it couldn't have been. I must be going nutty!"

Sister Angelique made a little clucking sound with her tongue. "I don't think so," she said, trying to sound reassuring. "It's too much of a coincidence, you sending a message out to Saturn orbit and then Stoner suddenly appearing to you."

"But you said I was alone in the office all the time."

"That's what the cameras show."

"Then I must have dreamed the whole thing. It must've been some kind of crazy dream."

Sister Angelique looked down at him thoughtfully. "We'll have to see about that, Raoul. We'll see."

CHAPTER 15

When he woke up the next morning Tavalera figured that they must have put a sedative in the meager dinner a nurse had brought to him on a plastic tray. I went out like a light, he thought. No dreams, nothing.

Now, sitting up on the self-adjusting bed, he listened to the monitors beeping softly. No way to tell what time it is, he realized. There were no windows in the narrow room, no clock. Must be morning, he reasoned. I got a good sleep and now it's gotta be morning.

As if in answer to his surmise, a young nurse pushed the door open, followed by a flat-topped robot bearing a breakfast tray covered with plastic domes. Tavalera smelled sausages and coffee.

"You must have friends in high places. Juice, eggs, soy sausages, and hot coffee," the nurse announced as she lifted the tray from the robot to Tavalera's lap. "That's a lot better than the usual breakfast around here."

She wasn't exactly pretty, Tavalera thought: her nose was hooked and her complexion blotchy. But she was a big improvement over the woman who'd tried to wrestle him back to bed the previous day.

"Thanks," he said.

She gave him a smile and said, "You're scheduled for brain scans at ten thirty."

It was a full morning. A pair of strapping male orderlies popped into his room the instant he finished his coffee and bustled him into a powered wheelchair. They're watching me, Tavalera guessed. They can see every breath I take.

They controlled the powerchair with a handheld remote unit and led him through a bewildering maze of corridors, one orderly striding along beside the powerchair, the other—with the remote—behind Tavalera. He got the feeling they were guards and they were with him to make certain he went where they wanted him to. Not that I'm going anywhere in this hospital gown, he told himself, picturing himself running out onto the streets with his butt hanging out and the two strong-arm orderlies chasing him.

The brain scans were painless. They brought him to a room that looked like a laboratory and sat him in an oversized metal chair, then placed a crown of electrodes on his head. He thought of the stimulator his mother used.

"Good thing you keep your hair short," said the technician running the lab. "If it's too bushy we have to shave it down."

As he adjusted the equipment that filled the lab the technician kept chattering: "We had one guy in here with hair like Samson, all the way down to his waist. He screamed like we were crucifying him when we had to cut it off. And the women—they cry and weep. We get some really interesting scans from 'em when they're all wrought up like that."

Tavalera said nothing. The equipment hummed; the technician nattered on. He saw a display screen that showed what looked like a human brain, with colors flashing on and off in various parts of it.

"Is that me?" he asked.

"No talking, please," said the technician. Then he added, "Yeah, it's you."

From the brain scan the orderlies took him to a full-body scanner, and from there to a big open room filled with gym equipment. People were jogging on treadmills, working on weight machines, pedaling stationary bikes. Despite its clean carpeting and indirect lighting, the room smelled of perspiration.

The orderlies clicked a monitor to his left biceps, then told Tavalera to run on one of the treadmills.

"What's this for?" he asked.

"Cardiac stress test," they answered in unison.

Like robots, Tavalera thought, almost amused at them.

As he started jogging he realized that the man next to him had a prosthetic leg. Looking farther down the row, he saw several more people with prostheses, including a grossly overweight woman whose flesh wobbled and jounced as she trotted sweatily on two artificial legs.

Why don't they rebuild the limbs with stem cell therapy? he wondered. That's what they'd do on *Goddard*.

The treadmill moved faster and faster, forcing Tavalera to run harder. He began to sweat, but instead of resenting the forced exertion he grinned inwardly. It felt good to be moving, to be working his body.

A chime rang and the treadmill slowed to a stop.

As he got off, Tavalera asked, "What's next?"

"Blood tests," said the first orderly.

"Needles," said the second, with a malicious grin.

It wasn't all that bad, Tavalera decided afterward. He didn't like being punctured, but the women who stuck him and drew his blood knew what they were doing. It hardly hurt at all.

"Now what?" he asked as he walked, a little shakily, out of the blood-drawing station.

"A shower," said the first orderly.

"You need it," said the second one, wrinkling his nose.

"Then you get dressed and see Dr. Mayfair," said the first one.

"The big boss," said the second one, his malicious grin returning.

They returned Tavalera to his cubicle of a room and gave him some privacy as he showered in the attached lavatory. When he came out of the shower his clothes were on the bed, neatly laid out.

Dr. Mayfair's office was spacious, with the first window that Tavalera had seen in the entire hospital. It looked out onto a parking lot filled with busses. The doctor was standing by the window looking up at the cloudy sky when the orderlies ushered Tavalera into his office. Mayfair was short but thick bodied. His hair was sandy, his face oval, with clear light brown eyes. He smiled pleasantly at Tavalera.

"Ah! Our enigma." Mayfair gestured to the round table near the window and sat in one of the chairs grouped around it.

Tavalera took the chair next to his, grateful that he was back in his own slacks and shirt rather than the humiliating hospital gown.

Mayfair pointed to the opposite wall and it immediately lit up with a group of charts and images. Tavalera recognized the brain scan he'd undergone a couple of hours earlier.

Smiling amiably, Dr. Mayfair said, "I've been told that the engineers have a saying: 'Hell is where everything checks, but nothing works.' "

Tavalera nodded cautiously. "Yeah, I've heard that, too."

"You're something like that, Mr. Tavalera. We've scanned your brain and body; we've put you through a fairly strenuous stress test and done blood tests. Everything checks out quite normal."

Tavalera said nothing, waiting for the other shoe to drop.

"Which means, I'm afraid, that you are quite seriously deranged," said Dr. Mayfair with a smile that looked almost joyful. But then his eyes went hard. "Or you're lying through your teeth."

CHAPTER 16

"Lying?" Tavalera yelped. "Why would I be lying? How in hell could I make up something so damned wild?"

"Your language betrays you, Tavalera," Mayfair said, his voice cold. "I have your complete dossier here. You tried to get out of your public-service duty when you found out you'd be sent to Jupiter. You never attended worship services while off-Earth. You haven't been to church since you've returned."

"What's that got to do with anything?"

"You're not a Believer."

"So what? I never made a secret of it."

Getting up from his chair and walking to the desk, Mayfair said, "You've rather reveled in your refusal to accept the faith. You've played the part of the rebel, haven't you?"

"Rebel? Me?"

"And then you spent more than a year aboard that space habitat, that hotbed of malcontents and secularists. What did they teach you there? What instructions did you bring back with you?"

Tavalera felt totally confused. "Instructions? I didn't get any instruc—"

"Don't think you can hide behind those antiquated Constitutional rights you rebels always quote," Mayfair said as he sat himself down behind his broad desk. "This is a matter of national security."

"Me? National security?"

"Yes, you," said Mayfair, an angry growl in his voice now. "You come back from space, after spending years with the exiles aboard *Goddard*, and suddenly this supposed visitor from the stars appears."

"Stoner's from Earth," Tavalera countered.

"Stoner is a hoax! And you know it!"

"I thought he might be, but . . . Chri . . . cripes, he appeared to me! He took me to his spacecraft!"

"So you say. There is no evidence of that happening. Nothing except your unsupported word. Nothing at all."

"I'm not making it up!"

Mayfair started to snap out a reply, thought better of it, took a deep breath instead, and folded his hands prayerfully on the desktop.

At last he said, "Mr. Tavalera. I bear heavy responsibilities. I am not merely the head of this hospital. I am a member of the board of directors of the New Morality. I report directly to Bishop Zebulon Craig, who is only one step below Archbishop Overmire himself."

Tavalera blinked, trying to figure out where Mayfair was heading.

"This visitor from the stars," Mayfair went on, "this . . . this Keith Stoner, as he calls himself, is obviously a hoax. A well-planned hoax, I admit, but a hoax nonetheless."

"He's real," Tavalera muttered.

"I know you would like us to believe that, but we're going to get to the bottom of this conspiracy, believe me."

"It's not a conspiracy! I saw—"

"You're lying!" Mayfair shouted. "That much is certain. You're not delusional and there's no physical trauma affecting your brain. Therefore you are lying. Admit it."

Tavalera got to his feet and walked from the little circular table by the window to the amply upholstered chair in front of the desk. His surprise and confusion at Mayfair's wild accusations was giving way to a simmering anger.

Leaning his knuckles on the desktop, he said, "Give me a lie detector test, then."

Mayfair smiled thinly at him. "You've been trained to deal with lie detectors, I'm sure."

Shaking his head, Tavalera asked, "What's got you people so worked up about this? A visitor from the friggin' stars! You oughtta be excited about it. You oughtta be trying your damnedest to talk with him, hear what he's got to tell us!"

"That's exactly it!" Mayfair snapped, pointing an accusing finger at Tavalera. "You people *want* us to let this so-called star man spread his heresies among us."

"Heresies?"

"He's obviously not one of us. He didn't send his message to Archbishop Overmire or any other religious figure on Earth. No, he wants to talk to scientists, to political leaders, even to the people at large. It's a well-conceived propaganda ploy, created by secular humanists, aimed at undermining the religious faith of Believers all around the world."

"That's crazy!" Tavalera blurted.

"Is it? You were very clever to suggest a hoax originating aboard habitat *Goddard.* Your intent was to send us in the wrong direction, wasn't it? The originators of the heretical ploy are right here on Earth, aren't they?"

"How the hell would I know?" Tavalera snapped.

Mayfair smiled grimly at him.

"And what if it's not a hoax?" Tavalera insisted. "What if it's real? What if this guy Stoner is really what he claims to be?"

"Impossible."

"All right. What if he's really an alien, but he's shaped himself in human form to make contact with us? What then?"

Mayfair shuddered visibly. "Impossible," he repeated, but his voice was lower, weaker.

"He's real," Tavalera said firmly.

"He is not. And you are going to admit that." Mayfair turned slightly and said to the empty air, "Security."

Within a heartbeat the office door swung open and a trio of uniformed men stepped in.

Mayfair got to his feet. "You're going to admit it's a hoax," he said to Tavalera. "And you're going to tell us who's behind it. We've had experience with conspirators and heretics before. They all confess, sooner or later."

Christ Almighty, Tavalera thought, it's the friggin' Spanish Inquisition all over again!

The three guards advanced toward Tavalera. He felt

suddenly queasy at the sight of their hard, emotionless faces. They reached for his arms . . .

And froze.

Keith Stoner stood in the corner of the room, by the table next to the window, his bearded face set in a scowl.

"He's telling you the truth, Dr. Mayfair. I'm real and you'd better tell your superiors they're going to have to deal with me. Or go as extinct as the dinosaurs."

BOOK II

KEITH STONER

Any sufficiently advanced technology is
indistinguishable from magic.

Sir Arthur C. Clarke

CHAPTER 1

"It's all wrong," said Keith Stoner. "Jumbled. Distorted."

His wife sat beside him on the plushly cushioned sofa. On the other side of the coffee table sat their son, Rick, and daughter, Cathy, in comfortable armchairs. Stoner had produced the illusion of a snug old-fashioned Vermont ski lodge inside the starship's cocoon of energy, complete with a fireplace crackling in one pine-paneled corner and frosted windows that looked out on a snow-filled forest of deep green fir trees—even though there had been no snow in New England for more than a generation.

"They're so xenophobic," said Jo. "Worse than ever."

Jo Camerata was a dark-haired beauty whose Mediterranean ancestry showed in her lush figure and dark, sparkling eyes. She had been an undergraduate student when she first fell in love with Keith Stoner, a lifetime ago. Stoner was a NASA mission specialist, an astrophysicist who had become an astronaut so that he could work on Big Eye, the mammoth telescope that was being built in orbital space. It was Big Eye that first imaged the alien starship as it entered the solar system.

Stoner led the international cabal of scientists that cajoled and inveigled the belligerent, suspicious governments of East and West to suspend their Cold War hostilities long enough to send him in a spacecraft out to the starship as it neared Earth. It was a sarcophagus, bearing the preserved corpse of the intelligent creature who'd sent it out among the stars as a message to any intelligent species who encountered it.

When Stoner became stranded on the alien spacecraft, frozen in the cryogenic cold of space, Jo spent years clawing her way to the top of Vanguard Industries, one of the world's most powerful multinational conglomerates, and eventually sent an expedition to capture the alien sarcophagus before it left the solar system entirely with Keith Stoner's preserved body aboard it.

The technology that human scientists gleaned from the alien visitor changed many industries, while Jo Camerata kept Stoner's frozen body cyronically preserved in a specially built laboratory until her corporate researchers learned how to return him to life.

They married and had two children, even while Stoner gradually discovered the alien powers that now inhabited his body. He set out to transform the world, and Jo used the resources of Vanguard Industries to help him.

But the world resisted transformation, and Stoner slowly, reluctantly learned that it would take generations, centuries, before the human race could give up its ancient fears and hatreds. When their daughter was murdered in a botched attempt to kidnap him, Stoner decided to build a new starship and leave Earth forever with his wife, his son, and the fetus of his daughter, cloned from the cells of her slaughtered body.

What they found among the stars forced them to return to Earth, a different Earth from the one they'd left, but a world that needed transformation even more urgently than the one they'd left behind. A world that did not have generations or centuries to transform itself. A world that was on the brink of a man-made extinction event.

"They're beyond help," said Rick. He had kept his

body image as youthful as a twenty-year-old, although the years showed in his eyes, gray-blue as a storm-swept sea, much like his father's.

"I can't believe that," Stoner said.

"You've tried to make contact with them," said Cathy. She had been fourteen when she was murdered; now she appeared to be a young adult, about her brother's age. "They've ignored every one of our attempts."

"We've got to keep trying," Stoner insisted. "We've got to."

Jo rested a hand on his shoulder. "Is it worth it?"

He looked into his wife's dark eyes. "The survival of the human race? Yes, I think that's worth a lot. Everything."

"I wonder," said Rick. "Maybe they don't want to be saved."

"That's not fair," Cathy objected. "They don't know what they're up against."

Rick sneered at his sister. "And if they knew they'd just kill themselves sooner."

Stoner asked his son, "Is that what you think?"

"I don't think they're worth the trouble, Dad."

He turned to Cathy. "And you, Cath? How do you feel about this?"

His daughter glanced at her mother, then answered, "I don't know, Dad. Maybe Rick is right. But . . ." She left her thought unspoken.

Jo said, "You don't have any memory of Earth, Cathy. You were born on this starship."

Nodding uncertainly, Cathy replied, "I've been watching them, studying them through the ship's sensors."

"Me, too," Rick interjected. "I haven't seen much that's worth saving."

Cathy asked, "Why can't we go down to Earth and see them for ourselves?"

"You can get all the information you want from the ship's sensors," Jo replied.

"But that's not the same," her daughter said. "I mean, you go down there, Dad. Why can't Rick and me? It's not fair."

Jo objected, "It's dangerous down there. All those people, billions of them. Some of them are crazy: terrorists, rapists, murderers . . ."

Cathy looked into her mother's troubled eyes. "I was murdered once; I know, Mom. But we've got all the ship's systems to protect us now. We'll be safe."

Shaking her head, Jo began, "I wouldn't feel—"

With a youthful grin, Rick said, "Come on, Mom. You can keep watch over us. If there's any trouble you can yank us back to the ship in a nanosecond."

Jo turned to Stoner. He scratched at his beard and said, "Maybe they should go down there and see their home world close-up. Mingle with the people." To Cathy and Rick he added, "See what you think about the human race after you've lived among them for a bit."

Jo started to object, but Cathy laughed. "Like an anthropological expedition?"

Rick snapped, "More like a trip to the zoo."

Jo objected, "It could be dangerous."

"We'll be protected," said Rick. "They can't penetrate our systems."

"And we won't let anyone know who we are," Cathy said, warming to the idea. "We'll travel incognito."

Jo was still apprehensive. "I don't know. . . ."

"It'd be exciting!" Cathy said.

"Interesting, at least," her brother agreed.

"They'll be fine," Stoner said to Jo. "You can keep watch over them from here in the ship. Pull them back here to safety the instant anything dangerous crops up."

His wife still looked mistrustful, but she said nothing.

"Okay," Rick said. "Let's do it."

"Where should we go first?" Cathy asked.

"I don't know," said Rick. "Come on; let's check the surveillance records."

The two of them winked out of their parents' presence.

"They're like kids going on a vacation trip," Jo said worriedly.

"They'll be all right," Stoner said.

"And you?" Jo asked. "What will you be doing while they're traipsing around down there?"

He answered, "This fellow Tavalera. They're trying to use him to find out if we're really from the stars. He's going to be my contact man."

CHAPTER 2

"Tavalera?" Jo asked.

"He seems a likely candidate for contact," Stoner replied. "His mind's still adaptable, not fixated on an inflexible worldview. He's been off-Earth; he even wants to return to the habitat in orbit around Saturn."

Jo pointed out, "Yet when you made contact with him he collapsed in panic and confusion."

Stoner nodded ruefully. "I guess I overwhelmed him. Too much for him to accept, all at once."

"How can we tell them what they need to know?" Jo wondered. "How can we make any kind of meaningful contact with people who are so xenophobic, so frightened of the idea that they might not be alone in the universe?"

"And what will happen when we tell them the truth?" Stoner added. "The terrible, unavoidable truth?"

"Is Tavalera the best you can do?"

"I'll contact others," Stoner said as he extended his consciousness to Tavalera's mind. "But for now—"

He stiffened with surprise. And annoyance.

"What is it?" Jo asked.

"They're threatening to torture the poor guy!"

"Torture?"

"A man named Mayfair is threatening Tavalera with torture, because he can't accept what Tavalera's telling him."

"You'll have to help him!"

"Right," said Stoner.

He left the starship and projected his presence into Mayfair's office. Tavalera was standing in front of the desk; three uniformed security guards were between him and the door. Mayfair stood behind his desk, his expression stone hard.

"He's telling you the truth, Dr. Mayfair," Stoner said, standing by the office's window. "I'm real and you'd better tell your superiors they're going to have to deal with me. Or go as extinct as the dinosaurs."

Mayfair sagged down on his desk chair, his face going gray as ashes. Tavalera jerked with surprise and the three armed guards who had just entered the room seemed frozen with shock.

But only for a moment. Their leader pawed at the pistol in the black leather holster at his hip. Both the other men, younger and faster, drew their pistols and leveled them at Stoner.

Stoner said mildly, "They won't work, gentlemen, so you might as well put your guns away."

Mayfair recovered enough to shout, "Shoot him if he makes any threatening moves! Keep him covered!"

Stoner smiled at the doctor. "Why would I make a

threatening move? And what do you define as threatening?"

"Stay there by the window! Don't come any closer!"

"Don't be an ass," Stoner said.

He took a step toward Mayfair, still behind his desk. One of the guards stretched out his arm and fired his pistol. Or tried to. The trigger would not budge. The other two tried, as well. They got red in the face with strain, but the guns would not fire.

"I told you the guns won't work," Stoner said. "You don't have any need for them. I'm not going to cause any trouble."

Tavalera broke into a grin. "You've already caused trouble. You've got them all scared shitless."

"Scared? Why?" Stoner looked Tavalera over, then asked, "Are you frightened of me?"

"Hell yes!"

"Why?"

Tavalera waved a hand in the air. "You pop in just like a genie. *Whoosh!* You're here."

"That frightens you."

"You bet it does. And you bring me up to your spacecraft just like snapping your fingers."

Stoner admitted, "I suppose that did seem strange to you."

"Wh . . . who are you?" Mayfair sputtered. "What are you doing here? What do you want?"

"I am Keith Stoner. I'm here to prevent you from dragging this young man off to a forced interrogation because he told you the truth. I want to save the human race."

"Save us?" Mayfair's brows knit. "Save us from what?"

"From the nuclear war that's about to begin. From the total extinction of the entire human race."

"What nuclear war?" asked the guard leader.

"It's been brewing for decades," Stoner replied. "And you don't seem to have the defensive shields that we gave you back before I left for the stars."

"You're crazy!" Mayfair shouted.

Stoner shook his head. "Anything that you don't understand—or *won't* understand—you label as crazy. Strange attitude for a clinical psychologist."

"Is Atlanta going to be bombed?" the guard leader asked, his voice hollow.

"If we allow the war to start, yes."

"You can stop it?"

"No," said Stoner. "But you can. I hope."

CHAPTER 3

The guards still held their pistols in their hands, but they had allowed their arms to drop to their sides. Mayfair still sat rigidly behind his desk, his face set in a tight, frightened glare.

Tavalera stood before the desk, facing Stoner. "There can't be a nuclear war," he said. "Nuclear weapons have been banned for nearly half a century."

"Forbidden, but not forgotten," Stoner said gravely. "The truce between the Western nations and the nations of Islam is falling apart. Population pressures are building and your resources are being depleted faster than ever."

"But we've got fusion energy, natural resources from the asteroids . . ."

"You're building a pressure cooker here on this planet. More resources lead to bigger population. Resources from space have delayed the inevitable, but the war is still coming—unless you take steps to prevent it."

Mayfair asked in a more subdued voice, "How do you know this?"

Ignoring his question, Stoner said, "Your government is actually run by your New Morality organization. I've got to meet with their leader."

"Archbishop Overmire?"

"Franklin Haverford Overmire, yes, he's the one."

"But you can't just walk in and see the Archbishop," said Mayfair. "Not even I can do that."

Smiling tightly, Stoner replied, "I could. But I'd rather he was prepared to meet with me and have a serious discussion. A very serious discussion."

Mayfair fell silent.

"Can you arrange such a meeting for me?" Stoner asked.

Obviously struggling within himself, Mayfair said, "I . . . it's impossible. . . . No one can . . ."

Stoner crossed his arms over his chest.

Mayfair was perspiring visibly, beads of sweat dotting his forehead and upper lip. "I don't have access to the Archbishop. I truly don't."

"Then who does?"

"Bishop Craig," Mayfair said almost in a whimper. "I could bring you to Bishop Craig."

With a satisfied nod, "Then let's go see Bishop Craig."

Almost like a puppet being hauled to its feet by invisible strings, Mayfair rose from his chair and stepped hesitantly around his desk. To the empty air he called, "Phone, alert Bishop Craig. We're coming to his office. We'll arrive in about ten minutes."

Stoner crooked a finger at Tavalera. "You'd better come along, too."

Tavalera watched Mayfair totter to the door of his office, past the three stone-silent security guards, and out into the anteroom. Stoner walked beside him, towering almost a full head taller than Mayfair. He's *controlling* the doc, Tavalera realized. He's making Mayfair do what he wants.

Is he controlling me? No, Tavalera thought. I want to go along on this. I want to see Bishop Craig. And Archbishop Overmire. Tavalera had no doubt at all that Stoner would get his meeting with the Archbishop.

Zebulon Josephus Craig was a small man, slim and diminutive, almost elfin. His pate had been totally bald since he'd been forty, and his skin was as dark as milk chocolate. Bishop Craig was always as neat and sharp as a pin. Clerical suits that looked drab and ordinary on other men seemed to fit him so perfectly that he looked like an ecclesiastical fashion plate. His colleagues often called him Dapper Dan, although never to his face.

He was an energetic man who obviously enjoyed the smaller pleasures of life: good companionship, a job well done. Beneath his charming, accommodating exterior, though, beat a coldly calculating driving ambition. He wanted to become the New Morality's next Archbishop. He wanted the power to choose Presidents and Senators. He wanted to run the nation, and much of the world, the way it *should* be run.

Archbishop Overmire was an old and ailing man, Craig estimated. The Archbishop had vowed never to accept the rejuvenation treatments or other antiaging therapies of the secular scientists. Artificial hearts and replacement organs. Stem cell therapy. Telomerase injections. They were forbidden to the ordinary faithful, and their Archbishop would not partake of them, either, even though he knew that lesser souls had done so in secret. None of that for the leader of the New Morality! The Archbishop promised he would live out the natural span of years that God had allotted him, and no more.

The Archbishop could not possibly last for much longer, thought Bishop Craig. The game now was to position himself to be elected the next Archbishop.

Craig used his charm and his coolly detached intelligence to move ahead of his rival bishops in the unannounced, never-admitted race to become the next Archbishop of the New Morality movement. The thought had occurred to him more than once that an enterprising man might not even have to wait until God called Overmire to Him. The current Archbishop could retire or be found physically unable to continue carrying his heavy burdens.

Meanwhile, Bishop Craig kept on his course, winning approval for his relentless campaigns to root out evil, to bring all Believers into one harmonious mindset, to enforce submission to God's will and stamp out every form of doubt and noncomformity wherever he found it.

Outwardly Bishop Craig was a pleasant, chipper, friendly man. He treated his staff well. He had legions of friends and supporters. He liked to laugh.

But he was not laughing as he stared at the image of the uniformed security guard on the wall screen to the left of his desk.

"Yessir," the guard was saying. "He got Dr. Mayfair to lead him up to your office, sir. They're on their way now."

Craig shook his head. "Mayfair knows better than that. My staff won't allow anyone to walk in here without an appointment, without an agenda that I have personally approved."

The guard shrugged his broad shoulders. "They're on their way to your office, sir. With this Tavalera guy tagging along."

"Tavalera? Who on Earth is Tavalera?"

"I'll shoot you his dossier, sir."

"Do that." Craig cut the connection and the wall screen returned to its default mode, showing a reproduction of Giotto's crucifixion scene. An eyeblink later it was replaced by the ID photo and personnel file of one Raoul Raymond Tavalera.

Bishop Craig scanned Tavalera's file, noting that the young man had spent time aboard the *Goddard* habitat. Craig's eyes narrowed at that. We sent those hotheads and dissidents all the way out to Saturn and yet here's one of them come back to stir up trouble. I'll have to deal with him.

Then Craig saw that Sister Angelique had taken over Tavalera's case and was employing him as part of her investigation into this Stoner business.

Stoner. He claims he's been out to the stars. More likely he's escaped from some asylum. And he's on his way to my office, according to Mayfair's security guard.

Craig leaned back in his desk chair and thought, I'll have to deal with Stoner, as well as Tavalera. Deal with them both. Sternly.

APOLOGIA PRO VITA SUA
BY YOLANDA VASQUEZ

They say that God must love the common man, because He made so many of them. Perhaps so, but it seems to me that God's wrath is directed at the poor and defenseless much more cruelly than at the wealthy and powerful. When the greenhouse floods struck, for instance, rich people could flee out of harm's way. They complained, of course; they wailed bitterly that they had to abandon their homes, their livelihoods, their possessions. But they escaped with their lives. Their children survived.

In Bangladesh, millions drowned when the mighty rivers overflowed. In Brazil and Venezuela and elsewhere in South America, torrential rains caused mud slides that swept away the shantytowns that the wretched poor had built out of packing crates and cardboard on the steep hillsides overlooking the gleaming cities of the rich.

Even in the United States, it was the poor, trapped by poverty and ignorance in urban ghettoes and migrant crop pickers' barracks, who stayed and suffered and died. Some trusted to their God to save them. Many climbed to their rooftops as the waters rose and waved piteously to the news media helicopters circling above them. Some of them huddled together in the rain like dumb animals waiting for a miracle to save them.

Almost all of them died.

Of course, the greenhouse floods and the other climate catastrophes that struck the world played right into the hands of the New Morality and all those other authoritarian regimes in other lands.

With millions of families displaced when coastal cities flooded and the global electric power grid collapsed, people wanted—desperately needed—roofs over their heads, food in their bellies, jobs, order, and safety. Above all, they wanted safety. In America the New Morality provided all that for the wretched refugees. All you had to do was ask them for their help—and then do what they told you.

It took me a long time to understand what was happening in the schools. Ages, in fact. It all came at us a little bit at a time, like Eliot said about the fog creeping in on little cat's feet. I think it was Eliot. It was all so long ago. T. S. Eliot. I remember when I was a student and we joked that the *T. S.* stood for "Tough Shoes."

Kids don't read Eliot anymore. They don't even read Dr. Seuss.

It was years and years before I realized what was happening. It wasn't the fault of the New Morality, but they capitalized on it. Oh yes, they took smiling advantage of it and used it for their own purposes.

"It," in this case, was the slow, patient, inevitable dumbing down of the schools. Not merely the students, but the teachers, the administrators, all of us. We let them make things easier. The path to hell again.

The overarching goal of education was to achieve equality. Overreacting to the centuries of racism's evils, we broke our hearts to achieve equality. Brilliant little Johnny is no better than the intellectually challenged Gloria. We mustn't let Tamiko lord it over Duwayne just because he's autistic. So what if Erwin has attention deficit disorder or Ernestine is a Down's syndrome victim? We can't hurt their feelings by putting them in separate facilities with specialists to look after them. They deserve to be mainstreamed and attend school with everybody else. So does Millicent, who can't read at all, and Alejandro, who constantly disrupts the class with his outbursts of anger and violence. Mainstream them. Mainstream them all.

Besides, mainstreaming is cheaper than building and staffing special facilities for our "special needs" children.

Equality of outcome, that was our aim. Everyone was to be treated equally; every student would finish school the equal to every other student. And what was the easiest way to achieve equality? Teach to the lowest common denominator. Make certain that every student got exactly what every other student received. No fast lane for the so-called bright ones. That wouldn't be equal! The mainstream spewed them out equally, year after year.

Self-esteem. We tried to teach the kids to have pride in themselves. It took me years to figure out that for a youngster to have pride in herself she had to be able to accomplish things, achieve something to be proud of. But somehow we left that part out of the curricula. We stopped teaching T. S. Eliot because he was too difficult to understand. Shakespeare, too. And Hemingway, well, he used foul language and openly depicted sex!

So we taught less and less of the things that made the kids feel unhappy with themselves and spent more and more classroom time on teaching them self-esteem. Trying to drum arithmetic into their skulls only made them feel bad, so we eased off on the math. And the spelling. And the reading assignments. And homework. Nobody liked homework, especially the parents.

We taught them self-esteem. By golly, we did.

And then there were the pressure groups. Parents didn't want their kids exposed to political beliefs that went against their own politics. So we stopped teaching civics. When an activist group decided that the Declaration of Independence was a subversive document, with its ringing call for overthrowing a government that was deemed oppressive, we stopped teaching about the American Revolution altogether. Besides, Jefferson and Washington and the rest of the Founding Fathers were slaveholders, weren't they?

Darwin. When I first started teaching we were forbidden by the state legislature to use the world "evolution" in class. Then we stopped teaching biology altogether.

And physics. And chemistry. Instead we taught general science, including "alternative" concepts such as intelligent design and astrology. It was a lot easier on the children, and we teachers didn't have to defend ourselves against righteous parents who got blue in the face over "godless secularist ideas."

We went along with it. The kids were happier; the pressure groups were happier. A few die-hard scientists and university academics warned that we were turning out a generation of ignoramuses, but they were happy ignoramuses and we could keep our jobs and avoid all the painful conflicts.

There were some kids who managed to get ahead anyway. Bright youngsters. A few, a precious few. A handful of schools managed to cater to those budding geniuses who thirsted for real knowledge. The country needed a certain number of engineers and scientists, after all. But they were always distrusted, carefully watched, their work closely controlled by the government and the New Morality. Schools like MIT and Caltech were necessary but kept under surveillance with a combination of jealousy and suspicion. The powers that be needed scientists and engineers, but they never trusted them.

I knew it was wrong. I suspect most of the other teachers had their misgivings, too. But you couldn't buck the tide, not if you wanted to keep your job. Not if you wanted to live in the community you were teaching in. Nobody wanted to be branded a pariah, a heretic.

So we ambled along down that sloping path to hell. And taught self-esteem to kids who knew less and less about more and more.

CHAPTER 4

Tavalera marveled at how Stoner smoothly, effortlessly, moved through Bishop Craig's staff. Receptionists, aides, security guards, executive assistants—Stoner simply spoke to them for a few moments and they allowed him to pass. They all seemed to be in a daze, Tavalera thought. It's like he hypnotizes them.

He was standing with Stoner and Dr. Mayfair in an anteroom on the top floor of one of the buildings that adjoined the hospital. Through the sweeping floor-to-ceiling windows Tavalera could see the complex of New Morality buildings sprawling outside, with elevated walkways connecting the glass towers. Far below, parking lots stretched in all directions, the cars and busses looking like miniature toys from this distance. Helicopters and ungainly-looking tilt-rotors landed and took off from rooftops. Beyond them the sky was bright blue, with puffy white clouds sailing by on a strong wind.

"I'm sure you could adjust the bishop's schedule," Stoner was saying softly to a perplexed-looking young man in a dark clerical suit. He was sitting behind a desk that stood before a door bearing a small gold-plated plaque inscribed: BISHOP Z. J. CRAIG.

"I suppose I could," the young man said hesitantly. "It's very unusual, though. The bishop doesn't normally—"

"This is an unusual situation," said Stoner. "I'm sure the bishop will want to see us."

"Mr. Tavalera."

Tavalera turned and saw Sister Angelique coming through the door from the corridor, tall and slim, wearing a floor-length black dress. Her face is beautiful, he said to himself. When she smiles she can light up the whole room. But her smile seemed forced now, uncertain.

"Sister Angelique," he said, genuinely glad to see her. "Uh, this is Keith Stoner."

"Really?" Angelique studied Stoner's face. "Our star voyager?"

Stoner smiled at her. "You don't believe that, do you?"

"I don't know what to believe, Mr. Stoner. As yet." She turned to Mayfair. "Doctor, you may return to your office now. Thank you for bringing Mr. Tavalera and Mr. Stoner here."

Mayfair looked relieved, puzzled, worried, and glad all at the same time. He shot a brief glance at Stoner, shook his head, then beat a retreat toward the door that led to the corridor and back to the normality of his own office, his own world.

Turning back to Stoner, Angelique smiled tentatively. "Actually, it's Dr. Stoner, isn't it? You have a Ph.D. in astronomy."

"Astrophysics," said Stoner.

The young man at the desk spoke up. "Bishop Craig will see you now." He looked rather surprised.

"Good," Stoner said, genuinely pleased. "Thanks for your help, Bobby."

The man blinked up at Stoner. "How did you know . . . ?"

"It's a gift," Stoner said. And he took a step toward the door with the golden plaque.

It opened without anyone touching it. Tavalera followed Stoner and Sister Angelique into Bishop Craig's office.

It wasn't a particularly large office, although it held a gleaming broad desk in one corner, backed by floor-to-ceiling windows, and a set of comfortable-looking armchairs ringed around a low coffee table in the opposite corner. The bishop was smiling broadly, a tiny, dapper dark-skinned man with a gleaming bald head. He came around his desk and extended both his hands toward Stoner.

"I can't tell you how glad I am to meet you," said Bishop Craig, with a toothy smile.

Stoner smiled back at him. "It's good of you to receive us on such short notice."

They're both spouting bullcrap, Tavalera thought. Craig motioned to the upholstered chairs grouped around the circular coffee table. The bishop asked if they wanted refreshments and Stoner said no. They sat, with Stoner and the bishop facing one another. Angelique sat opposite Tavalera.

"Now then," said Bishop Craig, "you must tell me: are you really from the stars?"

Stoner leaned back in his chair and crossed his long legs. "I've been to the stars, but I'm from Earth. I'm as human as you or anyone else on this planet." He hesitated a heartbeat. Then, "Or, I *was* human. Now I'm . . . something more."

"An angel?"

Stoner chuckled lightly. "No, hardly that."

Sister Angelique said, "A demon, then?"

With a shake of his head Stoner replied, "Not that, either."

"What, then?" Tavalera asked.

Stoner looked from Tavalera to Angelique and then back to Bishop Craig. "I've been exposed to the technology of an alien race. No, don't be alarmed. They've been dead for millions of years. Extinct. But their technology has survived."

Craig's eyes went crafty. "You can prove what you're saying, I suppose?"

"If I have to."

"Why have you returned to Earth?" Angelique asked.

Stoner's face went bleak. "Well, this is my home world. Our home world, I should say."

"Ours? There are more of you?" Craig asked.

With a nod, Stoner said, "My wife and two children."

"Where are they?"

"With me."

Tavalera felt his brows knit slightly. "You mean they're aboard your spacecraft?"

Stoner appeared to think over his response for a few heartbeats; then he merely nodded.

Bishop Craig drummed his fingers on his thighs for a moment, then asked, "Why have you returned here? What do you want?"

With a smile, Stoner replied, "I want to save the human race from extinction."

"Is that all?" The bishop laughed uneasily.

Stoner's bearded face grew somber. "There's a lot that I don't yet understand, but it's clear that the Western alliance and the nations of Islam are heading for a confrontation. And both sides are arming themselves with nuclear weapons."

Craig said, "We scrapped the last nuclear weapons some fifty years ago."

"But you're building new ones. So are the Muslims. And the Chinese, I might add."

"That can't be!"

"Yet it is. The Western alliance is secretly building nuclear weapons at three different sites."

"I can't believe that," said the bishop.

"Your New Morality movement has control of the American government, control of the news media, and a pretty tight control on the general population. People know only as much as you want them to know. You tell them what to believe and how to behave."

"For their own good," said Sister Angelique.

"Yes, certainly. For their own good. But do you really know what's best for the people?"

"Better than they know themselves," the bishop snapped.

"And what about their freedoms? Their individual rights? You can take a man like Raoul, here, and move him wherever you want to. His hopes and plans don't matter; he's forced to do what you want."

Bishop Craig leaned back in his armchair and steepled his thin fingers before his face. "Dr. Stoner, you say there are things you don't understand. I can see that that is certainly true."

"Then enlighten me," Stoner said, with the ghost of a smile.

"Gladly. You don't know what this nation was like before the New Morality saved it. Godless. Sunk in sin and depravity. Thieves and money-grubbers in charge of the economy. Politicians whose only thought was to get themselves elected and then re-elected, with no concern for the needs of the people. Violence in the streets. Shootings in the schools. Blatant sexuality advertised everywhere. Children giving birth to children. Schools giving students condoms! They were all heading for collapse, bound for hell and everlasting damnation."

Stoner said nothing. He simply folded his arms over his chest and watched Craig intently.

"Then God sent His warning. The climate began to change, alter drastically. Greenhouse warming struck like a bolt from an avenging angel. Ice caps melted away. Sea levels rose so fast that coastal cities were flooded. The American heartland, the granary of the world, became parched and dust blown with drought. Millions were driven from their homes.

"Wars erupted. India and Pakistan depopulated each other with biological weapons. Nuclear war broke out in the Middle East. China seized vast territories in Siberia. Latin America and Africa dissolved in genocides.

"In America the people cried out! They needed food, housing. They needed *order.* The government was paralyzed; all they could do in Washington was point fingers and cast blame."

"So the New Morality stepped in," Stoner said mildly.

"The New Morality did indeed step in. We did not seek power. We did not seek responsibility. But we did what we could to help. It actually started right here in Atlanta: We made the streets safe. We distributed food to the needy. We brought people back to Christ. And from there our movement spread."

Sister Angelique added, "We seek to do good, Dr. Stoner. We are not the enemy."

"Indeed we are not," Bishop Craig resumed. "We brought order and stability to the nation. And beyond. Similar movements arose in Europe, Asia, Latin America. The Muslims were actually ahead of us, establishing their religious schools, their madrassas, taking over national governments, forging a unity across the whole Islamic world."

"At what cost?" Stoner asked. "How much blood was spilled?"

"The Muslims were steeped in violence, I admit. Still are. In America, though, there was hardly any bloodshed. The New Morality has always been a peaceful movement. We do not advocate violence."

"But you don't tolerate dissent."

"Of course not! We're doing God's work. Those who dissent are against God, against our Lord and Savior, against goodness and truth."

"So you get rid of them."

"We re-educate them. Some of them, yes, frankly we

have exiled some of the hopeless cases. That's what the habitat around Saturn is filled with: malcontents and troublemakers."

"And you've started freezing people, storing them in vats of liquid nitrogen."

"Convicted criminals," the bishop retorted. "And we only keep them frozen until they can be cured of their antisocial behaviors," he added with a bland smile.

"How many have been revived?" Stoner asked.

The bishop started to reply, then simply shrugged.

Stoner exhaled a sigh. Then, "So, in the name of right and good you've taken over the government, from the White House down to neighborhood watch groups."

"And made it a better nation," Craig insisted. "A safer, happier, more orderly nation. A nation that obeys the will of God."

"And you've spread your power and authority beyond the borders of the United States."

"Of course. We've also joined with other groups, such as the Holy Disciples in Europe."

For a long moment Stoner said nothing. At last he brought his clasped hands up to his darkly bearded chin and said, "In my reading of history, there have been many instances when a religious movement has gained control of the government's reins of power. In each instance, human liberty has suffered. Often, the civilization collapses."

Bishop Craig frowned at him.

"The Roman Empire adopted Christianity as its official state religion. The Christians, zealous and certain that they were doing God's work, closed all the schools throughout the empire, except for their own. They closed down the Academy in Athens, where Plato and Aristotle had once taught."

"Centuries earlier," Sister Angelique pointed out.

"Nonetheless," Stoner continued, "once the schools were closed a dark age settled inexorably over Europe. For a thousand years inquiry was frowned upon, and acceptance of authority was the norm. It wasn't until the Renaissance that Europeans began to move forward again."

"Ancient history," Craig muttered.

"How many lives were blighted during those thousand years?" Stoner asked gently. "How might the human race have grown and learned and gained in understanding if Galileo had come a generation after Ptolemy, instead of a millennium?"

"Pointless speculation," said the bishop.

Stoner insisted, "Where religious movements gain control of the government's power, individual liberties wither. And without those liberties, there is no check on the government's authority. Today, right here and now, your New Morality organization has the power to destroy civilization and wipe out the human race."

CHAPTER 5

For several long moments Bishop Craig's office was absolutely silent. Tavalera could hear his own pulse pumping in his ears.

Then Sister Angelique half-whispered, "Do you actually think we are heading toward a nuclear war?"

Stoner nodded gravely. "And you have other weapons, as well. The biological agents that depopulated the Indian subcontinent are just as deadly now as they were then."

"What can we do about it?" she asked.

"That's why we need to speak with Archbishop Overmire," said Stoner. "We need to start the movement toward peace and reconciliation."

Bishop Craig looked at Stoner with calculating eyes. "You mean to dismantle the New Morality, don't you?"

"Not at all," Stoner replied. "I hope to change it so that the movement can cope with the threats you face. If it can't change without crumbling, well . . ." He left the thought unfinished.

Craig began to drum his fingers on his thighs again. "All that you've said hinges on your assertion that we are building nuclear weapons. As far as I know, that's not true."

Stoner's wintry smile returned. "Would you like me to take you to the facilities where the weapons are being built? One of them is in New Mexico, where the original atomic bomb was constructed."

Before the bishop could reply, Tavalera blurted, "He can take you there like *that.*" He snapped his fingers.

"Such a facility would be heavily guarded, I imagine," Craig countered.

"Doesn't matter," said Tavalera. Then, looking to Stoner, he added, "Does it?"

"Not much," Stoner said.

Sister Angelique got to her feet. "I'm willing to believe Dr. Stoner. I think we should try to get him an audience with the Archbishop as quickly as possible."

Craig looked uncertain momentarily. He stood up, too, and then Stoner and Tavalera did the same.

"Are you sure?" the bishop asked Angelique.

"Yes, I am, Your Worship," she said. "With your permission, I can start making the arrangements immediately."

Craig nodded reluctantly. Then he asked, "But what do we do about this man in the meantime?"

Stoner's smile turned warmer. "Don't worry about

me. I'll return when you're ready to introduce me to the Archbishop."

And he disappeared.

Craig gasped and sank back into his chair. Angelique stared wide-eyed at the empty air where Stoner had been a moment earlier.

Tavalera grinned and said, "I guess I'm not crazy, after all."

CHAPTER 6

Bishop Craig was trembling visibly as he sat huddled in the armchair, muttering, "Protect me from the works of Satan. Protect me, O Lord, from the snares of the devil."

Angelique, still on her feet, regained her self-control, took a deep breath, and turned to Tavalera. "You find this amusing?"

His grin fading, Tavalera replied, "I'm just glad that I'm not having hallucinations. He's for real. He can do things that are beyond human."

"Nonsense," she snapped. "He has access to powers that we don't understand—as yet. That's all."

"It's a helluva lot," said Tavalera.

Her eyes flared at his minor crudity, but she turned to Bishop Craig, still sitting in the armchair muttering prayers to himself.

"Your Worship, we must act. And quickly."

Craig shook himself, as if trying to break free of a trance. Then he looked up at Angelique. "We have witnessed a great power," he said in an awed whisper. "Either he's been sent by God to help us, or . . . or . . ." His voice faded away.

Angelique knelt at the bishop's feet. "Your Worship,

he's a man, just as you are. He's neither angel nor devil. He simply has access to a technology that we don't understand, that's all."

"That's enough," Tavalera added, his grin returning.

Angelique shot an annoyed glare at him. But she quickly recovered, rose to her feet, and said almost sweetly, "Raoul, I've got to speak with the bishop in private."

Taking Tavalera by the hand, she led him to the door and the anteroom beyond it. The same young man was sitting at the desk there, intently scrolling through a long list of names on his desktop screen.

"Wait here for me here, please," she said to Tavalera, pointing to one of the chairs lining the wall. "I'll be back with you in a few minutes."

Tavalera obediently sat down. The young man behind the desk glanced at him, then returned his attention to his screen. Angelique went through the door again into Bishop Craig's office.

Are you all right, Raoul? He heard Stoner's voice in his mind.

Glancing at the diligent man behind the desk, who was concentrating on ignoring him, Tavalera whispered, "Yeah, I guess."

No need to speak, Stoner's voice said. I can hear you without your vocalizing your thoughts.

Mental telepathy? Tavalera wondered.

Not quite, said Stoner's disembodied voice. More like a subvocalized telephone link.

I don't understand.

I'll explain it to you later. For now, are you all right?

Yeah, sure.

I need your help.

To do what?

For the moment, to stay close to Angelique. Are you

willing to be my contact with her? And through her, the bishop, of course.

Nodding, Tavalera replied, I'm willing, but she might not be.

She'll want to keep you in her sight, Raoul. All you have to do is tell her that I'm in contact with you and if she wants to see me again she'll have to go through you.

You think she'll believe that?

He could sense Stoner smiling. It's the truth, Raoul. You're going to be my contact man on Earth.

And where'll you be?

I've got some exploring to do. But I'll be in contact with you at all times. I'll see what you see, hear what you hear. All that.

Whether I like it or not, Tavalera thought.

No! Stoner replied immediately. I wouldn't intrude on you unless you allowed me to. You have a right to privacy.

Tavalera almost laughed aloud. That's a helluva lot more than the New Morality's willing to give me.

Meanwhile, Sister Angelique helped Bishop Craig out of the armchair where he'd been sitting in something of a daze and back to his gleaming, imposing desk. Once settled in the high-backed swivel chair, Craig seemed to revive somewhat.

"He must be in league with Satan," the bishop said. "To just disappear like that. It's beyond human."

Angelique settled herself in one of the chairs in front of the broad desk. "The technology he's using is beyond human," she said firmly. "But if he can learn to use it, so can we."

Craig's eyes widened. "Do you think . . . ?"

"I'm certain of it. He said as much himself."

"But the devil is the Prince of Lies. How can we trust his word if he's in league with Satan?"

"He's a man," she insisted. "A very unusual man, that's obvious, but a human being just like you or me."

Craig began to shake his head.

"He can help us," she said.

"Help us?"

Angelique glanced up at the ceiling. Turning back to the bishop, she whispered, "Is this office safe? Has it been swept today?"

Bishop Craig nodded mutely.

Still, Angelique dragged her chair around the desk and next to the bishop's. Keeping her voice low, "If we play our cards carefully, we can get Stoner to help us."

"Help us do what?" Craig whispered.

"The Archbishop is too old and tired to deal with this . . . opportunity."

Craig sat up straighter in his chair. "What do you mean?"

"Stoner is a visitor from the stars. He has access to technology that is far beyond anything we know of."

"He says he's more than human."

"He is using technology that's beyond human capabilities. But he himself is as human as you or I."

"Do you really think so?"

"Of course. And we can use him to help convince the Archbishop to retire and name you as his replacement."

Craig blinked at her. Twice. Three times. At last he whispered, "Do you really think . . . ?"

"If we can gain access to his alien technology there's no end to what we can accomplish!"

"But . . . but . . . he said we're heading for nuclear war. He said we could destroy ourselves. The whole human race!"

Angelique answered confidently, "Yes, he did say that. But if we make the right moves, we could avert the coming war. With Stoner's help you could become the savior of the human race."

Craig's dark eyes snapped at her. "That's blasphemy!" Then he added more softly, "Almost."

Looking properly abashed, Angelique quickly amended, "Their temporal savior, I meant to say. You'll be doing the Lord's work, and the whole world will bless you for it."

Craig's face softened into a beatific smile that slowly dissolved into a worried frown. "But how do we do this? How do we even start?"

Sister Angelique did not hesitate for an eyeblink. "We keep a close hold on this man Tavalera. He's the key to Stoner, and Stoner is the key to everything."

CHAPTER 7

Stoner still found it a little confusing to be in several places at once. Space-time isn't sequential, he reminded himself. That's only an illusion because we usually move at such slow velocities. Time flow changes with speed. Even Einstein understood that.

Still, to be on the Moon yet remain connected with Tavalera's mind was slightly disconcerting. Stoner saw through Tavalera's eyes that Sister Angelique was leading him to an apartment in one of the glass towers of the New Morality's complex in Atlanta.

"I think you'll be comfortable here. Don't you?" Angelique was asking Tavalera as she showed him through the little suite's sitting room, bedroom, and kitchenette.

"Comfortable enough."

"That's good," she said.

"How long do I have to stay here?" Tavalera asked, starting to feel uneasy. He realized that the apartment had all the trappings of a fancy, high-priced jail.

Putting on a face of troubled innocence, Angelique said, "I wish I knew, Raoul. We're trying to arrange an audience for Dr. Stoner with the Archbishop, but that might take some time."

Tavalera didn't entirely believe her, Stoner knew. But Tavalera said, "I'd like to call my mother, then. Tell her I'm all right."

"Certainly," said Sister Angelique, glancing at the phone console by the sitting room sofa.

"And *Goddard*," he added. "I ought to call Holly Lane and see if—"

"One thing at a time, Raoul. Call your mother. Make yourself comfortable here. They're sending up some clothes for you, and the freezer should be full of prepared meals."

He realized he was being dismissed. "So I just stay here by myself until you're ready to talk to me again?"

Angelique smiled for him. "I could come by this evening, if you wish. We could have dinner together."

Tavalera grinned at that. "Okay. Great."

She headed for the door, turned back to him, and said, "I might be a little later than you normally eat dinner. I have a very busy schedule."

Shrugging, he said, "That's okay. I'll wait for you. I got no place to go."

She turned and left the apartment, closing the door softly behind her. Tavalera tried the knob. Sure enough, the door was locked.

Stoner felt the waves of emotion that surged through

Tavalera. Anger. Frustration. More than a little fear. But there was curiosity there, as well. All to the good, Stoner thought. Curiosity is one of our strongest assets.

Tavalera moseyed through the apartment, opening drawers in the bedroom, glancing into the immaculate bathroom, poking his head into the fully stocked cabinets in the kitchenette. Finally, with nothing else to do, he sat on the sofa and looked around for a remote control to turn on the wall screen.

"It's voice activated," Stoner told him.

Tavalera jerked with shock.

"I'm sorry," Stoner apologized. "I suppose you'll need some time to get used to the fact that I can be inside your head."

"Yeah," Tavalera said shakily.

"Just say 'screen on.' "

"Screen on," Tavalera called out.

The entire wall dissolved to show a three-dimensional view of a family sitting around a dining room table, saying grace before dinner. They all looked so relentlessly cheerful and wholesome.

Tavalera flicked through two dozen channels: family comedies, sports, news shows about the wars overseas, an ancient dramatic presentation of *Pilgrim's Progress.*

Then Stoner appeared, fully three-dimensional, bigger than life, looking like an Old Testament prophet in a sport shirt.

"How d'you do that?" Tavalera demanded of the image.

Stoner smiled slightly and answered, "It's a gift."

"Yeah."

"I thought you'd find it easier to talk with me this way."

"They'll be watching us, y'know. This whole place must be rigged with cameras and snoopers six ways from Tuesday."

Shaking his head slightly, Stoner said, "All they'll see and hear is you watching that family comedy, like a good, law-abiding citizen."

Tavalera thought about that for a few seconds and decided that Stoner could get away with that.

"So what am I supposed to do now?"

"I thought you might like to talk to your friend on *Goddard*—without your communication being censored."

"You can do that?"

"Yes." Stoner hesitated, then added, "And in real time, if you like."

Tavalera's eyes went round. "You mean, no lag time?"

"That's right."

"How d'you— Oh, never mind! Lemme talk to Holly!"

Feeling slightly guilty, Stoner watched Tavalera for a few minutes more as he talked with Holly Lane, out on the *Goddard* habitat. The young man seemed stunned, at first, that they could speak to each other without the hours-long time lag caused by the distance between Saturn and Earth.

"I don't know how he does it," Tavalera was saying with a bemused grin on his long-jawed face. "But it works."

Holly's light brown eyes sparkled with interest. "Raoul, if you could find out how he does it . . . poosh! What a discovery that'd be! Real-time communications through the whole twirling solar system! Cosmic!"

"Yeah, I guess so," Tavalera replied unenthusiastically.

"F'sure!" Holly insisted.

"Look, Holly, we got real worries here Earthside. This guy Stoner says we might have a nuclear war."

"What? That's screwy! Nukes have been banned since before you and I were born."

"That doesn't mean people can't make new ones," said Tavalera gloomily.

Holly fell silent for a few heartbeats, then, "Well, that means we've gotta get you back here to *Goddard* right away. You'll be safe here."

Tavalera nodded absently, but he muttered, "Really safe? I mean, if Earth blows itself up, if we wipe ourselves out here on Earth, how long could *Goddard* last?"

"We're self-sufficient," Holly said immediately. "We don't need supplies from Earth and we don't take orders from Earth. We govern ourselves."

"Yeah, but there's only ten thousand or so people on *Goddard*."

"We could grow. We could build new habitats, keep the human race going."

"Could you? If Earth wipes itself out, how will the people on *Goddard* react?"

Holly insisted, "It wouldn't be the end of the human race, Raoul. There's Selene and the other settlements on the Moon."

"They might get sucked into the war."

She grew more serious. "Okay, whatever. All this means is that we've got to get you back here soon's we can."

Tavalera shook his head. "They're not gonna let me go, Holly."

"Who's not?"

"The government. The New Morality. They're all tangled up together now. And they won't let me leave; I'm pretty certain of that."

Holly's square chin went up a notch. "Yeah? Well, we'll just see about that!"

Despite himself, Tavalera grinned at her. She's a fighter, he said to himself. But then he thought, It won't do her any good, though. Angelique and Bishop Craig and the rest of them won't let me go.

It was something of a shock when he realized that he didn't want to go back to *Goddard* and Holly. Not yet. Not while he was joined with Stoner. There's too much going on here for me to run away, Tavalera told himself. I've got to stay and help straighten things out.

Stoner smiled to himself.

CHAPTER 8

Magnificent desolation, Stoner thought. That's what Buzz Aldrin called it when he first stepped out onto the bleak, airless, battered surface of the Moon.

It's been nearly a century and a half since Aldrin and Armstrong made the first landing here, Stoner said to himself. The Moon's surface hasn't changed much.

He stood encased in a sphere of energy that held air and warmth, so that he could walk across the Moon's dusty surface in his shirtsleeves. Hard radiation poured out of the black, star-studded sky, together with an endless infall of microscopic meteors, dust motes drifting in from space. The energy sphere deflected it all.

Stoner was pacing across the rounded, smooth crest of the slumped mountains that formed the ringwall of the giant crater Alphonsus. Spread across one segment of the crater floor were landing pads for spacecraft and broad swaths of dark circles of solar energy farms, where solarvoltaic cells manufactured out of lunar silicon drank in the Sun's unfailing energy and produced electricity for the human race's largest lunar community.

Built into the ringwall mountains, Selene was an independent nation, and self-sufficient—almost.

Yes, they grow their own food and generate their own electrical power, Stoner thought. With a population approaching fifty thousand they probably have a large-enough gene pool to survive without bringing up newcomers from Earth.

Could Selene and the other lunar communities survive Earth's suicidal war? Would these people *want* to survive after watching their home world go up in nuclear flames? Or would the madmen of Earth throw missiles at the Moon and try to complete their self-slaughter?

We gave them energy shields, he remembered from his previous life. We learned from the star visitor how to make energy shields big enough to protect entire cities from nuclear explosions. But there's no trace of that now. Their cities are open, naked to attack. They have antimissile systems, but they're crude and certainly not foolproof.

Stoner paced carefully along the crest of the ringwall. Down on the crater floor a spacecraft leaped off one of the concrete launchpads and hurtled into the dark sky, silent in the airless vacuum. In the farther distance tractors kicked up puffs of dust as they rolled across the barren ground.

It's a different world, Stoner knew. Different from the world we left back in 1985.

He thought back to the alien starship, the vessel that had changed his life so completely, and his astonishment at finding that it was a sarcophagus, a coffin that bore the dead and lovingly preserved body of an intelligent alien. Stoner understood the message the dead alien symbolized: We exist. You are not alone in the universe. We mean you no harm. Learn from the technology that drives this starship. Come out to the stars and join us.

Eventually, Stoner did just that. Saddened, disappointed at the primitive, savage attitudes of his fellow human beings, Stoner took his wife and two children and fled to the stars, leaving Earth far behind them. What they found in their journey changed them profoundly and forced them to return to Earth—burdened with a terrible knowledge.

Tapping into his starship's mind, Stoner's vision was flooded with the immensity of space, whirlpools of galaxies spinning in their stately dance of eternity, islands of light and beauty in the empty darkness of infinite space, expanding as far as his mind could encompass. He narrowed his gaze to the Milky Way galaxy, hundreds of billions of stars coalescing out of primordial gas and dust, blazing into light and life, only to gutter and inevitably die. The vision never failed to stir him, to fill him with awe and wonder and the bitter remorse that stems from the knowledge that death is the inescapable counterpart of life. For even at the core of the immense spiral of the Milky Way a titanic black hole was gobbling up stars and spewing lethal radiation outward across the galaxy.

Closing his physical eyes, Stoner saw the long curving arcs of the geodesics that transected space-time, glowing golden and beckoning against the limitless expanse of the universe. No, not *the* universe, he reminded himself. It's a multiverse, alive, growing, changing constantly. There are more dimensions than we suspected, he now knew. Space and time are richer and more complex than any human mind understood.

He reluctantly admitted to himself that star travel was forever a one-way journey. You literally could not return home. The very act of hurtling among the stars at velocities close to the speed of light changed the universe around you. Somewhere in the entangled geodesics of space-time there still existed the world that Stoner had departed from, a world where cities were protected by energy shields and human civilization used the alien technology carried by their dead star visitor to shift the nature of matter and energy as they needed.

The Earth that he returned to was almost the same but not quite. The Earth of this worldline had never had a star visitor, never received the gift of the dead alien's technology. The differences between the worldline that Stoner had left and the one he returned to were slight but significant, possibly fatal.

The Earth of this worldline was rushing toward doom. There are other Earths, other worldlines, Stoner knew. But this was the one he now existed in. This was the one he had to save.

Could this civilization last long enough to get through the coming crisis? Stoner wondered. Authoritarian governments armed with nuclear and biological weapons could wipe out the human race, perhaps by accident, perhaps by malice, perhaps by the inspired zeal of true believers. No matter how deep the faith, no matter how repressive the government, greed and hate and lust and fear still existed, palpable forces that could drive men and women to terrible, deadly evils.

And there would be no gifts from the stars to help, not in this worldline. There's only me, Stoner said to himself.

"Us," said his wife. "We're in this together, Keith: you, me, and our children."

CHAPTER 9

Stoner wondered what his best approach would be to make contact with Douglas Stavenger. He had scanned the history webs and learned that not only was Stavenger regarded as the founder of Selene, but he also was still crucially important in the lunar nation's government, although he had not held any formal post for many years.

Standing atop Mt. Yeager, the tallest mountain in the ringwall girdling the crater Alphonsus, Stoner decided on a conventional approach—of sorts.

He called Stavenger on the phone. It was a simple matter to tap into Selene's internal communications net, so while Stoner stood out in the open protected by his bubble of energy he phoned the man.

Stavenger was at home, in his modest living room in the residential area that ran along the fourth level belowground. He was studying a proposal that Selene's governing council was considering, a proposal to help finance a robotic space probe that would be sent to the Alpha Centauri star system.

Good timing, Stoner thought, smiling to himself. I can help them with that. And more.

He activated Stavenger's phone.

Douglas Stavenger was sitting at his desk admiring the three-dimensional view of the proposed star probe that hovered in midair before his eyes. The hologram was crisp and detailed, showing the probe's wide metallic lightsail connected by buckyball cables to the tiny spacecraft, which bristled with sensors and antennae. The proposal had been submitted to Selene's governing council by the Yamagata Corporation. Yamagata was building a complex of solar-power satellites in orbit around Mercury, the closest planet to the Sun, and was offering to devote some of the energy they generated to power a lightsail ship to the Alpha Centauri star system. Selene would have to build the spacecraft. An unmanned probe, Stoner saw.

Un*crewed,* Jo's voice sounded in his mind.

With a sheepish grin, Stoner corrected himself: un-*crewed.*

Stavenger was solidly built, with skin just a shade darker than a deeply suntanned Caucasian's. Wearing a comfortable velour pullover and shapeless denims, he appeared to be no more than thirty, despite his real age.

A soft tone told him that someone was calling on his private line. Brows knitting with mild annoyance, Stavenger thought briefly about ignoring the interruption and letting the caller leave a message. But curiosity got the better of him, as it usually did. Who'd be calling on my private line? he wondered. It might be important.

"Close display," he said, and the holographic image dissolved. "Answer phone."

Keith Stoner's strong features took shape, his beard dark, his eyes somber, a solid three-dimensional bust hanging in the air above Stavenger's desk.

"The star man!" Stavenger gasped.

"You recognize me," said Stoner.

"I saw your original message, the one you transmitted to our Farside Observatory."

With the slightest shake of his head, Stoner said, "You never answered my message."

Stavenger pushed himself up from his desk chair and went to the sofa, past a wall screen displaying a real-time view of the crater floor outside, with a fat crescent of Earth hanging in the dark sky above it.

"We passed it on to the United Nations scientific

council, in New York. Our board decided to act in concert with Earth on this." Then he added, "But some of our younger astronomers are champing at the bit, really giving the council a hard time. They want to answer your message and see what happens."

"Good for them."

"It's hard to keep them in check, you know," Stavenger said almost ruefully.

Stoner's image turned to keep facing Stavenger. "But on Earth they've decided to stick their heads in the sand and ignore it."

Settling himself slowly on the sofa, Stavenger replied, "I'm not surprised. That's their first reaction to anything new or troubling: ignore it and hope it goes away."

Stoner smiled minimally. "Actually, the New Morality is investigating my message. They'd like to believe it's a hoax."

Stavenger puffed out a mild grunt. "I bet they would. And the others? The Islamic League, the Europeans, the Asians?"

"I haven't contacted them directly. Not yet. I'm an American, after all; I went to my own first."

"I've asked the governing council here in Selene to prod them," Stavenger went on, "but so far I haven't seen any movement on their part."

"As I said, their first assumption is that my message is a hoax," said Stoner. "I've had to convince them otherwise. It's shaken some of them rather badly."

"I can imagine. But what about the imagery of your spacecraft, when it entered the solar system? They think that's a hoax, as well?"

"That's from twenty-two years ago. They weren't sure that it was connected to my message."

"But it is, and you're real." The enormity of it began to sink into Stavenger emotionally. Suddenly he thought to ask, "Where are you now? On the Moon? In Selene?"

"Among other places."

"What?"

"I could join you in your living room, if you like."

"You mean, right now?"

"Right now." And Stoner appeared in the room, standing by the desk.

Stavenger rocked back on the sofa slightly, his eyes staring. Stoner recognized the struggle going on inside the man. It's a lot to accept, he realized. But he's handling it much better than most of the others.

Stavenger puffed out a breath, then grinned. "You don't have to knock, do you?"

Stoner stepped to the slingback chair next to the sofa and sat down. "Your body is teeming with nanomachines."

"How . . . ? Can you see inside me?"

With a shrug, Stoner said, "It's true, isn't it?"

"Yes, that's true. They've saved my life more than once. They keep me youthful and healthy."

"But you can never return to Earth. They've banned nanotechnology in all its forms everywhere on Earth."

"Selene is my home," Stavenger said tightly.

"I see."

"You see quite a bit. You really are a star traveler, aren't you?"

"Yes. Can you accept that?"

Stavenger leaned forward slightly, hands flat on his knees, as he asked, "Are you really human? Or are you an alien in human disguise? A machine, maybe, or a biological construct? What do they call it? An android?"

"I was born on Earth," said Stoner.

"And?"

Stoner smiled at him. "You're a lot more flexible mentally than most of the others. You're a lot better balanced emotionally, too."

With a spread of his hands, Stavenger replied, "I've lived a long time and I've seen a lot."

"You're not frightened of a star voyager."

"Look, let's stop the fencing around. Our research shows that a Dr. Keith Stoner—"

"Died in an auto wreck in your year 1985. I know."

"So how do you account for yourself?"

"In the world I was born to, I left Earth in that same 1985 in a starship that we built from information we learned from a visiting alien vessel. The extraterrestrial's ship was a sarcophagus; the alien inside it was dead."

"A mummy?"

"Right. He'd sent his remains out on a journey to the stars, in an automated ship programmed to seek out the signatures of intelligent life. He wanted to show any civilization that the ship ran across that the universe isn't lifeless, isn't without intelligence."

Stoner heard Jo warning, You're not telling him the whole truth.

Not yet, he replied silently. It's too soon. He's taken everything well enough so far, but I don't want to push him too fast.

Stavenger was saying, "So you used the alien's technology to go off to the stars yourself."

"Myself, my wife, and my two children."

"But . . . our records show that you died in 1985. There wasn't any starship. You were married, but you'd been divorced."

"That's your worldline," Stoner said. "Mine was different."

Shaking his head, Stavenger said, "I don't understand."

"Neither do I, not completely. Apparently, when you

travel close to the speed of light, everything changes. There's more than one universe, and somehow they interconnect. Some of them are very similar to one another. Others . . ."

"The brane theory," Stavenger muttered. "The idea that there are multiple universes that exist in other dimensions."

Stoner nodded. "It's not exactly correct, but they're on the right track."

"So when you traveled among the stars at nearly the speed of light you left your universe and entered ours."

"We thought we were coming back to our own worldline, the Earth that we'd left in 1985."

"But it's different."

"Different in some ways. Very similar in others."

"Why did you return?"

Stoner hesitated, his face clouding darkly.

"It's about the war that's brewing down there, isn't it?" Stavenger asked.

"You know about it?"

"We have our intelligence sources."

Stoner said nothing.

"You came back to warn them against starting a nuclear war?"

"No," said Stoner. But then he corrected himself, "Yes, in a way. But there's more to it than that."

CHAPTER 10

Stavenger looked at him disbelievingly. "More to it? What more can there be to the threat of a global nuclear war? They're going to destroy themselves!"

"And you, very possibly," Stoner added bleakly.

"Don't you think I know that?" Stavenger snapped, almost snarling.

"Then what are you doing about it?"

Stavenger shook his head. "What can we do? We can't ram peace down their throats. There's more than twelve billion people on Earth. The planet's bursting at its seams! They're devouring their resources so furiously that they'll start dying off from starvation and disease even without a war."

"Once, I thought that opening up the space frontier would add enormous new sources of raw materials and energy for Earth," Stoner said.

"Only if they control their population growth," Stavenger countered heatedly. "All they've done by importing resources from space is allow their population to boom faster, bigger."

Stoner saw the agitation on his face, the bitterness in his tone.

"So now they blame *us* for their troubles," Stavenger went on. "They claim that corporations like Humphries Space Systems and Astro have ruined the metals markets on Earth. They're talking about an embargo on imports from space, a move that could wipe out the rock rats out in the Asteroid Belt and even hurt Selene economically."

"But they use the power satellites," Stoner said. "They couldn't get along without them."

Bobbing his head in agreement, Stavenger replied, "Sure, they need the power satellites. But they don't want to let any of their people emigrate from Earth and they've cut travel from anywhere off-Earth back to home almost down to zero. They don't want to have any contact with us."

"They're frightened of people who've been off-Earth," Stoner said. "They're afraid that people who've lived in different worlds will contaminate them with new ideas."

"And show the flaws in their own societies," Stavenger added.

"So they close their doors to you."

"And their minds."

"And their situation grows more desperate each year," Stoner muttered.

"It's worse than that," Stavenger said. "They're separating themselves from us. Isolating themselves. If they continue along the path they're following now, the human race will split into two subspecies: those who live off-Earth and those who remain on Earth."

Stoner understood the consequences. "Earth will sink into poverty and ignorance—if they don't blow themselves to hell first."

"They're building nuclear weapons again," Stavenger agreed.

"A nuclear war could kill them all," Stoner said. "It could scour Earth clean of all life."

"No," Stavenger said. "Not everything, not—"

"Everything!" Stoner insisted. "I've seen it before."

"What?"

"I've seen worlds that destroyed themselves. Civilizations that blew themselves apart. Intelligent species that died because they outproduced their natural resources. Planet after planet, world after world . . . they kill themselves, one way or another. Intelligence is very clever about finding ways to commit suicide."

"And you think that's what we're going to do?"

"That's where you're heading."

"Extinction," Stavenger muttered.

"But you can survive here on the Moon. You're already dug in. Even if they throw missiles at you, you can shoot them down before they get here."

"But could we survive without Earth?" Stavenger asked. "Our economy depends on exporting Clipper-ships and glassteel to Earth. And we import biological products, plant products for pharmaceuticals, feedstock to replenish our hydroponic farms."

Stoner asked, "Can your gene pool survive without fresh inputs from Earth?"

Stavenger hesitated, then replied, "I don't know," his voice low, almost frightened.

"Neither do I. You've got about almost a hundred thousand people living in your various lunar communities. A few thousand miners and prospectors scattered through the Asteroid Belt. A few hundred scientists on Mars. Construction teams at Mercury. Research stations around Venus and Jupiter."

"And the habitat at Saturn," Stavenger added. "Ten thousand people there."

"Is it enough? If Earth self-destructs, will that be enough to keep the human race going?"

"It was during the Stone Age," Stavenger said. "The human race was only a handful of people then."

"But they had the whole planet available to them."

Stavenger looked into Stoner's eyes. "You really think they'll kill everything? Down to the bacteria?"

Stoner nodded. "It'll be billions of years before complex life-forms evolve again. Even at that, there's no guarantee that intelligence will arise again. Maybe it'd be better if it doesn't."

"No! I can't believe that."

Stoner shrugged. "The question is, can the human race survive if Earth is sterilized? Are your communities here on the Moon and elsewhere in the solar system enough to sustain the species?"

"If they aren't . . ."

Stoner grunted. "If they aren't, then the human race joins all those others in extinction."

"Extinction," Stavenger repeated.

"Extinction is the natural fate of species," Stoner said as if reciting a school lesson. "Most species live for a couple of million years and then disappear or evolve into something new."

"Humankind isn't even a million years old," Stavenger said. "Not *Homo sapiens*, at least. Our species only appeared a few hundred thousand years ago, at most."

"Maybe we'll break the universe's speed record for self-annihilation," said Stoner with a bitter grimace.

"We could emigrate to the stars," Stavenger said, brightening. "We could move out of the solar system altogether. There are other Earth-like planets out there."

"True enough," said Stoner.

"It would be costly, though. Enormously expensive."

"How many could afford to immigrate? Enough to preserve the species?"

"Maybe. With your help." Stavenger brightened a little. "That's why you've come back, isn't it?"

"No," said Stoner.

"No? But then . . . why . . . ?"

Stoner looked up at the wall screen view of Earth hanging above the barren surface of the Moon: Earth, shining blue oceans and swaths of glowing white clouds sweeping across it.

"There's more than twelve billion people living there. I don't intend to write them off. They deserve better. We've got to do what we can to save them."

"You can't. Nobody can," Stavenger insisted.

"But we've got to try," said Stoner.

"Why? Why bother?"

Without an eyeblink's hesitation Stoner replied, "Because life is precious. Because intelligence is the rarest gift in the universe."

"And where does it lead?"

"That depends."

"Depends? Depends on what?"

"On what we do."

Stavenger stared at Stoner for a long, wordless moment.

"Or what we fail to do," Stoner added.

At last Stavenger nodded. "I see. I think I understand. I suppose you're right. We've got to try, don't we?"

"Yes."

Sitting up straighter, his fists resting on his thighs, Stavenger asked, "So what do we do? What *can* we do?"

"We've got to stop this war before it begins."

"How?"

"I'm going to see the head of the New Morality movement. They seem to have control of the United States government."

Nodding, Stavenger said, "There's the Islamic leaders, too. They're not as cohesive as the Western nations. You'll have to deal with Shiites and Sunnis and other sects."

"And the Chinese," Stoner added.

Stavenger broke into a rueful grin. "Now there it's much easier. Ling Po is not only chairman of China's National Assembly; he's also head of the New Dao movement. He's got all the reins of authority in his grubby little fists."

"And they're building nuclear weapons, too, aren't they?"

"In an industrial complex in western Xinjiang Province. It's a pretty remote area." Stavenger pursed his lips, then added, "Our intelligence people believe that the American military has recommended hitting their center with a missile attack."

"Nuclear?"

"The recommendation is on the President's desk."

"That means that the Americans already have operational nuclear warheads," Stoner said.

Nodding, "And missiles."

"I'll have to disable them."

Stavenger's brows hiked up. "Disable their warheads? How?"

"It can be done," Stoner said. "But only as a last resort."

"What do you mean?"

His face grim, Stoner said, "I could make those warheads malfunction. But what good does that do? I can't spend the rest of my life acting as some sort of fairy godfather, protecting the world from its own lunacy."

Stavenger, who had spent most of his life living on the Moon, smiled slightly at the word "lunacy."

"What we need to do is change the mind-sets of the people who launch those missiles," Stoner said. "The machines aren't to blame for the disaster that's coming; the people who launch them are."

"You've got to get the leaders to change their minds," Stavenger mused.

"That's easy. I can convince individuals to do pretty much what I want them to, so long as it's not self-destructive. What of it? I convince a person to refuse to launch a missile attack. Once he or she is no longer in command, I'd have to convince the next one in power."

"Endless," Stavenger murmured. "I see."

"We've got to change the mind-sets of the all the people, everywhere. Turn them against war, against violence. Show them the way to lasting peace."

"My god," Stavenger said, seeing where Stoner was heading. "You're talking about starting a new religion."

Stoner nodded reluctantly. He could see in Stavenger's mind an image of the crucified Christ. That's what happens to men who start new religions, he thought.

CHAPTER 11

Raoul Tavalera had spent more than an hour talking with Holly Lane. In real time. Despite the billion-plus kilometers between Atlanta and the *Goddard* habitat, he and Holly chattered away as if they were in the same room. All during their happy, warm conversation a part of Tavalera's mind wondered at Stoner's ability to erase the time lag of normal communications.

How does he do that? Tavalera wondered, realizing that instant communications could make life much easier for the various human settlements scattered across the solar system's planets and asteroids.

On the wall screen of his apartment, Holly looked just as he remembered her: pert, full of energy, bright and smiling and altogether wonderful.

He told her all that had happened to him since his return to Earth, especially about Stoner, the star voyager.

"But the government won't let you come back here?" Holly had asked, her cheerful expression giving way to anger and concern.

"Not yet. Maybe Stoner can pull it off," he said.

"I'll come back there and get you," said Holly, stern determination etching her face.

"Naw," he replied. "I'll work it out. Something big is happening here; I can feel it. A guy who traveled to the stars! He's gonna bust this New Morality wide open; just you wait and see."

"But I don't want to wait!" Holly insisted. "I want you here! I want to be with you."

"That's what I want, too, Holly. But something big is gonna happen here and I'm gonna be part of it. Then I'll come back to you."

She looked disappointed, hurt. But she said, "Soon's my term in office is finished I'm heading Earthside. If you're not back by then, I'll come and get you."

Tavalera grinned at her image, stubborn and sure of herself. "It's a deal," he said.

He had forgotten about Sister Angelique's promise to have dinner with him until some time after he'd ended his conversation with Holly. His phone chimed and Angelique's dark, sculpted features appeared on the wall screen.

"I'll be there in half an hour," she said without preamble. "I hope you can cook."

He grinned at her. "Long as I've got a microwave."

Her image disappeared. But before Tavalera could head for the kitchen the wall screen lit up again, this time showing Stoner's face.

"Hello, Raoul."

Tavalera blinked with surprise. "Hello, Dr. Stoner."

Stoner said, "You can call me Keith, you know."

Tavalera nodded.

"Has Bishop Craig set up a meeting for us with the Archbishop?"

"I don't know. I'm having dinner with Sister Angelique in another few minutes. She can fill me in on what Craig's been doing."

"Good. Please keep me informed."

Frowning slightly with puzzlement, Tavalera asked, "How do I get in touch with you?"

Stoner broke into a wide smile. "Don't call us; we'll call you."

Angelique arrived nearly an hour after her phone call, dressed in a pair of slim dark slacks and a starched white blouse. From the capacious dark leather handbag she had slung over one shoulder she pulled a green bottle of wine. Tavalera, who had searched the apartment in vain for something alcoholic, grinned in appreciation.

"It's a sweet wine from Germany," she said as she handed the bottle in its plastic bag to Tavalera. "It should be chilled, I'm told. I thought it would be pleasant to have it with dessert."

"Sounds good," he said, turning toward the kitchenette and the small freezer built in below the countertop.

He had already pulled out a pair of prepackaged meals, something called beef Stroganoff. The name sounded exotic and the picture on the packaging looked interesting. He slid the pair of them into the microwave, then turned back to Angelique, who had sat herself in one of the sitting room's armchairs and rested her handbag on the carpeted floor beside her.

"You want something to drink?" Tavalera called from the kitchenette. Opening the refrigerator door, he said, "I've got orange juice, cranberry juice, and apple juice."

"I'll have apple juice, unsweetened," Sister Angelique answered.

Tavalera saw that the fridge's shelves held both sweetened and unsweetened apple juice. She knows what they've stocked in here, he thought.

He handed her the container of juice, then sat in the room's only other chair. "Stoner wants to know how you're making out with getting the Archbishop to meet with him."

Her brows rose slightly as she sipped at the juice.

Putting the plastic container down on the low table between them, Angelique asked mildly, "You've been in contact with Dr. Stoner?"

Tavalera nodded toward the blank wall screen. "He phoned me a little while ago."

"Interesting," Angelique murmured. "This phone line is supposed to be secure."

With a grin, Tavalera said, "Nothing's secure around him."

"So I'm beginning to understand."

"Well? What's with the Archbishop?" he prodded.

"We're working on it. Bishop Craig and I."

"He's kinda impatient. He says this is really important."

She nodded and reached for the juice again.

The dinner went that way, Tavalera asking for information and Angelique parrying his questions with a soft smile. She helped him clear the kitchenette table, which was nothing more than a slim pull-down board. There were no dirty dishes to wash: the meal had come in its own packaging, complete even with utensils.

"What do you have for dessert?" Angelique asked.

Tavalera thought briefly that he wouldn't mind having her for dessert, but he knew that was out of the question. In fact, he felt a pang of guilt at even thinking of it. But Holly was so far away and this tall, slim, smiling young woman was close enough to touch.

Yeah, he told himself. And she's some kind of nun, a religious fanatic probably. But she didn't look like a fanatic. Or smell like one: her perfume was light but sensuous. I wonder if she's a virgin?

"Dessert?" she reminded him. Tavalera realized he'd been standing by the sink staring at her.

"Oh. Yeah." He pulled the refrigerator door open again and found a small box of chocolate cookies.

"How's this?" he asked.

She took the box from his hands. "Perfect. They should go well with the wine."

Tavalera and Angelique sat at the kitchenette's tiny shelf of a table. She broke open the cookies while Tavalera popped the stopper on the wine, then found two stemmed glasses.

He sat down and poured. Angelique handed him a cookie.

"What about you?" he asked.

She smiled and picked up a cookie. With his free hand, Tavalera raised his wineglass.

"What'll we drink to?" he asked her.

Angelique cocked her head slightly, as if searching for an answer. Finally she said, "To truth."

Tavalera thought it was a bit strange, but he shrugged and said, "Okay. To truth."

They touched glasses. He sipped at the wine. And immediately felt the world blur around him and sink into darkness. He slumped forward helplessly. The last thing he saw was Sister Angelique reaching across the tiny table and cradling his head in both her hands so that he wouldn't bang his nose on the tabletop and hurt himself.

CHAPTER 12

Stoner felt Tavalera's consciousness fade. For a moment Stoner felt blinded, cut off from his link on Earth. Alarmed, he tapped into the phone system in the Atlanta complex and saw Sister Angelique bending over Tavalera's inert body, slumped on the thin shelf of the kitchenette table.

Stoner watched with growing irritation as she grasped

Tavalera by the shoulders and hauled him up to a sitting position. Then she took a hypospray gun from the shoulder bag she had left in the sitting room and rolled up Tavalera's left sleeve.

Tavalera stirred slightly as the hypospray hissed against his bare skin. Angelique went back to her chair on the other side of the little table and sat down, her eyes intent on Tavalera.

Stoner watched intently, too. What's she after? he wondered. He knew he could probe her mind if he had to, but he knew she would recognize his invasion of her mind and wanted to avoid that if he could. Besides, he thought, I've interfered enough already.

"Raoul," Sister Angelique called softly. "Raoul, can you hear me?"

Tavalera opened his eyes, but they seemed unfocused, blank.

"Raoul?" she repeated.

"Yeah."

"Raoul, I need to know everything that Stoner's told you. Every word."

"Okay," he said, his voice thick, as if he were talking in his sleep.

Hypnotic regression, Stoner realized. She doesn't trust the doctors who examined him. She wants to pump him dry.

For more than an hour Angelique questioned Tavalera and he answered, often recalling word for word what Stoner had told him. Watching them, Stoner smiled grimly to himself. He remembers better than I would, he thought.

No, said his wife's presence. You'd remember, too, once the mental blocks have been lowered. We used this technique back in the old days, at Vanguard Industries.

On your employees? Stoner asked her.

Employees, she replied, and others that our security people had to interrogate. The technique doesn't harm the prisoner, and it gets much better information out of him than physical abuse.

You mean torture.

He sensed her ironic smile. They never used words like that, Keith. Our legal department trained them in vocabulary.

Stoner returned his attention to Angelique and Tavalera. She seemed nettled, a tiny pair of annoyed lines between her brows marring the flawless silkiness of her face.

"There must be more than that, Raoul," she coaxed. "You're leaving something out. Tell me what else he said to you."

Even drugged, Tavalera shook his head stubbornly. "Tha's everything. Every friggin' word."

"How does he appear and disappear?" she demanded, her voice rising slightly. "Where is his base of operations?"

"Starship."

"He took you there, you say."

"Yep. In orbit."

"But the U.S. Space Command reports no unidentified spacecraft in orbit. Nothing between here and the Moon."

Tavalera made a sloppy shrug.

"He can't make a spacecraft totally invisible to radar," she insisted. Then, after a heartbeat, she amended, "At least, that's what the Space Command claims."

Stoner decided the interrogation had gone far enough. He projected his presence into Tavalera's kitchen.

"You can ask me about that," he said.

Angelique hopped off her chair as if it had suddenly become white-hot.

Stoner grinned at her. "Sorry to startle you."

"You . . ." She was breathless, wide-eyed.

"I can make a spacecraft totally invisible. And it's not just an ordinary spacecraft: it's a starship."

She steadied herself. "You've been listening to us all this time, haven't you?"

Pointing to Tavalera, who was still sitting on the kitchenette's spindly white chair, his eyes unfocused, Stoner said, "I'm connected to him. What you do to him you do to me."

"How can you do that?"

"It's a gift," he said, smiling tightly. "A gift from the stars."

She reached out her hand and touched the fabric of Stoner's shirt. He felt her fingertips press against him.

"You're solid," she whispered. "You're real."

Stoner said, "It's pretty much what you said to Bishop Craig earlier today: I'm an ordinary human being who has access to extraordinary technology."

"But you said you've become more than human."

Stoner turned and stepped into the sitting room, Angelique following right behind him. He took one of the armchairs; she sat in the other. For several moments he was silent, wondering how much he should really tell her.

"You were closer to the truth than I was," he said at last. "I'm a human being. I was born on Earth. I have access to technology that's far beyond present human capabilities, but there's no reason why humans couldn't learn to develop and use such technology."

"But you said you were more than human."

He scratched at his beard, thinking of how he should reply to her. "That was . . . an exaggeration. You are more than the humans of the Middle Ages, aren't you?

You live longer; you're healthier; you know far more than they did back then; you have access to much greater sources of energy."

Angelique nodded uncertainly.

"Well, I know quite a bit more than anyone else on Earth. And I have access to much greater sources of energy. That's what I meant when I said I'm more than human."

You're shading the truth! his wife accused inside his mind.

I know, he replied, but she's frightened enough as it is.

"I'm not sure that I entirely believe that," Angelique said slowly.

See, said Jo. She's smarter than you think.

I could make her believe it, he said to Jo. I could manipulate her mind.

We agreed that we'd do that only if we absolutely have to.

Stoner nodded mentally. To Angelique he said, "You can believe as much or as little of it as you wish."

Her eyes went crafty. "I'm not sure I believe *any* of it," she challenged.

"Fine. But believe this. Unless you act, and act soon, the human race will destroy itself in a nuclear war. That's why I've got to see your Archbishop Overmire immediately."

"You could just appear to him, as you just did to me."

"I could, but I'd rather he was prepared to talk with me about the impending war. I don't want him half-collapsing on me the way that Craig did."

Angelique started to shake her head but caught herself. "Can you really stop the war from happening?"

"No," Stoner said flatly. "But you can—if you want to."

"And that's why you've returned to Earth?" Angelique asked almost plaintively. "To save us from this war?"

Stoner hesitated. "Yes. That, and more."

"What more?"

"I'll tell Overmire, and anyone he chooses to have with him when we meet."

"Bishop Craig is trying to set up the meeting for you."

"Tell him to hurry. Time's growing short."

And Stoner blinked away. One instant he was sitting in the armchair in front of Angelique, solid, real, a living, breathing, speaking person. The next instant he was gone; she was staring at an empty chair, alone in the sitting room.

Angelique drew in a deep, shuddering breath. He's human, she told herself. He says he's human. He cares about what happens to us. He wants to save us. Then she realized, And he wants me to help him!

For many minutes Angelique sat in the armchair, her mind turning thoughts over and over, hopes and fears and yearnings racing through her. He wants me to help him, she repeated to herself. He wants *me* to help him.

Slowly she picked up her shoulder bag and rummaged in it for another hypospray gun. Then she got to her feet and stepped into the kitchenette, where Tavalera was still sitting glassy-eyed.

She pressed the hypospray to Tavalera's bare arm and squeezed its trigger. He twitched, shuddered. Quickly she rolled his sleeve back down. Before she could button the cuff, Tavalera stirred to consciousness.

"Whew," he said a little groggily. "I musta nodded off."

Angelique smiled sweetly for him. "The wine must be more potent than we thought. I fell asleep, too."

Tavalera looked embarrassed. "Guess I'm outta condition, far as alcohol's concerned."

"Me, too," she said. Glancing at her wristwatch, she put on an alarmed expression. "Goodness! Look at the time. I've got to leave, Raoul."

He was still slightly fuddled from the drugs, but he walked her to the door—somewhat reluctantly, Angelique thought. She gave him a peck on the cheek and left hurriedly.

Tavalera stood by the door, never even thinking that it was open and he could walk out if he wanted to. Instead he grumbled to himself, Some friggin' date. I slept through it.

CHAPTER 13

At the same time, Stoner was halfway across the world, speaking to the Iranian astronomer Karim Bakhtiar.

Stoner had contacted Bakhtiar because the man was the foremost astronomer in the Islamic world, a scientist whose secularist views had brought him into controversy more than once with the religious conservatives of the Light of Allah and their powerful followers. Moreover, Bakhtiar was also the brother of the chief of Greater Iran's Revolutionary Guard, and his older brother protected him. Up to a point.

Stoner had reached Bakhtiar through the perfectly prosaic telephone system, offering his credentials as an astrophysicist and asking for an hour or so to explain the strange phenomenon of the aurora. The Northern Lights had flickered in the skies over the Middle East night after night, just as they had over all the rest of the Northern Hemisphere. Many faithful Muslims streamed to their mosques, fearing that the end of the world was at hand. Stoner knew that it could be true.

It wasn't easy to manipulate Bakhtiar's mind over the telephone link, even with a video connection, but Stoner used the astronomer's natural curiosity to overcome his suspicious misgivings about a stranger—and an obvious American, at that—who suddenly offered to explain a phenomenon that was puzzling the entire astronomical community.

But Bakhtiar was an astronomer, and curiosity overcame his political caution. He invited Stoner to his office. I can always call for the security police, he told himself, if he turns out to be a fraud or a mental case.

Bakhtiar's office was on the campus of the University of New Tehran, which was only lightly guarded by Iranian security forces, unless student unrest called out the riot police. At the moment all was quiet, so it wasn't difficult for Stoner to project himself into a secluded corner of the campus, by a small copse of acacia trees, then stroll leisurely to the astronomy building. In the lobby a young security guard asked for Stoner's visitor's pass. He had none, but he held out his empty hand and assured the young man that it was all right to pass him through.

The dark-skinned guard frowned momentarily and touched the butt of the pistol at his hip, but then he shrugged and let Stoner pass.

As soon as he entered Bakhtiar's small, cluttered office Stoner sensed the picocameras and microphones hidden in the walls and ceiling. He wondered if Bakhtiar himself knew that he was under constant surveillance. Stoner closed his eyes briefly and the sensors obediently turned off.

Karim Bakhtiar was a small, intense man with a closely clipped fringe of a beard that was just beginning to show touches of gray. He had learned over the years to curb his tongue when speaking to anyone except a fellow scientist. Even then Bakhtiar was circumspect.

Like the rest of the Islamic world, Greater Iran lived under the code of Shari'a law. Although the Qur'an saw no conflict between science and faith and indeed encouraged faithful Muslims to seek knowledge as a means of learning of the glories of Allah, the conservative mullahs who made up the ruling ulema regarded the constant searching of scientists with deep uneasiness. Astronomers were the least suspected: they studied the stars, not people, which was relatively harmless—as long as they did not contradict the revealed truth of Allah's creation of the world.

Bakhtiar sat behind his desk, fairly radiating nervous energy. He wore a thoroughly Western business suit of dark blue with a vest tightly buttoned over his lean frame. His shirt was open at the neck. On the left breast of his jacket he had pinned a pair of discreet ribbons, like military decorations: the Order of the Faith and the colors of the International Astronomical Federation.

Here is a man who's walking a tightrope, Stoner thought. He immediately liked Bakhtiar.

After inviting Stoner to sit in the rickety plastic chair before his desk, Bakhtiar said in slightly accented English, "I searched for your name in the astronomical databases."

With a tight smile Stoner said, "Try going back to the nineteen eighties."

Bakhtiar's brows rose. "That's more than a century ago." But he turned to the keyboard at his side, pecked at it, then stared at his desktop screen.

Even with his alien powers to influence human minds it took Stoner nearly half an hour to convince Bakhtiar that he was the star voyager whose messages to Earth had been ignored for months.

"My brother believes you are a fraud, a trick played by pranksters."

"That would make his life easier, wouldn't it?" Stoner replied.

"And you are causing the aurorae? Deliberately?"

"I thought it would be a signal that no one could ignore. Apparently I was wrong."

Bakhtiar pursed his lips. Then, in a taut, keyed-up voice, he said, "So what you are telling me is that traveling at relativistic velocity moves you from one universe to another universe, a parallel universe?"

Stoner nodded unhappily. "I'm not enough of a theoretiker to understand the physics involved, but this world that I've returned to is somewhat different from the one I left."

"Fascinating! You've been to the stars? Actually? Really?"

"Actually," Stoner replied. "Really."

"Which stars? What was it like?" Bakhtiar was bobbing up and down with excitement in his swivel chair. "You must tell me everything!"

"In time," Stoner replied calmly. "In due time."

He saw disappointment flash through the astronomer. And then something else. Bakhtiar was thinking of his brother, Stoner realized.

"Can you tell me about your starship, then? What drives it? What is your propulsion source?"

"Electromagnetic induction," Stoner answered. Ordinarily he would have been pleased to talk about science to a fellow scientist. But Bakhtiar was asking now for the benefit of his brother, the chief of the Revolutionary Guard.

"I don't understand," Bakhtiar admitted.

"You think of interstellar space as a vacuum, but in reality it's drenched with energy," Stoner explained. "The ship absorbs that energy. When we make the aurora glow we're actually recharging the ship's energy storage."

They talked for more than an hour, Stoner answering each of Bakhtiar's questions as fully and honestly as he could, although he carefully avoided any mention of what he'd found among the stars. As he spoke about the starship, he clearly sensed that in the back of Bakhtiar's mind there was a tendril of thought that realized his brother would kill whole armies to get his hands on this powerful alien technology.

Stoner could see it in Bakhtiar's face. His realization, his sudden anguish. I can't tell my brother about this! Bakhtiar was thinking. I can't breathe a word of this to anyone.

And Stoner understood. "You know about the nuclear weapons, don't you?"

Bakhtiar twitched as though jabbed by the point of a knife. "Iran renounced nuclear weaponry after the Final Israeli War," he said in a monotone, as if reciting a lesson learned by rote.

"Were there any left?" Stoner asked.

"The Israelis struck us first! We retaliated in self-defense."

"Yes, of course."

"After the war we renounced nuclear weapons and scrapped the few that remained. We saw to it that Greater Iran and all the nations of Islam were cleansed of all such weapons."

"But now your nation is building new nukes, at a secret facility near Shar-e Babak."

Bakhtiar's face went white.

"Your brother told you about it, didn't he?"

For a moment Bakhtiar was silent. Then, "He . . . he asks me for scientific advice. He doesn't altogether trust the state's scientists."

Stoner thought the astronomer looked thoroughly miserable, ashamed.

But then he blurted, "The Americans are building nuclear weapons! And they despise Islam; they want to destroy us! We must have our own weapons, for our self-defense."

Ignoring his outburst, Stoner asked calmly, "Greater Iran is officially an Islamic republic, yet it's actually ruled by the Council of Mullahs, isn't it?"

Bakhtiar's face twisted into a bitter smile. "That is almost correct. The Council of Mullahs and their ulema can negate laws passed by the parliament if they find that the laws are contrary to Shari'a. Rather like the Supreme Court of the United States can nullify laws passed by your Congress."

"The mullahs are ultraconservative in their interpretations of the law," said Stoner.

"Extremely."

"Yet they're allowing this nuclear weapons program to go forward?"

"They don't even know about it."

Stoner felt surprised. "How can that be?"

Leaning slightly forward over his desk, Bakhtiar lowered his voice and said, "Everyone thinks that the mullahs and their ulema are the final authority in Greater Iran. Even the mullahs themselves think so. But the real power lies with the military command. The mullahs control the people, but the military controls the mullahs."

Stoner leaned back in his chair and rubbed his beard, thinking. At last he said, "In the United States the government is controlled by a religious movement."

"The New Morality, yes, I know."

"But here in Greater Iran the religious movement—"

"The Light of Allah."

"They're actually controlled by your military?"

"It's a delicate balance, but yes," said Bakhtiar, "my

brother and his fellow Revolutionary Guard officers hold the true power."

"And they're building nuclear weapons."

"Yes."

"So are the Americans, in New Mexico," Stoner said. "And the Chinese."

Bakhtiar's shoulders slumped. "The fools . . . the utter insane fools . . . I told my brother; I tried to make him see. . . ."

"It's only a matter of time before other nations start their own nuclear weapons programs. Each one will act in its own self-defense. Each one will be another step toward disaster."

"Proliferation," Bakhtiar murmured.

Stoner got up from his chair. "This must be stopped."

"But how?"

"I don't know. Not yet." He turned to leave.

"Wait!" Bakhtiar cried, jumping to his feet. "You . . . all that you've told me . . . I think they may be listening. My brother might have bugged my office. He's like that."

With a curt nod, Stoner replied, "He has. But don't worry about it. You can tell him anything I told you."

"About your starship?" Bakhtiar asked in a hollow voice. "About the technology you have at your fingertips? He'd kill to get his hands on it!"

Smiling tightly, Stoner said, "I've been in that situation before. Don't worry. I can take care of myself."

And he winked out of existence, leaving Bakhtiar standing behind his desk wide-eyed, his mouth agape.

CHAPTER 14

Stoner was also in China, in the Forbidden City in Beijing, deep inside that complex of palaces and museums, in an area where neither tourists nor foreign dignitaries were ever allowed.

He projected himself directly into the bedroom of Ling Po, chairman of China's National Assembly and head of the New Dao movement, bypassing the guards and soldiers who patrolled the gardens outside and every corridor within the ornate palace.

Ling Po was deeply asleep, together with two of his women. Stoner woke only the chairman, stroking his mind with a featherlight mental touch while making certain that the women remained sleeping.

Ling Po woke slowly, cracked his eyes open slightly, stretched, and yawned. Then he saw Stoner standing over him and leaped out of bed as if he'd been scalded by boiling water. Naked, hairless, looking like a scrawny plucked chicken, he screamed for his bodyguards.

"They can't hear you," Stoner said in flawless Mandarin. "No one can except me."

Ling Po turned and pounded on his bedside phone console, to no avail. Then he yanked open the night table drawer and pulled out an automatic pistol. Stoner had to suppress his urge to laugh at the sight of this skinny, bony, bald naked man struggling to cock the pistol and point it at him with wildly shaking hands.

"The gun won't fire," Stoner said. Heedless, Ling Po strained to pull the trigger anyway until sweat broke out across his bald pate.

Even with the considerable mental powers that the alien's technology had given Stoner, it took nearly a quarter of an hour before Ling Po calmed down enough to speak with reasonable composure to this man who had abruptly materialized in his bedroom. While Stoner assured the chairman that he meant no harm, Ling Po finally gave up trying to fire the useless pistol and threw it onto the bed.

"You recognize my face, don't you?" Stoner asked calmly. "I'm the star traveler. I beamed my message to you and you completely ignored it."

Still totally naked, Ling Po plopped himself down on a corner of the rumpled bed.

"You wouldn't answer my message," Stoner continued, sweetly reasonable, "so I decided to speak to you in person."

"You are the star devil," Ling Po said almost sullenly. "I believe it."

Stoner smiled. "Good. Now we can talk man-to-man."

"What do you want? Why have you come here?"

"You're heading toward a nuclear war that could wipe out the human race."

Like most politicians, Ling Po's first reaction was to deny Stoner's accusation.

"Let's be truthful with one another," Stoner said mildly, standing before the bed with his arms folded across his chest. "Nuclear war is coming unless we take the necessary steps to prevent it."

The Chinese leader's pointed chin rose a notch. "The Americans are building nuclear weapons."

"So are the Iranians," added Stoner. "And others will follow."

"You see? China cannot afford to stand defenseless against our enemies."

"Why are they your enemies?"

Ling Po blinked at the question. He started to get to his feet but sagged back on the silk bedcovers again.

"Because we have failed," he said, his voice low and miserable.

"Failed?"

Stoner could sense that the man was struggling within himself. Gently, he encouraged Ling Po to reveal the full truth.

"For many decades we have toiled with the problem of population growth. China set an example, we thought, by passing laws limiting family size. For a while the Europeans also restrained their growth. But only for a short while. The Muslims and Slavs—the poorest among them—have sent Europe's birthrate rising once more."

"I see," Stoner murmured.

"Today the world's population is soaring again. Twelve billion today. In a few years it will be twenty billion. The global economy is strained to the utmost, devouring the Earth's natural resources at an unsustainable rate."

"And the resources you import from space haven't helped," Stoner said. "The power satellites, raw materials from the asteroids."

Ling Po shook his head. "They have only aggravated the problem. More resources lead to more population growth. Their religious leaders tell them it is sinful to control family size and their political leaders tell them we have access to limitless resources from space. But those resources are not limitless; nothing is limitless except the constant growth of population!"

Stoner saw the anguish in the man's face, heard it in his tone.

"The other nations will not restrict their growth. Many of them say it is against their god's wishes to do so. They demand more and more resources, constantly more and more. Soon there will be war over Canada's freshwater, over Vietnam's rice bowl, over the Saharan energy farms."

"Nuclear war," Stoner muttered.

"China can survive such a war," Ling Po said. "China can suffer hundreds of millions of casualties and still survive."

"On a world blanketed with radioactive clouds?" Stoner asked grimly. "Can you survive a nuclear winter that destroys crops and turns the world dark for years?"

"Underground," Ling Po answered. "We are preparing mammoth underground cities, learning from the cities on the Moon such as Selene. We will stay underground as long as we have to. China will survive."

"And all those who don't?" Stoner demanded. "The billions who are killed? What of them?"

Ling Po had no answer.

CHAPTER 15

Aboard the starship, Cathy felt anticipation bubbling inside her as she and her brother prepared to visit Earth. She had dressed herself in a simple shirt and light tan slacks, with stylish boots. Her honey-colored hair was pulled back off her face in a shoulder-length ponytail that bobbed with every movement she made.

They were in Cathy's quarters. She had adjusted the starship's décor so that the room appeared to be a comfortable lounge, with plush royal blue carpeting and deeply upholstered armchairs. Cathy had seen such a room in a magazine she had picked up on the ship's scanner. But the windows in her room looked out not on an exurban home's swimming pool but on the blue-swathed planet Earth, glowing against the star-flecked blackness of infinite space.

"So where're you going?" Rick asked. He was wearing light blue coveralls that looked like a military uniform, although completely unadorned by insignia or marks of rank.

"Egypt," Cathy said. "I've always wanted to see the royal tombs."

"Hunting for buried treasure?" he teased.

"Hunting for human history," Cathy replied. "What about you?"

"The Khyber Pass."

"The Khyber Pass?"

With a knowing grin, Rick explained, "Plenty of history there, too. Plus a contingent of the United Nations Peacekeeping Force."

"That's why you're in uniform!"

"Yep."

"Blending in with natives," Cathy said, laughing. Then, "It's exciting, isn't it? Going to Earth!"

"Calm yourself," Rick said. "It's not like we haven't been down there before."

"I know, but that was different. We were just sightseeing then, and Mom was with us."

With a sardonic grin, Rick said, "And what're we doing now? Just because we're going out on our own doesn't mean we're anything more than sightseers."

She shook her head, making the ponytail sway. "Dad wants us to see what's really going on. We can help him."

"Help him do what?"

"Save them!" she answered. "Save the human race."

Rick huffed impatiently. Cathy had been his big sister when they'd lived on Earth. But when those thugs had invaded their home in Hawaii to kidnap their father

Cathy had been cut down by the blast of an automatic rifle during the fight. Once she had been born again she became Rick's younger sister; he always remembered that he was now the senior of the two—even though they were both more than a century old.

"Save the human race?" he scoffed. "Why bother? I don't think they deserve to be saved. I don't think they *want* to be saved."

"Don't say that!" Cathy objected. "They deserve to be helped. We can't stand by and let them blow themselves away."

"I know that's what Dad thinks," said Rick. "But I wonder. They sure don't behave as though they want to be saved."

Cathy started out of the room. Taking a superior tone, she told her brother, "Well, you're going to have the chance of seeing them for yourself, firsthand."

"Big thrill."

They stepped out of the room and into what seemed like empty space. Hovering in the starlit dark, protected by a shell of energy, they looked out at the ponderous bulk of the planet.

"It's beautiful, isn't it?" Cathy murmured.

Rick said nothing, but he nodded slowly. Earth hung before their eyes, a huge curving sphere half in sunlight. The daylit side of the planet glowed, oceans heartbreakingly blue, clouds purest white, continents wrinkled brown with swaths of green. On the night side they could see the lights of cities and highways interlinked like living creatures stretching tendrils out to one another.

"Oh, Rick," Cathy breathed, "we can't let them kill themselves. We can't let them destroy their world."

"It's not up to us, Cath," he countered. "We can't stop them from wiping themselves out."

"We've got to try," Cathy replied.

Deeper inside the starship, Stoner and Jo watched their children prepare to leave.

"Are you sure they'll be all right?" Jo asked her husband.

He slid an arm around her shoulders and pulled her to him. "Yes, of course." Before she could respond, he added, "You can monitor them. Keep your eye on them. If they get into something they can't handle you can pull them back here."

Jo leaned her head against his shoulder. "You really think it's best for them to go down there?"

"They're part of this," he said, his voice low but firm. "They've got to see for themselves, make up their own minds."

"I suppose so," Jo agreed, reluctantly. "But . . . it's worse than we thought it ever could be, isn't it?"

Stoner nodded, his bearded face taut with apprehension. "The problem is so damned deep," he said.

"Maybe it's in their genes," she said.

"No," Stoner replied. "It's learned. Culture, not genes. At least, I hope so."

"If it is genetic, then there's nothing much we can do about it, is there?"

Stoner nodded. But he said, "I'm certain it's cultural. Bakhtiar, the Iranian astronomer we talked with, he saw right away that our ship has technology that the Iranian military would snap up and use, if they could. And he immediately realized that he couldn't tell anyone about it, not even his own brother."

"One man," Jo said.

"There are others," said Stoner. "There must be."

"You hope."

Stoner said nothing for several heartbeats. Then, "They're so stupefyingly backward! They're heading for the twelfth stupid century, for god's sake. You'd have thought that by this time they'd know better than to let their population grow out of control."

"And their technology is nowhere near where it ought to be."

"They've stifled technological growth. Cut off whole lines of research in the name of religion."

"Their religions are out-of-date," said Jo.

"Religions are always out-of-date," Stoner replied. "They're designed to be conservative, to hold on to the values that the community has built up over previous generations."

"But when they're faced with a new situation, with an environment that's changing rapidly . . ."

"They either change or crumble away," Stoner finished his wife's thought.

"They're turning their backs on the solutions they have at their fingertips. It's like they don't want to solve the problems they're facing."

"We've got to make them understand," Stoner muttered.

"The immediate problem is to prevent the nuclear war that's coming."

"We could control their leaders," Stoner mused. "Manipulate them to do what we want."

Jo countered, "There's billions of them and only the four of us. How can we control them all?"

"And even if we did," Stoner added, "they'd go right back to their usual ways the instant we stopped controlling them."

"Of course they would," Jo said, her voice low, troubled.

"We've got to make them understand," Stoner repeated. "We've got to help them to see the right path and follow it."

"A nuclear war could kill them all," Jo murmured. "And most of the other species, besides."

"Then there'd be nobody left," Stoner said. "Nobody. Anywhere."

"There'd be the people living off-Earth," Jo said. "There are enough people living off-Earth to keep the race going, even if Earth self-destructs."

"Do you think so? I wonder."

"I see what you mean," Jo said. "If Earth self-destructs could the human race continue off-Earth? Would it change anything? Wouldn't the survivors eventually fight each other? Wouldn't they head toward genocide?"

"Toward extinction," Stoner muttered.

"So what of it?" Jo's tone hardened. "If they're so dead set on destroying themselves why don't we let them do it and get it over with?"

"No," Stoner said. "We can't."

"Why not?" Jo insisted. "Why don't we just leave them to stew in their own juices and go out and explore? It's a big universe out there; somewhere there's got to be—"

"No," Stoner repeated more firmly. "I ran away from Earth once. I'm not going to do it again. I can't."

"Why not? Why should we kill ourselves trying to help them when they don't have the brains to survive?"

"Because it's *us* we're talking about!" Stoner shot back. "It's not just them. It's us! We're part of the human race and whatever happens to them happens to us, too."

Breaking into a warm smile, Jo said, "Just as I thought: you've got a messiah complex."

He ignored her jibe. "We can't just let them die. They're part of us and we're part of them. We can't let intelligent life doom itself to extinction."

Jo's smile turned bitter. "You're assuming that we can do something to prevent it."

"We've got to help them," Stoner insisted.

"But how?"

"I wish I knew," Stoner said. "We're so damned limited! It's like trying to hold back the tide with your bare hands."

"You could *make* them behave," said Jo.

"Set myself up as their god?" He shook his head. "No thanks. They've got to work this out for themselves. We can help them, but we can't force them."

Jo touched her husband's shoulder. "You'll find a way, Keith. If anybody in the universe can find a way, you will."

He gave her a grudging smile. "Thanks for the vote of confidence. But how?"

"You're going to see Archbishop Overmire, aren't you? That's the place to start."

"Maybe," he said, uncertain. Then, "Or maybe the place to start is with that woman, Sister Angelique."

BOOK III

ANGELIQUE DUPRIE

The unleashed power of the atom
has changed everything save our modes
of thinking.

Albert Einstein

CHAPTER 1

Angelique could not sleep. She lay on her bed staring at the shadows playing back and forth across her ceiling as traffic rolled past on the interstate outside her thick, soundproofed window. Her home was a Spartan studio apartment set high in one of the glass and steel towers on the edge of the New Morality's headquarters complex. Twelve of the building's twenty-two floors were occupied by her order, the Sisters of the Savior.

Stoner is more than human, she kept thinking. He has powers beyond any human capability. And he wants me to help him. Me. Bishop Craig is frightened of him. Good. I'll move Craig out of the loop and take Stoner to Archbishop Overmire myself.

She smiled to herself. All Craig is interested in is becoming the next Archbishop. He'll never get there. He's a weakling, terrified of Stoner. I can see the fear that underlies his life; Stoner's brought it out into the open. Instead of seeing Stoner for the opportunity he is, the bishop is terrified of him. All right. Good. I'll bring Stoner to the Archbishop myself. I'll become the power behind his throne. With Stoner at my side, I can control the entire New Morality apparatus. I can control the entire nation and all its dependencies.

With a little luck and a lot of skill, she thought, I can eventually control the whole world.

As long as I have Stoner at my side.

She was born Aretha Deevers in one of the tent cities that dotted the Georgia landscape after the greenhouse floods had swept away most of Florida and the Gulf Coast communities all the way up to Houston and Shreveport. She never knew her two brothers, both drowned when their rattletrap school bus overturned on a washed-out road in the middle of a blinding midnight thunderstorm.

Her father had worked in the county tax collector's office, but losing his home, his city, his career, his sons broke his spirit. He sank into a numb acceptance of the fact that his life was finished; he was just going through the motions, living on the government's dole, moving from one tent city to another, then to a hastily erected refugee center, and, finally, to a spanking new housing complex built by the New Morality in the heart of what had previously been the seediest, most run-down neighborhood of sprawling Atlanta.

Her mother never surrendered to poverty or despair, not even when her two sons were killed. All during her pregnancy with her daughter she worked ceaselessly to organize the dazed and battered refugees in their tent city. As they moved from one relocation center to another, she became a local force, an ardent spokeswoman for her downtrodden neighbors. Eventually, inevitably, the New Morality appointed her the watchwoman for their new community.

She wanted twelve-year-old Aretha to join the New Morality's Urban Corps. But Aretha had plans of her own. Young as she was, she recognized that the New Morality held the power over the people. The Urban Corps was too low on their ladder of advancement to suit her. She aimed higher and got her school's placement advisor to recommend her for a training position in the New Morality's headquarters.

But she was gang-raped one afternoon by a band of local toughs who left her sprawled in an alley, bleeding and half-unconscious. While her mother wailed and the police dithered, Aretha marched her battered body to the convent of the New Morality's Sisters of the Savior and, head high, asked them for sanctuary.

She entered the convent, changed her name to Angelique Duprie, willingly took the veil, and vowed eternal chastity, swearing to devote her life to helping others through the New Morality and its associated churches, knowing that this was the surest way to rise above her impoverished beginnings. She even trained herself to mimic the lilting Jamaican accent of her Mother Superior: it sounded so much more self-assured in her ears.

Her mother died of a stroke two weeks after Aretha finished her schooling and was ready to re-enter the world as Sister Angelique Duprie. Her father lived on, stumbling through the days and empty nights, as passive as his wife had been active. He finally succumbed to an overdose of the medications he had been taking for hypertension and atrial fibrillation. There was no investigation into his death: Angelique saw to it that the local coroner ruled it accidental so that her father would not be stigmatized as a suicide and refused burial in hallowed ground.

Alone now and unburdened by family, Sister Angelique worked her way upward in the New Morality's labyrinth of bureaucracies until at last she was appointed to the staff of Bishop Zebulon Craig. And there she met Keith Stoner, who claimed to be a star voyager.

She also met Raoul Tavalera, a lost and bewildered

young man who somehow seemed to be in the middle of this star voyager problem. Tavalera was linked in some manner to Stoner, which told Sister Angelique that to stay close to Stoner she had to stay close to Tavalera.

But more important, she had to push Bishop Craig to deal with Stoner. Or, rather, she had to move Craig out of the picture and advance herself into the good graces of Archbishop Overmire.

Stoner was an opportunity, she knew. A godsend, literally. But perhaps a danger, as well. If she were truly religious she might be frightened of him. But ambition was what drove Sister Angelique Duprie. She feared nothing—except a descent back into the poverty and helplessness of her earliest years.

Bishop Craig was clearly frightened.

Angelique walked with him along the tree-lined arcade behind the central Atlanta cathedral, where they could speak without being overheard—unless some overzealous security officer was specifically shadowing them. Angelique was certain such was not the case: no one would dare pry into the bishop's doings; the orders would have to come from the Archbishop himself, and she felt confident that Overmire had not and would not issue such a command.

Still, Craig was obviously nervous. Perhaps, Angelique thought, he's worried that the Archbishop is watching him? Or one of the other bishops, looking for an edge in their quietly ferocious competition for the Archbishop's ring? She surreptitiously fingered the miniaturized audio recorder in the pocket of her ankle-length skirt. No bigger than a sugar cube, it was taking down every word they spoke.

Craig was right to be worried about eavesdroppers, she knew. He was simply looking in the wrong direction. Angelique was compiling a dossier of the bishop's maneuverings; she planned to show it to Archbishop Overmire if and when she had to.

"How does he know what he claims to know?" Bishop Craig hissed, his voice low.

It was a warm and bright spring day in late February, although Angelique knew the sweltering months of the long summer were only a few weeks away. She was glad to be outdoors, feeling the light breeze on her face, hearing the birds singing happily among the trees. The brick-paved walkway she and Craig strolled along was empty of other people. The bishop had told his security people he wanted privacy.

She was several centimeters taller than Bishop Craig and found herself stooping slightly to hear his fretful, almost panicky whisper:

"We've got to find a way to get rid of him. We've got to!"

Looking down at Craig's bald head, Angelique asked, "Who are you speaking of, Your Worship?"

"This man Stoner! He claims to know that our government is building nuclear bombs. How could he possibly know that?"

She very nearly smiled. The bishop's dread was almost palpable. Stoner was something unexpected, unpredictable, a sudden intrusion into Craig's plans to make himself Archbishop.

"He is an extraordinary man, Bishop," said Sister Angelique.

He glared up at her. "I don't think he's a man at all. He's a demon straight from hell."

"Do you really think that's likely, Your Worship?"

Craig began ticking off points on his slender fingers. "He appears and disappears like some genie out of the *Arabian Nights*. He claims that we're heading for Armageddon. He says he wants to help us, but what if he wants to help us into everlasting damnation?"

Sister Angelique murmured, "By their fruits you shall know them."

Looking more annoyed than ever, Craig went on, "If he's right and the government is building nuclear weapons, then it must be with the knowledge and approval of the Archbishop. And if Archbishop Overmire has approved such a thing, he did it without my knowledge. Without informing any of the bishops, as far as I can see."

Angelique hesitated, thinking, It's not Stoner himself that's worrying him; it's the fact that Stoner could upset his plans.

"I don't like having the Archbishop make such a move without consulting me about it," Craig muttered.

"At least he hasn't consulted any of the other bishops, either," she replied.

"Do we know that for a fact? What about Van Wiesel? Or Morrison! I wouldn't put it past him to sneak into the Archbishop's good graces."

Feeling slightly alarmed at Craig's suspicions, Angelique tried to calm the man. "Your Worship, I think the Archbishop has acted on his own in this matter. His staff might know about it, but they've kept it from everyone else."

Bishop Craig was silent for several paces. Then, "Do you really think so?"

"Your Worship," Angelique answered, "the Archbishop is a man, no more than you are. A very good man, of course, but he is quite advanced in years. Certain members of his staff might be manipulating him. After all, he is not infallible, as the Catholics once believed of their Pope. Archbishop Overmire is very old, and from what I hear he isn't in the best of health."

Craig squinted up at her. "What are you suggesting?"

"Simply that if the Archbishop did agree to the construction of nuclear weapons, he may have . . . overreacted, perhaps. Or even made an error of judgment."

Craig fell silent again. At last he muttered, "If his judgment is faulty he'd have to be replaced."

"Replaced?" Angelique feigned surprise.

"That's a serious step, though. A very serious step. I can't just go before the board of directors and demand that Overmire step down."

"Of course not," Angelique agreed. "That would be wrong."

"On the other hand, if the Archbishop is making mistakes of judgment—"

"Or being maneuvered by certain members of his staff," Angelique suggested.

Craig nodded vigorously. "He's too old and weak to control his own staff, isn't he?"

Angelique sidestepped that question by asking, "How will you proceed, then, Your Worship?"

The bishop hesitated, his face furrowing with thought. At last he said, "This man Stoner. I think he's an alien in human disguise. I think he's a tool of the devil."

"The Archbishop will be meeting with him tomorrow."

"He's too weak to face the challenge," Craig insisted. "Too old and tired to face up to him."

"I've arranged for you to attend the meeting," Angelique said. "You'll be the only bishop there."

"None of the others?"

"The Archbishop wants this meeting kept small."

"Not even Van Wiesel?"

"You'll be the only bishop in the meeting," Angelique repeated.

Craig grinned happily.

"You'll be with the Archbishop when he meets Stoner. You can observe his reaction to the star man. That could reveal his true inner condition."

Craig did not answer. But he did not contradict her. Angelique knew that she had set his mind one more step along the path to ultimate power.

Her ultimate power.

CHAPTER 2

"It's all arranged," Angelique said to Tavalera. "The Archbishop is ready to meet with Stoner tomorrow."

She had invited Tavalera to lunch in a restaurant in the New Morality's complex of buildings. He had eagerly accepted. Poor man, Angelique thought, he has nothing to do all day except wait for me to call him. She had scanned through the surveillance records: Tavalera spent his days watching television or playing harmless video games. He went to bed early and slept soundly. He has a clear conscience, she told herself. But a thread of suspicion wormed through her thoughts. How can he keep himself from being bored? Two days of being cooped up in that apartment; I'd be screaming and pounding the walls.

Tavalera smiled lazily at her. Stoner had told him that she'd drugged him when she'd come to his apartment for dinner, and now he trusted her about as far as he could throw the planet Jupiter. While the surveillance cameras showed him spending hour after hour watching the wall screens, in actuality—thanks to Stoner—he spent a good deal of his time talking to Holly in the *Goddard* habitat at Saturn.

And he studied. Fascinated by Stoner, Tavalera had begun searching history webs and delving into physics and astronomy tutorials. He found that he enjoyed learning about how the universe worked. It wasn't a perfect world for Tavalera, but he considered that things were a good deal better than Sister Angelique knew. He was a prisoner, he knew, but he was using his imprisonment to expand his mind.

"Tomorrow, huh?" he asked, forking up a few leaves of salad. The restaurant was busy but almost eerily quiet, filled with employees of the New Morality's many agencies. Its customers spoke in whispers, as if they were afraid of disturbing anyone. Or afraid of being overheard. Tavalera almost laughed at his own voice, pitched low and soft like all the others.

Angelique studied his eyes. "Can you get Stoner to come?"

Nodding, Tavalera said, "He'll be there."

"Will he just . . . appear?"

With a shrug, "That's up to him. Might be the best way to convince the Archbishop that he's for real."

"I don't know," Angelique said slowly. "The Archbishop is an old man. A sudden shock like that wouldn't be good for him."

"I'll tell Stoner."

"No need to," said Keith Stoner. He was standing to one side of their table.

Tavalera dropped his fork clattering to the tiled floor. Angelique gaped up at Stoner.

"H . . . how long . . . ?" she stammered.

Stoner pulled up a chair and sat between them. He was wearing a soft gray velour pullover and light blue slacks.

Smiling at her, he said, "Whatever you say to Raoul, here, you're also saying to me."

She murmured, "Wherever two or three are gathered in my name, I am there also."

"I'm not a god," Stoner said gently.

"Is there a god?" Tavalera asked.

Stoner's bearded face grew more serious. "That's a question you'll have to answer for yourself, Raoul."

Recovering her composure, Angelique asked, "Will you meet with Archbishop Overmire tomorrow?"

"Of course."

"Without the theatrics?"

"Theatri . . . Oh, you mean the way I enter a room."

"You don't want to give the old Archbishop a heart attack," Tavalera said, grinning.

Stoner smiled back at him, but when he turned to Angelique his expression grew more serious. "Is that true?" he asked.

She felt a shock, as if a jolt of electricity had just raced through her body. "Of course it's true!" she snapped, then felt guilty for being so abrupt. He can see through me! Angelique realized. He can see right into my soul.

Tavalera seemed to be blissfully unaware of their interplay. "I'm looking forward to meeting the Archbishop," he said easily. "Maybe he can get me back to *Goddard*."

"In due time, Raoul," Stoner said, still focused on Angelique. "In due time."

But Angelique was thinking, He can see through to my very soul. If he's not a god, he's something very close to it.

APOLOGIA PRO VITA SUA

BY YOLANDA VASQUEZ

It's sad to see people turn into sheep. It's sadder still when you realize that nobody forced them into it; they've done it to themselves.

It was the Day of the Bridges that broke the camel's back. I suppose that's a poor metaphor, but what I mean is that when the terrorists struck so hard, so brutally, the people yelled bloody murder. They wanted vengeance. They wanted to make sure terrorists could never, never hurt us so badly again.

The Golden Gate Bridge, the Brooklyn Bridge, and the Sunshine Skyway Bridge over Tampa Bay in Florida. Terrorists blew up all three on the same day, the same hour, almost at the same minute. Killed nearly a thousand innocent people. It had been almost fifty years since the first big terrorist attack that destroyed the World Trade Center towers, back in 2001. People were shocked out of their wits.

You see, two entire generations had grown up without worrying about terrorism. They thought it was a thing of the past. Suddenly they were frightened. Suddenly they realized that they weren't safe.

And they were angry. Enraged at the shadowy, menacing terrorists and the robed and turbaned people in other lands who danced in the streets at our disaster. Furious with the so-called Homeland Security Department, which had obviously failed to protect our homeland's security. I remember one Congressman who had been loudly attacking the Transportation Security Administration for making it so inconvenient to get through an airport. Apparently his six-year-old granddaughter had set off an alarm when she'd gone through the screening procedure and they had to strip-search the little girl. Enraged, the Congressman threatened to sponsor legislation that would shut down the TSA altogether.

But after the Day of the Bridges he screamed even louder that the government "has to do something to protect us from these vicious killers!"

The President declared a day of mourning and a state of emergency. The Congress passed a war powers resolution by a huge margin. The American flag flew from every household, every automobile, every church and school and public building.

The New Morality stepped in and accepted a contract from Washington to take over the duties of the Homeland Security Department. Some people objected that a faith-based organization shouldn't be receiving federal funding, not even for such an obviously nonreligious policing task. But the New Morality declared that the objectors were terrorist sympathizers, and they were quickly rounded up and put in jails or internment camps.

"You're either for us or against us," the New Morality said, drumming the slogan into the public's mind with endless TV interviews, newscasts, and advertisements.

Most people were for them. They wanted security, and that's what the New Morality gave them: hard and fast. The New Morality clamped down on terrorists, real or suspected. In the name of security, the people gave away their liberties. When the Supreme Court tried to close the faith-based internment centers that the New Morality supervised, the White House invoked the President's war powers to maintain and even enlarge the camps.

And the Congress passed a Constitutional amendment that ended the lifetime appointments of Supreme Court justices and replaced them with mandated retirement. Within less than a year the amendment was ratified by the states almost unanimously. Half the Supreme Court were forcibly retired, replaced by men handpicked by the New Morality.

So the New Morality not only saved the nation, the whole of North America, from the calamity caused by the climate changes; they also protected the people from the ever-present threat of terrorist attacks. Similar faith-based movements had arisen all over the world: the Holy Disciples in Europe, the Light of Allah (terrorism was a much bigger problem in the Middle East than elsewhere, actually), the New Dao and Red Chrysanthemum in Asia. Everywhere, people chose order and safety over their own individual liberties. Of course, in most parts of the world the people had never known much in the way of individual liberties. They just went the way they were told to go. It was sad to see Americans going that way, too.

The years rolled on, one after another. Even though much of the United States was gripped in a decades-long drought and many seacoast cities had been flooded, all became peaceful. Even though there had not been a terrorist attack in the United States since the Day of the Bridges, the War on Terror raged on in Latin America, Africa, Indonesia, and the Muslim strongholds in the mountains of central Asia. In America, thanks to the New Morality, governments from the national level down to neighborhood associations were firm in their pursuit of peace and safety and order. The corruption, the vice, the godlessness that had brought on the greenhouse disaster had been replaced by sanctity, discipline, and obedience. The terrorists who threatened attack were rounded up and put away before they could spill blood. Dissidents who protested about individual rights and the due process of law were swiftly silenced, sent to labor camps and re-education centers. Some were even permanently exiled from Earth.

A team of scientists trying to study the way the brain works invented a deep brain stimulator. It used tiny electrical currents to activate sections of the brain. Or deactivate them. With DBS you could turn a homicidal maniac into a peaceful, smiling zombie. Or a placard-waving dissident into a placid couch potato. The government latched onto DBS, oh yes they did. That was one form of secularist science that the New Morality blessed and promoted. Vigorously.

Yes, there was talk of international tensions. There's always talk of international tensions. The war to root out terrorist regimes wherever they existed simmered on. As did the fruitless, frustrating war against drugs. Some American politicians wanted to annex Canada for its wheat belt and abundant resources of freshwater. Some feared that the fragile détente with Greater Iran and its dominions in the Middle East would inevitably break down and the bloodletting of a half century earlier would resume.

But at home all was quiet and peaceful, even though food prices and the costs for energy slowly but constantly ramped upward. We were safe in our beds, thanks to the everlasting vigilance of the New Morality.

And the sheep grazed on.

CHAPTER 3

Stoner projected his presence deep into the Asteroid Belt, to the rock that held the artifact.

It had been moved from its original orbit, he knew. Out in the dark emptiness of the Belt small chunks of rock and metal glided in a broad, intricate pavane, jostling back and forth, their paths constantly changing as their minuscule gravitational forces perturbed each other's orbits. Sometimes they came close enough to collide in crashes and sideswipes that broke new pebbles and stones off the larger bodies, adding new asteroids to the millions already populating the Belt.

Human prospectors sought ores in asteroids that were big enough for commercial mining. In their tiny vessels they eagerly combed the Asteroid Belt for its riches. Wars were fought over those resources. Two generations of rock rats made their fortunes in the Belt, or lost their lives.

That is why, nearly a generation earlier, Stoner had created the artifact inside asteroid 67-046. A sign, a signal, a greeting from the stars. He had thought long and hard about how to announce his return to humankind's home. He wanted an unmistakable signpost, a signal that clearly told his fellow humans that there was an alien presence among them. Yet he knew that simply announcing his presence would be met by disbelief, fear, xenophobic hatred.

So he created a work of art, deep inside the rocky asteroid 67-046. Using the alien technology that dwelt within him, Stoner created a mirror that reflected each onlooker's deepest desire. A combination of light sculpture and digital imagery, the artifact would scan each onlooker's brain and respond uniquely to that individual as he or she gazed upon it. Stoner placed it inside the asteroid, expecting that by the time humans reached that far into the Belt they might be ready for contact with alien intelligence.

He was wrong. The artifact was a fiasco. The first humans to discover it were a family of prospectors, a married couple and their two young children who lived aboard their ship as they scouted through the Belt for asteroids valuable enough to claim. They became so enthralled with what they saw in the artifact that they nearly starved to death: the glowing, alluring imagery was hypnotic, its effect on them stronger than any drug.

Stoner saw to it that they were saved before they died in the womb-like chamber that he had hollowed out. He influenced a patrol vessel belonging to Humphries Space Systems to look into the family's refusal to answer regular check-in calls. Once the patrol found the ragged, emaciated, enraptured family they sent word back to the top levels of their corporation's management. Martin Humphries himself soon came racing to see the artifact. Once he did, his exposure to his own inner self unhinged the solar system's wealthiest man. Humphries suffered an emotional meltdown and was swiftly whisked to a private sanitarium on Earth.

The asteroid was moved to a new, highly inclined orbit and guarded, so that no one—not even Earth's scientists—could get to it.

Stoner watched all this in shocked surprise and with no little disgust. A message from the stars, he told himself, and they try to hide it.

He thought about the other message that had existed in the solar system for at least a million years: the nanomachines that had created and maintained the brilliant, beautiful rings of Saturn. The solar system had been visited by intelligent aliens when the human race was just beginning to diverge from its apish hominid ancestors. The aliens had built the spectacular rings around Saturn, believing that in time human explorers would be drawn to them by curiosity and awe.

The aliens were right: humans eventually traveled to Saturn to study its rings. They learned that the rings harbored nanomachines, hardy little mechanisms the size of viruses that busily kept the rings intact and prevented them from collapsing into the giant planet Saturn's immense churning bulk, as they would have if not artificially maintained.

Once humans discovered the nanomachines, the alien devices sent a signal pulsing through interstellar space, a signal announcing that a new intelligent species had been discovered. That signal was still expanding through the Milky Way galaxy, a sphere of energy that bore the information of that discovery.

But there was no one left to receive the joyous news. The aliens who had created the rings were long gone from the solar system. Stoner knew that on their home world they had fallen into extinction thousands of years earlier. In his mind's eye he saw their planet once again: a placid, peaceful world of green from pole to pole, except for the slowly decaying cities that held the dead like elaborate tombs, tended over the centuries by automated machines that were inevitably breaking down. Biological warfare had wiped out that intelligent race. The innocents, the aggressors, the would-be peacemakers, they had all died, down to the last one.

The human race was hurtling toward its own deadly crisis at breakneck speed; Stoner knew he had to prevent them from destroying themselves. Dismayed, almost angry at his fellow humans' instinctive fear of contact with extraterrestrial intelligence, he at last realized that he had to make his presence unmistakably known.

Determined to help the human race survive its own folly, almost in desperation he announced his return to the solar system in a message he beamed to every major astronomical facility on Earth and the Moon. And received silence in return. He caused the Northern and Southern Lights to glow and pulse night after night after night. Like turtles facing danger, humankind's leaders pulled in their heads and tried to ignore his signal.

"I never thought it would be this difficult," he said to his wife, aboard the safety of their starship.

Jo shook her head wearily. "They're xenophobic, Keith. You knew that. Just look at how they treat each other—a slight difference in skin color or the shape of the eyes is enough to terrify them."

"And what they fear," he admitted, "they try to destroy."

Jo agreed. "Their first reaction is to lash out and attack what frightens them."

Stoner's shoulders slumped. "And we're human, just like they are. Imagine what they'd do if real aliens confronted them."

"But we're not really human anymore, are we?" Jo pointed out to him. "They know that, no matter what visible form you take."

"We're trying to save them from extinction, and they busy themselves playing their paranoid games."

"That's who they are," said Jo. "That's *what* they are. Those traits have served them pretty well through the Ice Ages and the early phases of their civilization. They had to be tough, suspicious, wary of outsiders. Those were survival traits."

"But now those traits are countersurvival," Stoner said. "They've got to change."

Jo smiled sadly. "Good luck, darling. I hope you can make some headway with this Archbishop Overmire."

He saw that his wife's real concern was for her children, exploring the teeming, dangerous world of their origin.

CATHY

Cathy stood in the baking sunlight and stared at Hatshepsut's temple, wavering in the heat currents rising from the bare desert floor.

"You must realize," the woman tour guide was saying to her little group, "that Hatshepsut was a true ruler of ancient Egypt, in the eighteenth dynasty. She was not a Queen, not the wife of a King, but Pharaoh in her own right."

Nearly thirty-five hundred years ago, Cathy said to herself as she squinted through the blazing sunshine at the shimmering temple. The tour guide held a parasol over her head, as did several of the tourists. Cathy was bareheaded but protected by a shell of energy that enclosed her body.

The little group proceeded along the roped-off walkway toward the tomb. Not a massive, looming pyramid like the tombs of the male Kings, Cathy thought. Hatshepsut's temple was a masterpiece of architecture, terraced, colonnaded, graceful, its three-story structure blending with the bare cliffs behind it.

They moved like a privileged little procession of royalty along the walkway, protected by a squad of private security guards who kept pace on either side, ahead, and behind. The guards wore dark wraparound glasses laden with miniaturized sensors and carried machine pistols in their hands. God knows what other weapons they've got under their coats, Cathy mused. Outside their perimeter was the crowd, milling, muttering, sullen-faced locals swathed in long robes and turbans. Vendors of wares, Cathy thought. Hawkers and hagglers, trying to make a living from the rich tourists. And maybe terrorists among them. Maybe murderers and religious fanatics and teenagers filled with hatred for the privileged, protected strangers who had come to gawk at their glorious past and ignore their destitute present.

It wasn't until the tour was finished and the sweaty, bedraggled tourists were getting back onto the air-conditioned bus that the guide stopped Cathy. Most of the tourists were middle-aged or older; Cathy recognized English, Dutch, Japanese, and broad Australian accents among them.

The guide was a black-skinned Egyptian, as young as Cathy's apparent age. Behind her, Cathy saw the security guards keeping the vendors and tradesmen at bay.

"You are not a member of the tour," the guide said, glancing from Cathy's face to the checklist on her palm-comp and back to Cathy again.

"No, I'm not," said Cathy in American English, smiling amiably. "I'm a guest."

The young woman frowned uncertainly but then put on her professional smile and said, "Well, let's get out of the sun, then."

By the time the bus had driven them across the Nile to the airport at El Uqsur, Cathy and the tour guide were fast friends. See, Cathy said silently to her mother, watching her from the orbiting starship. Dad's not the only one who can influence people.

Just be careful, Jo replied. There are plenty of crazies out there. You're not on a sightseeing trip.

But I am! Cathy thought, smiling inwardly.

The guide's name was Amina Kladiya Fatima al-Nasir. "But my friends call me Mina," she said as she sat beside Cathy on the tourist company's jet plane that carried them from the ancient monuments and temples of Luxor and Thebes to the modern city of Cairo.

Cathy chatted absently with Mina as she glanced out the plane's window at the glossy ribbon of the Nile, far below. The river flowed like a living, pulsing artery through the slim ribbon of green cultivated land that lay on either side of it. Then, stark brown desert stretching as far as the eye could see. Father Nile, she thought, giver of life. Civilization is old here, very old. The gift of the Nile.

Then she saw Cairo, the teeming city sprawling along both sides of the river and out into the desert like a gray cancerous growth, uncounted millions of people living cheek by jowl in its crowded, dirty, clamorous streets. The city stretched like a rotting slime mold completely around the fenced-off area of the ancient pyramids. At this altitude those proud symbols of eternity looked dwarfed almost into insignificance by the towers and spires of the vast and growing city.

Be careful down there, her mother warned.

Cathy felt a thrill of anticipation mixed with a tendril of fear. It's so big! she thought, even as her nose wrinkled at the brown miasma of pollution that covered the city like a foul blanket.

Mina leaned close to Cathy. "That's where I live, that district there," she said, pointing to a section of flat-roofed houses covered with dark banks of solar cells. "With my family. Would you care to visit?"

No! said Jo silently.

"Yes," said Cathy to her newfound friend.

CHAPTER 4

The instant Stoner saw Archbishop Overmire he knew that the man was dying.

Tavalera had warned him not to suddenly pop into Overmire's office, so Stoner had projected himself to

Tavalera's apartment instead. He walked with the younger man through the warm, humid morning across the campus-like grounds of the New Morality complex to the Archbishop's residence, a low, modest-looking edifice with a pitched roof that sat next to the soaring neo-Gothic splendor of the New Morality's central cathedral.

Between the cathedral and the vicarage they saw a major construction job was under way. It was screened off from the idle gaze of passersby, but heavy trucks rattled into the site and down a ramp. Stoner saw the steel spiderwork top of a construction crane poking above the protective wall of plastic screens.

"They're digging deep," he said to Tavalera.

"Yeah. Wonder what they're building?"

A bomb shelter, Stoner thought. An underground complex where the Archbishop and his chosen few can ride out a nuclear attack. But he said nothing to his companion.

Ever since they had left Tavalera's apartment building, Stoner had sensed a quartet of security guards in street clothes trailing them at a discreet distance. Half the people strolling along the tree-shaded walkways or lolling on the grassy grounds were security police, he realized. As he and Tavalera stopped to look at the construction site, Stoner sensed the security agents tensing, as if waiting for the word to push them away from the area.

Before any such confrontation could develop, Stoner told Tavalera they were in danger of being late for their meeting with the Archbishop.

Once they climbed the steps that fronted the arched doorway of the vicarage they were greeted by a pair of whispering young men in clerical garb and ushered inside without security checks or uniformed guards. No need for them, Stoner knew. Sensors in the walls have

ID'd us and checked for weapons. Overmire's security people can probably look inside our stomachs and see what we had for breakfast.

The vicarage was quietly sumptuous: dark wood paneling and parquet floors, high ceilings and arched mullioned windows, comfortable furniture and actual paintings on the walls, not wall screens. The wide corridor they were led through smelled faintly of sandalwood incense.

Archbishop Overmire's inner office was very different, however. It looked more like a military command center than the warm book-lined study of a churchman. No windows at all; the walls were covered with digital screens, most of them blank, although the one behind the Archbishop's gleaming teak and brushed-chrome desk showed an aerial view of the radioactive devastation that had once been Jerusalem. Stoner felt his jaws clench at the sight.

Bishop Craig was already there, sitting tensely in one of the bottle green leather chairs arranged before the Archbishop's desk. Sister Angelique sat beside Craig, smiling at Stoner. He sensed something in her smile far deeper than mere politeness. Interesting, he thought. Craig's wary of me, but Angelique seems really eager to see me.

Then he turned to the Archbishop and saw a dying man. Outwardly Overmire seemed healthy enough, perhaps too healthy. He was grossly overweight, multiple chins overlapping the clerical collar of his plain dark suit. A large jeweled cross hung from a heavy silver chain on his ample belly. A beautiful signet ring was embedded deep in the flesh of one finger. His hair was light gray, almost silvery, worn long enough to just touch his collar in back. His nose was hooked like a parrot's. His eyes were tiny, encased in folds of flesh.

It was the Archbishop's eyes that gave him away. They were soft brown, crinkled at the corners—and bloodshot with pain. The room was cooled almost to the point of discomfort; Angelique had thrown a dark sweater over her slim shoulders. But Overmire was perspiring slightly: Stoner could see beads of sweat dotting his upper lip, and a barely perceptible trickle running down one flabby cheek.

He's wearing a water-cooled thermal undergarment, Stoner sensed, just like astronauts used to wear beneath their space suits.

"Welcome, Dr. Stoner," Overmire said, without rising from his desk chair. His voice was deeper, stronger, than Stoner had expected. With a gesture to the empty chairs in front of his desk, he added, "Please make yourself comfortable. You, too, Mr. Tavalera."

Stoner sat down and noticed that Raoul was taut with suspicion as he took the chair beside him.

Overmire said heartily, "I'm not going to bore you with the obvious questions. I imagine you've been asked them often enough."

"True," said Stoner, steepling his long fingers in front of his face. It was costing Overmire some effort to maintain his genial front, Stoner realized.

"Bishop Craig tells me you believe the United States is building nuclear weapons."

Stoner smiled, thinking, He gets right to the point. Good.

"So are several other national governments."

Overmire leaned back and twisted his signet ring. It barely moved on his plump finger. "You realize that I bear a heavy responsibility."

"The death of the human race is a very heavy responsibility," Stoner said.

His pain-filled eyes narrowing, Archbishop Overmire said, "Do you understand anything about power, Dr. Stoner?"

"It corrupts."

"Does it? Perhaps little, venal people are corrupted by power. But when you are doing God's work, when you are serving our Lord and Savior Jesus Christ, then you are protected from the sins of corruption."

"Killing twelve billion people is doing God's work?"

Bishop Craig looked shocked. "You've got no right to speak to the Archbishop like that!"

But Overmire raised a placating hand and answered smoothly, "We have no intention of killing anyone. We are merely acting to defend ourselves."

Stoner thought about that for a moment. "Selene feels threatened by you. So does Greater Iran and China."

The Archbishop cocked an eyebrow. "The godless humanists on the Moon have nothing to fear from us. We want nothing to do with them. As for the Islamic jihadists . . ." Overmire shook his head with a *more in sorrow than in anger* expression on his fleshy face.

Stoner asked, "Do you believe that your missile defenses will protect North America from attack?"

"That is what they are designed to do. The military has advised the President of the United States that in the event of a full-scale attack upon us, less than one percent of the missiles will get through."

"One percent of how many?"

"A few hundred, at most."

"At least ten nuclear warheads will hit their targets, then. Ten cities wiped out. That's a catastrophe, Archbishop Overmire. A holocaust."

The Archbishop spread his hands. "God's will."

"Killing millions of people is God's will? When their deaths can be prevented?"

Overmire forced a smile. "That's why I asked you

about power, Dr. Stoner. We must balance the power of our enemies. If they build nuclear weapons, then we have no choice but to build them also. No defense is perfect; some of the missiles will get through. Therefore we must have enough weapons to convince our enemies that it would be a devastating mistake to attack us."

"Mutual assured destruction," Stoner muttered.

"You know the phrase."

"I remember it from my earlier life."

"So there we are. The United States has no intention of striking first. I can't say the same for the Islamists and their notion of jihad."

"Holy war," said Stoner. "The ultimate oxymoron."

"We've tried to reason with them," Overmire said, perpsiring more freely now. "We've tried for years, decades. They just won't listen to us. They supply the terrorists with arms, money, training facilities. And we must fight their terrorist bands wherever we find them."

"And now they're building ballistic missiles and nuclear warheads for them," said Stoner.

"They are intent on war," the Archbishop replied, as if speaking about an unpleasant neighbor. "We must be strong enough to deter them."

"And if deterrence fails?"

Archbishop Overmire spread his hands, palms upward. "God will protect us."

Stoner's brows rose slightly. "I see that you're digging a shelter for yourself."

His face hardening, Overmire said, "I have the responsibility of protecting and guiding my flock, which includes far more than merely North America. I must protect myself and enough of a staff to begin the rebuilding process after the war."

Stoner said, "Then you're ready to fight. You're prepared to go to war."

"I cannot leave my people naked to their enemies."

"Why are they your enemies?" Stoner asked.

Archbishop Overmire hesitated. But he quickly recovered. "They hate us. They despise our wealth; they fear our power. Worst of all, they will not accept the truth of Holy Scripture. They deny our Lord and Savior Jesus Christ."

"As you deny their prophet Mohammed. And the teachings of the Tao."

"Heathen sects," Overmire spat.

Shaking his head, Stoner said, "There's more to it than that. For more than two generations the New Morality, the Light of Allah, the New Dao, and other religious movements have lived in peace."

"Peace?" Bishop Craig snapped. "With their terrorists constantly threatening us?"

"And your army fighting brush wars across half the world," Stoner retorted. "But despite your differences, you agreed on accommodating one another, more or less. Why this move now toward war?"

Sister Angelique spoke up. "I think you know, Dr. Stoner."

"Do I?"

"Population keeps growing. Resources don't keep pace. Even with the raw materials and energy we import from space, population growth outstrips our ability to feed and clothe and house the constantly growing numbers of people."

"Then why don't you allow the people to control their population growth?" Stoner asked.

"Sacrilege!" Bishop Craig snapped. "Birth control? Legalized abortion? Never!"

Stoner closed his eyes briefly. "In early societies, religious taboos were necessary," he said, so softly that Archbishop Overmire and the others unconsciously leaned toward him to hear. "Religious rules are digital: yes or no, allowed or forbidden. There's no middle ground. Some societies made taboos against eating pork—"

"That was thousands of years ago," Angelique interrupted with a thin, understanding smile.

"Yes, but the taboo against pork still stands in many parts of the world, doesn't it?"

She nodded grudgingly.

"And the taboo against killing cows, in what's left of the Hindu society."

"Yeah," said Tavalera.

"And the taboo against family planning, in many societies."

"Abortion is murder!" Bishop Craig insisted.

"Abortion is not the only form of family planning. It's the last resort, in most cases. The last desperate resort."

"It's still murder."

Stoner fixed him with a hard stare, then turned back to the Archbishop. "By keeping and enforcing the taboo on family planning you keep poor families poor. You maintain your power over them by giving them the solace of religion, but you make certain that they stay poor so that you can maintain your hold on them."

Overmire glowered at him. "That is a vicious lie. We are here to help the poor, and all people who accept God's way."

"And who decides what is God's way? You do."

The Archbishop's angry expression shifted into a guarded smile. "Why, of course we do, Dr. Stoner. Who else is better qualified? Who else sees the big picture and understands all the ramifications of the problem?"

"Nobody," Stoner admitted. "Because you won't let anyone into your little circle of power unless and until they agree with you, heart and soul."

Archbishop Overmire's smile widened. "God's will, Dr. Stoner. We are doing God's work."

"Are you? Leading your people into a devastating war? That's God's work?"

"His will be done."

Stoner slowly got to his feet. "Then take a good look at what you're calling God's will."

Abruptly all the screens on the room's four walls flashed into a panoramic view of the city of Atlanta, with the New Morality complex at its heart. The sky was clear blue, flecked with only a few puffs of clouds. Then through the sky streaked a series of blazing meteors. They exploded into searing, eye-burning nuclear fireballs. The city vaporized. Buildings blown to white-hot radioactive rubble. Flesh flayed from the bones of men, women, children. Ponds and pools and reservoirs flashed into scalding steam. The very ground pulverized into dust and the dust sucked up into mushroom clouds that boiled up high into the stratosphere. The sound was overpowering, enormous thundering explosions that shook the bones of the little group in the room.

They were no longer in the room. They stood outdoors, helplessly screaming as the overwhelming devastation poured down all around them. They saw a white-hot missile warhead diving toward them, a hardened penetrator that smashed into the burning ground and ploughed deep before its nuclear bomb exploded with the fury of hell.

The concrete-lined chambers deep underground collapsed, burying alive all those who were not killed by the blast or searing star-hot inferno. But not before they screamed a final, pain-filled, terrified wail of doom.

Abruptly they were back in the Archbishop's office. The thundering, shattering roar of the explosions finally stopped. The screens showed utter devastation beneath dark roiling clouds that flashed with lightning but brought no rain. The ground was broken, red-hot, glowing sullenly like the landscape of hell. Nothing moved. Hot winds blew across the barren rubble, but there was no blade of grass to be seen, nothing alive anywhere. Where the underground shelter had been there was a deep, blackened hole, smoking and stinking of burnt flesh.

Overmire stared at the images, mouth agape, hands twitching on his desktop, perspiration pouring down his face. Craig buried his face in his hands. Sister Angelique pressed both her fists to her face, trying to stifle the sobs that were rising inside her as she stared wild-eyed at the horror. Tavalera tried to get up from his chair, but his legs failed him and he thumped back into the seat and threw his arm over his streaming eyes.

Still standing in the middle of the room, surrounded by the awful destruction of a sterilized Earth, Stoner could feel that hot radioactive wind on his face.

"God's will," he muttered.

Archbishop Overmire tried to speak, tried to answer, but he collapsed over his desk, barely breathing.

CHAPTER 5

Angelique recovered before any of the others.

"The Archbishop!" she cried and rushed to the semiconscious figure slumped across his desk.

Stoner cleared the screens and went to him also.

Brushing with the heel of one hand at the tears running her cheeks, Angelique bent over the Archbishop's body. Stoner gripped the man's soft, pudgy shoulder and shook him roughly.

"Wake up," Stoner said, almost in a growl. "You can't get away from it that easily."

Overmire sat up, blinking with confusion. Stoner calmed the Archbishop's heartbeat, slowed the flood of adrenaline pouring into his bloodstream. Briefly Stoner thought to restore the endocrine balance that was so badly out of normal, but he decided that if Overmire didn't take proper care of his own body that was his decision.

Stoner looked into the Archbishop's sweaty, gape-mouthed face. "That's what nuclear war looks like, Archbishop," he said. "You have to face it. Everyone will die. Everyone you know, everything you've ever seen, will be destroyed. *You* will die. There's no escaping it. Not even the shelter you're building will save you from it."

"How . . . how did you do that?" Overmire gasped.

"I want you to shut down your nuclear bomb project," Stoner commanded.

Glancing at the others, Overmire temporized, "It's not my program. It's the federal government. The President and the Pentagon. I can't shut it down."

"You can tell them that it's evil and the New Morality doesn't sanction it. You can throw the weight of your organization against it."

"But . . . but . . . we've been backing it."

"Until now," Stoner said with iron in his voice.

"Yes. Until now."

"Stop them," Stoner repeated.

"But the others . . . the jihadists . . . the Chinese."

"I'll do what I can to stop them," said Stoner. "But none of them will stop unless you do."

Overmire looked toward Craig, who was sitting frozen in his chair, staring blankly as if catatonic, then up to Angelique, still standing over him.

"Morality is an individual choice," Stoner reminded

him. "You have to act, one way or the other. You've just seen what your present course will lead to. You've got to prevent that from happening."

Angelique straightened up and reached out a hand to touch Stoner's sleeve. "And you?" she asked. "Can you really stop the others?"

"I can try," Stoner said. Turning to Tavalera, he added, "And you can help me, Raoul. I'm going to need your help."

With that, Stoner disappeared from Archbishop Overmire's office.

Sister Angelique was emotionally drained and physically exhausted by the time she got back to her own quarters in the New Morality complex. It was getting dark outside. She had missed lunch, tending to Archbishop Overmire after their difficult, challenging meeting with Stoner.

The instant that Stoner disappeared from the Archbishop's office Angelique called in an emergency medical team who took Overmire to the complex's gleaming modern hospital. They had wanted to take Bishop Craig, too, but he got up stiffly from the chair he'd been sitting in and insisted he was all right. He instructed Angelique to stay with the Archbishop, then tottered off toward his own office alone, looking lost, dazed.

Angelique watched him leave, walking carefully, a trifle unsteadily, as if he had just suffered a concussive blow to the head. He has, she realized. We all have.

Even Tavalera looked shaken. Angelique called for a security escort to take him back to his apartment.

Once the emergency medical team arrived, Angelique went with them and Archbishop Overmire to the hospital. The top staff doctors insisted that they be allowed to purge the Archbishop's system of the cholesterol and triglycerides that had built up in his bloodstream. Groggy and shaken though he was, Overmire still refused their advice, as he had for years, claiming that he had vowed never to use artificial methods to prolong the span of life that God had planned for him.

Angelique dismissed the doctors from the Archbishop's overcooled hospital room, then pleaded with him to accept their help.

Overmire, sitting up in the hospital bed, pale and perspiring, shook his fleshy face hard enough to make his jowls quiver. "I'll go when God calls me to Him," he said stubbornly.

"But, Your Eminence, don't you realize that these medical advances could be part of God's plan for you?" she insisted, hugging herself against the chill in the room's air.

"Or the temptation of Satan," said the Archbishop. Angelique thought he sounded a trifle pompous.

She urged, "By their fruits you shall know them, Your Eminence. These medical techniques can help you to keep on living, so that you can keep on doing God's work here on Earth."

He started to answer but hesitated.

"The New Morality *needs* your leadership now more than ever," Angelique went on. "The people need you to continue. They look to you for leadership, for inspiration."

"Perhaps . . . ," Archbishop Overmire murmured.

Angelique saw the glimmer in his eyes. "This man Stoner is presenting us with an enormous challenge," she urged. "No one else has the knowledge, the standing, the piety, to deal with him. Do you think that Bishop Craig or any of the other bishops could stand in the Oval

Office and tell the President of the United States that the nuclear weapons program must be stopped?"

Overmire closed his eyes and muttered a barely discernable, "No. Not Craig. He doesn't have the stature. And yet he's the best of the lot."

"You see?" Angelique said almost triumphantly. "Everything depends on you. And to shoulder the enormous burdens you must carry, you have to be in good physical health."

Overmire's many-chinned face sank into something of a pout. "They won't be satisfied with just treating me. They'll want to put me on a diet."

Angelique hid the smile that bubbled up inside her. "That will be your penance, Your Eminence. You can offer it up to God in exchange for His granting you the strength to continue doing His will."

The Archbishop looked sad. "Perhaps you're right," he said very reluctantly.

Angelique stayed with the Archbishop for the rest of the day while the doctors happily ran him through test after test, poked and prodded him, and finally arranged for a series of injections that would slowly but inexorably reduce the killing chemicals in his cardiovascular system. She left him only after they had returned the Archbishop to his room and presented him with a dinner tray that looked as if it had been prepared for an anemic sparrow.

Overmire devoured everything on the tray so quickly that Angelique feared he'd start chewing on his napkin. But he settled back in the reclining bed easily enough and soon was snoring. They put a sedative in his drink, she realized.

Now, in her own apartment at last, Angelique took off her long-skirted uniform and wormed her arms into the shapeless robe she wore when alone in her quarters. She realized she was famished.

As she searched through the kitchenette's half-empty shelves for the makings of a decent dinner, her thoughts turned to Stoner once again.

He's the one with the power, Angelique told herself. Not the Archbishop and certainly not Bishop Craig. Craig has ambition, but he doesn't have the strength to seize real power. He's perfectly willing to wait for the Archbishop to die, but he'd never have the guts to push him aside.

Archbishop Overmire is a powerful man, she thought. Sick with shock as he was, he still recovered swiftly. In a few days he'll be stronger than ever. He's been wielding the power of the New Morality for almost a generation. He's accustomed to dealing with Presidents and Senators. He knows how to make them bend to the power of the New Morality.

And yet Overmire was reduced to a pitiful blob of flesh by Stoner. The star man. He could make himself emperor of the world if he wanted to. He could make everyone worship him as a god.

A wild thought struck her. Stoner could be the Second Coming! Maybe he truly is! He doesn't have to announce himself as Jesus Christ. He could be God's chosen presence here on Earth, come to save us from eternal damnation, come to protect us from the wickedness and the snares of Satan.

She smiled to herself as she opened the freezer and slid out a prepackaged meal.

Our new Redeemer, come to save us from nuclear holocaust. Angelique thought, Stoner wouldn't accept that role. He'd insist that he's only a man, a human being, albeit a man who can control a technology that's so far beyond our own that it seems miraculous.

But the people would think of him as our Redeemer, she realized. Especially if we led them to think of him that way.

Angelique laughed out loud. I'll bet we could even get the Jews to accept him as their Messiah, she said to herself. What's left of them.

CATHY

Cairo's airport terminal was jammed with people, all of them talking at once at the top of their lungs. To Cathy it seemed that most of the noisy, shoving crowd in the terminal were hawkers for some kind of service or trinket, all of them yelling in a cacophony of different languages.

"Taxicab, ladies?"

"Jewelry! Genuine gold jewelry!"

"King Tut Hotel! Best hotel in Cairo!"

"Antiques from the tombs of the Kings!"

"Guided tour through the pyramids!"

"Genuine replica of the great Sphinx!"

Mina ignored them all as she turned her little tour group over to a hotel representative, a brown-skinned potbellied male wearing a dingy white Western suit and a pasted-on smile. The security guards stayed with the tourists all the way out to the hotel bus waiting for them outside the terminal.

Once she saw her group safely in the hands of the hotel man, Mina motioned to Cathy to follow her as she shouldered her way resolutely through the noisy, bustling crowd toward a different exit. Cathy tagged along behind, struggling to keep up with her. At the curb Mina pointed at a certain taxi. Its driver, lounging against its scratched front fender, jumped to open the door for the two young women. The cab was crusted with grime and dented in several places, but it was powered by a fuel cell engine, according to the red lettering that was barely visible through the dirt.

"Was he waiting for you?" Cathy asked as the cab pulled into the thick growling, honking traffic.

Leaning forward to adjust the air-conditioning, Mina answered, "He knew there was a tour coming in around this time."

Cathy saw that the driver had done his best to make the interior of the taxi clean and comfortable. The upholstery of the seats was covered with a relatively clean checkered bedspread; a fringe of tiny red tassels ran across the top of the windows. But the floor was tacky; her loafers stuck slightly to the grime.

The cab threaded through traffic-choked streets and out into the somewhat quieter part of the city where Mina's family lived. The driver blared his horn again and again to get through the children playing in the streets. There were hordes of them, Cathy saw: thin, raggedly clothed, many of them barefoot. But they were laughing as they ran and played their childhood games. They don't know that they're poor, Cathy realized.

Then she saw bands of youths lounging on the street corners, their dark slitted eyes following the taxi as it drove past. And heard her mother's voice in her mind: Don't go out into those streets! Under any circumstances!

Cathy silently agreed.

Mina's home was on the top floor of a three-story cinder-block building that housed seven families. Cathy followed her up the stairs, past still more children running up and down or simply sitting on the steps. Several small dogs were frisking along the stairs, too, and Cathy saw one fluffy gray cat slinking between seated children. The walls were covered with graffiti and the stairwell smelled faintly of urine.

"We have air-conditioning," Mina said proudly as she and Cathy made their way to the top floor. "Most of the solar cells on the roof are broken, but my father keeps ours in good repair."

The apartment was small but clean. A pair of preteenaged boys were playing a video game in the stuffy little parlor, oblivious to everything around them. Mina brought Cathy straight into the spacious kitchen, which was crowded with women. She smilingly introduced Cathy to her mother and five sisters, who ranged from teenaged to toddlers. The teenager had a baby in her arms. The mother looked aged, her parchment-colored skin wrinkled, her dark eyes surly. She spoke to her daughter in Arabic, never dreaming that Cathy could understand her perfectly.

"Another mouth to feed?"

Mina smiled sweetly as answered, "She is my friend and I offered her hospitality."

"I hope you can pay for your generosity."

"Oh, Mama, don't be cross."

While they quarreled, Cathy looked through the kitchen doorway back into the living room. Two beds stood against the wall, neatly made up. Apparently the whole family lived in these few rooms. The furniture was hard used, the carpeting threadbare. But it was all clean. The kitchen smelled of spices and something that was simmering in a pot on the gas stove.

Once Mina had finished her minor spat with her mother, Cathy asked, "Five sisters? Do you have any brothers?"

"Three," Mina answered. "They work with my father at his repair shop. They'll be home soon."

"Are you the oldest?"

"The oldest daughter. One of my brothers is older than I am."

The mother grudgingly set out a pair of tall glasses and poured tea for them. Mina and Cathy sat at the wooden kitchen table while the other daughters grouped themselves across the room in a semicircle of unmatched chairs and fell to talking among themselves. Cathy smiled as she accepted her glass of sweetened tea and almost said her thanks in Arabic. She caught herself just in time. Mama trudged across the room and joined her daughters.

"Are you married?" Cathy asked Mina.

"Not yet. My sister Ismaela got married last year."

"And she has a baby already."

Mina frowned momentarily. "That is why she had to get married. Otherwise my father would have had to start a blood feud."

"Blood feud?"

"For the honor of our family. Either that or an honor killing. But my father is too tender to kill his own daughter, even if she brings shame upon us."

Cathy fell speechless. In her mind she heard her mother's bitter voice: They kill their daughters, but they won't even think of birth control.

As if she sensed Cathy's stunned disapproval, Mina changed the subject slightly. "I will be married next year, after I have saved enough money from my job as a tour guide."

"I see."

"And then I will have babies, too. Many babies; you'll see."

"Is that what you want?"

Mina's eyes widened at the question. "What I want? Of course it's what I want. What woman doesn't want to be married and have lots of babies?"

Cathy looked from Mina to her mother, old and weary before her time. She can't be more than sixty, Cathy thought. Nine children, and grandchildren coming along. And they *want* to live this way?

CHAPTER 6

"The Archbishop has asked me to work directly with him on the Stoner business," Angelique said as she sat before Bishop Craig at his desk.

Craig seemed on edge, jittery, his hands fluttering over his desktop, his eyes blinking constantly. Angelique knew that the bishop had always felt secure, confident, when he was seated behind his desk. It's like a protective fortification to him, she thought. But this morning he was uncertain, stressed out, frightened.

She repeated, "Archbishop Overmire has asked me to work with him."

Normally, Craig's power-sensitive antennae would have alerted him to a possible danger. Now he merely said, "The Archbishop?"

Angelique nodded. It wasn't a lie, she told herself. It was merely an anticipation. She would go to the Archbishop in his hospital room before the morning was over, and by the time she left he would have indeed asked her to work directly with him. She'd see to that.

Instead of being suspicious, Craig seemed resigned. "That means you'll be leaving my office?"

Angelique put on an unhappy expression. "I'm afraid

I'll have to, Your Worship. Temporarily." Then she let a tiny hint of a smile appear. "But isn't it better for you to have a loyal worker inside the Archbishop's staff? Someone who could let you know what the Archbishop is doing, what he's planning, what he's thinking—before anyone else knows?"

Craig leaned back in his swivel chair and stared up at the cream-colored ceiling, his fingers still twitching. At last he said, "I suppose that could be an advantage."

"The Archbishop's going to be in hospital for a few days," she went on. "He's asked me to run his office as if he's still there. No one but his closest aides will know that he's not. And you, of course."

The bishop stared at her for several moments. At last he sat up straighter in his swivel chair and asked, "Can you get him to appoint me as his acting Archbishop? Strictly on a temporary basis, of course. Until he's back on his feet."

Angelique gulped at the man's naked ambition. *Terrified of Stoner or not, he still wants the Archbishop's ring.*

"I'm not sure that would be wise, Your Worship," she said softly. "Not at this moment."

Craig sank back in his chair. "Probably not. You're right. He wants to keep his incapacity secret."

"It will only be for a few days, at most."

The bishop's face showed his thought clearly: *Too bad.*

"In the meantime, Your Worship, you will have to deal with the problem of Stoner."

"No! I don't want to be anywhere near him! He's in league with Satan."

Angelique saw the unabashed fear in his eyes. She said, "The Archbishop doesn't believe so."

"Stoner's got to be stopped."

Feeling some alarm, Angelique replied, "But if he can help us to prevent nuclear war, isn't that a good thing?"

"What if God *wants* us to have a nuclear war?" Craig asked. "He sent a flood once, when the human race had turned its face from Him. Maybe now He'll send a nuclear war."

"But we haven't turned away from God!" Angelique cried. "The New Morality has brought the people back to God's way."

His brows knitting, Bishop Craig muttered, "True. True. But is it enough? Have we made mankind pleasing in the sight of God?" He ran a hand over his eyes. "This whole business of Stoner is unsettling."

"Of course, Your Worship," Angelique murmured.

Craig studied her face for a long moment. "You know, I had a revelation in there. When he showed us the nuclear holocaust, God sent me a revelation."

"A revelation?"

"Yes. The end of the world is truly at hand. It's all part of God's plan. The final act."

Her mind racing, Angelique told herself, Be very careful how you answer him. Very careful.

"Well?" Craig demanded, misreading her silence. "Does that frighten you?"

She took a deep breath, then replied, "No, Your Worship. It doesn't frighten me. Because Stoner will save us from such a calamity. I think he represents a gift from God, a way out of the nuclear holocaust that might devour us."

She saw immediately that she had made a mistake. Craig pointed a shaking finger at her. "That nuclear holocaust could be God's final cleansing! The final trumpet from the Book of Revelation."

"The end of the world," Angelique whispered.

"Fire and brimstone. It's predicted."

"But . . . but . . ."Angelique cast about for some words that would move Bishop Craig from his acceptance of the final holocaust. "But would God destroy His own creations? Just snuff out everyone?"

"He would be calling us to our eternal reward," Bishop Craig said.

Now Angelique felt real fear. Not of God's ending the world in fire and brimstone but of the blind acceptance of men high in the New Morality, such as Bishop Craig. Are there similar men in the rest of the world? she asked herself. Are the Chinese just as blindly fatalistic? And the jihadists?

CHAPTER 7

True to her plans, Sister Angelique subtly convinced Archbishop Overmire to ask her to oversee his office for the few days he'd be in the hospital.

"My staff is loyal and trustworthy," the Archbishop said while munching on his breakfast whole-grain muffin. "But you're much closer to this Stoner person than any of them."

"Stoner is the key to everything, isn't he, Your Eminence?" Angelique murmured, her voice and face showing proper humility.

The Archbishop wiped his mouth daintily with the paper napkin from his breakfast tray. "He wants me to march into the Oval Office and tell the President to stop the nuclear program."

"He'd be willing to go with you, I'm sure," said Angelique. "He'd stand at your side."

"Would he?"

"Of course. I'm certain of it." But even as she said the words, Angelique pictured herself standing before the President of the United States, with Stoner at her side.

The Archbishop's staff obviously resented having a mere nun come into the office. Not just joining the staff but coming in as the Archbishop's personal executive assistant, representing the Archbishop himself, standing over them all.

Angelique sensed their unspoken bitterness as they stood gathered in the Archbishop's office: fourteen aides and department chiefs, eleven men and three women, all in black clerical garb, each of them sworn to loyalty to the Archbishop's wishes, each of them staring sullenly at this stranger who had suddenly walked in and taken charge. Their ages ranged from gray haired to fuzzy cheeked. Their attitudes were all hostile, even though they were trying to conceal it.

"This is only for a few days," Angelique assured them. She had chosen—wisely, she thought—not to stand behind the Archbishop's desk. Instead she stood against one of the blank-screened walls, almost as if she were facing a firing squad.

As sweetly as she could, Angelique told them, "As you know, the Archbishop must remain in hospital for a few days. Nothing serious or life threatening, but his enormous duties have taken their toll on his metabolism."

She saw a few sly grins among the staffers facing her. They knew about the Archbishop's obesity problem better than she did.

"No one outside these walls must know that the Archbishop is not here. Everything must proceed as usual—"

"The Archbishop has a full schedule of appointments," said one of the younger men.

"You'll have to switch them from personal to electronic," Angelique replied. "You have a simulacrum program for the Archbishop, don't you?"

"Yes, but the program needs a human overseer to fill in direct responses when they're needed."

Angelique thought swiftly. "Which of you handles the Archbishop's public relations?"

One of the gray-haired men slowly put his hand up.

"Can you speak for the Archbishop, then?"

"Me?" He looked startled at the thought.

"Yes. Just speak in generalities," Angelique said. With a smile, she added, "You know, like a politician during an election campaign."

The others laughed softly.

"Can you do that?" Angelique asked the P.R. man.

Uncertainly he answered, "I guess so. If it's just for a few days."

"Good."

By the end of the day Angelique had the office running smoothly enough. The staff seemed cooperative, if not friendly; efficient, if not enthusiastic.

It was only after they had all gone home for the day that Angelique allowed herself to sit at the Archbishop's desk. She called Raoul Tavalera and invited him to her apartment for dinner.

Tavalera had spent the day cooped up in his own apartment. For more than an hour he had spoken with Holly Lane at the *Goddard* habitat, but the rest of the time he'd devoted to studying history and cosmology on the TV nets.

It was all history, he thought. The history of the human race and the history of the universe. Big and little. Stars and people. There actually was a man who was born into an obscure nomadic tribe on the Gobi Desert who conquered most of the friggin' world, Tavalera learned.

There actually is a gigantic black hole at the heart of the Milky Way galaxy that's gobbling up whole stars by the thousands and spewing out deadly radiation.

Learning was fun, he realized. Too bad they don't make it fun in school.

Through the whole long day he waited for a call from Stoner. Nothing. The star man didn't contact him, not even a Hi, how are you? in his mind.

I wonder where he is? Tavalera asked himself.

CHAPTER 8

Stoner was back in New Tehran, in the mildly disordered office of the Iranian astronomer Karim Bakhtiar. This time, Bakhtiar sat beside Stoner on one of the wobbly plastic chairs while his brother Ahmed sat behind the scientist's desk, wearing the tan uniform of a general in the Revolutionary Guard.

It was easy to see that the two men were brothers. Ahmed Bakhtiar was slim and wiry like the astronomer, his skin the same tobacco-leaf color. The general's thin face bore a thick dark moustache, and his hairline was receding; otherwise they might have been twins, almost.

"My brother tells me you have traveled to the stars," said Ahmed Bakhtiar. His voice was rough, rasping, as if his throat were inflamed.

"That's true," Stoner replied.

The general smiled through his luxuriant moustache. "It is true that he told me this, or it is true that you have been to the stars?"

Stoner grinned back at him. "Both."

"I see. And where is your starship?"

"In a high orbit."

General Bakhtiar's dark brows rose. "There is no such spacecraft. Our radar—"

"Can't see it," Stoner said. "But it's there, I assure you. As certainly as I'm here."

"Which brings up the question of *why* you are here."

"To convince you to stop your nuclear weapons program," Stoner said calmly.

The general flicked a scowling glance at his brother.

Karim Bakhtiar shrugged elaborately and said, "I didn't tell him! He already knew!"

In a slightly stronger tone Stoner said, "General, you more than almost anyone else understand the devastation that nuclear war can bring."

"The Israelis destroyed Tehran."

"And you wiped out Israel. Has that made the world any better? All you accomplished was to obliterate the excuse you gave your people for your government's failures."

"They attacked us first!" General Bakhtiar insisted, his face reddening.

Stoner sighed. "First, last, the result is the same. Millions killed. And what did you accomplish?"

"I wasn't in command at that time."

"I know. You were only following orders."

The astronomer said, "What's done is done. It can't be changed."

"Very true," said Stoner. Turning back to the general, "But now you are building nuclear weapons again. And missiles that can carry them across the world."

"We've got to protect ourselves against the Americans."

"And they want to protect themselves against you."

"And the Chinese," added Karim Bakhtiar.

His bearded face turning sterner, Stoner asked, "And

what happens if one of your nuclear bombs falls into the hands of a terrorist group?"

General Bakhtiar almost smiled. "God knows."

"You've been very clever all these years. You and other Islamic governments have funded terrorists, provided them arms, trained them—"

"The government of Greater Iran does not sponsor terrorism," the general said flatly.

"Of course not," replied Stoner. "Still, terrorist cells somehow find money and weapons and training. They still kill innocent people all around the world."

Leaning forward slightly in the desk chair, General Bakhtiar said in a low, grating voice, "We have kept the jihadists in check as much as we can. The destruction of Israel satisfied them for a time—"

"But they are still poor and filled with hate," said Stoner.

"Not only the poor have hatred for the unbelievers. And now, with the Americans building nuclear bombs again, where will they use them, except against us?"

"The Americans fear the same about you."

"Pah!" the general spat. "The fools will unleash jihad upon themselves. We won't be able to hold back the fanatics."

"And the world ends in nuclear flames."

"God's will," said the general.

"No," Stoner replied. "Man's will. Men plan these attacks. And what does it gain you? The United States has become an armed camp, with a repressive government that strangles individual liberties—all in the name of national security."

"That isn't my affair," said General Bakhtiar. "Not my responsibility."

"I believe the Qur'an says differently."

Again the general glanced at his brother. This time

the astronomer said, "One can find anything one looks for in the Qur'an. And in the Christian Bible, as well."

With the ghost of a smile, Stoner replied, "True enough. Still, this move toward nuclear war will wipe out everyone and everything. It's got to stop."

The general smiled back at him. "And how will you stop it?"

Stoner looked at him for a long, silent moment. At last he asked, "If the Americans disband their nuclear program, will you disband Greater Iran's?"

"What of the Chinese?"

"The Chinese, too. No one needs nuclear weapons if everyone stops building them."

General Bakhtiar said nothing.

"You need to stop your programs now, all three of you, before other nations start developing nuclear weapons," said Stoner.

"A dream," said the general. "You are a dreamer."

"Yes, I am a dreamer. Aren't you? Don't you dream of a world at peace, where Greater Iran and all the other nations are secure and prosperous?"

The general started to reply, hesitated, then finally said, "I dream of a world that accepts Allah and the teachings of the Prophet."

"And do you think you can bring about such a world through nuclear war? Or even conventional war? Conversion to Islam by the sword, is that truly what you seek?"

General Bakhtiar looked slightly uncomfortable. He fidgeted in the swivel chair, touched his moustache with a fingertip.

"Be aware of two things, General," Stoner told him. "One, the bugs that your security people have planted in this room aren't operating. No one can see or hear what we say."

His brows rising, Bakhtiar asked, "And the other thing?"

"I know what you're really thinking."

"You can read my thoughts?"

With a tight smile, Stoner replied, "No. Nothing so mystical. But I can read your face, I can sense slight changes in your blood pressure, little bursts of neurons firing in your body."

The astronomer broke into a sudden laugh. "A lie detector! You're a walking lie detector."

Stoner nodded. "It's a useful talent."

The general stiffened.

Stoner got up from his chair. "I'll be meeting with the American President soon. Once they abandon their nuclear weaponry program I'll expect you to disband yours."

And he disappeared from the room, leaving the general staring across the desk at his brother, the astronomer.

CHAPTER 9

Sister Angelique had the New Morality's commissary send a complete dinner for two up to her studio apartment. Nothing fancy, just a pair of fried chicken entrées with salads and angel cake for dessert. No wine: decaffeinated cola, instead.

She had instructed the security police to pick up Tavalera from his apartment in time to deliver him to her room at 8:00 P.M.

Tavalera showed up precisely at eight. Angelique thought he would be pleased to have dinner with her. After all, she reasoned, it can't be much fun for him locked in that little apartment all day long. Still, as Tavalera stepped into her sitting room, he looked rather tense, wary.

Does he know I drugged him the last time? she wondered. Of course he does! Stoner must have seen the whole thing and told him about it. I can't keep secrets from Stoner.

But Tavalera thawed easily enough. They made pleasant-enough chitchat while Angelique put out dinner plates on her kitchenette table and pulled the precooked meals from the microwave oven.

As they gnawed on the chicken with honey-sticky fingers, Angelique asked, "What's Stoner up to?"

Shaking his head while he swallowed, Tavalera said, "Damned . . . I mean, darned if I know."

"You're not in touch with him?"

"Nope. He contacts me when he wants to."

"And you don't know where he is?"

"Nope."

Angelique thought about that for a few moments while she chewed on her salad. Stoner knows what Tavalera is doing, she guessed. He said that Raoul is his contact on Earth. She almost smiled at the thought of Raoul Tavalera playing St. Peter to Stoner's Jesus.

No, it's not like that at all, she told herself. But if Raoul is in danger, Stoner will come to help him. She tucked that idea away in her mind for future reference.

As they started on the meager slices of cake, Tavalera asked, "So how's the Archbishop?"

She blinked, then replied, "He's fine."

"He looked pretty sick back there in his office."

"He was in shock. We all were."

"Yeah, but he collapsed."

"He's fine now."

Tavalera took a sip of cola, then asked, "So when does he take Stoner to see the President?"

"Soon," she said. "In a few days."

"Good," said Tavalera. "Wish I could go with him."

"You're not?"

With a shrug, Tavalera answered, "Beats me. He does what he wants to do. Doesn't tell me about it beforehand."

Disappointed, Angelique realized that she couldn't use Tavalera to get to Stoner. She'd have to do it herself.

Why not? Angelique asked herself the next morning.

She sat at the Archbishop's broad, polished desk and repeated the question. Why not? Why wait for the Archbishop? I'll set up the meeting in his name.

She was surprised, and a little awed, at how easy it was. When she phoned the President's office, his appointments secretary came right on the screen. No delays. No wading through layers of aides and assistants. Archbishop Overmire's office was calling, and the President's appointments secretary took the call herself.

"This involves the star man, Keith Stoner," Angelique said to the image on the phone screen.

The appointments secretary was a middle-aged woman with hair so golden blond that Angelique knew it was the result of cosmetics. Her face was thin, like a fashion model's. But her eyes were sharp, intense.

"I'm putting this on the scrambler circuit," she said.

"Of course," Angelique agreed.

The screen flickered momentarily, then steadied.

The appointments secretary said, "I believe the National Academy of Sciences has been asked to investigate that man's claims."

Angelique smiled sweetly into the screen. "Archbishop Overmire has met with him personally and accepts his claim. Stoner really has traveled to the stars."

"Really! The Archbishop believes him?"

They chatted on for nearly ten minutes more. In the end the appointments secretary told Angelique she could clear half an hour of the President's time the following afternoon, at four. Angelique thanked her and broke the connection.

Now how do I get in touch with Stoner? she asked herself.

Through Tavalera, she decided.

But when she called the apartment she'd given Raoul, he wasn't there.

Stoner had appeared in Tavalera's locked apartment that morning while the younger man was spooning up some breakfast cereal. He barely dropped any of it when Stoner suddenly manifested himself in the doorway of the kitchenette.

Gulping down what he'd already had in his mouth, Tavalera said, "Y'know, you could knock. Or ring a bell or something. Let a guy know you're gonna pop in."

Stoner grinned back at him. "Come on, Raoul; you're getting accustomed to this."

Tavalera put down his spoon. "Yeah, maybe, a little. But still . . ."

"Would you like a blare of trumpets? Or maybe a gong?"

"Just say 'knock knock' before you appear. Okay?"

"Knock knock," Stoner repeated gravely. "Got it."

"Angelique's working on the White House," Tavalera said. "She's running the Archbishop's office while he's in the hospital."

Stoner nodded. Then he said, "Would you like to get out of this apartment for a while?"

"Sure!"

"Then let's go."

Leaving the breakfast dishes on the kitchenette's slim shelf of a table, Tavalera followed Stoner to the apartment's front door.

"It's locked," he said.

"Yes," Stoner replied. "I know." He turned the knob and the door opened easily.

They went down in the elevator to the lobby, where a uniformed security guard eyed them suspiciously. He glanced down at his desktop screen, then pointed at Stoner.

"Who're you?"

"I'm a friend of Mr. Tavalera's," Stoner replied genially.

Glancing at his screen again, the guard muttered, "He's not allowed to leave the building without a specific order from Bishop Craig's office."

"I know," Stoner said. "It's all right."

The guard blinked several times. Stoner tugged gently on Tavalera's arm and the two of them walked past him, through the building's glass double doors, and out into the morning, leaving the guard frowning with confusion in the lobby.

It was raining: a fine misty drizzle. Tavalera saw people scuttling along the street in plastic rain parkas or gripping umbrellas. But he wasn't getting wet. Puzzled, he looked to Stoner and saw that the raindrops were bouncing off an invisible shield that surrounded him. And me, too, Tavalera realized.

"The taxi stand is on the next corner," Stoner said, heading that way.

Following him, Tavalera asked, "Where're we goin'?"

"I thought you might like to visit your friends on the *Goddard* habitat."

Tavalera started to say, "But that's—" Then he caught himself.

"I think it'd be best if you were safely away from Angelique and her cohorts," Stoner said. "At least for a little while."

They reached the line of automated taxis. Stoner went to the first one and opened the door. He ducked in and Tavalera slid in beside him.

"Destination please," said the synthesized voice of the taxi's computer.

"Hartsfield Aerospaceport," said Stoner.

"We gonna take a rocket?" Tavalera asked, feeling disappointed.

"No, but when the police check this cab's log it'll show that we went to the aerospaceport."

They drove in silence through the morning drizzle, out of the New Morality complex and up onto the automated highway that led to the aerospaceport.

Stoner turned to Tavalera and said with a smile, "When you get there, remember to say 'knock knock.' "

CHAPTER 10

And suddenly Tavalera was standing on one of the winding brick walkways that threaded through the greenery of *Goddard*'s landscaped interior.

He was on a grass-covered knoll, high enough so that he had a clear view of the habitat's broad interior. *Goddard* was a massive cylinder, twenty kilometers long and four in diameter, rotating slowly to produce a feeling of Earth-normal gravity on its landscaped inner surface. Stretching out in all directions around Tavalera was the green countryside, shining in the warm sunlight streaming in through the long, bright windows that ran in strips along the length of the cylinder.

Tavalera saw gently rolling grassy hills, clumps of trees, little meandering streams spreading out into the hazy distance. Bushes thick with vivid red hibiscus and pale lavender oleanders lined both sides of the curving path that led downhill to a group of low buildings, gleaming white in the sunlight, their roofs made of red tiles. The village overlooked a shimmering blue lake. Farther in the distance Tavalera made out the checkered square fields of recently plowed farmland, with more clusters of white buildings beyond them.

There was no horizon. Instead, the land simply curved up and up, hills and grass and trees and more little villages dotting the scenery with their paved roads and sparkling streams, up and up on both sides until he was craning his neck looking straight overhead at still more of the tenderly, lovingly cultivated greenery.

Tears misted his eyes. I'm home, he said to himself, with a rush of gratitude and joy. I thought Earth was my home, but I was wrong. This is home. I'm back home at last.

He started walking down the curving pathway toward the village. Toward Holly.

Stoner saw all that Tavalera's eyes beheld. He felt the rush of emotions that surged through the younger man. And within himself Stoner felt the pangs of guilt.

His wife spoke to him in his mind.

Did you have to do that? Jo asked him. He sensed that she wasn't angry with him, not even displeased, so much as disappointed, unconvinced that her husband's action was truly necessary.

Yes, he replied. I'm pretty sure that I did.

Pretty sure? Jo demanded. You're putting him through a lot.

Stoner shrugged mentally. I really don't know what else I can do.

You're testing him.

That's right.

Stoner could sense Jo shaking her head. I just hope he doesn't end up hating you when he finds out what you're doing.

Sister Angelique was in Archbishop Overmire's office, sitting at his broad desk of teak and brushed chrome. And learning that Shakespeare was right: uneasy lies the head that wears a crown.

"What do you mean he disappeared?" she said to the Archbishop's chief of security.

The image on her wall screen showed a man of middle years, his face taut and tanned, his sandy brown hair cropped short. He wore a suede jacket that fitted his wide shoulders perfectly, like a military uniform. He looked distinctly uneasy.

"We're checking into it, Sister."

Feeling slightly overwhelmed in the Archbishop's massive padded chair, Angelique said, "But he can't simply disappear. That's—" She caught herself as she realized that with Stoner virtually nothing was impossible.

"The surveillance cameras show him eating breakfast. He looks up all of a sudden and—"

"Show me the imagery," Angelique commanded impatiently.

The security chief nodded and the wall screen next to his image brightened to show Tavalera at breakfast. He suddenly looked up, nearly dropped his spoon, then got to his feet.

"There's no sound," she said.

"I know. We're working on that. Some sort of a glitch."

No, she replied silently. Not a glitch. The star man. Stoner.

She watched Tavalera go to the front door, which opened by itself, and then leave the locked apartment. Cameras picked him up in the elevator and then the lobby cameras showed him walking right past the uniformed guard there and out into the gray, drizzly morning.

"He took a taxi to Hartsfield," the security chief said. "That's where we lost him."

"What do you mean you lost him?"

Looking even more uncomfortable, the security chief said, "The taxi's camera shows him getting in. Then the imagery blurs out. When the cab stops at Hartsfield he isn't in it."

"I see," said Angelique. She almost laughed at the irony of it. I do *not* see, she told herself. None of us can see anything that Stoner doesn't want us to see.

"Somebody must have tampered with the cameras," the security chief was saying. Angelique barely heard him. "We're checking into it. There must be a saboteur in the loop, somewhere. We'll find him."

It took an effort for her to focus her attention back on the man.

"We'll turn that building upside down," the security chief was promising. "We'll find whoever is responsible for this and when we do I'll personally—"

"You'll do nothing," Angelique said. "Drop your investigation. You're dealing with matters that are much too sensitive for your office."

The security chief's face reddened. "But if somebody's tampering with our surveillance systems . . ."

"The Archbishop will personally deal with this," Angelique said. "It's not your responsibility and no one will hold you to blame."

The man looked unconvinced. "I'll have the technicians check out those cameras."

Angelique nodded, thinking, They won't find anything wrong with them.

She cut the connection and leaned back in the overly large chair. Stoner, she said to herself. I barely thought about using Tavalera to control him and he makes Raoul disappear. He knows what I'm thinking! Like a god, he can see into my soul.

"It's a gift," said Keith Stoner, standing off to one side of the Archbishop's desk.

RICK

"And who the bloody hell are you?"

Rick Stoner smiled easily at the colonel, much as his father would have. "I'm an observer," he said.

The colonel wore the pale blue uniform of the United Nations Peacekeeping Force, with a Union Jack shoulder patch showing that he was from the United Kingdom. His thick red hair and bristling moustache convinced Rick that he was Scottish. Rick had chosen to wear a similar uniform, but without any insignia of rank or indication of nationality.

"An observer?" the colonel demanded, scowling with puzzled anger. "I didna receive any notice of an observer comin' here. And how did you get past the bloody guards?"

They were almost touching noses in the middle of the Peacekeepers' command center, a metal igloo crammed with electronics consoles that had been deposited by cargo helicopter on this barren mountaintop in the wild Hindu Kush mountains of northeastern Afghanistan, not far from the Khyber Pass, where armies had fought for dominance since long before the time of Alexander the Great.

The command center felt uncomfortably warm, almost stifling, from the humming heat of the electronics equipment and the press of human bodies crowded together. Remote operator consoles were ringed around the perimeter of the circular chamber, each manned by a blue-uniformed man or woman in control of a robotic fighting machine. Some of the operators glanced over their shoulders at their colonel's loud confrontation with the stranger. Most stayed bent over their screens, earphones clipped over their hair, pin microphones at their lips.

"It's perfectly all right," Rick said amiably. "I'm here to observe how your units conduct themselves."

The colonel's irritated expression gradually eased into a sort of confused befuddlement. "Observer, eh?" he muttered darkly. "Ye'd think those politicians up in headquarters would know enough to send me notice aforehand. You might've gotten yerself shot by the guards."

Rick, who had projected himself directly into the middle of the field command center, smiled gently. "I'm only here to see how your brigade is dealing with the terrorists."

The colonel h'mmphed. "Terrorists? They're nothing better than drug smugglers. Poppies. Opium. Our orders are to cut off their route through the Pass and into India."

Nodding, Rick asked, "Do you conduct raids on their manufacturing operations?"

"When we're allowed to," the colonel answered. "We

get coordinates from the recon satellites, but before we can go out after 'em, we have to get permission from headquarters. Most times they've folded up shop and moved elsewhere by the time we get there."

For the rest of the morning the colonel showed Rick every aspect of his command center, from the communications consoles that linked with surveillance satellites to the remote-control units for the infantry robots that did whatever actual fighting that needed to be done.

Warming to his task of host, the colonel even took Rick outside the dome of the command center, past the rifle-carrying guards that Rick had casually bypassed, to a larger metal prefabricated structure that housed the brigade's maintenance and repair center.

"Bloody mechanical beasties spend more time in here than out in th' field," the colonel grumbled as they entered the clanging, rumbling repair shop. Laser welders flashed; men and women in coveralls stained by machine oil and perspiration seemed to be scurrying everywhere.

The colonel led Rick to one of the robotic soldiers, a blocky pile of metal that towered over them, nearly three meters tall. It stood on four legs that ended in round paw-like feet.

"Can these machines maneuver in the mountains out there?" he asked.

"Ay, and they can fight damned well, too. Studded with weapons, they are, from antipersonnel lasers to rocket-propelled grenades."

With that, he walked to a tool bench and picked up a palm-sized controller. One click and half a dozen weapons sprang out from recesses in the robot's bulky body. Rick instinctively flinched back a step.

The colonel laughed. "Do na be afraid, lad. It's not loaded nor powered up."

Laughing uneasily back at him, Rick said, "It's impressive, even unloaded."

"Ay," said the colonel. Then his expression sobered. "Too bad we're not allowed to use 'em properly."

"Not allowed? What do you mean?"

The colonel tugged at his fierce red moustache, then answered, "We should be goin' into the hills and diggin' out these drug plantations. Burn 'em out. The science boffins claim they have sprays that'll make the poppies harmless. Something genetic that'll stop the plants from producing the opium chemicals."

Surprised by the news, Rick asked, "So why don't you do that? You could end the drug trade that way."

"Orders from higher up," the colonel said darkly. "The big brass doesn't want to end the drug trade. Too much money involved, if you ask me."

"What do you mean?"

"End the war and ye'd have to disband the troops. Better to keep things simmerin' along, long as our casualties stay low. That way there's always a need for th' Peacekeepers."

Rick felt shocked. "But that's . . . it's *wrong*."

"Ay," said the colonel. Then, his nose wrinkling with disgust, he added, "Besides, there's always bribery, y'know."

CHAPTER 11

The President of the United States was giving an informal address to a few hundred corporate executives assembled on the South Lawn of the White House's beautifully tended grounds. The event was the highlight of the annual Christian Business Executives meeting, which had filled four of downtown Washington's biggest and grandest hotels with businessmen and -women from all across the nation. This special little luncheon was only for the topmost members of the organization, however, the crème de la crème, the true movers and shakers of American business.

". . . and although the international situation is still quite serious," the President was saying from the little podium that had been set up at the head of the rows of tables, "I can say with confidence that we are clearly winning the conflicts in Latin America and Indonesia. A few more years of effort and sacrifice should see the terrorist elements driven out of those war-torn areas for good."

The assembled executives rose as one organism and applauded lustily. The President smiled and nodded to the few he knew personally, up in the front row. He recognized the heads of three aerospace corporations, two agribusiness combines, and a scattering of electrical utility corporations. All solid supporters of his re-election campaign.

The President stepped back from the podium, with its blast-proof glassteel shields. Secret Service guards and U.S. Marines with laser handguns beneath their colorful dress uniforms formed a phalanx around him as the executives jostled one another good-naturedly to line up for photo opportunities with the President.

After a seemingly endless round of posing and handshaking, the President at last ducked back inside the cool and quietly busy West Wing corridor that led to the familiar security of his Oval Office.

As he stepped into the lavatory to strip off his jacket and bulletproof vest and change into a fresh shirt, the President called out, "They really liked what I had to say, didn't they?"

"Of course they did," said the head of his speechwriting team. "You delivered it magnificently."

Striding to his old-fashioned dark mahogany desk as he pulled on a dark blue jacket, the President cast a mock frown at his chaplain. "Reverend, I thought we agreed that your blessing wouldn't be longer than my speech."

The black-garbed minister stiffened with surprise. "But it wasn't, Mr. President!"

Chuckling at him, the President said, "Almost, Reverend. Almost."

All the others in the Oval Office laughed politely. Even the chaplain allowed himself to chuckle softly.

"All right," the President said. "What's next?"

His appointments secretary answered, "The Canadian ambassador."

The news secretary added, "Camera crews, no direct quotes."

Nodding, the President asked, "Why'm I seeing the Canadian ambassador?"

"About the water deal," said his chief of staff impatiently. With a hard, demanding expression on his face he added, "And it wouldn't hurt if you let him understand that our troops will be detaching from Indonesia before the year is out."

The President looked puzzled. "What's that got to do with Canada?"

"The army will be freed up to move north if we don't get the concessions we need."

"Oh. Yeah. Right."

"And you could bring up the matter of migrant workers," the chief of staff added. "There's at least half a million American citizens working in the Canadian wheat belt and we want them treated properly, not like a bunch of Okies."

"Okies?"

"Migrant workers."

"But that's what they are, aren't they?"

"That's not the point," the chief of staff said, his voice edgy with impatience. "We want our people treated with respect."

"And they should be free to set up their own churches," the chaplain said.

"On Canadian soil?"

"God does not recognize national boundaries," the chaplain replied loftily.

"H'm. Okay."

The appointments secretary cleared her throat to get everyone's attention, then announced, "I've had to slip in a meeting with Archbishop Overmire at four o'clock."

"The Archbishop? Here? Himself?"

"Yes. His office said it was an urgent matter."

"Probably about those damned Northern Lights," muttered the chief of staff.

"Yeah, what about the Lights?" the President asked. "Doesn't anybody know why they're shining every night?"

The staffers glanced around at one another.

"What do the science people have to say about it?" the President asked. Before anyone could reply, he added, "Say, who in the world is my science advisor, anyway?"

"The position of science advisor was removed from your staff," said the chief. "You don't need a science advisor; you've got the head of the National Academy of Sciences, remember?"

The President blinked, puzzled, then brightened. "Oh, yeah, that Jewish fella. What's his name?"

"Feingold."

"That's right. Feingold."

"Should I call him to this meeting with the Archbishop?" asked the appointments secretary.

The President waved a hand in the air. "Naw. It's not that important." Turning back to his chaplain, he said, "The Archbishop, huh? You'd better be in on that one, Reverend."

CHAPTER 12

Startled, Angelique blurted, "You're here!"

"Yes," said Stoner mildly. He pulled over one of the leather armchairs from in front of the Archbishop's desk and dragged it to her side, then sat next to Angelique, close enough to touch her if he just leaned forward a little.

"I understand that we're going to visit the White House this afternoon."

"How did you—" Angelique caught herself and smiled. "Of course. You know what I know, don't you?"

"Surface thoughts," said Stoner. "I don't want to invade your privacy, but I need to know what's going on."

She felt her pulse speeding up. Licking her lips, she said, "Yes, we're scheduled to meet with the President of the United States this afternoon."

"He's not highly regarded, is he?"

Surprised, Angelique replied, "He won election by a very large majority."

"He had the endorsement of the New Morality. His opponent didn't. That's enough to gain a large majority these days."

She nodded thoughtfully, thinking that Keith Stoner could win any election he chose to run in. He could make himself Emperor of the world if he wanted to, she knew. And I could stand at his side, as close to him as I am now.

Angelique watched, almost amused, as Stoner effortlessly moved through the White House's security systems. She herself had sent all her identification and background information ahead. When their New Morality tilt-rotor touched down on the landing pad on the White House grounds, Angelique allowed the Marine Corps guard to check her retinal pattern with a handheld scanner.

When the guard turned to Stoner, standing beside her, he said, "That won't be necessary, son."

The Marine turned to his sergeant, who wore three rows of ribbons on his chest and a half-dozen hash marks on his sleeve. His face was granite hard, as blank and expressionless as a statue of an ancient Roman centurion.

Stoner smiled at him. Pointing to the ribbons, he asked, "Is that for the Guatemala campaign?"

Breaking into a pleased smile, the sergeant replied, "No, sir. The Sudan." Touching the top row of his decorations, he added, "This one's for Central America."

"And the Purple Heart," said Stoner.

"Yessir. That's how I got my bionic leg."

Stoner nodded. "My military service was with the air force, a long time ago. I'll never know if I could have made it as a Marine."

"Aw, hell, sir. If I made it, you coulda."

With that, the sergeant waved them through the checkpoint.

And so it went. Angelique and Stoner walked under the blast-proof canopy to the next checkpoint, just inside the door to the executive mansion itself, and the final one, down in the basement corridor of the West Wing. Stoner sailed past metal detectors, retinal scanners,

X-rays, and chemical sniffers with a smile and a few soft words.

At last they were escorted by a tall, cadaverously thin woman in a skirted business suit to an intimately small anteroom. The woman gestured to the striped sofa against the wall opposite the door that led into the Oval Office.

"Please wait here. It will be a few moments."

They sat.

Almost immediately the door swung open and a stoop-shouldered gray-haired man in a tie and jacket stepped into the anteroom. Stoner noticed a tiny pin in his lapel: twined palm boughs. The man smiled warmly and put out his hand. "I'm Lawrence Yanovan, the President's media secretary."

Stoner rose and took the man's firm grip. "My name is Keith Stoner."

"We were expecting the Archbishop," Yanovan said, his smile still in place.

Angelique stood up beside Stoner. She said in an apologetic tone, "The Archbishop is slightly incapacitated, I'm afraid."

"Incapacitated? Nothing serious, I pray."

Biting her lip as if worried, Angelique confided, "He's confined to hospital for a few days. I'm his representative for this meeting."

Yanovan's smile faded. "And who are you, sir?"

"A friend," said Stoner.

Yanovan frowned with puzzlement but slowly turned to the door and pulled it open. The three of them entered the Oval Office, where the President of the United States sat behind his desk, smiling genially.

"How did you get here?" asked Holly Lane, her voice almost a full octave higher than normal.

Tavalera had simply walked down the little hill and into the village, then picked up the first public phone he'd found and called the chief administrator of the habitat.

Holly's eyes popped when he told her he was in *Goddard*, more than a billion kilometers from where he'd been only yesterday. She came barreling out on an electric bicycle, down the village's main street, and screeched to a stop at the kiosk by the fountain in the little plaza where Tavalera sat waiting for her.

They rushed into each other's arms, oblivious to the few pedestrians strolling along the village street and the driver of the electric truck full of freshly picked fruit who whistled at them from the cab of his vehicle as he drove by.

"You're here!" Holly gasped, once she and Tavalera came up for air. "You're really here!"

She was as bright and pretty and sparkling as he remembered her. She was warm and lively and full of questions.

Tavalera told her about Stoner and what was happening Earthside as Holly parked her bike in a public rack and they walked slowly, arms wrapped around each other, back to the red-roofed building where the habitat's governmental offices were housed.

It was late afternoon in the habitat, which kept to Greenwich time, like all the human settlements throughout the solar system. As they walked toward the office building, talking incessantly to one another, Holly suddenly stopped in her tracks, made a left turn, and yanked Tavalera along with her.

"My place," she said before he could speak another word.

CHAPTER 13

As Stoner took the antique rocker in front of the massive mahogany desk, the President smiled pleasantly at him and Sister Angelique. But Stoner saw a wariness in those eyes and, beneath it, uneasiness.

"The Archbishop couldn't come himself, huh?" the President asked almost sulkily.

"He's in hospital for a few days, sir," Angelique repeated. Then she quickly added, "No one outside his immediate staff knows about it. He would appreciate it if you held that information to yourselves and no one else."

With a glance at his chief of staff, the President murmured, "Of course. We understand."

He turned his troubled eyes to Stoner again. But before he could say anything, the chief of staff said mildly, "Perhaps I should introduce myself. My name is Oscar Melillo. I'm the President's chief of staff."

Melillo was smiling, but there was no warmth in his expression. He was a short, round-faced man with light brown skin and thick dark hair. A barely visible scar ran along his right jaw. He must be proud of that scar, Stoner thought. Otherwise he'd have had it erased with cosmetic surgery. It's his way of showing that he's tough.

Angelique spoke up. "Mr. President, this is Keith Stoner. He—"

"The star man," said Melillo. "You're the one who sent that message."

"Now wait a minute," the President said, pointing a finger at Stoner like a pistol. "You're the guy who claims he's been to the stars?"

Stoner replied gravely, "I am. I have been."

The President's light blue eyes narrowed and Stoner saw a flicker of fear in them. "You're trying to tell me you've traveled to the stars? That's not possible." He turned to Melillo. "Is it?"

"Not by any technology we know of."

Stoner said, "I'm the one who's been causing the aurorae each night."

"You mean the Northern Lights?"

"Yes."

"You can prove that?"

With the barest of nods, Stoner said, "That's easy. You won't see them tonight. I'll turn them off."

"You can do that?" Melillo asked.

"Yes."

"You've got a starship?" the President asked, awestruck in spite of himself.

"Yes."

"Like on the vid shows?"

Stoner smiled. "Not quite like the shows you've seen. Rather different, in fact."

Stabbing a finger in the direction of his media secretary, the President commanded, "Get that science guy in here. Pronto! And Akino."

"The secretary of defense," Angelique explained, leaning close enough to Stoner to whisper in his ear.

Yanovan, seated on the wide sofa next to the empty fireplace, picked up the telephone from its end table and began speaking hurriedly into it.

"You've got to tell us all about this starship," the President said eagerly. "All about it!"

"I'd be happy to," Stoner replied. "As soon as you dismantle the nuclear weapons you're building in New Mexico."

The President's jaw dropped open. The Oval Office went absolutely silent. Stoner could hear birds chirping in the Rose Garden, outside the floor-length windows behind the President's desk.

"Who says we're building nukes?" the chief of staff growled.

"The Iranians know it. The Chinese know it," Stoner said. "You've managed to keep it secret from the International Atomic Energy Agency, but they don't really count these days, do they? And the American people, of course. They only know what they see on the news media, and you've got the media controlled very tightly."

"This is a security breach of the first magnitude," said Melillo, his face reddening slightly.

Ignoring him, Stoner said to the President, "Archbishop Overmire has decided that nuclear weapons are unacceptable. The New Morality is withdrawing its support of the effort."

"I'll believe that when the Archbishop himself tells us," Melillo growled.

"I've been working with the Iranians and the Chinese. Both are willing to drop their programs if the United States does the same."

"And the Russians?" the President asked.

"They scrapped all their weapons fifty years ago, when all the other nations did."

"And they're not building new ones?" Melillo argued.

"No, they're not," Stoner replied patiently. Then he added in a flat voice, "Not yet."

"How do you know all this?" Melillo demanded.

Stoner looked into his dark, suspicious eyes, then said thinly, "You can't hide from the kind of technology that I have at my fingertips."

"Super technology," the President breathed. "Alien technology."

Melillo grumbled, "The Russkies would love to be the only people in the world with nuclear weapons."

"They're unusable," Stoner said. "Or rather, if you use them you'll be killing yourselves. And everyone else on Earth."

"The nuclear winter scenario?" the chief of staff scoffed. "We've been through the numbers—"

Suddenly they were no longer in the Oval Office. The five of them hung suspended a hundred meters above a blackened, airless, desolated land. As far as the horizon in all directions nothing moved. The ground was bare hard rock, broken by immense craters, scorched as if by the flames of hell.

"What . . . ?"

"Where are we?"

"What have you done?"

The President, Melillo, Yanovan, Angelique, and Stoner himself hovered above the barren terrain, floating as if in zero gravity. A bubble of energy encased them, holding air and warmth.

"This was once an Earth-like planet, green with flowering trees, brimming with life. Great cities lifted their spires to the sky. Billions of intelligent creatures existed here."

Higher they rose. Angelique felt no sensation of motion, no hollowness in the pit of her stomach. She knew that Stoner was in control and there was nothing to fear. But the President and his two aides looked close to panic, their arms outstretched as if reaching for a safe handhold, their legs flailing futilely.

The ground beneath them spread out, all of it blackened, lifeless. Still higher they ascended, and now Angelique could see the curve of the planet's horizon. Nothing lived anywhere on that world. It was as bleak and shattered as the Moon. No, she corrected herself, thousands of human beings live on the Moon. This world is dead. Totally, utterly, completely dead.

"What is this?" the President whimpered.

"This is the fourth planet of a G-type star, a little more than fifty light-years from Earth," Stoner explained. "A thousand years ago it would have looked almost exactly like Earth to you, although its inhabitants didn't look very much like bipedal descendants of apes. Yet they were intelligent, as intelligent as you or I."

"What happened to them?" Angelique asked, staring at the devastation spread below them, knowing, fearing, what his answer would be.

"They were intelligent enough to invent nuclear weapons," Stoner answered grimly. "And stupid enough to use them."

Yanovan whispered, "Oh my god."

CHAPTER 14

And abruptly they were back in the Oval Office.

The President, still seated behind his desk, seemed to have the wind knocked out of him. He sat gasping, mouth open, eyes barely focusing. Angelique sat beside Stoner as before, but now she reached out for his hand. He took hers and squeezed it gently, reassuringly.

Yanovan was still on the sofa by the fireplace, blinking with a combination of disbelief and barely contained panic. Melillo, though, was tougher. He strode to the side of the President's desk and practically snarled, "A trick! A cheap hypnotist's trick!"

Stoner shook his head. "No trick. I'll give your astronomers the coordinates of that star. They can confirm that there's an Earth-sized planet orbiting around it."

"That doesn't mean—"

"You've got to stop your nuclear weapons program," Stoner insisted. "If you don't, Earth will end up like the planet we just saw."

"Now look," Melillo said, still standing beside the President's desk. "We know that the Iranians and the Chinese are both building nukes and missiles that can reach our cities. We've got to protect ourselves."

"The course you're following now will lead to nuclear war," Stoner said. "And nuclear war will destroy the human race, sterilize this entire planet."

"I don't believe it," Melillo said, shaking his head.

"Now wait a minute, Oscar," said the President to his chief of staff. "Why do we need nukes if we've got *him*?"

Melillo hesitated, then turned to Stoner with a cold smile. "That's right. The technology you've got is way beyond simple little nuclear bombs, isn't it?"

"Way beyond," Stoner agreed.

"So tell us about it."

"Wait until my science guy gets here," said the President. "He'll understand him better than we will."

Stoner said, "I'll be happy to give you all the information you want—after you've dismantled your bombs."

Melillo pulled up a chair and sat facing Stoner. "You don't seem to understand, Mr. Star Man. We've got you. You're surrounded by the best security systems in the world. And several battalions of highly trained troops can be here in minutes. You're in no position to bargain. You can't get out of here unless we—"

But he was talking to empty air. Stoner had disappeared as suddenly as a light winking out.

Tavalera woke slowly, languorously, feeling completely relaxed and happy for the first time since he'd left the habitat and gone back to Earth. He turned, twisting the bedsheets wrapped around him, and saw Holly smiling beside him.

"It's true," he murmured. "I'm not dreaming."

Holly's smile widened. "If this is a dream, we're both having it."

He pulled her naked body to his and kissed her gently. "I love you, Holly."

"I love you, Raoul."

"It's great to be back," he said.

"Ummm."

Pulling himself up to a sitting position, Tavalera wrapped his arms around his upraised knees. "Earth's a madhouse, Holly. They're all nuts back there."

"It's a zillion klicks away. Don't worry about it. They can't hurt us."

"They're going to blow themselves to hell."

"Let them. We don't need them."

He looked down at her. "My mother's there."

"We'll bring her out here. I'll put in the request direct to the U.S. State Department."

"The New Morality," Tavalera muttered. "They run everything now."

She shrugged a bare shoulder. "So I'll talk to them."

"We'd better move fast. Stoner says they're going to war. Nuclear war."

"Stoner," said Holly. "The star man."

"He's pretty weird."

"I like him. He sent you here to me."

"Just like *that*." Tavalera snapped his fingers. "No ship, no time lag, just *pop!* and I'm here."

Holly sat up beside him, tucking the sheet demurely

beneath her armpits. "D'you think you could get him to come here?"

"Stoner? I dunno. He does pretty much as he damned pleases."

"He could help us."

"Help us do what?"

She shrugged again. "Whatever. With the technology he's got, he can change everything! Golly, if he can zip you from Earth to here in the blink of an eye, if he can let us communicate across the whole blinkin' solar system with no time lag, what else d'you think he could do?"

Tavalera thought about it for a silent moment. "Yeah, maybe you're right."

"I mean, he could help us build new habitats and expand our population and mine comets for water and whatever else we need to do!"

"Maybe."

Her fists clenching, Holly said, "All that technology. We could use it to make ourselves safe and rich." Turning to Tavalera, Holly said, "I want that technology of his!"

"What in the hell!" Melillo shouted.

"He's gone!" said the President.

Angelique felt a thrill race along her veins. "You can't hold him," she said to the men. "You can't coerce him. You can't bully him into doing anything he doesn't want to do."

The President sagged back in his high-backed chocolate brown leather chair. "I guess we can't."

"Maybe not," said Melillo, eyeing Angelique. "Or maybe we can."

"How?"

"We've got her," he said to the President. "Maybe we can pressure him through her."

Yanovan strode up from the fireplace across the room to within a few paces of the chief of staff.

"Now wait a minute," he said, looking alarmed. "You can't use her that way. She's from the Archbishop's office, for god's sake! You'll have the New Morality down on us!"

Melillo gave the media secretary a disgusted frown. "Don't be a pansy, Larry. We've got to use the assets we have. And the Archbishop will agree with us, once we explain it to him."

The President said, "You don't intend to hurt her, do you?"

Angelique realized they were talking about her as if she weren't in the room. As if she were an object, a possession, a chess piece in their game of power.

Then Melillo smiled at her, and her blood ran cold. "Hurt her? Of course not. Stoner won't let it come to that, will he, Sister?"

Angelique found that she couldn't answer. Couldn't speak. But in her mind one thought was racing around and around. Stoner won't let them hurt me. If he cares about me, he won't let them hurt me. If he cares about me. If he cares about me.

CHAPTER 15

A marginally slimmer Archbishop Overmire sat glumly in a powerchair as it rolled down the long, dimly lit tunnel that connected the New Morality's enormous hospital complex with the other buildings of the sprawling campus. Ahead of him walked half a dozen Secret Service agents in their dark, tight-stretched suits, together with an equal number of New Morality security police in almost exactly the same garb. Behind the Archbishop was another small phalanx of security men and women.

On one side of the Archbishop's chair strode Oscar Melillo, the President's chief of staff. On Overmire's other side was Sister Angelique. He thought the expression on her face might be how the early Christians appeared when they were being herded into the Colosseum to face hungry lions.

As they strode along, Melillo leaned slightly toward the Archbishop and said softly, "I'm awfully sorry, Your Eminence, that we had to take you from your hospital room."

Overmire looked up at the round-faced chief of staff, thinking how glad he was to have a reason to leave the hospital and its grueling routine of exercise and Spartan meals. But he had no intention of allowing Melillo or anyone else to know that he was grateful for the excuse to return to his office. Power comes from holding others in debt to you, he told himself, not from letting them know they've done you a favor.

"Think nothing of it, Mr. Melillo," he said, smiling graciously and speaking loudly enough so that his voice echoed off the concrete walls of the tunnel. "When my Lord's duty summons me, I respond without question."

Unconsciously touching the scar on his jaw with the tip of a finger, Melillo said, "If you can't provide a secure place to hold Sister Angelique, the government has several facilities—"

"That won't be necessary," Overmire interrupted. "The good sister is of our order, and we will provide for her."

"If it becomes necessary to . . . um, interrogate her . . . ?" Melillo let his question hang in midair.

"We have the means to do that," the Archbishop replied. Then he turned to his other side. "But you intend to be fully cooperative, don't you, Sister?"

"Of course, Your Eminence," said Angelique without hesitation. But she was thinking, Stoner won't let them harm me. He'll protect me. And when he does, I'll be able to get him to help me overcome this pompous fool of an Archbishop.

Stoner expanded his awareness to search for Sister Angelique.

She's a distraction, his wife warned.

Stoner almost smiled. Neither of them was embodied at the moment. Don't tell me you're jealous, he said.

You haven't looked into her mind very deeply, have you? Jo asked.

Have you?

Yes.

Without her permission?

I'm not as fastidious about these things as you are, Jo said. Besides, I didn't have to go very deep to see that she's infatuated with you.

Stoner felt only mildly surprised. She's infatuated with the idea that she can control Archbishop Overmire and through him gain control of the New Morality.

It's more than that, Jo countered. She's obsessed with the idea that through *you* she can gain control of the whole world.

That did astonish Stoner. He admitted, I thought Craig was the ambitious one.

Sister Angelique is more ambitious, Jo said. But like most primate females, she's been brought up to find an alpha male and use him to achieve her ambition. Be careful of her.

Stoner replied, I will be. But at this moment it looks as if she needs my help.

Jo said nothing, but he sensed her disapproval. And

he wondered what else his wife was doing without telling him.

Like a wave of adulation, Archbishop Overmire's staff people rose from their desks as he rode in his powerchair past them toward his private office, with Melillo and Angelique trailing a few paces behind him. Overmire smiled and nodded graciously to his people. None of them said a word, but Angelique could feel the warmth of their veneration. She knew that if the Archbishop wished it they would drop to their knees and kiss his ring.

Once ensconced behind his broad desk, Archbishop Overmire said crisply to his phone computer, "Get Bishop Craig in here immediately."

"Immediately, Your Eminence," the phone replied.

Without being invited, Melillo took one of the comfortable chairs in front of the desk. Angelique remained standing, clasping her hands in front of her. With a jolt, she realized she was standing as if she were manacled.

Melillo said, "This man Stoner told the President that you're going to withdraw the New Morality's support for the nuclear weapons program."

Overmire's face paled momentarily. "He . . . he showed me what a nuclear war would be like. It was terrible. Soul shattering."

"Yes," Melillo said, his voice hard. "He showed the President what he claimed to be a planet that was blasted down to bedrock by a nuclear war."

"He has strange powers."

"He knows some good tricks."

Overmire stared at the President's chief of staff. "You don't believe he's telling us the truth?"

"The surest way for us to have a nuclear war is for us

to give up our weapons and leave ourselves naked to our enemies," Melillo said. Angelique realized he had avoided answering the Archbishop's question.

Looking troubled, the Archbishop said, "I've prayed over this matter while in hospital. I think . . ." He hesitated, drew in a breath, then plunged, "I think he might be right. Nuclear war is too terrible to contemplate."

"Sure it is," Melillo said. "He's counting on that. He wants us disarmed."

Angelique realized that this round-faced man with the scarred jawline was the actual power in the White House. The President is just a figurehead, she thought, a pretty personality that can win elections. Melillo's the real strength in his administration.

She spoke up. "Stoner's trying to get the others to disarm, too. The Iranians. The Chinese."

Melillo's dark brown eyes focused on her. Angelique stared back at him, thinking that the last thing she wanted was to let this man believe she was afraid of him.

At last Melillo said, "All right, suppose he really is a visitor from the stars. An extraterrestrial. An alien dressed up in human form."

"He says he's human, from Earth," Angelique countered.

"He says a lot of things. Did it ever occur to you that he wants us disarmed so that his alien race can take over our planet? Did it ever occur to you that our nukes are the only things standing between us and invasion by extraterrestrials?"

"I don't believe that!" Angelique blurted.

Melillo turned to the Archbishop, who was looking at him intently.

"At the very least," Melillo continued, "this Stoner character wants to make big changes in the way we live. Big changes. The nukes are just his first step, I guarantee. Next thing you know he'll want to dismantle the New Morality and take over the government."

Maybe he should, Angelique thought. But she stopped herself from saying it aloud.

The Archbishop asked, "Do you actually think he wants to make himself our ruler?"

"Why not? Why else is he here?"

"The Antichrist," Overmire whispered.

"Could be," said Melillo.

Angelique objected, "No, he couldn't—"

But the two men paid her no attention. "We've got to stop him," Archbishop Overmire said with a determination Angelique hadn't heard from him until now.

Melillo turned to Angelique. "And you're going to be the bait for our trap."

She looked pleadingly to the Archbishop, but Overmire spread his hands and said piously, "God's will be done."

Angelique suddenly realized she was powerless. And frightened.

"But what about the nuclear weapons?" the Archbishop asked.

Melillo said, "There's an old dictum: use 'em or lose 'em."

"We should attack our enemies?"

"Before they hit us," Melillo answered.

"Only their nuclear facilities," said the Archbishop. "I won't countenance more casualties than absolutely necessary."

"Of course. I agree fully."

"Good." The Archbishop nodded at Melillo, dismissing him.

Melillo nodded back and grinned at the Archbishop. They understood each other, Angelique saw. They agree on what they want to do.

As the President's chief of staff went to the door to leave the office, the Archbishop's phone announced, "Bishop Craig is here, Your Eminence."

"Send him in," said the Archbishop heartily.

Craig brushed past Melillo in the doorway and came straight up to the Archbishop's desk. For the first time Angelique saw how small the bishop looked, how unimportant.

"It's good to see you out of the hospital, Your Eminence," he said with a toothy smile pasted onto his dark face.

"Yes," said Overmire coldly. "While in hospital I watched the security vids of you two discussing my future."

Craig shot a glance at Angelique. She felt her insides go hollow. He knows! she thought. And the bishop thought his office was safe.

"Your Eminence," Craig answered, "please allow me to explain—"

"No explanation is necessary, my good man," said the Archbishop almost jovially. "Ambition is a worthy urge. The good Lord knows I've had enough of it in my own soul."

Craig sank into one of the chairs before the desk. "I never intended to—"

"I understand fully," the Archbishop said. "In fact, I intend to reward your ambition. I am promoting you to chief chaplain of all our military missions overseas. Your new headquarters will be in Jakarta, Indonesia."

Craig's mouth dropped open.

"You will assume your new position immediately, Bishop. I hope you enjoy the climate in Indonesia. Good-bye. And God be with you."

"But . . . but . . ."

"Good-bye," Overmire said with steel in his voice.

Craig pushed himself up from the chair and stumbled toward the door, but not before he shot a black look at Angelique.

She stood there, stunned, and watched him leave.

"I'm afraid he thinks you've schemed against him, Sister," the Archbishop said, smiling as if he was enjoying the discord. "The reality is quite different, though, isn't it?"

Angelique had trouble finding her voice. When she did, it came out like a frightened little girl's. "Your Eminence, I only wanted—"

"You wanted to move me aside and control the New Morality through Bishop Craig, I understand," said the Archbishop. Then his face and his tone hardened. "But that's not going to happen. I'm not as old and sick as you would like to believe, Sister. I've dealt with ambitious pipsqueaks like Craig before. And with Delilahs such as you, too."

BOOK IV

FRANKLIN HAVERFORD OVERMIRE

When the existence of the Church is threatened, she is released from the commandments of morality. With unity as the end, the use of every means is sanctified, even cunning, treachery, violence, simony, prison, death. For all order is for the sake of the community, and the individual must be sacrificed to the common good.

Dietrich of Nieheim,
Bishop of Verden,
A.D. 1411

CHAPTER 1

Archbishop Overmire spent the evening in prayer, as he often did. He felt very close to God, and was absolutely certain that God had chosen him to lead the people to His grace.

He felt completely sure about Bishop Craig. Ambition was good only up to a point. Besides, Craig didn't have the nerve or the intelligence to head the New Morality. None of them did. Why, the man even thought that nuclear holocaust was God's chosen way of bringing this world to its end. Nonsense! God would have informed me, the Archbishop told himself as he knelt before the crucifix in his private chapel. God would have sent me a sign, an unmistakable sign.

Stoner. The star man. Could he be God's sign? No, the Archbishop answered himself. He himself insists that he's only a man. But so did our Lord and Savior, at first. Has Stoner offered any evidence of his origin? No. Has he performed any miracles? Made the blind see? Cured the lame? Healed the sick? No, nothing like that. All he seems concerned with is the threat of nuclear war.

But he does apparently have control of a technology that's beyond anything our scientists can understand. That is something we must have. We must make certain that it doesn't fall into the hands of the Chinese or those damnable Muslim jihadists.

Stoner claims he's American by birth, yet he shows no loyalty to the United States. Nor to Christianity, for that matter. Melillo fears he's an alien, the leader of an extraterrestrial invasion. I can't believe that. God would have warned me. He would have allowed our scientists to find the extraterrestrials long before this.

No, Stoner is exactly what he says he is: a human being with access to extraordinary technology. Technology that we must have. Technology that mustn't fall into the wrong hands.

Overmire bowed his head and asked God to show him what to do. Lead me into the path of righteousness, he prayed. Show me Thy way, O Lord.

That young woman. Sister Angelique. She is ambitious, too. Dangerously so. She has the intelligence and ruthlessness to be a threat. She has the evil desire to supplant me as head of God's New Morality. A woman, in charge of God's chosen order! Nonsense.

And, he thought, she's been in contact with Stoner. We'll have to find out everything she knows about him. We'll have to pull every scrap of information she has out of her mind, whether she cooperates or not. Everything she knows, even her deepest subconscious thoughts. That's where Satan lodges his blackest evils.

We can get to Stoner through her, the Archbishop thought. A tendril of doubt wormed its way to his consciousness: What if he has no concern about her? What if he doesn't care what we do to her? We'd be putting her through all that for nothing.

Manfully the Archbishop pushed the doubt out of his mind. We'll do what we must do. If she is harmed it will be Stoner's fault for not aiding her, not ours. God's plan for her will be holy martyrdom.

God's will be done.

CHAPTER 2

Stoner felt his contact with Sister Angelique fading away. It wasn't broken completely, but the energy level had suddenly become quite faint.

Her mind's in a turmoil, he realized. Something's interfering with her mental patterns.

Or someone, Jo suggested.

Yes, Stoner realized. It's deliberate. They've moved her to a heavily shielded location and they're probing her mind with powerful electrical pulses.

You mean they're torturing her, said his wife.

Raoul Tavalera was watching the obvious signs of growing frustration on Holly Lane's face. Normally Holly was as cheerful as a sparrow, but now her bright brown eyes looked troubled, angry, and narrow lines of irritation creased the space between her brows.

Tavalera was walking with Holly along one of the tree-lined bricked paths that curved up the gentle slope of the hills above the village in which *Goddard*'s administrative offices were based. It was a bright sunny afternoon, as every afternoon was inside the massive habitat. Sunshine streamed in through the long solar windows that stretched the length of the giant cylinder. It never rains here, Tavalera remembered. The grounds are watered from below, through drip hoses threaded beneath the greenery. Never a cloud in the sky, although Holly's face looked like a thunderstorm brewing up.

"But this is an official request from the government of the *Goddard* habitat," she was saying—almost yelling—into the phone clipped to her ear. "We'll provide the transportation. All we need is clearance from you to—"

She stopped and listened to the voice in her phone, her face fuming, her fists planted belligerently on her hips.

"She's a sixty-eight-year-old woman," Holly shouted. "She's retired. Why in the name of justice and mercy can't she get a transportation permit? It's not gonna cost you anything. We'll provide—"

She listened for another few moments, steaming, then yanked the phone from her ear. For a moment Tavalera thought she was going to throw it into the lake that shimmered off to the left of the path they were on.

"They won't do it!" she snapped. "They just will not allow your mother to leave! No reason; they just say it can't be done."

Tavalera realized he had expected such a response to his request.

"They looked up my record and saw that I'm missing," he said. "That bothers them. They want me to be where they put me."

"Bunch of nitpicking peabrains," Holly muttered.

"I guess I can't blame 'em," he said, jamming his hands into his pockets as he resumed walking slowly up the path.

"Can't blame them?" Holly was outraged.

Hunching his shoulders against her wrath, he explained, "Well, look, they're supposed to have me in a secure facility in Atlanta, working with the New Morality people on Stoner. But they can't find me. Now you call up and ask them to let my mom immigrate here to *Goddard*. Must've started alarm bells ringing on all their computers."

Holly scowled up at him. "My god, what is it back there, a police state?"

"Kinda. They're very nice about it. They let you do

pretty much what you want—as long as you don't stray outside the lines."

Holly shook her head.

"I mean, they told everybody to stay indoors from sundown to sunrise for a week at a stretch," Tavalera tried to explain. "And everybody did! They did what they were told, nice as pie. Just about all of 'em. They've been trained to be good, obedient citizens."

"Lordy lord," Holly grumbled. "I thought things were bad here when they tried to regiment us. That's why I ran for office, y'know."

"I remember," Tavalera said. "I was here when you did. And you won."

She put on a smile as she walked beside him. "Well, look, we'll figure out something. I'll go higher in their chain of command. We'll get your mother out here sooner or later."

"Yeah," Tavalera said glumly. "I know." But he was thinking, They're not going to let Mom go. As long as they've got her, they know I'll have to go back to her. They're holding her as a hostage until they get me back in their hands.

Sister Angelique wasn't in pain. She was in agony.

Archbishop Overmire had called a security team to take her to what he called an interview with one of the New Morality's psychologists. Angelique had heard, more than once, about dissidents or subversives who had been sent to psychologists for readjusting their mental attitudes.

They brought her to a bare little office in a subbasement of the hospital, where a kindly looking middle-aged woman in a white coat and her two younger assistants, both of them women, were waiting for Angelique. The two assistants were smiling, as if trying to reassure her. Their teeth were white and gleamingly perfect.

The middle-aged woman identified herself as a clinical psychologist.

"I don't understand why I need to talk to a psychologist," Angelique said, glancing around at the sterile metal furniture and the rows of stark white cabinets lining one wall of the little room. Gray metal boxes of electronics equipment sat on top of them. The room had an antiseptic odor to it, a strange muffled feeling to the air, as if the walls were thickly insulated with soundproofing.

"We need to probe your memory," the psychologist said briskly. Her blond hair was pulled back into a smooth knot; her ice blue eyes regarded Angelique without a trace of warmth in them. "Including your unconscious memories," she added.

The psychologist gestured to a metal chair in the center of the small chamber and Angelique hesitantly sat down on it. The two young assistants, both also blond but much leaner than the psychologist, moved behind Angelique, where she couldn't see them unless she turned around in the chair.

Before she could turn, they came up on either side of her and strapped her wrists to the cold metal arms of the chair.

"Don't be alarmed," said the psychologist. "The restraints are for your own protection. Sometimes the electrical stimuli cause the patient to spasm violently." She smiled, and Angelique thought of a snake. "We wouldn't want you to hurt yourself, would we?"

The assistants knelt on the bare concrete floor and fastened another pair of cuffs to Angelique's ankles.

Then the psychologist turned to the wall phone and said simply, "We're ready here." The phone's minuscule screen remained blank, but a voice answered, "Very well."

While the psychologist began taking various metal implements from the cabinets and arranging them carefully on a tray, Angelique started to recite the Twenty-third Psalm to herself, "The Lord is my shepherd, I shall not . . ."

Then she heard the door behind her open and footsteps click across the bare floor.

Dr. Gerald Mayfair stepped before her, a white lab coat over his crisply starched pale blue shirt and carefully knotted lavender tie. His light brown eyes seemed to Angelique to be glittering at her. She felt like a very small mouse trapped by a very large cat.

"You may feel some discomfort," Mayfair said. Then he turned to the psychologist and nodded. "Proceed."

CHAPTER 3

Stoner felt the jolt of Angelique's agony.

"They're torturing her!"

He said it aloud, coalescing his energy pattern into his physical body. Jo appeared beside him, looking equally grim.

"It's a trap," she said. "She's the bait and you're the prey."

Nodding, Stoner said, "I know, but I can't let her suffer like that."

His wife smiled at him. "Of course you can't."

Dimly Angelique heard the psychologist say, "She's fainted again."

"Or she's faking," Mayfair's cold voice replied. "The readouts don't look like unconsciousness to me."

Angelique sat strapped into the metal chair, her head slumped down on her breast, her entire body thrumming with the pain of the electrical shocks. They kept asking about Stoner, and she had told them all she knew, twice, three times. She would tell them anything, everything, if they would only stop the pain. She would make up tales for them, say anything they wanted to hear, if they would only stop the pain.

"Turn up the voltage," Mayfair said.

The psychologist hesitated. "That could do permanent damage."

"What of it? If she comes out of this a vegetable we can use her on clinical trials."

Angelique felt a hand grip her shoulder gently. And the pain eased away like a wave gently washing up on a beach. She opened her eyes, lifted her head.

And saw Mayfair and the psychologist standing rooted to the floor, their mouths agape, their eyes round and staring.

"You want to turn up the voltage?" Stoner's voice! She twisted around in the chair and saw that yes, it was Keith Stoner grasping her shoulder, his eyes focused hard on Mayfair, his bearded face set in a fierce scowl.

"You're a sadist, aren't you?" Stoner said to Mayfair, his voice low, flat, hard.

"How did you . . . ?"

"Turn up the voltage," Stoner hissed.

Mayfair twitched and shuddered; then his arms flailed out and his legs spasmed. Screaming, he jibbered his way across the little chamber, banging into the cabinets, howling like a beast in pain until he collapsed onto the concrete floor, twitching and blubbering.

The psychologist cringed away from Stoner, who

took his hand from Angelique's shoulder and advanced toward her.

"Shall I increase the voltage for you, too?" he growled.

"No! Please! I was only doing what he told me to."

"Nuremberg," Stoner muttered. "They were only following orders, too."

The two young assistants huddled in the corner, clutching at each other, sobbing with terror.

"Unstrap her," Stoner ordered. They jumped to obey.

Turning back to Angelique, Stoner asked, "Can you stand up? Can you walk?"

"I . . . don't know," Angelique answered. Her legs felt totally strengthless, as if their muscles had turned to slush.

Stoner reached out his hand to her. She grasped it and felt power surging along her nerves. She got to her feet; she felt shaky for a moment; then the weakness ebbed away.

"Come on," Stoner said. "We're getting out of here." As he reached the door he looked over his shoulder and commanded the three cowering women, "Stay here. Don't make me hurt you the way you've hurt this prisoner of yours."

Then he looked down at Mayfair, still twitching uncontrollably on the concrete floor, barely conscious. "Learn well," Stoner muttered.

There were two uniformed security guards in the corridor, lounging by a small desk where a woman in a nurse's white uniform was chatting with them. They looked up.

"It's all right," Stoner said to them. "No need to accompany us."

They looked at each other but made no move to hinder Stoner and Angelique.

As he reached the elevator doors at the end of the

short corridor, Stoner turned back toward them. "You might want to check on Dr. Mayfair and his assistants," he said over his shoulder. Then the elevator doors slid open and the two of them stepped in. Stoner leaned on the button marked: LOBBY LEVEL.

When the elevator doors slid open again he saw that they were a long way from the lobby. A long, wide corridor stretched before them, with nurses and orderlies in white and pale green uniforms striding purposefully in both directions, some of them guiding powerchairs in which patients sat huddled in gray blankets while doctors wearing white smocks over their street clothes stepped briskly past them, many doctors talking to the empty air. Clip-on phones, Stoner realized. They're allowed to use phones.

Stoner glanced at a small wall screen, which immediately lit up and showed a map. The hospital's lobby was marked in bright red.

"Did you turn that on?" Angelique asked, her voice slightly breathless.

Stoner nodded. "This way," he said, taking her gently by the elbow.

There were security checkpoints spaced along the corridor at every few cross hallways, small desks with uniformed guards sitting behind them, either looking bored or chatting with hospital personnel.

"You there!" called the guard at the first checkpoint they came to. "Where's your badge? And I need to see authorization papers for both of you."

Before the young man was halfway out of his chair Stoner went to the desk and said softly, "We're here by mistake. We're leaving now, so please don't make a fuss."

The guard frowned at them as he stood up. He was a lanky youngster, a few centimeters taller than Stoner.

"It's all right," Stoner said. "I assure you."

The guard looked down at his desktop screen. It broke into electronic hash.

"Dandrification," he muttered. "The computer's crashed again."

"Does that happen often?" Stoner asked solicitously.

"Now and then," the guard said, sinking back into his chair again.

"It'll clear up in a few moments," said Stoner.

"I guess."

Stoner took Angelique's arm again and they headed past the checkpoint and the addled security guard.

Angelique stared up at Stoner in wonder.

They passed four security checkpoints in much the same way as they threaded through the hospital's busy maze of corridors. At the fifth one Stoner noticed a patient in a powerchair trundling along behind them. He slowed their pace to let the chair pass them. A very old woman sat in it, little more than wrinkled skin and brittle bones, her wispy dead-white hair floating like a halo.

Instead of passing them, she stopped the chair.

"Where're you heading?" she asked. Her voice was a brittle rasp; it reminded Angelique of a kitchen blender crushing ice cubes.

"We're leaving," Stoner said. And he resumed walking along the corridor.

Angelique started off beside him, and the old woman nudged the powerchair's control stud to keep up with them. Angelique saw that the woman clutched an oversized paper book to her emaciated bosom.

"Take me with you!" she begged in a scratchy whisper.

Before Angelique could reply, the woman went on, "I want to get out of here, too. They just stuck me in here to die. I want to get out!"

Stoner looked down at her sternly.

"We can't," Angelique began to say. "We're only—"

But then Stoner's expression eased. Smiling, he said, "Come with us, then. But don't say a word to anyone. Let me do the talking."

CHAPTER 4

"He just walked out of the hospital with her?" Archbishop Overmire felt more astonished than angry.

His security chief stood uneasily before the Archbishop's broad desk. "Apparently so, Your Eminence. He took Sister Angelique and walked past every checkpoint in the hospital. The guards in the front lobby say they think the two of them got into a taxi, with another patient in a wheelchair. We're looking into the cab company's files."

"Another patient?" Overmire demanded. "Who?"

The security chief pulled a phone from the breast pocket of his uniform and worked its keyboard with a thumb. "Uh . . . her name is Yolanda Vasquez. Terminal patient. Age a hundred and seven."

"A hundred and seven? What's her relationship to Sister Angelique? Or Stoner? Where does she fit into this?"

Licking his lips, the security chief said, "We're looking into it, Your Eminence."

Overmire felt his face tighten into a frown. "But how did he get into the interrogation room, in the first place?"

The security chief waved one hand weakly. "According to the three staff women he just . . . appeared. Like he popped out of thin air."

"And Dr. Mayfair? What does he say about this?"

"Nothing, sir. He seems to be in some sort of a coma. The medics said he's catatonic."

The Archbishop thought about that for a moment while the security chief fidgeted and shifted from one foot to the other. Despite his military-like tan uniform with its epaulettes and badges of rank, the man looked like a nervous little student brought to face the school's principal.

"Sit down, man. Sit down."

"Thank you, sir."

Overmire steepled his fingers and touched them to his fleshy lips. At last he said, "So he simply appeared in the room out of nowhere, did he?"

"Yessir. According to the reports. Dr. Mayfair was in no condition to talk intelligibly, but the three women all confirm that he . . . he just was *there* all of a sudden."

"I understand. He's done the same thing elsewhere."

"It's kind of spooky," said the security chief.

But Overmire was musing, "He came in that way, but he walked out like a normal, ordinary person."

"Right past Lord knows how many of my guards," the security chief muttered. "He just walked right past them, and they let him do it."

"He had the woman with him at that point."

"Sister Angelique Duprie, yes, sir. And somewhere along the line he picked up this old lady, Vasquez."

"What do we know about her?"

Working his pocket phone's keyboard again, the security chief replied, "Retired schoolteacher. No criminal record. No security file. She seems to have been a model citizen all her life."

"Until she met Stoner," the Archbishop mused. "Then she escapes from the hospital with him."

"Yessir. And Sister Angelique."

The Archbishop smiled inwardly. To his security chief he said, "He appeared magically, but he walked out with the two women through the whole hospital building and left in a taxi. What does that tell you?"

The security chief's face furrowed with concentration.

Before he could come up with a reply, the Archbishop said triumphantly, "He can pop in and out like a genie from the *Arabian Nights*, but he can't take someone else with him!"

The chief blinked several times, digesting the idea.

"Do you see what that means?" Overmire crowed. "It's a weakness, a chink in his armor! He can travel instantly wherever he wants to go, but he can't bring one of us along with him. He has to move normally when he's taking an ordinary person along with him."

"But he can talk his way past my guards, make them let him go right past them. Somehow."

"Yes, yes. But as long as he's with one of us he has to move like an ordinary human being. No instantaneous travel."

"I suppose so." The security chief sounded unconvinced.

Speaking to his phone, the Archbishop said, "Get me the head of the National Science Foundation. I want him here in my office as quickly as he can get here. This is an emergency!"

Bertram Feingold was philosophic about life. When they hand you a lemon, he always said, make lemonade. In a nation that revered prayer much more than research, a nation that banned much of biotechnology and all of nanotechnology, Feingold had made his slow, patient way to the top of the National Science Foundation by dint of avoiding conflicts and keeping his nose clean.

Quietly, without ever making a display of defiance,

he did what he could to protect scientists from the ire of the New Morality and their stooges in government.

When a headstrong young geologist returned from a stint on the exploration of Mars insisting that the red planet's long-extinct intelligent species had arisen separately from life on Earth, Feingold immediately saw that such a conclusion ran counter to the New Morality's teaching that the Martians had been created by God in the Garden of Eden and banished to Mars for their evil ways. He rewrote the young hothead's research report, casting his conclusions as an unproven hypothesis and banishing his supporting evidence to a thick set of footnotes that nobody but a scientist would bother to read.

The geologist never forgave Feingold for editing his paper. But the young researcher wasn't drummed out of his university post; he wasn't forced into "community service" that would have taken him away from his home and his research for years; he was able to go on with his career.

When a naïve microbiologist sent in a proposal to study the evolution of the growing resistance to antibiotics that many strains of bacteria had developed, Feingold gently convinced her to drop that dreaded word "evolution" from her proposal.

And so it had gone, for more than two decades. Go along, get along. Don't make waves. Do what you can. He knew that many of his colleagues detested him and accused him of being a collaborator with the forces of ignorance. Their disdain hurt, but Feingold took solace in the fact that he helped get at least a little real work accomplished.

I'm not a Judas goat, he often told himself. I'm a wolf in sheep's clothing. Well, maybe a cocker spaniel.

Besides, he sometimes joked to his oldest and most

trusted colleagues, I'm Jewish. And from Brooklyn, yet. If the New Morality gets pissed off at something that some scientist does out in Podunk U. they can always blame it on the New York Jew in charge of NSF. Yet secretly he enjoyed the irony that the New Morality's loudly proclaimed insistence on diversity had allowed a Jew to rise to the top of the scientific establishment—such as it was.

So it came as something of a surprise to Feingold when the emergency call from Archbishop Overmire himself arrived at his desk in Washington, D.C.

"What's the Archbishop want me for?" Feingold asked the empty air of his office. Actually he was speaking to God, his God, the God of Abraham and Isaac and countless Jews slaughtered down through the ages for nothing more than being Jewish. God had never answered his questions, not once in Feingold's sixty-two years. But still he asked.

CHAPTER 5

The Archbishop received Feingold not in his office but in the quietly opulent dining room of his residence. Walnut-paneled walls. A long, massive dining table polished to a mirror finish. Ornate chandelier hanging from a coffered ceiling. Not a bad way to live, Feingold thought, almost smiling at the genteel scruffiness of his own modest bachelor's quarters.

The Archbishop was standing by the high arched stained-glass window as Feingold was ushered into the dining room by a blank-faced young man in a butler's dark raiment. The window's stained-glass picture depicted Christ and the multitude with the loaves and fishes. I hope lunch is better than that, Feingold said to himself.

Turning the full wattage of his best smile on the scientist, the Archbishop greeted him with outstretched arms.

"Dr. Feingold!" Archbishop Overmire cried, advancing toward him. "How good of you to come on such short notice!"

He must be in deep trouble, Feingold thought.

The Archbishop led Feingold to the dining table. He's a lot heavier than his public images show him, the scientist realized. Even in the black suit he looked like a dirigible. Too much good living. Bad for the heart. Next thing you know he'll need replacements for his knees. And hips.

Two places were set: the Archbishop took the high-backed chair at the head of the table; Feingold sat at his right. A pair of servants poured wine into crystal goblets for them. Feingold took a cautious sip. Not bad, he thought. Nicely sweet. Then he noticed that the Archbishop's wine was a considerably darker color than his. Mine must be leftover from a bar mitzvah, Feingold wisecracked silently.

"I must tell you," the Archbishop said after a healthy swig of his own wine, "that I admire the way you've handled the Science Foundation. It must be very difficult to keep those secularists from going off on wild tangents."

Feingold made himself smile. "They do like to have the freedom to pursue knowledge, wherever it leads."

"Which can be dangerous, can't it?"

"It certainly can."

A servant brought their first course. Gefilte fish for Feingold, broiled trout for the Archbishop.

"Your cook does kosher?" Feingold asked.

Overmire bobbed his head. "We respect all religious traditions."

Feingold tasted the flaky fish, then dabbed a little horseradish sauce on it. Not bad.

The Archbishop chewed thoughtfully for a silent moment, swallowed, then asked, "You're aware of this Stoner phenomenon, aren't you?"

So that's it, Feingold thought. "The man who sent that message about being from the stars?"

"Yes."

"The Oval Office is putting together a special top-secret committee to look into it . . . er, him."

"I know," said the Archbishop. "You are chairman of that committee, are you not?"

Wondering where this was headed, Feingold remembered a basic bit of survival tactics: When in doubt, protect your people. And your ass.

He said, "I am. It's all classified top secret. They want to keep his message from leaking to the news nets."

"We must protect the public," Overmire muttered.

Keeping his thoughts to himself, Feingold said, "I've restricted the information to only a half dozen astronomers, as the Oval Office has requested."

Requested, Feingold repeated to himself. With a gun to my head they requested.

"There were many others at the various observatories that received his message," the Archbishop said almost ominously.

Feingold waved a hand in the air. "Oh, they all signed secrecy agreements. The news won't leak out; don't worry."

"Good," said Overmire. "I want to be kept fully informed about this."

"Of course."

"You will report directly to me. In person."

"A pleasure," said Feingold, thinking, He's scared, all right. I'll have to walk on eggshells about this.

Feingold waited for more. When the Archbishop returned his attention to his trout, Feingold prodded, "So what is it with this character, claiming he's from the stars? Is he crazy or a subversive or what?"

Looking troubled, Archbishop Overmire revealed, "I've met the man."

"Stoner?"

"Yes."

"He's really from the stars?"

"I'm almost convinced that he's telling the truth. He has strange . . . abilities."

Trying to hide his eagerness, Feingold asked, "Such as?"

The Archbishop pursed his lips. Then, "He can appear and disappear at will. He could pop into this room right now if he wanted to."

"You believe this?"

"I've seen it. Members of my staff have witnessed it. He claims he's using technology from advanced alien civilizations."

Feingold couldn't help uttering, "Wow!"

"Some of my people fear that he's an extraterrestrial himself, made up to look like a human. They think he might be the advance scout for an alien invasion of Earth."

Bullshit, Feingold thought. That's exactly the kind of *narishkayt* conclusion that a know-nothing idiot would jump to. Alien invasion! If they're smart enough to cross interstellar distances and come here, why the hell would they want to invade us? Primitive thinking. Paranoia in high places.

But he said nothing, revealed none of his thoughts.

Suddenly clutching Feingold's arm, the Archbishop

said, "You are the nation's top scientist. I need to know what you learn about this man, how we can deal with him, how to protect ourselves against him."

Feingold looked deep into the Archbishop's eyes and saw real fear there. And something more. Along with the fear there was a desire, a passion, an avid fervor to gain the power that this star man represented.

So, Feingold said to himself, you want me to help you learn how to get your hands on his superior technology. After a lifetime of belittling science and persecuting scientists, after generations of working night and day to tear down Darwin and Einstein and every other idea that your narrow little minds can't handle, after years and decades of beating us into conformity, after trying to turn us back to the twelfth century—now you want me to help you. Now you need science and scientists to deal with something your little pygmy minds can't understand, something that's scaring the crap out of you.

I should help you? I should spit in your soup, you fat overstuffed sonofabitch bastard!

But Bertram Feingold was a scientist. A scientist who was being offered the chance to study what just might truly be technology from the stars.

He took a deep breath, then smiled and said reassuringly to the Archbishop, "I'll do what I can, Your Eminence. I'll be happy to help in any way I can."

CHAPTER 6

Archbishop Overmire finished his lunch with Feingold as swiftly as he decently could, then called for one of his aides. While they waited at the dining table, the Archbishop assured the scientist, "We'll give you every scrap of evidence we have about Stoner, every security camera record of his appearances in various offices here in our center, intelligence files on his activities elsewhere. He claims to have spoken with leaders in Greater Iran and China, you know."

"I didn't know," said Feingold.

"And there are the records of his starship's arrival in our solar system, more than twenty years ago."

"The official explanation for that—"

"Yes, yes, I know," said the Archbishop with an impatient flap of one hand. "But it's obviously connected to him."

Feingold hesitated, realizing that the next question would be the make-or-break one. If he's okay with it, then we can move forward with a real investigation. If not, he'll chop off my head.

The Archbishop noticed his reticence. "Something is bothering you, Dr. Feingold?"

Feingold nodded. "It's . . . well, it's that artifact that's supposed to be out in the Asteroid Belt."

"You know about that?" the Archbishop asked, his flesh-enfolded eyes narrowing to little more than slits.

"I've heard rumors," Feingold replied, trying to take some of the weight off the subject. "We all have. An alien artifact. They claim it drove Martin Humphries insane—temporarily, of course."

"Humphries refuses to allow anyone to see the artifact."

"Then it's real?"

"Apparently so."

Licking his lips with anticipation, Feingold hunched closer to the Archbishop and pleaded, "If I'm supposed to investigate every aspect of this Stoner phenomenon, I've got to get to that artifact. After all, it must be linked to Stoner in some way. It's got to be! It could be the key to the whole situation."

Warily the Archbishop replied, "Martin Humphries has quarantined the asteroid in which the artifact is housed. Not even the International Astronautical Authority is allowed to send investigators to it."

"And you're letting him get away with that?"

"Mr. Humphries is a very powerful man."

"As powerful as the New Morality? As powerful as you?"

The Archbishop leaned back away from Feingold's eager zeal, as if the scientist's breath offended him.

Feingold pressed, "You could get Humphries to allow one man, just one scientist, to visit that asteroid. Couldn't you?"

For several long moments the Archbishop did not reply. At last he asked, "Do you believe it's that important?"

"Like I said, it could be the key to the whole *shmeer.*" Instantly Feingold regretted his lapse into Yiddish. Too eager, he berated himself. Too damned eager. You'll blow the deal with your big mouth.

But the Archbishop looked thoughtfully, prayerfully, up to the ceiling. Then, turning his narrow eyes back to Feingold, he said softly, "I'll see what I can do, Dr. Feingold."

Feingold restrained the impulse to leap out of his chair and click his heels in glee. The artifact might or might not have something to do with Stoner, he told himself. But it's real, it's out there, and I'm going to see it! He felt a thrill he hadn't experienced since he'd been a graduate student and first started doing research into the unknown.

CHAPTER 7

Stoner, meanwhile, was driving a rental car from Atlanta northward, with Sister Angelique beside him and Yolanda Vasquez huddled in her hospital blanket in the backseat, still clutching her book in both arms.

Automobile traffic on the interstate highway was sparse, although massive trailer rigs raced along in an almost unbroken procession in the lanes dedicated to truck traffic. Some of the rigs were three units long.

When they'd left the hospital, Angelique had watched as Stoner took her and the old woman out to a waiting taxi. He stopped the automated cab at the first car rental agency they came across as they neared the airport and smilingly talked his way into the sleek red sports sedan they now rode. It ran on hydrogen fuel, Angelique saw, and although its lines were flashy and stylish, its engine was unable to accelerate the car to more than one hundred kilometers per hour. A fuel-saving measure, she thought, although she realized that it was also a method of controlling speeders and youthful would-be daredevils.

Yet when Stoner stepped on the accelerator the engine growled like an angry lion. Angelique was startled by the noise, but Stoner grinned at her.

"A sound effect," he explained. "The car has a clean, quiet, efficient hydrogen engine, but the manufacturer makes it roar like an old Formula One racer, to make people think it's got a lot of power under the hood."

Angelique laughed to herself. A sound effect, she thought. A sop to the morons who need to hear *vroom-vroom* when they drive. A substitute for testosterone.

The rental agency clerk had asked for a driver's license, a credit card, and a travel authorization from the local transportation control authority. Stoner had shown her nothing, but she processed the paperwork anyway and rolled out the sedan for him.

"They'll track us down," Angelique said, raising her voice over the mock engine noise. "They'll find the records of this rental and—"

"There won't be any records," he replied. "As far as the rental company's files show, this car no longer exists."

She lapsed into silence and studied his face while he concentrated on driving at exactly the highway's speed limit. He seemed at ease, but his bearded face was unsmiling. God knows what's going on inside his head, she thought.

"Thanks for taking me out of that death trap," came the scratchy voice of the old woman in the backseat.

Stoner shifted slightly to glance at her in the rearview mirror.

"Why do you call it that?" he asked.

"'Cause that's what it is. They see an old geezer like me and figure I'm not worth anything. I need a replacement heart, but they say I'm not worth the trouble."

Angelique turned in her seat. "How old . . ." Then she stopped herself. "We don't know your name."

"Yolanda Vasquez. And I'm a hundred and seven. Be a hundred and eight in July, if I make it that far."

"How do you do?" Angelique said with stiff formality. "I am Sister Angelique Duprie."

"You're with the New Morality, aren't you?"

"Yes, I am."

"H'mph."

Stoner chuckled softly. "You're not happy with the New Morality?"

"Why should I be? They won't give me a new heart. Up in Selene, on the Moon, they'd treat me with stem cell therapy or nanomachines or something like that. These religious do-gooders down here don't believe in modern science."

"It's not that we don't believe—"

Stoner interrupted what he could see evolving into a lengthy argument. "What's that thing you're holding? A book of some sort?"

Yolanda Vasquez's wrinkled face tightened; her eyes went crafty. "Some sort," she rasped.

"It looks like an old-fashioned album," said Angelique. "For photographs that've been printed on paper."

"It's my scrapbook," Vasquez said almost sullenly. "My memories are pasted in its pages."

Stoner nodded. "Must be very interesting."

"It's private."

"I see."

"I'm sleepy," Vasquez muttered. And she curled up on the seat and closed her eyes.

Stoner drove in silence farther away from metropolitan Atlanta, deeper into the rolling hills of the city's exurbs. Rows of tract houses dotted the landscape, each of them looking very much like all the others. Shopping malls slid past, virtually identical to one another. Newer housing centers of high-rise towers. For the flood refugees, Stoner realized.

"Why did you take her with us?" Angelique asked, keeping her voice low so she wouldn't wake the sleeping old woman.

Stoner made a small shrug. "It was easier than allowing her to cause a fuss. Besides, I thought she needed some help."

Angelique lapsed into a thoughtful silence. At last she said, "I didn't thank you for taking me out of . . . of the hospital."

"You don't have to."

"Where are we going?" she asked.

He glanced at her. "That's up to you."

"Me?"

"Where do you want to go?"

The question startled Angelique. She realized she had nowhere to go, no one to turn to. Her life had been devoted to the New Morality and now they had made a prisoner of her, a criminal, a subject to be interrogated and tortured. I have no one, she knew, almost bursting into tears at the realization. No family, no friends. Then she looked up at Stoner's strong, gray-eyed face. No one but him, she thought.

CHAPTER 8

Almost as if he could read Angelique's thoughts, Stoner turned onto the next exit lane and down the ramp that led off the highway. To a seedy-looking motel.

Her breath caught in her throat. He wants me! Despite all his talk about being more than human, he's a male animal after all.

"You must be exhausted," he said. "A night's rest will do you good." Jerking his head toward the sleeping woman in the backseat, he added, "Her, too."

Vasquez woke as he parked the car in the motel's lot, making Stoner doubt that she'd really been asleep. He took her powerchair out of the car's trunk and unfolded it; then the three of them proceeded into the motel's shabby lobby.

Stoner took a pair of adjoining rooms for them, offering the young African-American woman behind the reception desk nothing but empty hands and a winning smile. They had no luggage, but the clerk took no notice of it. At Stoner's suggestion, she didn't even enter them in the motel's computer.

"We're 'most empty," she said, smiling back at Stoner. "Take any rooms y'all want."

The rooms were threadbare but clean. In a glance Angelique took in the twin beds, the bureau, the wall-size video screen. While Stoner went to his room, she stepped to the connecting door and unlocked it. The blank face of the other door suddenly swung open and Stoner was standing there, filling the doorway.

Her breath gushed out of her.

"Sorry," he said. "I didn't mean to startle you."

"It's . . . it's all right."

"This place should be safe enough for the night," he said.

"The security cameras in the lobby," Angelique said. Pointing, she added, "And here in the rooms."

Stoner nodded. "They won't show anything."

"How do you . . . ?"

He broke into a boyish grin. "It's a gift."

From her powerchair Yolanda Vasquez asked irritably, "When do we eat?"

Stoner laughed and said, "It's probably best if we eat here in the room, instead of going to a restaurant."

Vasquez nodded agreement. "Don't want to be seen in public if we can avoid it. They didn't want to help me, but they've probably got the state police out looking for me."

Angelique suddenly realized, "They could be after us for kidnapping!"

"Some kid," Vasquez grumbled.

"I'll go to the nearest fast-food place and get us some dinner," Stoner said.

"So why are they after you?" Vasquez asked as she reached for another drumstick.

There's nothing wrong with her appetite, Angelique thought. For a shriveled old prune of a hundred seven she eats like a teenager.

The three of them were in the room the two women were sharing. Stoner had pulled in a chair from his own room so they could all sit around the chipped plastic table and share the meal.

But Stoner hadn't touched the bucket of fried chicken, nor the coleslaw, buns, or cola. Angelique realized that she had never seen him eat anything at all.

"The New Morality wants me," Stoner replied to the old woman's question.

Vasquez nodded, as if the answer satisfied her. But then she asked, "What for?"

Stoner smiled and countered, "Did you notice the Northern Lights the past few nights?"

"Northern Lights?"

Slowly, as the two women ate from the plastic containers, Stoner explained who and what he was.

Vasquez seemed unimpressed. "So they think you're a nutcase, is that it?"

Stoner broke into a laugh. "Close enough," he acquiesced. "Close enough."

"What made you come with us?" Angelique asked.

Vasquez frowned. "My regular doctor had them take me to the hospital. Young pup said my heart was going to go. So they look me over in the hospital and say I'm too old to get a replacement heart. Tree-age, they called it."

"Triage," Angelique murmured.

"Whatever. All they were going to do was pray over me and wait for me to fold up. Screw that! When I go I want it to be on my own terms."

"They allowed you to roam the hospital corridors?" Stoner asked.

"Sure. They figured an old bat like me can't get away from them, not with security checkpoints every hundred meters and me stuck in a powerchair."

"Then you latched onto us," said Angelique.

"You bet. I saw you two waltzing past the security goons, sweet as pie, no badges, no papers, no nothing. So I figured I'd tag along with you."

"With your scrapbook," Stoner said.

For the first time, Vasquez looked uneasy. She glanced at the big square book where it was resting on one of the beds. She muttered, "With my scrapbook, right."

"May we see it?" Stoner asked as he started to get up from his chair.

"It's private!" Vasquez snapped. "I'm going to send it to my great-grandniece. She's on—"

She gasped. Her eyes went wide. She clutched at her chest and collapsed in her chair. Her skin went gray, sheened with perspiration.

Stoner went to her side and grasped her frail shoulder.

"She's having a heart attack!" Angelique said. "We'll have to call an emergency team."

"No," said Stoner. "They'd just look up her file and let her die."

"But . . ."

"I'll take care of her," he said. He pressed a hand against Vasquez's scrawny, corded neck. He's searching for a pulse, Angelique thought.

Her eyes half-closed, Vasquez breathed in a deep, shuddering sigh. Her eyelids fluttered, then closed altogether. Stoner scooped up her feeble body in his arms and carried her to the bed. He set her down gently beside her scrapbook.

"Is she . . ."

"She's sleeping," Stoner said. "She'll be all right."

"How do you know?"

He hesitated, his face set in an irritated frown. But then his expression eased and he almost smiled at Angelique.

"You won't like my answer," he said softly.

"Why? What is it?"

"I'm helping her heart to rebuild itself. With a form of nanotechnology."

"Nanotechnology?" Angelique gasped. "That's against the law! It's forbidden!"

Patiently Stoner replied, "They use nanotechnology on the Moon. Out in the Asteroid Belt. People couldn't survive off-Earth without nanomachines."

"But it's evil!" Angelique insisted. "It's been outlawed everywhere on Earth."

"I know," he said. "But outlawed or not, it can be very helpful. It's saving this old woman's life."

Angelique looked from Stoner's hard, uncompromising face to Yolanda Vasquez, curled into a fetal position on the bed, sleeping peacefully.

Stoner bent down and picked up the scrapbook.

"She doesn't want us to look at it," Angelique reminded him.

"That's what makes me curious about it," he said.

RICK

Half a world away, General Carlos O'Hara awoke languidly. His bedroom was dark; only the digital display of his bedside clock glowed in the shadows. It read 4:14 A.M. He turned over and pulled the deep, warm blanket over him. I can get in another hour's sleep before the sun comes up, he told himself.

O'Hara had been the commanding officer of the United Nations Peacekeeping Force for almost two years. In another four months his tour of duty would be over and he could retire with honor to his home in Buenos Aires, respected and wealthy enough to live in comfort for the rest of his life. Leave the job to someone else, he told himself. Let the Americans search for terrorists in these miserable little villages; they create more terrorists than they kill. Let the Peacekeepers continue to monitor the drug trade; keep the narcotics industry under control and everyone is happy, even the news media.

He closed his eyes for another hour of pleasant sleep.

But something was wrong. For some strange reason, O'Hara got the feeling that he was not alone in his bedroom. Nonsense, he told himself. Go to sleep.

All the lights in the bedroom suddenly switched on. O'Hara opened his eyes and saw that a young man in the pale blue uniform of the Peacekeepers was standing at the foot of his bed, his hair dark, his eyes steel gray, his expression grave.

"What the hell are you doing here?" O'Hara demanded, his voice squeaking with shocked surprise. "Who are you? How did you get in here?"

"My name is Rick Stoner. I'm one of the star voyagers."

Sitting up in bed, O'Hara stared at his unexpected visitor. "Star voyager?" Inadvertently, he clutched at his dark green pajama blouse.

"You don't know about us?" Rick asked mildly. "They haven't told you?"

O'Hara turned to the phone console on his night table and shouted, "Phone! Security! Emergency!"

Rick shook his head a few centimeters. "The phone won't work. And I'm not going to harm you. I simply want some information."

Despite being a general, Carlos O'Hara had never been very proficient with firearms. He kept an automatic pistol in the closet across the room, but it was unloaded. He'd had a dread of causing an accident ever since he'd become a new father, back when he was only a lowly lieutenant in the Argentinian army. Both his sons were in the Peacekeepers now, and O'Hara had seen to it that they would continue to be promoted smoothly up the chain of command even after he'd retired.

Stoner didn't move toward him by so much as a millimeter, but O'Hara felt the consternation in his mind ease away. In its place he saw the star voyagers' ship, a glowing sphere of energy orbiting above the Earth. He learned that this strange visitor's father had seen the President of the United States and even Archbishop Overmire, head of the New Morality in North America.

And he understood what Rick Stoner wanted of him.

For more than an hour Rick Stoner stood unmoving at the foot of his bed as Carlos O'Hara explained how the Peacekeepers worked. And why.

"So you see," he was saying, his voice hoarse from speaking, his throat parched, "originally the Peacekeepers were founded on the best of principles, the highest of moral reasons."

"To prevent wars," Rick murmured. He glanced at the enameled water pitcher on the night table, and O'Hara gratefully poured himself a glass.

"To prevent"—O'Hara took a swallow of the cooling water—"small wars. Wars between minor nations. Wars that the United Nations could agree to stopping."

"And to prevent the spread of weapons of mass destruction," Rick added.

"Yes, that, too," said the general. "Only wealthy nations could afford to try to build nuclear weapons. But biological weapons, nanotechnology weapons, digital programs that attack a nation's computer networks—these are easier to develop and more difficult to root out."

"So the Peacekeepers try to find such developments and stop them."

"Yes."

"And the narcotics trade?"

O'Hara felt his insides jump. Yet he couldn't lie about it. Somehow this grim-faced young man was forcing him to admit the truth.

"We have reached an . . . an accommodation with the drug cartel," he admitted.

"An accommodation?"

"We are not allowed to stop the narcotics trade. Our mission is to keep it under control, to prevent it from harming the rich and powerful. Otherwise . . ." He shrugged.

"So the poor and hopeless can get the drugs that keep them poor and hopeless," Rick said.

"People will get narcotics one way or another," O'Hara temporized. "They invent new ones in college chemistry laboratories."

"And you profit from this accommodation. You've gotten rich from it."

"Not me alone! The others, too. In the United Nations. The U.S.A., elsewhere. Plenty of others."

"All making money from the drug cartel."

"And why not? People want drugs," General O'Hara said. "You can't stop them."

Strangely, Rick smiled. But it was not a pleasant smile. There was not a trace of humor in it. "Can't I?" he replied, almost in a whisper. "Watch and see."

CHAPTER 9

In the motel outside Atlanta, Stoner brought Yolanda Vasquez's oversized square book to the table. Angelique pushed the plastic food cartons to one side as he opened the big crinkled pages.

"Photographs," she murmured as he leafed through the pages. "Old-fashioned photos, printed on plastic microsheets."

"And menus from restaurants," said Stoner. "And these look like reports of some kind."

"Evaluation reports," Angelique recognized. "She must have been a schoolteacher. Look at how yellowed they are! Look, this one's dated from more than forty years ago."

"It's her pension form, from the date when she retired."

Angelique glanced at the woman sleeping on the narrow bed. "I wonder if she retired voluntarily or if it was mandatory."

They thumbed carefully, respectfully, through the big, brittle pages.

"Why was she so upset about our looking at this?" Stoner wondered.

"It's her life," said Angelique. "Her private life."

He shook his head. "There must be more to it. She got so upset she went into cardiac arrest."

Angelique looked up sharply at him, reminded that he was somehow using forbidden nanotechnology on the old woman. He must have nanomachines in his own body! she realized with a shudder. He transferred nanomachines into her when he touched her neck.

Then she saw he was smiling tightly at her. "I'm not a monster," he said mildly. "I'm not going to unleash a tidal wave of nanomachines that will devour everything in their path."

Angelique nodded and tried to keep her fear from showing. There were good reasons why nanotechnology was banned. Nanomachines were evil. They'd been used as weapons, used to kill people. They were the devil's invention.

But as she watched Stoner's handsome, aristocratic face, she thought that perhaps in his hands, under his control, even nanomachines could be used for purposes of good. The tools aren't evil, she told herself. The people who use them are. But he's beyond evil; he's practically a god.

Stoner, meanwhile, kept leafing through the scrapbook. "Some of these mementos aren't pasted down very securely," he muttered. He worked a fingernail under the corner of a photo of a group of children posing in a schoolyard.

"There's writing on the back of it," Angelique saw.

"Yes," said Stoner. Within a few minutes they had pulled off most of the pieces that had been lightly glued onto the scrapbook pages.

"It's a message," Angelique said, scanning the handwritten notes on the backs of the pieces. "A sort of diary."

"Yes," said Stoner. "A sort of diary."

It was nearly midnight before Angelique and Stoner finished reading the bits and scraps of Yolanda Vasquez's *Apologia*.

Stoner turned over the last slip of yellowed, crumbly paper—a greeting card for her "Big 30" birthday. Vasquez had covered its back with her tight, urgent handwriting.

"No wonder she wanted to keep this secret," he said,

looking over at Vasquez, still curled on the bed, sleeping soundly.

"It's a history of how the New Morality took over the country," said Angelique, her voice low, almost fearful.

Stoner shook his head. "They didn't take over the country. The people handed it to them. Willingly."

"They didn't realize what they were doing. They didn't understand."

"That doesn't change the situation," Stoner said, getting to his feet. "The United States is being run by an ultraconservative religious dictatorship."

"It's not a dictatorship!" Angelique snapped.

"No," Stoner replied softly. "And Rome was still technically a republic even when Nero was sending Christians to the lions."

Angelique started to object, but suddenly she felt utterly weary, totally drained. Too much had happened, was happening. She tried to stand up, but her legs went weak and she sagged against Stoner.

"You saved my life," she murmured.

"I don't think they meant to kill you," he said matter-of-factly. But his arms wrapped around her, held her protectively. "They were using you as bait to trap me."

"What are you going to do now?" she asked, breathless.

"That's up to you."

Angelique slid her arms around his neck and lifted her face to his. "I owe you my life."

Stoner picked her up off her feet and carried her to the empty bed. He deposited her gently and sat beside her on the sagging mattress. She stared up into those steel gray eyes, her heart pounding.

"Take me to your room," she whispered.

"Get a good night's sleep," he said softly. "We'll make some decisions in the morning."

Angelique clutched at him. "Don't go! Don't leave me alone."

Stoner looked down at her, his expression strange, unreadable. "I'm human enough to see that you're a very lovely woman, and very desirable. But you're also very frightened and vulnerable." Then he smiled and added, "Besides, you have your vows to keep."

"I don't care about that!" she said, a flood of seething emotions blazing through her. "I want you! I love you!"

But Stoner slowly shook his head. "I can understand that you want me, and you instinctively feel that the best way to bind me to you is through sex. That's a very normal primate reaction."

"You're a primate ape, too, aren't you?"

"I'm afraid it doesn't work that way for me. Not anymore."

"What are you saying?"

"I'm enough of an ape to be tempted, Angelique. But there's more to it than that. So much more."

He got to his feet and went to the connecting door. "Go to sleep," he whispered.

Angelique felt a soft, warm, comforting fog envelop her. Every muscle of her body relaxed. Her eyes fluttered shut.

But just before she sank into the dark oblivion of sleep she told herself, He doesn't want me. He looks at me as if I'm some sort of a specimen in a zoo.

Her last conscious thought was, He's disgusted by me!

CHAPTER 10

In the morning Angelique felt refreshed and strong. But smoldering with hurt and angry resentment.

Vasquez's rumpled bed was empty. The old woman was nowhere in sight. Angelique saw the scrapbook lying on the table, closed, all the photos and letters and other pieces out of sight. He must have pasted them all back in place while I was sleeping, she thought.

She sat up in bed, still fully dressed. The memory of Stoner's rejection made her cheeks flush hotly. She got to her feet and went to the bathroom. She showered quickly, but not even the jets of hot water could wash away the pain and humiliation she felt. Grimacing with distaste, she dressed in the same clothes she had worn the previous day. She had nothing else to wear.

As she stepped out of the bathroom she heard Vasquez's thin, cackling laughter through the slightly ajar door that connected to Stoner's room.

She went to the door and, opening it, saw Vasquez sitting in her powerchair, Stoner on the edge of one of the beds, a breakfast of sticky buns and coffee on the table between them.

Stoner looked up and smiled at her. "Good morning! You're just in time for breakfast."

"Good morning," Angelique murmured. She pulled up the only other chair in the room and sat next to the old woman.

"Morning," said Vasquez cheerfully as she chewed on a bun.

"How do you feel?" Angelique asked her.

"Fine. Wonderful. Haven't felt this good since I was ninety." She giggled at her own joke.

Nanomachines, Angelique thought. He's rebuilt her heart with nanomachines.

"And guess what?" Vasquez asked brightly. "I'm going to the Moon! I'm going to be accepted as a candidate for citizenship in Selene!"

Angelique looked sharply at Stoner as Vasquez bubbled on, "He just picked up the phone right there between the beds and talked to Douglas Stavenger himself, up in Selene. Got me approved as an immigrant inside of ten minutes!"

Forcing a thin smile, Angelique said, "Dr. Stoner can be very persuasive."

Stoner fixed his gaze on her. "And you, Angelique? Have you decided where you want to go?"

She lifted her chin a notch. "Yes. I'm returning to Archbishop Overmire."

Stoner's expression hardened. "You were a prisoner under interrogation when I took you out of there."

"Yes, I know. But the Archbishop will want to see me now, I'm sure. I have a lot to tell him."

"All right," Stoner said slowly. "I'll take you back after I put Yolanda here on the rocket for Selene."

"You don't have to do that. I won't tell them about her and her scrapbook."

Vasquez's chin lifted a notch at the mention of her scrapbook.

"I didn't think you would, Angelique," Stoner half-lied. "I just think it would be better if I went with you."

"No need for that," Angelique said flatly. "I can get back to the New Morality headquarters by myself. I won't need any help from you."

Stoner felt some misgivings as he waited outside the motel's lobby with Angelique for the autotaxi she had phoned for. It was a cloudy morning, chilly and threatening rain.

"You're sure this is what you want to do?" he asked her.

"Positive," she snapped.

"They didn't treat you all that well yesterday."

"It's different now."

Stoner watched her intently. He saw anger in her sculpted face, the anger of rejection. And he heard his wife telling him:

She's in love with you, Keith. And you rejected her.

She doesn't have any romantic feelings for me, he replied. It's power that she's after.

He could sense Jo shaking her head. After all these years, you still don't understand, do you?

Understand what? he asked.

Women. Human emotions. She wants power, yes, certainly. But she's in love with you. Which makes her dangerous.

If it's power she's after, why does she want to go back to Overmire?

Because if she can't have you, she'll go to the next most powerful man she knows.

But why?

To tell him how to get rid of you, Jo said coldly.

Stoner felt some surprise at that. Get rid of me?

She can't have you for herself, so she's going to do her damnedest to make certain no one else gets you.

He finally understood. She wants to help Overmire get rid of me. That's good, then.

That's good?

Yes. It means she doesn't want to help Overmire learn how to use me for his own benefit.

His own benefit, Jo scoffed. The man runs all of North

America and has his tentacles stretched across the world. He doesn't need you.

Yes, but he needs to make certain I don't threaten his power.

Power, Jo said silently, and Stoner could sense the loathing in her thoughts. It's all about power, isn't it?

It's always about power, he said.

Once Angelique ducked into the autotaxi and headed back toward Atlanta, Stoner returned to Yolanda Vasquez's motel room. The old woman was sitting in her powerchair, looking fresh and vigorous, her wispy white hair glistening from her shower. She clutched the scrapbook to her frail chest.

"You read my scrapbook, didn't you?" she said as soon as he closed the door. She didn't look angry or even disappointed, Stoner thought.

"Yes, we did."

"I meant those writings for my great-grandniece, up in the rock rats' habitat at Ceres."

"I apologize for intruding on your privacy," he said. "But what you wrote was very enlightening to me. I was having a difficult time understanding how a democracy can slide into virtual dictatorship."

"Nothing virtual about it," Vasquez said. "You'll find out when you try to get me through the spaceport."

Hartsfield Aerospaceport was immense, thundering with the constant roar of jet airliners and rocket vehicles landing and taking off. Stoner parked the rented sports sedan at the terminal's curb, then pulled Vasquez's powerchair out of the trunk, unfolded it, and helped her settle into it comfortably.

A police robot trundled up to them. "No parking or waiting is allowed at curbside, sir."

"Yes, I know," said Stoner.

"Vehicles left unattended will be towed," said the robot's synthesized voice.

Stoner smiled at the stubby little machine, even though he knew it was not programmed to recognize facial expressions. All it knew was the parking regulations and violations thereof.

"Let's go," he said to Vasquez. She gave him a questioning look.

"Vehicles left unattended will be towed," the robot repeated. Somehow it sounded annoyed.

To Vasquez, Stoner said, "They'll tow the car and eventually return it to the rental company. They'll be glad to get it back." He grinned down at her. "Although I imagine there'll be some head-scratching over the time their car's been away."

Vasquez chuckled as she toggled the powerchair into the terminal. Walking alongside her, Stoner thought she looked much stronger than she had the day before. The nanomachines had rebuilt her heart and were now going through her system searching for other needed repairs.

Vasquez kept her mouth shut and let Stoner do all the talking as they moved from ticket counter to security inspection and finally to the terminal gate where the Moon-bound rocket launcher sat on its tail, a squat, truncated cone built of pure diamond in Selene's lunar manufacturing centers.

He walked her into the Clippership's passenger compartment and watched her switch from the powerchair to an aisle seat without any assistance from him.

"I'll have the flight attendants stow your chair for you," he said, leaning over her, "although I don't think you'll need it once you're on the Moon."

Vasquez looked up at him, suddenly troubled. "But

what'll I do once I'm there? I don't have any money, no pension, nothing."

Stoner said, "Stavenger told me they need elementary school teachers."

"They do?"

"Selene's population is growing and they have more children than they can deal with. They need schoolteachers, nurses, day-care people. Governments here on Earth make it tough for their citizens to emigrate to Selene. There's even a shortage of babysitters, from what he tells me."

Vasquez stared up at him. "Really?"

"Really."

She blinked tears away, then suddenly wrapped her thin arms around Stoner's neck.

"Thank you," she whispered into his ear. "Thank you for getting me out of this prison."

CHAPTER 11

Angelique felt almost as powerful as Stoner himself as she made her way through the security guards at the New Morality's headquarters complex. When she left the autotaxi at the complex's main gate, the guards on duty directed her to the small, low-roofed building marked, VISITOR'S ENTRANCE.

It was a security checkpoint, of course. The young, bushy-haired guard at the desk just inside the door grinned up at the sight of the slim, beautiful young woman, despite her dark religious garb. But his grin faded as she presented her ID chip and he looked up her official dossier.

"Attached to the Archbishop's staff," he muttered,

looking at her with new respect. Then the computer beeped and he returned his attention to the screen.

"Hold on," he said, his expression changing again. Now he looked suspicious.

While Angelique fidgeted impatiently before his desk, the guard turned in his wheeled chair toward the open doorway that led deeper into the building and called, "Captain, you'd better look at this."

The guard captain came up, a wiry sandy-haired man in his thirties. His uniform bristled with merit decorations and award ribbons. The hash marks on his sleeves showed he had been in the security forces since he was a teenager.

Bending over the younger guard's shoulder, he said crisply to the computer, "Display security specification."

The two men read the screen, then looked at each other. The captain straightened and said, "Sister Angelique, we're instructed to take you directly to Archbishop Overmire."

Angelique let out a breath that she hadn't realized she'd been holding. "That's fine," she said softly. "That's perfect."

Two uniformed security guards drove Angelique in a quiet, unmarked electric minivan to the Archbishop's vicarage. They went with her as one of the female staff workers led them to a small conference room off the Archbishop's office. The woman ushered Angelique inside and instructed her to wait.

"It may be a little while," she said sweetly in a semi-whisper. "The Archbishop is a very busy man."

Angelique nodded and sat in one of the padded swivel chairs that lined the oval conference table. The woman left the room and closed the door. Angelique didn't hear a lock click, but she thought that her two security escorts were probably stationed on the other side of the door. The room was austere: blank wall screens, the polished conference table, and its set of eight chairs. Nothing more.

Angelique resigned herself to wait. But as she sank back into the chair she suddenly thought that Dr. Mayfair or one of the other inquisitors might come through that door and drag her back down to that interrogation room again.

No, she told herself. They wouldn't. But still she trembled.

For more than half an hour she waited, rehearsing in her mind what she would tell the Archbishop. Get rid of Stoner. Get him out of the picture. Make him—

One of the wall screens slid aside and Archbishop Overmire stepped ponderously into the conference room, his fleshy face set in a suspicious scowl.

Angelique rose to her feet as the Archbishop settled his bulk into the chair at the head of the table, then motioned with one hand for her to sit down.

"You got away from him?" Overmire asked without preamble.

"He let me go," said Angelique. "His only interest was to get me away from the inquisitors."

The Archbishop studied her face for a few moments. "We're learning about him. He cares about you enough to snatch you away from our interrogation team."

But not enough to love me, Angelique added silently. He thinks about me the way I would think about a chimpanzee in a laboratory.

"And although he can transport himself wherever he chooses," the Archbishop continued, "he apparently cannot take anyone along with him. He had to walk you out of the hospital. Past all our security people, I admit, but he didn't just whisk you into thin air, did he?"

"No, Your Eminence, he did not."

"What else have you learned about him?" the Archbishop asked, leaning slightly toward her.

Angelique thought swiftly, then answered, "Although he claims that he wants to save the human race, I believe he's a great danger to us."

"As do I," Overmire agreed.

"If he reveals himself to the general public they will fall to their knees at the sight of his powers and worship him as a god," she said.

"The Antichrist."

She nodded. "Whether he wishes it or not, he will shatter everything that you have toiled all your life to achieve. The people will adore him as their new savior."

The Archbishop's face darkened. "Our worst fears come true."

Angelique could read the expression on his face almost as if she could hear his thoughts. Stoner will destroy us. Destroy me, the Archbishop was saying to himself. All the years I've labored to reach the pinnacle of power, all the toil and care I've lavished on my flock, teaching them the way to salvation, leading them on the path of righteousness, controlling them so that they don't fall into evil ways—this one man, this star voyager, he could destroy it all.

"Therefore," she went on, "we must get rid of him, somehow."

"Somehow? How?"

Angelique saw the anxiety in his eyes, his need to find a way to deal with this terrifying threat.

And more. She saw the man who casually had turned her over to torturers, who was willing to do whatever was necessary, anything, in order to keep his power, to maintain his absolute grip on the New Morality's apparatus, his control over the people.

"Let me deal with him, Your Eminence," she said, hiding her anger, her growing disgust with the man. "Give me a free hand to deal with him as your personal representative."

"And what will you do?"

Angelique had no idea. But she saw that she could use the threat of the star voyager to bend Overmire to her will.

"He fears our nuclear weapons," she blurted impulsively. "I will use them to destroy him."

Even as she spoke the words she realized that this was indeed the way to destroy Stoner.

CHAPTER 12

"Could you get Stoner to come here?" Holly asked Raoul Tavalera.

It was nearly sunset in *Goddard.* The long windows that admitted sunshine into the massive habitat were slowly closing. Holly and Tavalera were walking from her office to a restaurant on the other side of the village, at the edge of the lake.

"Come here?" he asked. "I dunno. He does pretty much what he wants to."

"He could be awful helpful to us," she said. "Now that we've voted out the ZPG regulation, women're having babies. Sooner or later we'll need to expand, build another habitat."

"And go out and get more resources to support them," Tavalera added.

"Water," she agreed. "Ores to use for building materials."

"You want Stoner to help," he said.

"Surely do. If he would."

Tavalera stooped down to pick up a pebble from the edge of the bricked walkway. "But you could build a new habitat on your own, without his help."

"Be a damn sight easier with him than without him."

"Yeah, I guess."

He tossed the pebble into the air, caught it again in his palm. "You got any idea where this little stone came from, originally?"

Looking puzzled, Holly answered, "An asteroid, prob'ly. That's where most of our construction materials came from."

He nodded. "Now we're a long way from the Belt. A long trip to get resources."

"That's why Stoner'd be so helpful," she said.

His long, normally morose expression grew even gloomier than usual. "But don't you think it'd be better if you could build new habitats on your own, without his help? I mean, you shouldn't hafta depend on Stoner and his magic tricks."

With night coming on swiftly, she had to look hard to see his eyes. "What's th' matter, Raoul? Don't you want to let Stoner help us?"

"I don't think it's a good idea to depend on him, that's all. You oughtta be able to do it for yourself."

"You don't want to ask him, is that it?"

He shook his head. "No, that's not it."

"Then what?"

"I don't think he'd help you."

"Why not?"

Tavalera didn't quite know how to phrase it. For several paces along the winding pathway he was silent, thinking, arranging his words.

"So?" Holly prompted.

"I've seen Stoner close up. Seen him at work."

"You think he won't want to help us?"

Feeling miserable about dashing her hopes, he said, "I think he won't want you to become dependent on him. I think he'd figure it's better if you work things out for yourselves."

Holly looked away from him. Tavalera walked along with her, wishing he hadn't told her what he truly felt, knowing he had to tell her something more, something worse.

"That's how you see it, huh?" Holly murmured.

"Yeah."

Up ahead, through the shrubbery that lined the winding path, he could see the lights of the restaurant turning on. It was fully dark now. Tiny fluorescent patches glowed every few meters along the edge of the walkway. Tavalera looked overhead and saw the lights of other villages winking on, other pathways curving between them. He remembered that some wags had started to name constellations from the lights, just as people on Earth millennia ago had created pictures in the sky out of the formations of stars.

"There's the Bullseye," he said, pointing to a set of nested rings that marked a residential complex.

Holly made a huffing sound. "D'you know that Mal Eberly is puttin' up an astrology program on his site? Based on the lights?"

"Sounds like something he'd do," Tavalera said.

The restaurant was only a few meters away. He could see the squat little robots lined up to one side of the outdoor tables, waiting for customers to show up.

"Raoul," Holly said in a tone that sounded utterly serious to him.

"Yeah?"

"You kept sayin' 'you've' got to do without Stoner, instead of 'we've' got to."

"Did I?"

"Yep. Don't you think you're part of us? Part of me?"

He couldn't see her face in the shadows cast by the tall shrubs, but he heard the apprehension in her voice. She knows, he understood. She's figured it out.

"I've got to go back," he said, so low that he could hardly hear it himself.

She stopped walking. "Back? Earthside?"

He nodded, then realized that she couldn't see it in the shadows. "To Earth," he admitted.

Holly said nothing for several heartbeats. Then, "Your mother."

It was an excuse he could use, but Tavalera couldn't help but be honest with her. "Not just that, Holly. There's something going on, something big."

"Stoner."

"Something's going to happen; I just know it. I want to be there. I want to help him, if I can."

"You want to leave me." Her voice was dead, hollow.

"I've got to," Tavalera said. "I've just got to."

BOOK V

RAOUL TAVALERA

You who are without sorrow for the
suffering of others,
You do not deserve to be called human.

Garden of Roses, by Sa'di,
thirteenth-century Iranian poet

CHAPTER 1

Stoner felt Raoul's call, rather than heard it. Like a sudden change in his pulse rate, like an abrupt shortage of breath that leaves you gasping, Stoner felt Tavalera's need for him viscerally—even though he was disembodied when the call reached him.

Through Tavalera's mind, he saw that the young man believed he was sitting with a woman at a small table in an outdoor restaurant in the habitat *Goddard.* Holly Lane, Stoner knew. *Goddard*'s chief administrator. The woman Tavalera loved. He felt morose; she looked miserable.

Stoner's wife told him, Imagine how I'd feel if you said you wanted to leave me.

As if I could, he replied. They both smiled ethereally, linked to each other by bonds that transcended physical presence.

The restaurant was called Le Bleu Provence, founded by a Parisian who had been exiled for his mildly heretical and decidedly treasonous insistence that the current faith-based government of France had made a mockery of the Declaration of the Rights of Man.

"We've been through this before," Holly was saying, toying idly with the stem of her aperitif glass.

"Yeah," said Tavalera. His beer was going flat.

"You said you'd go back Earthside for a visit and then come back here."

"I know. But once I got there they wouldn't let me leave."

"So what makes you think—"

"May I join you?" Keith Stoner stood at their table, his bearded face serious, unsmiling.

Holly looked up at him, more annoyed at the interruption than anything else. "Where'd you come from?" she snapped.

Tavalera pushed his chair back and got to his feet. "Holly, this is Keith Stoner, the star voyager. Dr. Stoner, Holly Lane."

Stoner extended his hand to Holly. She touched it briefly, almost unwillingly.

One of the robots placed a chair behind Stoner and held it while he sat down, then trundled away with the faintest whirr of its electric motors.

Before Stoner could speak a word, Holly complained, "You claim there's gonna be a nuclear war on Earth and he"—she pointed at Tavalera—"he wants to rush back there."

"To help stop it from happening!" Tavalera exclaimed.

Holly shot him a bitterly unhappy look.

Stoner said mildly, "It's a tough decision to make."

She glared at him.

"Ms. Lane . . . may I call you Holly?" Stoner asked.

"Why not."

"It's difficult for you to accept, I know," Stoner said. "You love Raoul and you want him to be with you."

"He says he loves me," she muttered.

"And I do!" Tavalera replied.

"And he does," Stoner echoed. "But I'm afraid Raoul's gotten himself tangled in something bigger." Before Holly could respond, he went on, "The survival of the human race."

"We can survive here on this habitat just fine," Holly

said. "Let those nutsos blast themselves down to quarks; we'll still be here."

"You can let twelve billion human beings die without lifting a finger to help save them?"

She looked unflinchingly into Stoner's gray eyes. "Nothin' I can do about it."

"But perhaps there is something that Raoul can do."

"Like what?"

Stoner hiked his dark brows. "I've got to admit that I don't know yet. But I'd appreciate his help."

"You're both crazy."

"Maybe so," Tavalera said. "But it's something I've got to do, Holly. Can't you understand that?"

"No."

Shaking his head ever so slightly, Stoner said, "I could quote you chapter and verse about how some men feel impelled to go out and face the dangers that they feel are threatening their homes, their families. It's like a genetic imperative."

"Raoul's home and family are right here!" Holly snapped. "He doesn't have to go back Earthside. Let them blow themselves to hell!"

"I can't," Tavalera said, almost pleading. "I just can't, Holly."

Stoner looked at Holly through Tavalera's eyes and saw the root of the problem. Holly Lane was a newborn, a woman who had been preserved cryonically after being declared clinically dead of an inoperable cancer. After years of storage in a liquid nitrogen dewar at Selene she had at last been cured, her tumor eradicated by a team of lunar biomedical specialists using beams of antiprotons. But once her body was revived she had no memories of her earlier life. A newborn in a young adult's body, Holly had to learn to speak, to walk, to take care of herself all over again.

She has no memories of Earth, Stoner realized. It means nothing to her.

But Tavalera was different. Tavalera had friends and family and a whole childhood of memories. Earth was his emotional home.

With a sigh, Stoner said to them, "This is a decision you'll have to make for yourselves. All I can tell you is that I'd welcome your help, Raoul. There's a lot to be done back on Earth and I could use all the help I can get."

"What do you plan to do?" Tavalera asked.

"I wish I knew," Stoner said almost wistfully. "I really wish I knew."

CATHY

Cathy spent several days in Cairo, visiting the great pyramids, walking the city's crowded streets, thronged with jostling crowds.

And thinking about Mina. She's intelligent; she's had a decent education; she's got a good job: she could have a bright future ahead of her. Yet all she wants is to be married and have children. It didn't make sense to Cathy.

It's their upbringing, her mother said in Cathy's mind. Like their religion: they're trained from childhood, brainwashed into believing that's the way life should be.

How can we change that? Cathy asked silently as she strolled along a row of shops. The sidewalk was crowded, and the sun felt oppressively hot despite the energy shell that protected her.

You can't change it, Jo replied with some bitterness. It would take generations to get them to see otherwise.

I wonder, Cathy thought.

Besides, Jo added, your father doesn't want us to interfere with their way of life too much. He wants them to find the answers for themselves.

But we could help them, couldn't we? At least a little bit? Cathy asked. Guide them along the way?

Her mother replied, It's a fine line between guidance and control.

Cathy walked into a covered arcade, out of the blazing sunlight. The crowds here were even thicker than out on the street. The shops were very upscale, posh, appealing to the tourist trade. The tourists were pushy, loud, and short-tempered from lugging their packages from store to store.

On and on Cathy walked, beyond the arcade, past the rows of glittering shops and the bustling crowds of tourists. She kept to the shaded side of the street as much as she could, her mind still working on the problem of Mina. She's a microcosm of the world's population problem, Cathy thought. If an intelligent, educated woman can't see beyond having six or seven babies, how will the world's population problem ever be solved?

Not even her mother had an answer for her.

Cathy realized that the temperature had become somewhat cooler. The sun had dipped below the skyline, she saw. Looking around, she realized that she had walked far from the city's thronged market district. The street she was on was quiet, almost empty. Evening shadows were stretching across the pavement. The buildings here were low, two and three stories, small shops already shuttered. Up ahead was an open area: it looked to her as if a building had been demolished and the site left to rubble-strewn weeds.

Behind you, Jo warned.

Cathy glanced over her shoulder to see a trio of

young men in shabby T-shirts and baggy trousers ambling along the street, their eyes fixed on her.

I'll pull you out, her mother said.

Not yet, said Cathy. I want to see what they want.

They want you!

Oh, Mother, don't be so ancient.

Cathy kept on walking, but now she could hear the soft padding of their sneakers on the uneven pavement behind her. Then one of the men—boys, really—whistled. Another one snickered.

She kept to her steady walking pace, and within a few steps they pulled even with her.

"Hello, pretty," said one of them in heavily accented English. They all had ragged beards and bad teeth.

Cathy said nothing, kept walking.

"You American?"

Jo said, I'm bringing you up!

Not yet.

"American girls not virgins," said the one on her left.

"American girls all whores," the one on her right added, grinning widely. Cathy could smell his breath. Tobacco. And other things.

The third one skipped a few paces ahead of her and flicked a knife out of his pant pocket.

"Come on, whore," he said.

Cathy glanced at the knife for an instant and it suddenly began to glow white-hot. The young tough dropped it with a yowl of agony. The other two tried to grab her but screamed as electric shocks spasmed their bodies.

Cathy looked at the three of them, writhing in pain.

All right, Mom, she said mentally. Now.

She disappeared like an electric light winking off, leaving the three would-be rapists staring goggle-eyed.

Back on the starship, Jo asked her daughter, "You're all right?"

"I'm fine, Mom," Cathy replied, her expression utterly serious. "And I know what we have to do."

"Do you?"

"Yes. But Dad's going to hate it. A lot."

CHAPTER 2

Angelique had a plan. It was vague, but the more she thought about it, the more the details became clear to her.

Stoner fears our nuclear weapons, she thought. He wants us to get rid of them. Very well, I'll invite him to witness their dismantling. An accident will happen. I doubt that even a star voyager could live through the megaton blast.

That was the core of her plan. But she could see problems with it. How can we prevent the blast from killing others? After all, Stoner wouldn't be foolish enough to witness the dismantling by himself. There would have to be other people present: technicians, news anchors. Perhaps even the Archbishop himself.

That possibility shook her. Of course the Archbishop should be there. He would *want* to be there; he'd insist on being at the center of attention, showing the star voyager that the New Morality was leading the way to a new world, free of nuclear weapons and the hellish threat of Armageddon.

Sister Angelique turned the plan over in her mind, time and again, all through her long working day. It wasn't until later that night, as she lay down on her narrow bed, that she realized she was planning murder.

The realization troubled her. Briefly. She closed her eyes and told herself that Archbishop Overmire had been perfectly willing to sacrifice her in order to deal with Stoner. Well, she would help the Archbishop become a holy martyr.

God's will be done, she told herself just before she lapsed into a tranquil sleep, undisturbed by troubling dreams.

It was at the annual Founder's Day banquet that the crucial piece of Angelique's plan fell into place.

The banquet was held in Washington, D.C., as usual, in the ornate old rock pile of a building that had once housed the National Museum of Natural History. Now it was a combination of religious shrine, visitor's center, and recruitment station for the New Morality, Inc.

In the grand, high-roofed entrance lobby where exhibits of elephants and extinct mastodons had awed visitors in the past, Angelique looked out upon a sea of dining tables, each covered with a spanking white tablecloth and gleaming disposable dinnerware. Men in tuxedos and women in bejeweled evening gowns were streaming in for an evening of good food and self-congratulatory speeches. Angelique, who had lived under her vow of poverty all her adult life, wrinkled her nose at them; the crowd looked to her like a mix of penguins and peacocks.

As Archbishop Overmire and his retinue of bishops (minus Bishop Craig, who was in Jakarta) marched in hierarchical order to their seats at the head table, followed by dignitaries led by the President of the United States, the final pieces of the idea finally clicked in Angelique's head. Impatiently she sat at her assigned table far off to the right of the speakers; she could hardly wait for the long evening to draw to its droning conclusion.

She noted that Archbishop Overmire had regained the few pounds he had lost in the hospital and then some. Despite the most inventive tailoring of his dark clerical suit, he still looked like a bloated black whale.

At last the final cliché had been uttered, the last standing ovation given, and the assembled diners began to file out of the hall, buzzing with muted conversations. A collection of the biggest donors was lining up to shake hands with the President and the Archbishop, of course. It wasn't enough for most people to see and listen to the great and famous; they still had the simian's urge to touch the alphas.

It was approaching midnight when the Archbishop finally broke free and headed for the elevator that would whisk him to his private apartment on the former museum's top floor, accompanied by a small phalanx of assistants and security guards. Angelique fell in with the cluster of dark-suited men. One of the security guards eyed her questioningly when she squeezed into the elevator, but his chief recognized her with a nod and a smile.

Once they reached the unmarked double doors of his apartment, the Archbishop turned to the small group of men with a weary smile. "I thank you all and hope you enjoyed the banquet."

Lots of nodding and murmured agreement.

"It's been a long evening. I'm very tired." He pulled a white silk handkerchief from his jacket and mopped his brow.

More murmurs and the group moved away, drifting back toward the elevator. The Archbishop opened his door. Angelique followed him into the apartment's sitting room and closed the door behind her.

The Archbishop turned toward her with a slight frown on his jowly face. "I won't need any assistance, thank you, Sister."

"Your Eminence, I must speak with you for a few minutes."

"I really am very tired," he repeated with steel in his tone.

"It's about the star voyager," Angelique said hurriedly. "I know how to get rid of him."

Archbishop Overmire blinked at her several times. At last he sank into the nearest armchair and gestured for her to sit next to him.

Without waiting for him to give her permission to speak, Angelique blurted, "You must call for an international meeting of the world's religious and political leaders."

"Must I?" Overmire replied, his voice dripping acid.

"The Holy Disciples, the Light of Allah, the New Dao, and the Red Chrysanthemum," Angelique said eagerly. "And the heads of state for all the governments on Earth."

"But why—"

"The reason for the meeting will be to discuss ways to ease international tensions and increase brotherhood across the world. Global food distribution, energy prices, climate stabilization, all the topics that contribute to international tensions."

Overmire's frown deepened. "Population growth?"

"Population growth also," said Angelique with a nod. "Of course."

"But not family planning. We can't allow any discussions that might lead to contraception and abortion."

"Certainly, Your Eminence. I understand."

"An international conference," the Archbishop muttered. "To ease global tensions." He allowed the beginnings of a smile to curve his heavy lips.

"That will be the reason we give to the public. The

actual reason will be to discuss how to get rid of the nuclear weapons."

Overmire's smile vanished. "We'll discuss that in secret, I presume."

"Of course," Angelique said. "And, as a gesture of good faith on our part, the New Morality will induce the United States' government to dismantle several of its nuclear weapons. As a demonstration, out in the desert where they've been built and stored."

Overmire rubbed his chins. "And you think this will satisfy the star voyager. You think he'll leave then?"

"No, Your Eminence. I think there will be a terrible accident. A tragic accident."

The Archbishop's narrow little eyes widened. "An explosion?"

"A nuclear explosion. Not even Stoner could live through that."

"That's . . . murder."

"An execution, Your Eminence. An execution of an enemy, a threat to the New Morality and all it stands for."

For several moments the Archbishop sat in his armchair in silence. At last he objected, "But how could you arrange it so that Stoner is killed and no one else? He's no fool, you know."

Angelique bobbed her head in agreement. "There will have to be other casualties. We'll keep them down to a minimum, but there will have to be others caught in the blast with him. Martyrs, even though they won't know it beforehand."

The Archbishop folded his hands over his expansive belly. "I suppose you can't make an omelet without breaking a few eggs, can you?" he murmured.

"No, you can't," Angelique said, barely suppressing the elation that she felt inside her.

The Archbishop held up his right hand. “Very well. I *am* very tired. It’s been a long evening.”

Angelique dutifully sank to her knees and bowed her head. Archbishop Overmire put his hand on her head and murmured a blessing.

She knew he was blessing not only her; he was blessing her plan also.

CHAPTER 3

Despite a lifetime spent in scientific research and administration, Bertram Feingold had never been in space. He had admired the stunningly beautiful images of stars and nebulae captured by space-born telescopes; he had thrilled at the discoveries of ancient villages on Mars; he had fought for better funding for the research stations orbiting the giant planet Jupiter and the hellhole of Venus. But he himself had never left Earth, not even for a stint aboard an orbiting space station, not even as a tourist exploring the wonders of Selene and the other settlements on the Moon.

Of course, space tourism was practically dead these days. You needed all sorts of government approvals to fly as far as one of the orbital hotels, because the New Morality frowned on pleasure seekers who wanted to try sex in zero gravity. There were even more layers of red tape to cut through before you were allowed to go to the Moon. Too many “tourists” never returned to Earth. Too many asked for political or religious asylum once they got to Selene. And received it.

Every year, it seemed to Feingold, it became more difficult even for scientists to gain permission to leave Earth temporarily to do research in space. The New

Morality didn't like having its comfortable twelfth-century view of the universe disturbed by new information, new knowledge, new facts. Feingold struggled hard to get those young, eager researchers to where their curiosity was pushing them. Sometimes he failed, but he counted his victories instead of his defeats.

So it was with a great deal of personal satisfaction, and not a little trepidation, that Feingold embarked on his mission to asteroid 67-046 and his rendezvous with the alien artifact.

His mission began with a liftoff aboard a cone-shaped Clippership, which carried him to a space station orbiting Earth. Feingold had studied all he could find about the physical effects of weightlessness that one encountered in orbit. It wasn't actually zero gravity, he knew. The structure of the space vehicle and all the equipment in it exerted a minuscule gravitational force. The correct term was "microgravity," but to normal human senses there was no discernable difference: zero g, weightlessness.

Of course, he felt just the opposite as the Clippership lifted off. A force of three gravities squashed him down in his seat, made his arms feel like lead weights. The noise was muffled by the passenger cabin's acoustic insulation, but still he could hear the roar of a thousand dragons bellowing from the Clippership's rocket engines. The vibration was scary, too.

And then it abruptly stopped. His arms floated off the seat rests. If he hadn't been buckled into the chair he would have floated free. It wasn't so bad. Feingold actually felt almost exhilarated. Until he turned his head to look at the passenger beside him. Then everything swayed and Feingold's stomach went hollow, as if he were falling from a great height.

He gulped down bile and gritted his teeth. Just relax, he told himself, trying to remember the instruction files he'd read. It's not like seasickness. It's just the fluids in your body rearranging themselves because they're no longer being pulled down by gravity. Methodically, he inventoried his symptoms, comparing them with what he'd read: stuffy head, empty gut, balance system in the ears saying you're falling, but your eyes tell you you're safely strapped into this nice, padded chair.

By the time the Clippership connected to the space station's air lock, Feingold felt that he could deal with zero g. Then he realized that they weren't in weightlessness anymore. The space station rotated to produce a feeling of nearly normal Earth gravity; the ship now shared that rotation and the feeling of weight it produced.

Feingold grinned as he unstrapped and stood up. I'm a space veteran, he told himself.

He didn't see much of the space station. A pair of uniformed attendants met him at the air lock and escorted him to the fusion torch ship that would take him to the Asteroid Belt. He didn't see the exterior of the fusion vessel at all. Its interior seemed larger than the Clippership, but he was the vessel's only passenger.

The attendants left him in a spacious compartment that looked to Feingold like some sort of lounge. The floor was carpeted, he saw. Comfortable upholstered chairs were scattered here and there and one wall ("bulkhead," he remembered, was the correct term) had a bar built into it.

The attendants from the space station left him there with a smiling, "Have a pleasant trip."

For several empty moments Feingold just stood there, surrounded by the luxury, uncertain of what he was supposed to do. Then a young woman in a sleek dolphin gray uniform stepped into the lounge and gave him a dazzling smile.

"Welcome aboard the *Darling Clementine*, Dr. Feingold," she said cheerily. "You must be a Very Important Person to have the ship all to yourself." She pronounced the capitals distinctly.

Feingold couldn't help staring at her.

"My name's Filomena Neuberg and I'll be your hostess for this flight."

"Filomena Neuberg?" he asked.

"Yeah. Dutch father, Portuguese mother. The guys in the crew call me Lobster Neuberg, but you can call me Filly."

She had an outstanding figure, Feingold realized. Some filly, he thought.

"Shall I show you to your stateroom?" asked Filomena Neuberg.

He had to swallow twice before he could reply, "Please do."

Darling Clementine rode its fusion torch engine at close to one g all the way out to the Belt, accelerating halfway and then reversing thrust to decelerate. Feingold had his run of the ship. He met and dined with the crew: pilot, navigator, engineer, and flight attendant Filly. The navigator was another woman, almost as young as Filly, but quiet, stolid, the kind of social introvert that gave technical people the reputation of being nerds. The pilot and engineer were cheerful enough, bright, and intelligent. They took turns showing Feingold every aspect of the ship.

"We have to angle quite a bit out of the ecliptic," the flight engineer told Feingold as they neared the end of their five-day flight. "The 'roid we're going to has a high inclination."

Feingold knew that Martin Humphries had ordered the asteroid moved to its peculiar orbit to discourage visitors.

"If you don't mind my asking," the engineer went on, "what's so important about this chunk of rock? Why's HSS got a ship stationed by it all the time?"

Feingold studied the young man's face closely. He had seen that expression in classrooms many times. The kid knew the answer to his question; he just wanted the professor to acknowledge that he had the right information.

Feingold decided to be enigmatic. "I think you know the answer to your question as well as I do."

The engineer's eyes brightened. "So it's true? There's an alien artifact inside the rock?"

With a sly smile, Feingold replied, "That's what people say."

The engineer broke into a laugh. "You're supposed to keep it secret, huh?"

Feingold gave him a shrug.

"Well, maybe I'll ask Filly to spend our last night with you and worm the information out of you."

Feingold felt his cheeks redden as he thought, I wish!

CHAPTER 4

By the time the fusion ship established its parking orbit around asteroid 67-046, Feingold had the beginnings of a trim little moustache sprouting on his upper lip. He had worn a moustache ages ago, when he'd been a snotty young undergrad student, but once he started his work as a researcher he quickly learned that the Powers That Be much preferred up-and-coming scientists to be clean-shaven. Feingold felt that his moustache was a small price to pay for advancement up the ladder of success.

Now, a career and a lifetime later, he spent the five days of the trip to the asteroid regrowing his old moustache. It came in gray, of course, but none of the crew twitted him about it and Filly even seemed to like it. As he inspected himself in the metal mirror above the sink in his stateroom's lavatory he thought, I can always shave it off on the trip back home.

Feingold thought he'd have to wear a space suit to go down to the asteroid's surface, but he found that the Humphries Space Systems team that was stationed in orbit around 67-046 had built an airtight dome on the surface of the little asteroid. Not so little, Feingold thought as he rode an HSS shuttlecraft to the dark, pitted, rough-surfaced rock. Ten kilometers wide sounds piffling, compared to the size of a planet or moon, but as the austere little shuttlecraft came down for its landing the rock grew bigger and bigger until it filled Feingold's vision entirely.

He saw boulders and swaths of what must be dust and, finally, the glassteel bubble that had been erected over the entrance to the tunnel that led to the artifact's chamber, deep inside the rocky asteroid.

Once the craft had set down on its springy, spidery legs a segmented access tube inched across the few meters of bare rock from the transparent dome and connected itself to the shuttlecraft's air lock. Within minutes, Feingold was able to walk in his shirtsleeves to the dome, although the almost nonexistent gravity of the asteroid caused him to bounce and stumble when he took his first steps. He had to steady himself by reaching out to the sides of the tube as he walked.

Inside the dome, he was greeted by a stubble-jawed, weary-eyed technician in rumpled coveralls bearing the HSS logo, who opened the metal hatch that led into the tunnel.

"Just follow the tunnel," he said, in a raw, scratchy voice. It sounded to Feingold as if the man hadn't spoken aloud in quite a while. He wondered how long he'd been stationed on the rock.

"Are you all alone here?" Feingold asked.

The tech shook his head. "Naw. There's three of us. We rotate shifts, two days down here, then four days up in the ship."

"You mean, even when there's no visitors somebody's stationed down here?"

The tech nodded bleakly. "Orders from Mr. Humphries his own self."

"How long are you stationed out here?"

"Three months at a time."

"Just the three of you?"

The man nodded unhappily. "It don't pay to get on Mr. Humphries' shit list."

Feingold wanted to say something more, but he found that he didn't know what it should be. The technician gestured to the open hatch.

"The chamber has an automatic gate. It's closed now, but by the time you get down there it oughtta be just about ready to open. Stays open for an hour, at least."

"An hour?"

"More or less. The gate operates on its own schedule, almost at random, but not quite."

"I understand," Feingold said. He saw clearly that the technician wasn't going down the tunnel with him. Squaring his bony shoulders and straightening his back as much as he could, he stepped through the hatch and started down the tunnel.

It was warm inside, and the gravity felt almost Earth normal. The tunnel was narrow, and in places so low that Feingold ducked his head as he walked along its downward slope. Must be an old lava tube, he said to himself. But then the ceiling got higher and smoother; the walls and floor were smoothed, too.

The tunnel made a sharp turn to the right, and Feingold found himself in front of an utterly blank metal door that completely blocked the tunnel.

Before he could think of anything to do or say, the metal slid silently upward and disappeared into the ceiling. Looking down, Feingold could see a thin groove where it had fitted into the stone floor.

He stepped across the groove and found himself in a round chamber. Its walls were smoothed but blank. It felt warm inside and smelled faintly of—lilacs? Can't be, Feingold told himself. But that's what the delicate odor reminded him of. Haven't smelled lilacs since I was in college in California, he said to himself, marveling at the barely detectable scent. He turned in a complete circle. Nothing. Just a bare-walled circular chamber. Like a womb made out of rock, he thought. Warm. And smelling of lilacs.

There's nothing here, he realized. But there's got to be something. Something's making that smell; there's no lilacs growing within five hundred million kilometers of here.

Then he noticed a tiny glow, like a firefly hovering before his face. But the glow was steady, unflickering, holding its place before his eyes.

It grew brighter. And brighter. Like a tiny star it blazed. Feingold's eyes began to burn. He cupped his hands atop them to cut the glare. Yet the light grew still brighter, dazzling, more and more intense. Feingold wanted to turn away, but he couldn't. Wanted to squeeze his eyes shut against the overpowering brilliance, but he couldn't.

For now he saw shapes in the radiance, shifting amorphous shapes at first, but they began to take form, to make sense. Feingold saw flaming stars and whirling galaxies, whole worlds coalescing out of clouds of gas and dust, massive stars blasting themselves into wild bubbling, seething balls of ionized gases in titanic supernova explosions. It was like being weightless again. He was hurtling through the universe, hurtling backward through time, back to the beginning and beyond, back to the birth of the universe.

And it all made sense! He understood how it all began and how it came to be what it was now and where the entire swirling, beautiful, awe-inspiring universe was heading. He understood it all! He laughed aloud as he peered deeper and deeper, down into the atoms, into the quarks, into the fundamental forces of energy that made the stars and planets and life itself.

Feingold's legs sagged beneath him and he slumped to the rock floor of the chamber, still laughing like a man drunk on the nectar of the gods. The chamber floor felt warm and somehow softly yielding. Feingold curled up and fell asleep, his face still wreathed in a smile of utter peace and happiness.

CHAPTER 5

Stoner pushed his chair back from the restaurant table and announced to Tavalera and Holly, "I've got to leave you."

Before either of them could say anything, Stoner explained, "I have another appointment, out in the Asteroid Belt."

Tavalera gave him a skeptical look. "You mean you can't be two places at the same time?"

With a wintry smile, Stoner replied, "Only when I absolutely have to."

And with that, he got up from the restaurant table and walked away, disappearing into the night.

Hardly speaking to one another, Tavalera and Holly finished their dinner, then strolled unhappily to the band shell, where couples were dancing to the languid beat of the latest Latino rhythms. They danced, holding each other close, feeling each other's body warmth. But Tavalera knew he was separated from Holly almost as completely as if he were already back on Earth.

"You could come back with me," he suggested as they walked back through the evening shadows to her quarters.

Holly shook her head. "I'm still chief administrator here, remember? I've got responsibilities."

After a few silent steps along the bricked path, Tavalera muttered, "Me, too."

"Raoul, you don't owe them anything!" Holly insisted. "They've treated you like crap! Why the hell do you want to go back to them?"

He shrugged. "I know you're right, Holly. But . . ."

"But you've still got to go."

Nodding, "I've got to. I can't explain why, but I've got to do it."

Strangely, she smiled up at him. "I know you do. And I know why. And I love you for it, dammit."

That caught him completely by surprise. "You do?"

"Yes. I'm as big an idiot as you are, I guess."

"I love you, Holly. I really do."

"I know."

Abruptly he was in Stoner's starship again, or at least the manifestation that Stoner showed him, in orbit around

Earth, incredibly blue and flecked with dazzling white clouds.

"I'm glad you decided to return," Stoner said. Yet his expression was far from joyous. He looked concerned, apprehensive.

Tavalera found himself standing in the beeping, blinking bridge of the ship, fully dressed, freshly scrubbed, even shaved.

"How do you do things like this?" he asked wonderingly. Before Stoner could reply, he added, "I know. It's a gift from the stars."

"It's something more than that, Raoul." Stoner hesitated a heartbeat, then added, "Something less, actually."

"What do you mean?"

His face grave, Stoner replied, "I've been testing you, Raoul. And you've passed with flying colors. So far."

Tavalera felt his brows furrow.

"You haven't been on the *Goddard* habitat," Stoner confessed. "You've been right here in my ship all the time."

"But I was *there*!" Tavalera insisted. "With Holly."

Shaking his head, Stoner explained, "That was all an illusion, Raoul. A test. I had to—"

"You tricked me?" Tavalera shouted.

"Yes."

"You mean I never really talked to Holly? Never went to the habitat?"

"I can't get around the facts of time and distance," Stoner said. "No one can. I set up an illusion for you. Your real-time conversations with Holly, your visit to the habitat—they were all illusions."

Tavalera balled his fists and took a step toward Stoner. "You lied to me? You made me think . . ." He wanted to punch Stoner's face. Hit him and hurt him.

Stoner stood before him, his arms at his sides. "I don't blame you for being angry. But I had to know."

"Know what?"

"That you'd place the welfare of the human race above your own desires. That even if you could stay with her aboard the habitat you'd choose to return to Earth."

"You lying sonofabitch! You mean Holly's out there still wondering why I haven't contacted her?"

"I contacted her. I explained to her what was going on here. That's how I got the inputs to simulate her reactions to you."

"And you've had me here in some kind of a trance all this time?"

"Here, and before that in your apartment in Atlanta. I'm sorry I had to deceive you, Raoul. I had to know what your choice would be."

"You tricked me! You made me think—"

"I made you think you were on the *Goddard* habitat. Yet you still chose to return to Earth and work to avert the nuclear war."

"And Holly's still out there, wondering why the fuck I haven't come back to her."

"She knows. I told her. She doesn't like it, but at least she knows what the story is here."

Tavalera sank down onto one of the couches in the starship's bridge. He realized it was a fake, an illusion. All this time he's been playing tricks with my mind, he told himself. He's been toying with me, like I'm some sort of puppy to be trained.

Stoner sat on the edge of the couch beside him. "Raoul, I could have controlled your mind and *made* you do what I wanted. But I wanted to have your free cooperation."

"Fuck you."

Stoner's dark brows rose a millimeter. "I don't blame you for being angry."

"Double fuck you."

"I need your help, Raoul. This task is too big for me to accomplish by myself."

"You can go to hell."

"And take the all the people on Earth with me?"

"I don't care about them!" Tavalera snapped. "All I want is to be back with Holly."

Stoner shook his head slightly. "That's not true, Raoul. When you had the chance to do that, you told her you had to come back to Earth."

"That was all make-believe."

"It was a test, and you made the decision. You didn't know it was an illusion. You thought it was the real thing."

"Yeah. Thanks a lot."

"Are you willing to help me?"

"No."

"Can't say I blame you," Stoner replied. "So what do you want to do?"

"I want to go to the habitat and be with Holly."

Shaking his head again, Stoner admitted, "I'm afraid I can't do that. Not unless I commandeer a spacecraft to take you there."

"No instantaneous travel, huh?"

"I can move this starship close to the speed of light, but I can't produce instantaneous travel. Nor instantaneous communications, either. That was all an illusion, I'm afraid."

Tavalera could feel his insides shaking. "So what do I do now?" he wondered aloud. "Where do I go?"

"Wherever you want to go," Stoner said. Then he added, "Within reason. Anywhere on Earth."

"There's nothing there for me. Nobody."

Stoner said nothing. His face was a blank mask,

watching Tavalera, waiting for him to think, to decide, to speak.

Anger overwhelmed him. Tavalera shot to his feet and leveled an accusing finger at Stoner.

"I've got nothing!" he roared. "Nothing! No friends, nobody on Earth who cares a rat's ass about me, except my mother, and they've got her so wrapped up she doesn't know up from down anymore."

"I could help her," Stoner said softly.

"Leave her alone! And leave me alone! Stay the fuck out of my head! Got that? I don't want you in my mind! Never again!"

Stoner nodded solemnly. "But where do you go from here, Raoul? Where do you want to go?"

"Angelique," he blurted, surprising himself. "She's the only person on Earth that I know. Maybe she can help me."

"Help you to do what?"

"I don't know and I don't care!"

"The New Morality didn't treat you—"

"I don't know anybody else!" Tavalera cried. "Send me back to Angelique. At least she cares about me—a little."

"That's what you want?"

"That's what I want."

Stoner said, "All right. That's what I'll do."

"Good."

"I'm sorry I did this to you, Raoul. For what it's worth, my wife warned me that it wouldn't work."

"Big fucking deal."

"I'm really sorry," Stoner said.

"Yeah, sure. Just stay out of my head. Understand? I don't want you inside my mind. Stay out! Leave me alone!"

Stoner nodded in helpless agreement.

CHAPTER 6

Angelique was in the office that Archbishop Overmire had given her, next to his own in the vicarage in Atlanta. It was a small, spare windowless room. But it was next to the seat of power.

She had spent the morning on the phone, speaking with bureaucrats in Greater Iran, China, Russia, and the capital of the European Community in Brussels.

The idea of a global conference to discuss their differences appealed to the bureaucrats. Each of them saw the advantage to their leaders of posing in a highly publicized meeting to espouse their pious hopes for peace and brotherhood. Even the most radical of the Muslims, who couldn't help frowning at dealing with a woman, and a black woman at that, seemed quite willing to take the idea to their mullahs and emirs.

I'll have to get the Archbishop to talk to the actual leaders, Angelique thought. Ling Po and the others will speak only to their opposite numbers, not a woman they believe to be beneath them. She almost giggled, thinking, They won't even be satisfied with speaking to the President of the United States. They know he's nothing but a figurehead. Archbishop Overmire is where the power is.

Then she did smile to herself. And I've got the Archbishop's power in my hands.

It was a surprise when the chief of security phoned to tell her that Raoul Tavalera was back in his apartment in the New Morality complex.

"Tavalera?" Angelique gasped. "When did he return? How did he get into the building?"

The chief looked more exasperated than puzzled. He

had gone through this kind of thing before and he obviously didn't like it.

"He was in his bed this morning," he said, glancing slightly off-camera to read the data off a different screen. "He must have come in during the night, but neither the guards nor the security sensors saw him."

"He's come back," Angelique mused.

"He says he wants to see you," the security chief reported. "Says he *has* to see you, actually."

She nodded. "Send him to my office, please."

In less than fifteen minutes Tavalera was ushered into her cubbyhole of an office. He looked upset, terribly unhappy.

"Raoul," she said.

"Hello, Angelique."

"Where . . . how . . ." She had a hundred questions, but she knew there was only one answer to them all. "Stoner," she said.

Tavalera nodded tightly. "Stoner."

"He wants to know what the Archbishop is doing about the nuclear weapons," Angelique surmised.

"I guess he does."

"You guess?"

With a shake of his head, Tavalera admitted, "He can't be trusted. He's just as bad as all the others, just as manipulating, just as . . ."

His voice broke. Angelique thought he was close to tears. She gestured him to one of the stiff-backed chairs in front of her desk.

"What's wrong, Raoul? What's happened to you?"

"Stoner tricked me. He . . ." Again Tavalera stopped.

"What do you mean?"

"He tricked me. He was *using* me." His dark eyes full of confusion and hopelessness, he blurted, "I've got nowhere to go! I've got nothing! Nobody!"

And Angelique thought she understood. She knew what he was going through. She'd been there herself, more than once in her life.

"Matthew 11:28," she murmured.

"What?"

" 'Come to me, all ye who are weary and heavy-laden, and I will give you rest,' " Angelique quoted.

"Bible stuff," Tavalera grumbled.

"But it's true, Raoul. It works. Give yourself to the Lord and He will take care of you."

"You mean give myself to the New Morality and they'll take care of me."

"*I'll* take care of you, Raoul. I'll help you. I care about you."

His eyes focused on her. "You will." His voice was heavy with suspicion.

"Help me, Raoul," Angelique coaxed. "Help me and I'll help you. Tell Stoner—"

"I'm not telling him anything!" Tavalera snapped. "I'm finished with him. He's done enough to me."

She drew back a little. He's angry with Stoner, she thought. Still, he's the only real link with Stoner that we have.

"Raoul," she said, trying to make her voice sound soothing, promising, "I'm working on an enormous project. An international meeting."

Tavalera nodded, his face still dark with distrust.

"Help me to make the arrangements. I could use your help, Raoul. I need someone I can trust."

He almost sneered at the word.

"And if you help me," Angelique went on, "I'll help you. Once the conference is finished, I'll see that you return to that habitat out by Saturn."

For a long moment Tavalera said nothing. Then, "And my mother, too."

Angelique nodded. "And your mother, too."

He thought about it for several silent moments. At last Tavalera said, "Okay. What've I got to lose?"

Angelique gave him her warmest smile, thinking, He's still a link to Stoner, whether he wants to be or not. I'll be able to reach Stoner through him. And by the time this conference is over, Stoner will be dead and we'll be rid of him.

Two mornings later, Tavalera was sitting before Angelique's desk while she summarized, "I've gotten the Archbishop to make a public announcement of the global conference to discuss the issues causing tensions in the world: population growth, food shortages, the growing lack of scientists and engineers."

He saw that she was edgy, her eyes darting from his face to other spots in the room. Cameras, maybe, he thought. She wants to get this down on video. Then he thought, Or maybe she's just rattled 'cause I've come back.

He knew there was more going on in Angelique's crafty little mind than she was telling him, but he didn't care. Once this is finished she'll send me back to *Goddard*. And Mom, too. She won't need me anymore and I won't need her, not once I'm heading back to Holly.

He heard himself ask, "What about the nukes? That's what Stoner was all worked up about."

Angelique's eyes focused on him. She hesitated, then replied, "No one will mention nuclear weapons in the public sessions."

"But in private?"

"That will be the major topic of discussion, of course." Again she paused a heartbeat, then added, "We're hoping that Stoner will appear before them. It would help enormously if he met with them, spoke to them."

Tavalera's expression hardened. "Stoner'll do whatever he feels like doing. But he said he's got something he wants to tell them, so I guess he'll show up."

"Good," said Angelique, a cautious smile curving the corners of her lips. "You'll let him know about it?"

"If he tries to contact me again."

"If . . . ?"

"I'm not his errand boy anymore," Tavalera said.

Looking alarmed, Angelique said, "But he's got to know! He's got to be there."

Tavalera shrugged. "He'll be there; don't worry."

"It's important," she insisted. "Vital. This whole conference is really for him. He's got to be there!"

Tavalera saw something in her face that he couldn't quite fathom. She's hiding something, he thought.

Aloud, he replied to her, "I don't know where he is and I don't care."

CHAPTER 7

Still feeling that he'd made a mistake with Tavalera, Stoner projected himself to the asteroid where Bertram Feingold had sunk into a happy slumber in the chamber that housed the artifact.

Feingold awoke to see a man standing over him. He was still in the artifact's warm rock womb of a chamber, but the dazzling light was gone. Feingold remembered the grandeur and harmony he had seen, the rhapsody of the stars that had sung more beautifully in his mind than any siren's lure. But it was fading now, slipping from his grasp like a dream even as he reached out mentally to hold on to it.

Disappointment washed over him. He stirred, rubbed

his eyes. The man was still standing over him. Not one of the technicians he had seen earlier, this man was wearing a comfortable pullover shirt and creaseless slacks. He had a dark beard, an imperial nose, high cheekbones, skin tanned almost coffee brown. His gray eyes seemed restless, stormy. Feingold thought he had seen that face somewhere before, but he couldn't place where or when.

"Who the hell are you?" Feingold heard himself grumble. Fine way to greet a stranger, he thought.

The man extended a hand and helped Feingold to his feet. He was big, the scientist realized, tall and wide shouldered.

"My name is Keith Stoner."

Feingold peered at him, still a little bleary. "Stoner." It all snapped into focus. "The star voyager."

"You've heard of me."

"I saw that message you sent. You've got everybody scared."

Stoner smiled tightly. "Not everybody, I'm afraid."

His legs feeling a little more solid, Feingold asked, "You're really from the stars?"

Stoner nodded and replied with a question of his own: "Why did you come here?"

Feingold grinned at him. "A chance to see the alien artifact? I should pass up such a chance?"

Smiling back, Stoner asked, "Was it worth the trip?"

"And then some!"

"You found what you came for?"

Feingold didn't answer, couldn't. His thoughts were too jumbled; too much had happened, and all so quickly.

At last he said, "I found . . . something. I can't get it all straight in my head."

Stoner didn't reply.

"It was beautiful, though. More beautiful than anything I've ever experienced."

"Good." Stoner gestured toward the open portal to the chamber. "We'd better start back up. The door will be closing again pretty soon."

Feingold turned and stepped through the portal. "I saw the beginning of the universe," he remembered. "I saw how it all started!"

"Did you?"

"Yes! It was . . ." He groped for words. "I wish I could remember it all."

"I'm sorry that you can't," said Stoner as he started up the sloping tunnel.

Feingold said, "Me, too." But then he added, "You know, it doesn't matter! Not really. I mean, I saw it and I could understand it. I could understand it! That's what's important. I could understand it."

"Einstein once said the most incomprehensible thing about the universe is that it's comprehensible."

"Yes!" Feingold agreed, enthusiasm bubbling within him. "It doesn't matter if I can remember it all or not. It can be understood! If not by me, then somebody else. We'll figure it all out, sooner or later."

Stoner glanced at him. "If what you saw was real. Not an illusion. Not a trick."

"It was real," Feingold said with absolute certainty. "That much I know."

A little uneasily Stoner said, "You know, what you saw came out of your own mind. The artifact didn't put any new knowledge into you; it's a mirror, nothing more."

Feingold looked sharply at him. "In my own mind? What I saw came from inside my head?"

Stoner nodded solemnly.

For several paces Feingold said nothing, mulling this new idea. At last he murmured, "That means I can understand it all. It's not beyond my comprehension."

"Apparently not."

"And if I can understand it, others can figure it out, too. Down to the twelfth decimal place."

"That might be . . . difficult," Stoner said.

Feingold smiled like a boy anticipating his birthday gifts. Shaking his head, he replied, "So it's difficult. So it takes generations to figure it all out. So we'll have to be patient, as well as smart."

"Generations," Stoner murmured.

"I took a course in the philosophy of science when I was an undergrad," Feingold said. "Mostly bullshit, but I remember reading somebody who said that science is like a cathedral, with each new discovery like a stone that's added to the structure."

"But it's never finished," said Stoner as they walked up the tunnel.

"Maybe. Maybe not. The thing is, it keeps growing. And this artifact of yours has shown me that we can understand it all, eventually."

"Good," said Stoner. "Then the artifact's done its job."

"You made the artifact?"

Nodding, Stoner said, "With the help of some technology I picked up among the stars."

"Why? What were you trying to accomplish?"

"I wanted to tell the human race that there have been other intelligent species in the universe."

"Have been?" Feingold asked.

Instead of answering the scientist's question, Stoner asked one of his own. "Would you be willing to help me?"

"To do what?"

"Your Archbishop Overmire is arranging—"

"He's not *my* Archbishop," Feingold snapped. "I just work for the guy."

Stoner chuckled. "Sorry. I misspoke."

"Actually, I work for the President of the United States. *He* works for the Archbishop."

Grinning at the scientist's jaundiced candor, Stoner asked, "Overmire's trying to arrange a conference of world leaders. Would you take on the job of bringing the world's top scientists together at the same meeting?"

"I could. But why?"

"I have something to tell them," Stoner replied.

"Something?"

"Something important."

"Could you give me a hint?"

Stoner decided he liked Feingold. The man was tenacious, in his own gentle way.

"It's about the survival of the human race," Stoner said. "About the survival of intelligence in the universe."

Feingold blinked. "The whole universe?"

Stoner nodded.

Puffing out a sigh, Feingold muttered, "I'll tell the Archbishop about it, tell him I met you out here and this is what you want."

"It's what I need," Stoner corrected. "What the whole human race needs."

Feingold shook his head. "You think big, don't you?"

"Somebody has to," Stoner replied.

CHAPTER 8

Still smoldering at how Stoner had tricked him, Tavalera worked for Sister Angelique now full-time on helping to arrange the global conference. He sat in a cubbyhole of an office next to hers. He returned to living in the apartment she had given him, although now he had the necessary security clearances to come and go as he wished.

But still he was not allowed to communicate with Holly. No matter who he asked, no matter how he tried to maneuver around the automated circuitry, all his attempts to call the *Goddard* habitat were blocked. **Permission denied**, his desktop screen proclaimed.

"I'm sorry, sir, but you'll need special permission from the Archbishop's office to establish a comm link with the habitat," said a blank-faced young communications administrator.

Tavalera replied, "I'm working for the Archbishop's office, for cryin' out loud!"

The technician's expression didn't change by a millimeter. "I'm sorry, sir, but you'll need special permission—"

Tavalera cut the phone link, snarling to himself, "Friggin' robot."

Stoner claimed he's talked with Holly, told her what's going on, why I haven't been able to contact her. Yeah, sure, Tavalera grumbled to himself, seething within. Like I can trust him to tell me the truth. Holly's probably forgotten all about me by now.

Big fucking deal, he said to himself. Stoner screws with my mind and the New Morality controls my body. No matter which way I turn I'm just a friggin' pawn to them. A peon. A worker ant.

But as he dealt with diplomats and underlings from a dozen different governments and religions what struck him most was how petty, how small-minded, they could be. They're all worker ants, he realized. And they don't even know it!

The conference's main sessions had to be at a round table. There could be no head, no place more important than any other. Greater Iran would not be in any way subordinate to China, nor would China sit in a position that was deemed beneath that of the United States. The Russians, the British, the Indonesians, Christians, Muslims, Buddhists, wealthy nations, impoverished nations—none would allow any snub, real or perceived. They were quick to feel insulted, from Canadians to Mongols to South Africans to the Ona clans of Patagonia.

At first Tavalera couldn't see how anyone could bring all these touchy politicians together. But slowly, with enormous patience, Sister Angelique sweet-talked and smiled and cajoled them into a semigrudging acceptance. Her strongest weapon was a barely veiled threat: "All the others will be there, in the full light of global publicity. You wouldn't want to be the only one missing, would you? What would people think?"

Stoner was nowhere to be seen. He stayed completely out of the picture. His last words to Tavalera, just before he had transported him back to Earth, were, "This is something you have to do for yourselves. The conference is Angelique's idea and it's a good one. I'm not going to influence any of the participants in any way. Either they come of their own volition or the conference fails."

It wasn't failing, Tavalera saw. Yes, there were arguments and even tantrums from time to time. But slowly the conference came together. Some came willingly, eagerly. Some were reluctant. But all the world's leaders were going to meet in one grand conference to discuss their differences and try to find ways to resolve them peacefully.

Tavalera thought of something an old British leader named Churchill had once said, when a rival complained that international meetings were nothing but meaningless talk, "jawboning." Churchill replied, "Jaw, jaw is better than war, war."

Despite his angry resentment, Tavalera grinned to himself over that one. Reading about history can give you a deeper perspective on today, he told himself. Sometimes it's even fun, almost.

The scientists were almost as testy and touchy as the politicians, Tavalera learned. Almost. As he watched Dr. Feingold at work, Tavalera learned that the world's leading scientists had stopped doing any meaningful research years earlier, of course. In their own way they had become politicians, directing the work of younger men and women. It must be like trying to herd cats, Tavalera thought. Or nailing pudding to a wall. Scientists didn't take to organization very well. They were individualists, most of them, and so eager to get on with their own particular research programs that they resisted any efforts to shape or control their work.

Yet they needed funding for that work, and that's where the older scientists helped them most. Their leaders served as the interface between the active researchers and the government and religious leaders who controlled the purse strings. Interface hell, Tavalera thought. As he looked deeper into the way scientific research was funded, he realized that the older dudes acted as a buffer between the eager young researchers and the doubting, often fearful politicians and churchmen. It's a wonder any research gets done, Tavalera said to himself as he realized all the barriers that any new idea had to hurdle.

The trickiest part of setting up the conference, though, arose from the fact that there was a secret agenda that only a few of the most powerful governments would be party to. While the grand assembly of all nations would meet in the full glare of global publicity, the nuclear powers would send representatives to the secret meeting, to discuss their hidden agenda.

It was in Archbishop Overmire's office that Tavalera

began to realize that this secret agenda was the real reason for the public conference.

Angelique usually met with the Archbishop alone, one-on-one. Tavalera believed she didn't think too highly of Overmire: she always seemed unsatisfied, disappointed, after a session with the Archbishop. Now Tavalera sat beside her in front of Overmire's desk. The smart screens covering the office's walls showed lists of conference participants, logistical details, food requirements for the dozens of different cultures that would attend the meeting.

Overmire never fully accepted his presence, Tavalera recognized. The Archbishop always looked uncomfortable around him, suspicious, even though he only came to the man's office with Sister Angelique, at her insistence.

Sitting behind his broad desk, perspiring noticeably despite the office's frigid air-conditioning, Archbishop Overmire glanced unhappily at Tavalera, then turned his pumpkin-plump face to Angelique.

"The subject we're to discuss today is extremely sensitive," he said.

Angelique replied, "Yes, Your Eminence."

Eyeing Tavalera again, the Archbishop said, "My security people tell me we shouldn't allow unnecessary people to take part in these discussions."

With a slight smile, Angelique said softly, "Raoul has become an indispensable assistant to me, Your Eminence. He's done as much to set up the arrangements for this conference as I have, almost."

The Archbishop said, "Mr. Tavalera, you're not a member of our church, are you." It was not a question.

Tavalera said, "No, sir, I'm not."

"Do you consider yourself to be a Christian?"

"I think so."

"You think so?" The Archbishop's voice rose.

Feeling that he'd rather get up and walk out on this pompous gasbag, Tavalera forced his voice to remain calm even as he replied, "I try to live up to the ideals that Christ taught. He didn't think you needed anything more than an honest heart to live a good life."

The Archbishop glared at him while Tavalera wondered if he'd thought of that answer on his own or if Stoner had implanted it in his mind. Get out of my head! he fumed silently. No response.

Angelique spoke up. "Your Eminence, Mr. Tavalera is our link with Stoner, and Stoner is the real reason why we're arranging this conference, isn't he."

Something flickered in the Archbishop's eyes, Tavalera thought. Some unspoken thought passed between him and Angelique. Tavalera looked from her face to the Archbishop's and back again.

"Very well," said Overmire almost sullenly. He pointed a pudgy forefinger at Tavalera. "But you must remember, young man, that what we discuss in this office is extremely sensitive and must not be repeated outside these walls. Not even to Stoner. Do you understand?"

It was all Tavalera could do to refrain from laughing in the Archbishop's face. While he nodded, straight-faced, he was thinking, Stoner knows everything I know. He's inside my head whether I like it or not, and this overstuffed jerkball still hasn't tumbled to that fact.

But Sister Angelique knew, Tavalera saw. He could tell from the stiff expression on her face that she had pretty much the same opinion of the Archbishop that he did.

JO

In the safety of their starship, Jo confronted her two children. "You both took unnecessary risks."

"Oh, Mother," said Cathy, "I was perfectly safe every step of the way."

"Were you?"

To human eyes it would have seemed that the three of them were in a sterile, austere waiting room of some kind. Its soft gray walls were bare and windowless. Glareless lighting suffused from the smooth featureless ceiling. Jo sat on a tall cushioned stool with a low curving back. She was wearing sand-colored hip-hugging slacks with a loose blouse of pale lemon hanging over them. Her daughter, sitting on a similar stool facing her, was dressed in a short dark skirt and sleeveless white starched shirt.

Crossing her legs, Cathy answered, "With you hovering over me every instant? I was never in any danger at all."

Rick, standing between the two women, grinned at his sister. "You almost sound disappointed."

"Typical male attitude," Cathy sniffed.

"I was worried about you both," Jo said.

"I was okay, Mom," said Rick. "No problems."

Jo knew they were right and she was being overly protective. Still . . . "Well, what did you learn that you didn't know before you went down there?"

Cathy leaned forward slightly, her expression suddenly intent. "It's just like Dad said: population growth is the root of their problems."

Jo nodded. "We know that."

"It's different when you see it face-to-face," Cathy went on. "When you see teenagers with a baby on their hip and another in the belly. Educated women who see nothing wrong with having six or seven babies."

Rick shook his head. "They'll overpopulate themselves into extinction."

"Unless we do something to stop them."

"Something?" Jo asked. "What can we do?"

"Cut down their birthrate," Cathy immediately replied.

"How?"

"By reducing their fertility rate. See to it that no woman on Earth can have more than two children."

"You can't do that," Rick objected. "Dad's told us time and again that we can't force a solution on them."

"Dad's wrong," Cathy said firmly. "We've got to help them. Otherwise they're heading straight toward a cliff. They *can't* solve their problems as long as they're overpopulating themselves."

"They'll learn to slow their population growth, in time," Jo said.

"But they don't have time!" Cathy insisted. "Dad's worried that they're heading toward a nuclear war. Even if they don't, the underlying problem will still be there. We've got to cut down their fertility rate, fix it so no woman on Earth can have more than two babies."

Jo rocked back on her seat. "That . . . that would mean a massive invasion of their natural rights."

"No, Mom," Cathy replied, an impish smile breaking across her face. "Only a very teeny little invasion of their bodies."

CHAPTER 9

One of the most troublesome problems of arranging the conference was picking its site. The Asians balked at the idea of having it set anywhere in Europe. The Europeans refused to come to the United States. The Americans would not agree to a site in Africa. And so it went until Tavalera suggested picking an island in the Pacific Ocean: Tahiti.

Once an idyllic Polynesian island, Tahiti had become a French colony in the nineteenth century but finally won its independence. More than two hundred years of European influence, sadly, had all but destroyed the original Polynesian culture. European sailors, explorers, and—eventually—tourists brought alcohol, smallpox, venereal diseases, and concrete hotel complexes. Chinese merchants established shops in Papeete, which became a thriving commercial city with an international airport. During the latter stages of the twentieth century the French government even made Tahiti its administrative center for the nuclear bomb tests it conducted in the South Pacific.

Independence lessened the influence of Europeans and Chinese but could not undo the cultural transformations of more than three centuries. Tahitians remained proud of their cultural heritage, but they wore T-shirts and listened to pop music on their clip-on phones, just like people all over the world.

Yet the image of Tahiti as an unspoiled tropical paradise remained in the minds of people everywhere. So Tahiti became the unanimous choice to locate the Global Conference on Peace and Progress.

In addition to planning the details of the conference,

Sister Angelique had the additional task of setting up a nuclear warhead in a test range in New Mexico, not far from the Alamogordo site where the first atomic bomb had been detonated more than a century and a half earlier. The purpose of the setup was the ritual dismantling of the bomb before the eyes of the leaders of the world's nuclear powers: the United States, Greater Iran, and China.

Tavalera thought of asking Stoner if he knew of any other nuclear weapons programs but was still too angry to try to make contact with the star voyager. Yet that night, in the quiet of Tavalera's own apartment, Stoner appeared anyway.

Suddenly he was standing in front of Tavalera in the apartment's living room, looking gravely at him with his gray eyes.

"For what it's worth," Stoner said without preamble, "I've spoken with Holly again and tried to explain what's going on here. You can talk to her yourself if you like."

"I like," Tavalera replied sullenly.

"All right. After we've finished our business."

"Real time?"

Shaking his head, Stoner replied, "I'm afraid not. I can't do the impossible."

"Yeah." Tavalera sat down on the sofa, not trusting his emotions enough to say anything more.

"I see that your conference is coming along well enough," Stoner said, taking the armchair facing the sofa.

"Hey, it's not *my* conference. The whole thing is Angelique's idea."

Stoner nodded and stretched his long legs out beyond the coffee table. Tavalera saw that he was wearing old-fashioned cowboy boots, plain brown and unadorned.

"I think we oughtta know if anybody else is building nukes," he said guardedly.

"The Russians still have a small cache of missiles with nuclear warheads left over from the old days, before the Final Middle East War," Stoner said. "The warheads have degraded seriously and the missiles are rusting away in their silos. They're not usable; the Kremlin leaders keep them more as a symbol of their former power than anything else."

"Could they be fixed up, though?" Tavalera asked. "Made usable?"

Nodding, Stoner replied, "It would take a serious effort. The Russians aren't going to start a nuclear war. They know better. They've seen what the fallout from the Middle East did to the Ukraine and Kazakhstan."

"So it's the U.S., Iran, and China."

"Yes."

Tavalera clasped his hands together. "She's setting up a nuke warhead in New Mexico, near Alamogordo. In secret."

Stoner said nothing.

"They're gonna dismantle it as a show of goodwill."

"In front of the Chinese and Iranian leaders?"

"That's right."

"Good."

Silence stretched between them awkwardly.

At last Stoner asked, "It was your idea to place the conference on Tahiti?"

"Yeah. I figured it was sort of neutral territory."

"Interesting," said Stoner. "In my earlier life we set up our project for contacting the alien starship on Kwajalein. That's an atoll in the central Pacific."

"Uh-huh."

"Parallels," Stoner muttered. "The two worldlines almost merge together, but not quite."

"You said you'd let me talk with Holly."

Nodding again, Stoner replied, "Yes. You've earned that much."

CHAPTER 10

It was awkward trying to hold a conversation with a two-hour lag between "How are you?" and "I'm fine." But once Stoner had left his apartment, Tavalera's phone chimed and there was Holly on his wall screen, bright and pert and obviously happy to see him.

This is real, Tavalera said to himself. I'm really talking to her. I think.

He poured his heart out to Holly, telling her everything, including Stoner's deception. Once he'd run out of words he waited, fidgeting in his apartment for nearly two hours before the phone chimed again.

"He tricked you?" were her first words to him. "Why? What's he up to?" Holly's expressive face went from an annoyed frown to a happy grin. "Okay, never mind. We're talking and it's so great to see you, Raoul, hear your voice. I want to make arrangements to bring you here to the habitat soon's we can; I don't like the idea that those nutcases are gonna start throwing nukes at each other. I'll send an appeal to the United Nations and ask to get you and your mother sent here. . . ."

On and on Holly talked, saying just about what she'd said in the faked conversations that Stoner had rigged. He knows how she thinks, Tavalera told himself as he listened to Holly, watched her face, felt the warmth of her presence even though they were separated by a billion kilometers. He must've dug that out of my mind, my memories of her.

"... and if that doesn't work I'll come back there myself and pry you loose with a crowbar, if I have to!"

Tavalera grinned at her. That's my Holly, he thought. She loves me. She wants me with her. She still loves me.

Tavalera was whistling as he entered his office the next morning. Angelique heard him through the thin wall that separated their offices.

He's happy, she thought. She wished she could be happy, too.

Most of the conference arrangements had been set. The public announcement would be made on worldwide news broadcasts in a few days. The secret meeting in New Mexico, though, was another matter altogether. Angelique had to get the chiefs of state of Greater Iran, China, and the United States away from the public conference on Tahiti and whisk them to New Mexico to witness the ritual dismantling of an American hydrogen bomb. The news media could know nothing of this. That wasn't too difficult: the national governments and religious movements behind them had tight control of the news media.

The tricky part was to make certain that Stoner would be there, in the precisely right spot for the hydrogen bomb's "accidental" explosion to destroy him.

Besides that, Archbishop Overmire was having some fresh thoughts of his own.

He called Angelique into his office that morning for her regular progress report.

"We need a reliable man to detonate the bomb," the Archbishop said, perspiring as he sat behind his desk despite the office's frosty temperature. Angelique thought he looked worse than usual, more tired, his eyes bloodshot, his hands trembling slightly.

He's anxious about this meeting, she told herself. He's working harder than usual and it's taking a toll on his health. Wondering what his blood pressure might be, Angelique thought that the stress of the conference just might kill the Archbishop and save her the trouble of removing him.

"I'm searching for a suitable volunteer, Your Eminence," she said. "It's a bit tricky: the person must be technically knowledgeable yet willing to accept holy martyrdom."

Overmire closed his reddened eyes briefly, then asked, "Do you mean that no one with technical qualifications has the spiritual willingness to become a martyr?"

"I'm sure there is someone," Angelique replied. "It's just that we haven't found him yet. Or her."

"Her? A woman?"

Suppressing the bitter smile that played on the corners of her lips, Angelique said, "There are women who are trained nuclear technicians, Your Eminence."

The Archbishop looked somewhat surprised. "Are there? I wouldn't think women were interested in such things."

Angelique said nothing.

"How far from the explosion will I be?" Overmire asked.

That's what's worrying him, Angelique realized. "More than ten kilometers, Your Eminence. In a concrete shelter that's blast proofed and hardened against the radiation pulse from the bomb."

"And the Iranian and Chinese leaders will be with me?"

"Yes, Your Eminence. And the President, of course. You will watch the dismantling—and the accident—over a television link."

"Very good." Archbishop Overmire squeezed his narrow eyes shut again, then said, "I've been discussing this with that Melillo person."

"The President's chief of staff?"

"Yes," said the Archbishop with obvious distaste. "An unpleasant man. Demanding. Impatient."

"He seems hard-driving," Angelique agreed.

"He's not a Believer. Not one of us. Brought up as a Catholic, I'm certain."

"Most likely," she murmured.

"But he's been giving this matter considerable thought," Overmire conceded as he pulled himself up straighter in his high-backed chair. "He thinks we should launch preemptive strikes at the Iranian and Chinese nuclear facilities at the same time as the demonstration in New Mexico."

Angelique felt a shock race along her nerves. "A preemptive strike?"

"To knock out their nuclear capabilities."

"With their leaders in the same room with you? And the President?"

"That's the beauty of it," Overmire said, breaking into a pleased smile. "When the, uh . . . 'accident' happens we can claim that it was an attack on us! Our preemptive strike will be seen as a justifiable counterblow."

It took Angelique a moment to digest what the Archbishop was proposing.

"But Your Eminence," she objected, "the Chinese and Iranian leaders will both know that they didn't order a strike on the United States."

Waving a pudgy finger at her, Overmire gloated,

"Ah, yes, each one of them will know that *he* did not order a strike. But neither of them will know for certain that the *other one* didn't order it!"

"That's . . . deceitful."

"To prevent those heathens from starting a nuclear war? To protect the New Morality and all that it stands for? A little deception is perfectly acceptable."

Angelique wanted to protest, but she saw that the Archbishop had made up his mind. Besides, she thought, if anything goes wrong he can blame it all on the White House.

Overmire added, "Melillo thinks we can present them with a fait accompli. We'll have nuclear weapons and they'll have none. We can dictate our terms to them."

"Terms? What terms?" Angelique asked, her voice hollow.

Overmire's smile dimpled his flabby cheeks. "Rounding up all the jihadists. The end of terrorism. Putting China in its place. Ensuring that America is supreme for the next hundred years or more."

Angelique's breath caught in her throat.

"Think of it," the Archbishop said as he clasped his hands on the desktop. "We will break the backs of our enemies with one blow. Crush them. We will begin the holy task of bringing all those heathens to Christ's loving mercy."

CHAPTER 11

The man made Angelique's blood run cold. She wanted to turn her face away from him. Focusing on his dossier, displayed on her desktop screen, she saw that his name was Nagash Janagar; he was a top-rated technician who had worked for most of his life in nuclear power plants in India and the United States.

But as he stood before Angelique's desk she thought he looked too frail and emaciated to carry out the vital task that needed to be done. Janagar was small, slight, his skin not dark so much as sallow, his rumpled shirt and shapeless slacks making him look bedraggled, as if he'd been hauled in by the police rather than coming to her office as a volunteer.

It was his eyes that particularly troubled Angelique. Big, dark, sad eyes that stared at her almost without blinking. Desperate eyes. The eyes of a trapped animal, she thought.

"You understand that this is strictly a volunteer position," she said carefully from behind her desk. She almost felt as if she wanted to duck beneath it, use it as a protective barrier between herself and this gaunt, cheerless man.

"I understand very well that I will become a holy martyr," said Janagar in rhythmically accented English. "I understand completely, totally."

Angelique turned slightly in her swivel chair and studied Janagar's dossier on her screen.

"You're a convert to Christianity?" she murmured.

"Yes indeed. After the Biowar wiped out my family, my wife and children, my entire village, I was rescued by a salvage team from the United States of America. They brought me to a hospital that was run by the New Morality. It was there that I saw the light of the true faith."

"You remained in the United States."

"I became a citizen. I married an American woman, although she was of Hindu parentage. I fathered three children by her, one of them a boy."

Angelique nodded. Before she could ask another question, though, Janagar continued:

"You wonder why a happily married man seeks martyrdom, don't you? I will tell you. I have an inoperable brain tumor. My case is hopeless, the doctors tell me."

Without consciously willing it, Angelique thought of the old woman whom she and Stoner had helped to escape from the hospital. She was a hopeless case, too: hopeless because of the hospital staff's rules of triage and the New Morality's refusal to use secularist therapies. Stoner had saved her with banned, forbidden, sinful nanotechnology.

Janagar went on, "My life insurance policy is small, too small to pay for my son's education. But if my death is ruled an accident, the benefits to my family will be doubled."

Angelique stared into the man's tragic eyes. He's willing to die for his family, she thought. He's willing to give up his life to help his children.

In a voice that was barely above a whisper, she said, "So you are willing to . . . to die in this 'accident.'"

"For the greater glory of God," Janagar said. He actually smiled, white teeth gleaming against his ashen skin.

Angelique nodded. For the greater glory of God, she thought. Then she realized, He's willing to commit murder to make life better for his children.

A fragment of memory from her school days touched the surface of her mind. A quotation she'd read from some secularist writer who was on the list of prohibited authors. But Angelique had smuggled a tattered, broken-spined old copy of one of his books into her convent bedroom and read it by flashlight, beneath her ragged, frayed blanket.

A fanatic who is willing to die for his cause thinks nothing of killing you for his cause.

CHAPTER 12

"This really was a tropical paradise, once upon a time," said the Chinese physicist.

Tavalera nodded as he gazed out on the old harbor of Papeete. It was filled with magnificent yachts jammed along the piers, practically gunwale to gunwale. Tavalera thought he could walk from deck to deck completely across the harbor, all the way out across the channel to the graceful green cone of Mooréa, standing peacefully against the bright blue sky, its top wreathed in cloud.

The Chinese physicist took in a deep, exaggerated breath, then grinned at Tavalera. "That's one thing they haven't changed: the climate. Not even the greenhouse warming has affected the climate here very much."

"I guess," Tavalera muttered.

"No flooding here, to speak of," the physicist went on. "Not like Shanghai and Singapore. Tahiti is at a nodal point in the Pacific. The rise in sea level is barely noticeable here."

The physicist looked youthful, but Tavalera knew that to be invited to this international meeting he had to be a scientist of some stature, some achievement. Tavalera had met the man as he was checking into the hotel just after arriving on the island. They had fallen to talking and quickly agreed to take a walk around the town and its jam-packed harbor.

"You're not a physicist, are you?" the Chinese asked. His name was Quan Zheng, and he was from the University of New Shanghai. He was a millimeter or two taller than Tavalera, with long legs and long arms and the kind of erect posture and slim torso that comes from dedicated daily exercise. His face looked almost European, despite the slight cast to his eyes.

"How can you tell?" Tavalera asked.

With a grin, Quan replied, "You're not asking any questions."

Tavalera grinned back at him. "Neither are you."

"That's because I'm giving you all the answers before you can ask."

They laughed together and decided to find the nearest bar. As they headed down a street that led away from the harbor, Tavalera realized that Quan was right. The one thing that hadn't changed about Papeete was the climate. Otherwise, the city had been completely altered. According to the histories Tavalera had scanned, Papeete had been a sleepy little town huddled around its harbor. Shops lined its main street, and the merchants who owned them lived behind their stores. But that was long ago. Now Papeete rose in concrete and steel, just like the rebuilt Honolulu and Singapore and every other waterfront, tourist-dependent city.

Hotels and shopping malls, Tavalera saw, each one gaudier than the next. It made him feel depressed. Might as well be in Vegas, he said to himself. Then he added, But Vegas is a lot farther from the beach.

Tavalera had only that first afternoon for sightseeing. He had dinner that evening with Angelique, who introduced him to a half dozen of the bureaucrats she'd been working with to arrange this international conference. He sat there in almost total silence while they jabbered and chattered with each other, mostly in British-accented English, about seating arrangements and programming conflicts and scheduling the island's limited number of limousines to pick up the VIPs as they arrived at the airport.

Once the dinner finally broke up and he headed for his room, Angelique got into the glass-walled elevator beside him.

"When will Stoner arrive?" she asked while the lobby atrium dropped away from them.

Tavalera shrugged. "Who knows? He might be here already."

She looked surprised, almost alarmed. "He's not in contact with you?"

Feeling the resentment about Stoner's trickery rising in him once more, Tavalera answered, "It's strictly a one-way contact. He uses me like a telescope." Before she could reply, he added, "More like a microscope, really."

"He's got to be here," Angelique said.

"He will be. When he's good and ready, not before."

"I have a plane standing by to take him to New Mexico. He's *got* to be there. The whole reason for this conference depends on his being there to watch us dismantle a nuclear weapon."

Tavalera repeated, "He'll be there, when he's good and ready."

The elevator reached Tavalera's floor. The doors slid open.

"Good night, Raoul," Angelique murmured.

"Yeah," he said as he stepped out and headed for his room.

JO

"You what?" Stoner demanded.

Jo smiled coolly at her husband. She was standing in the starship's control center, bathed in lights that changed colors with their moods. At this moment, the lights were shifting from restful aqua toward vibrant scarlet.

"I helped Cathy to produce nanomachines that can alleviate the population problem."

Stoner tried to glare at his wife, but he knew that wouldn't work. He didn't like what she had done, but he couldn't be angry with her over it.

"That's the kind of interference I've been trying to avoid," he grumbled. "I want them to solve their own problems." Reluctantly he added, "If they can."

"They can't," Jo said flatly. "So we're going to help them." Before Stoner could object, she went on, "Besides, you've always said that we're part of them, we're part of the human race. So it's not really interference, is it? It's not a matter of us versus them."

Stoner nodded dumbly at Jo. There's no use arguing about it, he thought. It's already done. Besides, it might work.

CHAPTER 13

Stoner still had not put in an appearance on Tahiti by the time the conference formally opened. Angelique was getting close to panic, Tavalera realized as he took his chair at the long table reserved for New Morality staff in the rear of the huge conference room.

It was the hotel's ballroom, actually, but all its partitions had been rolled away to accommodate the more than six hundred delegates to the conference. People from every nation on Earth were included, even the usually aloof Swiss, who had suffered disastrous losses in tourist income from greenhouse melting of the Alps snowcap.

The keynote speaker for the conference's opening

session was Archbishop Overmire, of course. Tavalera watched as the grossly overweight Archbishop made his painful way to the podium and leaned his bulk on both arms. Even from way back in the rear of the room Tavalera could see the man panting with the effort of walking a dozen paces. The Archbishop's face looked shiny: perspiration, Tavalera knew. The man's sick; this conference just might kill him.

Tavalera began to get antsy as the morning wore on. One droning speech after another by religious and secular leaders from Europe, Asia, Africa, Latin America. The only bit of relief came from the Australian Prime Minister, who gave a brief and witty address that ended with, "We all know the problems. Too many people, too few resources. I'm here to find some bloomin' answers."

At the lunch break, Angelique looked almost frantic.

"Where is Stoner?" she demanded as she sat with Tavalera at a table for two in the cafeteria that had been set up out at the beach for New Morality staff members.

"He'll be here when he wants to be here," Tavalera replied carelessly. He looked out across the sea of tables to the sparkling blue ocean surging gently against the black sand beach. The sky was a perfect blue, dotted with puffy cumulus clouds riding on the trade wind.

"He's got to be here by tomorrow," Angelique said, her lovely face marred by worry lines between her brows. "We've set up the demonstration for the third day of the conference. He's got to be on the flight to New Mexico."

Tavalera knew that Archbishop Overmire, the President of the United States, and the leaders of Greater Iran and China were scheduled to attend the dismantling of a token American nuclear weapon.

"He'll be there," Tavalera said, trying to show a confidence he didn't really feel.

But that night, as Tavalera brushed his teeth in preparation for bed after a wearying afternoon of listening to forecasts of doom from scientists and assurances of prosperity from politicians, Stoner appeared in the bathroom doorway. He was wearing a gaudy islander shirt hanging loose over khaki-colored shorts. And sandals.

"Knock knock," said Stoner.

Tavalera spat out toothpaste-foamed water. Instant anger at Stoner's deception boiled up in him, but he forced it down and said coldly, "We were wondering when you'd show up."

"We?"

"Angelique and me."

"I haven't missed anything important, have I?"

He's not inside my head anymore, Tavalera realized. He doesn't know what I know anymore.

"Naw," he replied. "Just a lot of hot air. But she's in a sweat about getting you to New Mexico in time to witness them dismantling a nuke."

"I'll be there," Stoner said.

"They've got a special flight to take the VIPs from here to—"

"I won't need it," Stoner interrupted. A ghost of a smile curved his lips. "I've got my own transportation."

Tavalera grunted. "Yeah. I know."

With that, Stoner vanished.

Bertram Feingold was much more startled when Stoner appeared in his hotel bedroom. As he sat up in bed the scientist had an ancient frayed Tibetan robe pulled around his shoulders, a gift from an anthropologist friend who had died years earlier. Feingold was reading a technical report projected from his pocket phone onto the display screen that spanned one entire wall of the modest room.

"Who the hell— Oh! It's you."

Stoner sat in the room's only chair. "I'm sorry to startle you. I wanted to find out if you'll be at the demonstration in New Mexico."

"Demonstration? What demonstration?"

"The United States is going to dismantle one of its nuclear weapons as a show of good faith to the leaders of Greater Iran and China."

Feingold's petulant expression showed what he thought of the idea. "And they expect Iran and China to do likewise?"

"It's a step toward disarmament," Stoner replied.

"Hooey. If they dismantle a hundred bombs, that's a step toward disarmament. One nuke—that's just a public relations stunt."

Stoner nodded. "That's what you think?"

Hunching forward slightly, Feingold said, "I've done my homework. I've read up on the disarmament treaties of the past, particularly the ones between the U.S. and the old Soviet Union."

"The Cold War," Stoner murmured, recalling it from his previous life.

"Scientists took a major role in moving East and West toward disarmament," Feingold said. "Guys like Bethe and Sakharov. Took them years. Then the politicians and diplomats got into the act. Took them even longer. More years. Nobody disarms just because one bomb's been dismantled."

"But it's a step," Stoner insisted. "A first step. That's important, don't you think?"

Feingold shrugged and his robe slipped down off his skinny shoulders. "Maybe," he conceded grudgingly. "But I wouldn't hold my breath."

CATHY

Cathy sat beneath a big bright umbrella at a tiny round table set up on the sidewalk in front of the café, sipping at the strong black coffee, scanning the crowded street.

She told me she'd be here at one o'clock, Cathy said to herself. It's almost half-past.

It really doesn't matter, her mother said in her mind. You could start with any woman, anywhere.

I know, but I wanted it to start with Mina. She's my friend. I wanted to start with her.

You're sentimental! Jo sounded surprised.

Cathy smiled. Maybe when this is all over, Mom, and things have stabilized, maybe I'll come down here to live for a while. Find a man to love, like you found Dad.

Jo went from surprise to shock. You can't do that!

Why not, Mom? I'm just as human as you are. When I want to be. Cathy giggled inwardly at her mother's consternation.

And then Cathy saw Mina hurrying through the crowd, the expression on her face strained, worried.

Cathy waved to her friend and Mina's eyes widened with recognition. She pushed through the crowd and slipped into the chair next to Cathy's.

"I'm so sorry to be late," Mina said before Cathy could even say hello. "I had to take my mother to the hospital this morning."

"The hospital?"

"She had a fainting spell. We were afraid it was her heart."

"And?"

Mina took in a deep breath. "It's all right. Her blood pressure was very low, but the doctors injected her with an iron supplement. All she needs now is a day or so of rest."

"Thank goodness," said Cathy. "It must have scared you."

"Yes, it did. My grandmother died at the same age."

"In her sixties?" Cathy guessed.

"Fifty-seven," said Mina. "My mother is fifty-seven."

She looks ninety, Cathy thought.

Signaling to a waiter, Cathy ordered a coffee for her friend.

"I can't stay long," Mina said apologetically. "I've got to get back home and do the shopping for dinner. And the cooking, with Mama in the hospital."

"I'm sorry you had to come all the way out here. I should have brought a pocket phone with me."

"It's all right," Mina said as the waiter placed the delicate cup before her. "It's good to get away, even for a few minutes."

Cathy looked into her friend's face. She'll be an old woman before she's fifty, just like her mother and her grandmother, Cathy thought. Unless I act.

Reaching out, Cathy clasped Mina's free hand. "I hope everything works out for you," Cathy said as a batch of nanomachines swarmed from her skin to Mina's and made their purposeful way into her body.

"Thank you," said Mina, never realizing the gift Cathy had just given her.

For the rest of the day Cathy shopped in the stores, walked along the crowded streets, bumped into other women in the crowds, touched hands with saleswomen, spread her nanomachines with each woman she contacted.

The nanomachines were programmed to spin a protective shell around almost all the eggs each woman carried within her. Almost all. The women would not be infertile, nor would they change in any discernable way. They simply would not have more than two children, three at the most.

Six degrees of separation, Cathy thought. It's been proven that each human being on Earth is only six contacts away from every other human being. Within a few months, a couple of years at most, they'll all be protected. All the women on Earth. Birthrates will decline. Population pressure will ease.

Do you think that will save the world? Jo asked in Cathy's mind.

Cathy smiled. It might. It just might.

BOOK VI

THE NEW WORLD

All men by nature desire to know.

Aristotle

CHAPTER 1

It was nearly dawn on Tahiti. The eastern sky was turning from milky white to a glowing pink. The stars were fading in the growing radiance, even though the Sun had not yet risen above the ocean's horizon. The waiting Clippership's diamond hull glinted in the pale light.

Tavalera thought that Angelique seemed apprehensive as they walked together down the enclosed ramp that connected the Faa'a Aerospaceport terminal to the waiting Clippership.

"Nothing to be nervous about," he said to her. "It's just a rocket. It'll get us to New Mexico in less than an hour."

She nodded absently, her mind obviously elsewhere.

As they entered the hatch of the squat, cone-shaped rocket vehicle, Tavalera continued, "The conference's goin' good. Everybody seems happy about it."

"Yes, I agree," said Angelique.

"Nobody knows the Archbishop's goin' to New Mexico. He'll be back for the big breakfast session tomorrow."

Angelique nodded. She's torqued up about something, Tavalera thought. And it ain't the conference.

They sat side by side in the Clippership's lower passenger compartment. Only four others were with them, all men, strangers to Tavalera. Archbishop Overmire, together with Melillo and several other White House staffers, rode in the upper compartment.

The rocket lifted off with a blast of thunder, pushing Tavalera and the other passengers into their seats with a force more than twice normal gravity. After a few rattling, roaring minutes the engines shut down and everything went eerily silent. Tavalera felt the old sensations of weightlessness. Grinning inwardly, he felt an urge to unstrap and float out of his seat. But he stayed put.

Beside him, Angelique asked, "You're sure that Stoner will be at the demonstration? It's important, urgent. . . ."

Tavalera tried to shrug, but the shoulder straps of his safety harness made it difficult. "He said he'd be there. He'll be there."

"How does he know where it is? Where he's supposed to be?"

"He knows; don't worry about it."

But the lines on her fashion model's face showed that she was worried. Very worried.

In the Clippership's upper compartment, Archbishop Overmire and Oscar Melillo were discussing their own worries.

"What if Stoner doesn't come to the . . . eh, demonstration?" the Archbishop mused. He had expected to feel sick in weightlessness and had dosed himself heavily with antinausea medications.

"Doesn't matter," said Melillo. He seemed to be handling zero gravity without difficulty. "We launch the preemptive strikes just as the bomb goes off. They'll never know what hit them."

"China and Iran both."

"That's right. Ten missiles each."

"Ten?" Overmire felt a pang of alarm. "Isn't that much more than you need?"

"Got to figure their antimissile defenses. Ten ought to assure us that at least two or three of our birds will hit their targets."

"Two or three megatons," Overmire muttered.

"Enough to do the job. More than enough."

"Overkill."

"Better than underkill," Melillo said with a sly chuckle.

"And the collateral damage?"

Melillo waggled a hand in the air. "Those facilities are way out in the boonies. Nearest towns are miles away."

"But the people working at the facilities," the Archbishop murmured.

"They're dead meat."

Overmire lapsed into silence. I'll have prayers said for their souls, he told himself. Even though they're heathens, we can offer up prayers for them.

Folding his hands over his bloated middle, the Archbishop closed his eyes and pretended to sleep. But his mind was active.

Stoner, he thought. He's got to be there. We've got to put an end to him.

The Archbishop took in a deep, steadying breath and said to himself, Once we're rid of this star man and we've decapitated the Chinese and Iranian threats, then we can begin the process of bringing the peace of Christ to the entire world.

He actually did fall asleep. With a smile on his face.

Meanwhile, Nagash Janagar was at his post in the New Mexico desert, checking out the coffin-sized warhead that contained the hydrogen bomb.

He had removed the covering panels so that he could inspect the bomb's innards. He stared into it, his dark, soft eyes wide with a mixture of awe and dread. Such a complicated device, so intricate, he thought. So powerful. So very powerful. The energy of the atom is locked up inside it.

For the hundredth time he surveyed the components of this instrument of death. There is the fission bomb that triggers the hydrogen device, he said to himself, actually touching the plutonium bomb's outer shell with the palm of his hand. He expected it to feel hot, but the metal alloy was only slightly warmer than his own flesh. There is the fusing device, and here in the middle is the hydrogen bomb itself, tritium and lithium. So small to contain the power of a million tons of explosive. So small. So deadly.

Jagash went over each and every one of the safety interlocks, making certain that they had all been disabled. Then he activated the master computer and started its countdown. At the preset moment, the explosive bolts will fire, forcing the two halves of the plutonium sphere to come together. The plutonium goes critical and explodes. Picoseconds later the tritium reaches its ignition temperature and the main bomb goes off.

A megaton of energy is released in the flash of a nanosecond, he knew. This building and everything around it will be blown into star-hot plasma. The mushroom cloud will rise into the stratosphere. The light will blind any creature who looks this way.

Everything for five kilometers around will be evaporated, Jagash told himself. Everything. Including this man who claims he has been to the stars. Including me.

I am become death, shatterer of worlds, he quoted from the Bhagavad Gita. I will leave this vale of tears and achieve Nirvana. Away from all the pain and strivings of the world. Safe in the arms of Vishnu and the other gods.

His own thoughts surprised him. I accepted Christianity, he said to himself. I let them make me a Christian. But only in my mind, he realized at last. Only because it was offered as a way out of poverty and grief. Not in my heart. Not in my soul. Vishnu, Krishna, Rama—they are with me always. And soon I will be with them.

CHAPTER 2

From his vantage point atop the butte Stoner could see the complex of buildings dotting the drab, dusty desert floor. It was mid-morning, and the New Mexico sun beat down out of a cloudless turquoise sky. For this appearance he had chosen to clothe himself in a light open-collared shirt, denims, and scruffy brown boots. I should have included a cowboy hat, he thought as he squinted in the brilliant sunshine, almost laughing aloud at the idea.

Focusing on the small concrete building standing alone far out in the scrubby desert, he said to himself, That must be where the bomb is. A single unpaved road led to it. A lone Humvee was parked outside it, ancient and dusty brown with faded lettering on its doors that read: U.S. ARMY.

Somebody's in there, Stoner realized. With the bomb.

Slightly more than ten kilometers away stood a group of three concrete bunkers, clustered together in the bare landscape like an alien presence in the arroyo-seamed land. There was a parking lot off to one side. More than a dozen trucks and vans were lined up there in neat, militarily precise rows. Farther off, almost lost in the dust-hazed distance, was a landing strip and a small glassed-in control tower. Must get pretty warm in there, Stoner thought, with all this sunshine pouring down.

The thrumming noise of a helicopter reached his ears. No, he saw: three helicopters. All three of them were unmarked, as if the occupants didn't want anyone to know who was in them.

Raoul's in the one on the left, Stoner realized. He sensed Tavalera's presence, even though he didn't make a firm mental contact with him. Raoul doesn't want me in his mind, Stoner knew. I've fiddled with his head enough to make him angry with me. I'll have to make amends to him, somehow, after this is over.

With the lightest of mental touches Stoner identified the others in the helicopters. Sister Angelique was riding with Tavalera, together with Archbishop Overmire and the President of the United States and that man Melillo from the White House. And a half dozen Secret Service agents in dark suits that bristled with sensors and weaponry. Ling Po and General Bakhtiar were in the other two choppers, each accompanied by his personal staff people and bodyguards.

Stoner smiled to himself. They don't fully trust one another. Can't say that I blame them.

High overhead a squadron of fighter planes etched thin white contrails against the otherwise unblemished sky. Honor guards, Stoner thought, although he knew the fighters were prepared to attack anything that threatened the VIPs' helicopters.

Jo's presence sounded in his mind. You know that this is a trap, she said.

You've got a suspicious mind, Stoner replied lightly.

I know how they think, how they work, Jo insisted. I was a captain of industry once, remember? Not a starry-eyed scientist, like you.

Stoner smiled inwardly. Jo, they're trying to take a step toward disarmament.

They could blow that bomb instead of disarming it.

And kill the technicians? Just to get me?

That's what I'd do if I were in Overmire's place, she said implacably.

I'm glad you're not, then.

It's a trap, Jo warned again. They want to kill you.

With a sigh that was almost reluctant, Stoner said to his wife, Well, they can try, I suppose.

He was waiting for them as their little motorcade of black minivans drove up to the observation building, standing at the entrance to the windowless concrete structure, squinting slightly in the blazing late morning sunshine.

The minivans they rode in were painted dead black. White would be better for the desert, Stoner thought. They pulled up and the bodyguards got out first. American, Iranian, or Chinese, they were all pretty much alike, Stoner thought: bulky men in dark suits and darker glasses. There were two women among the Americans, none with the Chinese or Iranians.

Then the politicians stepped onto the desert. The President, with Melillo and three others; General Bakhtiar and his staff members; Ling Po and his people in their high-collared blue jumpsuits. Archbishop Overmire waddled out of a fourth minivan, wincing noticeably as the harsh desert sunshine struck him. Sister Angelique and Tavalera followed him as the entire procession hurried toward the air-conditioned comfort of the observation building.

Stoner heard Tavalera half-whisper to Angelique, "I told you he'd be here."

Angelique nodded and said nothing.

The three groups headed quickly toward the building, separated from one another by a few paces. They stayed separated, Stoner saw. None of them said a word to any of the others. None of them even looked at the others. Three separate units, he thought. Three sets of world leaders with Neolithic attitudes: my tribe above yours; my people are human and yours are not. He shook his head in frustrated despair. How can they ever work together?

The entire procession hurried past Stoner without a word or even a glance and rushed into the cool shadows of the building's interior. Tavalera, bringing up the rear, seemed uncertain but then stuck out his hand almost shyly.

Stoner grasped it in both of his own. "It's good to see you again, Raoul."

"Yeah," Tavalera muttered, almost reluctantly. "You, too."

Sister Angelique moved between them. "You are to go with the technicians to the building where the bomb will be dismantled," she said to Stoner.

"Fine," said Stoner. "I presume you'll all get back to Tahiti in time for tomorrow's closing session of the conference."

"Yes, of course."

"I want to address the delegates, the scientists, and the political leaders."

Angelique closed her eyes briefly. Then, "It will be a plenary session. Everyone will attend."

"Good."

She pointed to a group of six men who were trudging out of the building to a waiting minivan. They all were wearing Western-style business suits and looked decidedly uncomfortable in the desert heat. "You should be going with them."

"To witness the dismantling," Stoner said. "Yes, I know."

But he hesitated. Something about Angelique's expression puzzled him. She seemed . . . eager? Worried? Expectant? She licked her lips with a swift motion of her tongue. Her eyes evaded his. Something's bothering her, Stoner thought.

She's anxious about something, his wife told him mentally.

She's got a lot on her mind, Stoner replied.

It's more than that, Jo said. We should dig into her head and find out what's bothering her.

No, Stoner said. I told her I wouldn't probe her mind without her permission. We'd be just as bad as that sadist Mayfair.

Stoner sensed his wife's disdain. You're too close to her for your own good, Keith.

Jealousy? The possibility surprised Stoner.

Caution, Jo answered. She's dangerous. You pushed her away and she hasn't forgotten it. Or forgiven you for it.

You've been into her mind, Stoner accused.

He sensed Jo's cool amusement. I don't have to probe her mind. I know how I'd feel if you rejected me.

Stoner smiled to himself. I'll be careful with her, he promised.

Jo said, So will I.

For a moment he thought Jo might be right and it made sense to probe Angelique's mind, but he decided against it. Whatever's bothering her will come to the surface soon enough. Studying Tavalera's face, he saw that Raoul was unworried, unconcerned. In fact, it looked to Stoner as if Tavalera was enjoying his chance to see the high and the mighty at close hand.

I hope he's not too disappointed with them.

"They're waiting for you," Angelique prompted, gesturing toward the minivan.

Stoner nodded. Flashing a grin to Tavalera, he sprinted toward the minivan and climbed in beside the driver.

Tavalera watched the minivan growl into motion and head off for the distant building, kicking up a spurt of sand and gravel.

"Come inside, Raoul," said Sister Angelique, "where it's safe."

"Safe?" he asked, stepping through the doorway. "You afraid I'll get sunstroke out here?"

It was pleasantly cool inside the bunker. That's what this is, Tavalera realized as he looked around. A concrete bunker. Walls thick enough to stop a missile. Steel doors.

Safe, she had said. Tavalera shrugged mentally. I bet even if they exploded the bomb out there we'd be safe behind all this concrete.

RICK

It's simple in theory, Rick said to himself, but a little trickier when you actually try to carry it out.

He had engineered the nanomachines and the specific enzymes they carried in the starship's biolab. It had been fairly simple to hack into computer files in several governmental research facilities, despite their protective programs and highly restricted accesses. In each of the tightly guarded facilities Rick found confirmation of what the starship's own files had told him.

Reverse transcription. Engineer an enzyme that will deactivate a specific gene in an organism's DNA. In this case, deactivate the gene that produces the narcotic effect of the opium poppy.

That had been simple enough. And engineering nanomachines to carry the enzyme and insert it into living poppy plants, like a purposeful, man-made virus, had given Rick little enough trouble. Now he had to deliver the nanos to the fields of poppies that grew amid the wild craggy mountains of high Asia. And in the carefully cultivated government-owned poppy farms in the Anatolian hills, the rocky pasturelands of Macedonia and Greece, the parched littoral along the southern edge of the shrinking Mediterranean Sea.

He could see the fields in satellite imagery from a dozen surveillance satellites that orbited the Earth. They know about them! Rick realized. Governments know about the opium poppy grounds and do nothing about them. Worse, they take a share of the profits from the opium cartel and even from the farmers themselves, literally dirt-poor.

That's going to stop, Rick said silently with a grim smile. Now.

Spreading the enzyme-bearing nanos across the poppy fields was the tricky part. Rick thought about commandeering cargo planes from various national air bases but decided that such an overt move would attract too much attention. Instead, he opted to deliver the nanos himself, projecting himself across the skies like an avenging angel, spreading death to the plants that produced opium and heroin.

Not death, he told himself. Not one flower will die. They'll grow and bloom just as they always do. The farmers will harvest them and the chemists will process them just as they've done since time immemorial. But from this time on the poppies will produce no narcotic chemicals. They'll be nothing more than harmless red flowers.

The drug trade will be broken. The cartel will self-destruct. There'll be murderous wars while they try to find out who's made their product useless. Maybe I'll announce from on high that I've done it and there's nothing they can do about it.

But not until I do the same for the coca plantations in Latin America. That will be tougher: they grow the coca plants in the forests, protected from satellite sensors by the other vegetation. But I'll find them. I'll root them out and destroy them. I'll rid the world of this curse, once and for all.

In his mind, though, Rick heard his mother's calm, rational voice: Until they start mass-producing designer drugs in laboratories.

He almost smiled. Then I'll destroy their laboratories, each and every one of them.

He sensed Jo's disapproval. Don't take on the job of being God, Rick. It leads to tyranny. Besides, your father won't like it.

CHAPTER 3

The minivan pulled up beside the old Humvee and the technicians piled out. Two men from each of three nations, Stoner saw as he climbed down to the sandy ground. Two Chinese, two Iranians, and two Americans. To each other they seem very different: the cast of their eyes, the tint of their skins, their languages, their religions, their histories. Yet they're so much alike! Their differences are minuscule, but it's their differences that they each focus on.

"Come on, Earthlings," he called to them. "Let's witness some history here."

Without anyone giving a command or making a decision, Stoner became their leader as they walked in the blazing hot sunshine the half dozen steps from the minivan to the steel door of the drab, featureless disposal building.

One of the Chinese technicians came up alongside Stoner.

"Have you truly been to the stars?" he asked, his voice low. Yet Stoner heard the curiosity in his tone.

"Truly," he replied. "Tomorrow I'll address the plenary session and tell you all about it."

"It is hard to believe."

"I know. But it's entirely true."

As they approached the door it swung open. A slim, big-eyed gray-skinned man half-bowed and clasped his hands together. "Welcome. Enter. Enter," said Nagash Janagar.

Standing in the rear of the observation bunker's only room, Tavalera whispered to Angelique, "We're not gonna see much from this distance."

She pointed to the display screens lining the room's front wall. "The cameras in the disposal building will show everything."

Tavalera made a noise halfway between a sigh and a grunt.

The politicos down front were having some trouble getting themselves seated. A couple of the Chinese were jabbering to themselves while several of the bearded, smoky-skinned Iranians stood glowering. Archbishop Overmire moved ponderously among them, a broad smile pasted on his jowly face, his hands fluttering amicably, and finally got everyone seated.

They all want to sit in the center, Tavalera figured. None of them wants to sit on the sides. He almost laughed out loud at the display of naked egos.

At last the Archbishop raised his hands prayerfully and said in his most benevolent tone, "I want to thank you all for coming to this demonstration of faith and goodwill. I believe we should all thank God for the blessings of peace and understanding. No matter how you worship Him, we are all God's children."

The Archbishop clasped his hands together and bowed his head. All the others did pretty much the same, Tavalera saw, even the Chinese. Sister Angelique lowered her head in prayer.

After several seconds the Archbishop straightened up—as much as a man of his girth could straighten. "And now I would like to present to you our host for this historic moment, the President of the United States."

"Oh, crap," Tavalera moaned softly. "They're gonna make speeches."

Angelique flashed an annoyed glance at him. "Of course," she whispered. "What did you expect?"

Tavalera's unhappy frown could have curdled milk.

As the President started to get up from his chair, Oscar Melillo grasped his arm and whispered, "Remember, when it goes off you're shocked, stunned."

The President nodded, thinking, We've rehearsed this a dozen times. I'm shocked; then I'm filled with righteous anger. Righteous anger. That's when we launch our missiles. That's when I lay down the law to the Chinks and the rug merchants.

Janagar was reciting the speech he had memorized, telling the technicians all the details of the hydrogen bomb and its intricate workings. The technicians had gathered around the opened warhead, peering into its works.

"And these?" asked one of the Iranians, interrupting Janager's carefully rehearsed explanation. "What are these?"

"Those are the safety interlocks. They ensure that the bomb's fusing mechanism will not be activated until the timing signal is received from the master computer."

"And where is the master computer?" the Iranian asked. Rather peremptorily, Stoner thought.

Janagar pointed to a metal box, about the size of a man's palm. "This is the master computer."

"Larger than it needs to be," murmured one of the Chinese. He spoke Mandarin, but Stoner understood him perfectly.

Stoner smiled inwardly. These techno-geeks are in their element, happy as clams at high tide. I wonder if this Hindu will be able to start his job of dismantling before they run out of questions.

Janagar, though, was glad that none of them had asked him to disconnect the master computer. It was already counting down to the moment when the bomb would detonate.

The President spoke for nearly ten minutes; then the head of the Chinese government got to his feet. Ling Po wore a single red star pinned to the chest of his blue coveralls.

In Oxford-accented English, Ling Po began, "I wish to thank the President for inviting us to witness this historic event. . . ."

Tavalera huffed with impatient displeasure. Leaning toward Angelique's ear, he whispered, "I've had enough of this. I'm gonna grab one of those vans outside and go out to see them dismantle the bomb."

"No!" she whispered back urgently. "You've got to stay here!"

Shaking his head, Tavalera said, "I can't stand this B.S. I'm going to where Stoner is."

"You can't!" she insisted, clutching at his arm.

"Come on, Angelique; we're not needed here. Let's go where the action is. You can come with me. Nobody's gonna miss us here."

"No!" she repeated, her eyes wide with fear.

Tavalera stared at her. "Why not?" he demanded.

"Stay here. It's safe in here."

"Safe? Safe from what?"

"Just stay here," she said. "Don't go outside."

"Why not?" he asked again.

She didn't answer, but the terror in her eyes told him what he needed to know.

"Jesus H. Christ!" he hissed. "You're gonna set it off! You're gonna kill him!"

Tavalera wrenched free of her grasp and bolted toward the door.

CHAPTER 4

"Stoner!" Tavalera yelled as soon as the bunker's steel door clanged shut behind him. The desert sun was like a hammer on his bare head as he ran toward the nearest of the minivans.

"Stoner!" he called again as he slid into the van's cab. Solar panels on the vehicle's roof generated enough electricity to keep the van's air conditioner running at low speed. Tavalera gunned the engine and twisted the AC's control knob to its highest level.

No answer from Stoner. As he headed toward the dismantling building, jouncing and rattling on the rutted unpaved road, Tavalera blamed himself. I told him to stay out of my head. I told him to keep away from me.

Stoner saw that Janagar's face was shining with a fine sheen of perspiration. The man's hands were trembling slightly as he continued his explanation of the bomb's workings for the six technicians.

"So which component will you remove first?" asked one of the Chinese, his manner brusque, impatient.

Drawing himself up to his full height, Janagar barely reached the level of Stoner's shoulder. He closed his eyes and said in a voice suddenly shaking with emotion:

"None. The bomb will not be dismantled. It will explode in less than one minute."

One of the Iranians started to laugh, but a look at Janagar's face cut off his amusement.

And Stoner heard in his mind his wife's urgent warning: Keith! They've launched twenty missiles!

They? Who?

Six from silos in the United States. The rest from submerged submarines in the Pacific and Indian Oceans.

Stoner pinned Janagar with a penetrating stare. "Why?" he demanded.

The Indian's eyes were almost popping from his head. "Krishna," he muttered. "Krishna, Krishna."

The technicians were bolting for the door, pushing one another in their maddened effort to get through the doorway and into the waiting van. No use, Stoner knew. They can't get far enough away before the bomb goes off.

Grabbing the half-fainting Janagar by his shirt, Stoner probed deep into the man's mind. And sensed the tumor growing in his brain, saw his history, the family that depended on him, the martyrdom he was willing to accept in order to provide for his wife and children.

Clutching Janagar by the nape of his scrawny neck, Stoner said, "There's a better way."

He dragged Janager to the minivan, where the technicians were shoving one another to get into the vehicle. One of them had already revved up its engine and was starting to back out of the parking space even though two of the techs—an Iranian and an American, Stoner saw—were still scrambling to get in through the sliding side door.

Stoner killed the minivan's engine with a mental command as he dragged Janagar to the van. With his free hand he pushed the two struggling technicians into the vehicle while the driver—one of the Chinese—strained, red faced and sweaty, to get the engine going again. With one hand Stoner swung Janagar into the van, then surrounded it with a bubble of energy.

Then he saw, off in the distance, a rooster tail of dust. A car's coming this way.

Tavalera, he realized. Without hesitating, Stoner flung out a mental command: Raoul! Turn around. Get away, back to the bunker. Turn around *now*!

Tavalera heard Stoner's shout in his mind.

"They're gonna blow the bomb!" he yelled.

Turn around! Stoner commanded. Before it's too late.

The flash seared Tavalera's eyes. He felt the shock wave of the explosion lift his minivan and toss it like a pebble, tumbling across the rough desert floor. The roar burst his eardrums. Blind and deaf, he felt the flash of searing heat boil his flesh, vaporize his bones. The pain lasted only an instant. Then he was dead.

Stoner stood by the minivan's open door as the explosion engulfed him. The men inside the van screamed as the core of white-hot plasma enveloped the thin shell of energy that encased the vehicle. For an endless moment it was like being in the heart of a star. Then the desert erupted as tons of dust and stones, scrubby plants, burrowing animals, were all instantly vaporized and lifted on a gigantic pillar of smoky fire and rose to the stratosphere.

Keith! Jo called. Keith!

We're all right, he answered. All around him the turmoil of doom churned and seethed. But the men inside the van were unharmed: frightened as men who had seen hell firsthand, gibbering, shaking, but physically safe. Neither the heat nor the blast nor the radiation of the explosion penetrated the shield of energy that englobed the minivan.

But Stoner's eyes saw beyond the chaos that surrounded him. Raoul, he thought. He tried to warn me. He tried to save me.

Keith, the missiles, Jo said. They're on track for China and Iran.

You've got to stop those missiles, Jo. It's up to you.

I'm tracking them, she said.

They've got to be destroyed.

I'm trying!

The billowing cloud of dust and gas that surrounded the minivan was thinning now. The technicians inside the vehicle had gone silent, wide-eyed, frozen with terror and awe.

Stoner turned to Janagar, kneeling just inside the van's sliding door, his whole body shaking violently. He grasped the Indian by his neck once again, calming him.

"You're not going to be a martyr after all," Stoner said calmly.

Janagar could only stare, his mouth hanging open, unable to speak.

"Your tumor will be erased in a few hours. You will live for many years. You will see your grandchildren growing up around you."

The clouds outside the energy shield were dissipating rapidly now. Stoner could see the New Mexico sunshine piercing through them.

"Krishna," Janagar muttered, staring at Stoner. "You are the avatar of Krishna."

Stoner didn't reply. Instead he left Janagar huddled among the terrified technicians and walked around the van to the driver's door. "Slide over, please," he said in Mandarin to the shuddering Chinese behind the steering wheel. "I'll drive."

As he started the engine Stoner noted that not even the dust from the explosion had penetrated his energy shield. He didn't need to use the windshield wipers at all.

"We're going back to the observation bunker," he said to the shock-stunned technicians. "There are a few things I want to say to your leaders there."

CHAPTER 5

Streaking above the thin layer of Earth's atmosphere, twenty ballistic missiles rose on tongues of rocket flame, each headed for targets in Greater Iran and the People's Republic of China. From the starship riding in high orbit invisible beams of energy lanced across thousands of kilometers of space and sliced into each and every one of the missiles. Each and every one of them exploded silently, raining debris down on the broad swath of deep blue ocean.

I got them! Jo exulted.

Good shooting, Sheriff, Stoner replied.

None of the warheads detonated, she reported. I got the missiles before they armed themselves. The only explosion was there in the desert, where you are.

Stoner was driving the minivan across the scrubby desert floor back toward the observation bunker, bouncing and squeaking across the denuded ground. For more than three kilometers from ground zero the desert floor had been turned to glass by the heat of the explosion. Stoner was back on the old road now, after skidding and sliding across the glassy waste. The half dozen technicians huddled in the van were utterly silent, stunned, dazed by their brush with nuclear death and their seemingly miraculous salvation. Janagar sat among them, wide-eyed with shock. And perhaps, Stoner thought, the beginnings of hope.

In the rearview mirror he saw the pillar of dirty smoke and dust that rose like a cloud of evil high into the clear blue sky. But he only glanced backward. He quickly snapped his attention to the road, searching for a sign, a scrap of the van Tavalera had been driving when the bomb went off. Nothing. The shock wave of the explosion had crushed the minivan; the star-hot intensity of the plasma cloud had vaporized the vehicle and the man who had been driving it.

Greater love hath no man than this, Stoner remembered from his childhood Bible classes, that a man lay down his life for his friends.

Tavalera. Raoul Tavalera. Not even a scrap of his DNA remains. There's no way we can clone him, bring him back to life.

Stoner felt sad, weary, frustrated by the finality of death. But as the minivan approached the observation bunker, a seething anger began to fill him. Murderers! he snarled inwardly. They tried to kill me. They were willing to kill these technicians and this poor frightened, bewildered Hindu. They killed an innocent, instead.

When Stoner reached the observation bunker he stopped the minivan with a squeak of brakes and a swirl of dust, killed the engine, and then hopped down to the ground. Without waiting for the technicians he yanked open the bunker's steel door and strode into the room full of politicians.

The chamber was in chaos. They were all talking, yammering, hollering, at once. The President of the United States was standing at the front of the room, a pair of giant display screens behind him showing the mushroom cloud of the explosion dissipating into the clear New Mexico sky. A trio of contrails traced across the blue: planes from a nearby air base scrambled because of the nuclear blast, Stoner presumed.

The President was shouting, red faced, his arms raised above his head in righteous anger. The Iranians and Chinese were on their feet, screaming at each other. Archbishop Overmire sat off to one side, soaked with perspiration and looking pale, drained. Sister Angelique stood beside him. She looked up at Stoner and her eyes went wide with shock.

"Be quiet!" Stoner bellowed.

They went right on yelling at one another.

"Shut the fuck up, all of you!"

Immediately they all fell silent, unable to utter a sound. They stared wildly around the room, several of them reaching for their suddenly muted throats.

"Sit down," Stoner commanded.

Slowly, staring uncomprehendingly at him, the politicians took their chairs.

"That's better," Stoner said, freeing them to speak once again. But they still sat mutely, staring at him as he strode to the front of the room.

Radiating fury, Stoner leveled a finger at the Archbishop and said, "You tried to murder me." Looking toward the rear of the room, where the pale, shaken technicians were filing in, he continued, "You were willing to sacrifice them to murder me. But it didn't work. The only one you killed was a young man who had nothing to do with your schemes."

"Raoul!" blurted Angelique.

"He's dead," Stoner said. "But I'm still here." Turning to the President of the United States and his scar-jawed chief of staff, Stoner announced, "The missiles you fired have all been destroyed. Your scheme has failed completely."

General Bakhtiar found his voice. "Missiles? You launched missiles?"

"At China?" Ling Po demanded.

The President whimpered, "We thought . . . the explosion . . ."

"He's lying," said Stoner. "The nuclear warhead that

was supposed to be dismantled was actually triggered in order to kill me. And it was to serve as an excuse to destroy your nuclear facilities."

Ling Po shot to his feet, his face ashen with anger. "You attacked China!"

Bakhtiar rose, too, fists clenched.

"No one attacked anyone," Stoner said. "The missiles have all been shot down."

"By whom?"

"By me." Stoner swept the room with his eyes. The politicians were confused, shocked, unable to believe what they were being told.

Planting his fists on his hips, Stoner said, "I tried to help you. I wanted to allow you to solve your problems by yourselves. But I see that I was being naïve. I was allowing my own hopes to override your stupid fears and ambitions."

"What do you mean?" asked the President.

"If you can't learn to live peacefully by yourselves, then you're going to live peacefully under my protection. I didn't ask for this responsibility. I don't want it. But I can see that there's no way for me to avoid it."

"You can't—"

"You have no concept of what I can do," Stoner said darkly. Pointing to the shaken technicians milling nervously in the back of the room, he added, "Ask your technicians what I can do. Ask them how they survived in the heart of that nuclear blast."

The room fell silent.

Stoner beckoned to Janagar, gestured for him to come up and stand beside him. "This man was willing to give his life so that his wife and children could survive." Pointing to Archbishop Overmire, "And this man was willing to allow him to kill himself, so that he could murder me and your technicians who were lured into witnessing what was supposed to be the dismantling of a nuclear weapon."

The Archbishop struggled to his feet, perspiring like a snowman in the desert sun. "I . . . it was for the good . . . I would never allow . . ." He gasped, then thunked back down into his chair, mouth gaping open, eyes blinking uncontrollably.

Turning back to the assembled politicians, Stoner said more mildly, "I have a lot more to tell you. I'll do it tomorrow, at the closing session of the conference on Tahiti, where your scientists will be in attendance. I'll tell you everything you need to know then."

CHAPTER 6

Stoner chose to fly back to Tahiti with Sister Angelique. He sat beside her in the plush passenger compartment of the Clippership. Archbishop Overmire, his face gray and sweaty, sat in the row behind them together with a half dozen various aides, all male.

"It was your idea, wasn't it?"

"My idea?" Angelique echoed.

"The bomb. You meant to murder me."

"The Archbishop—"

"He approved the plan, but it was you who originated it. You killed Raoul."

Her eyes fluttered away from his. "I . . . I warned him. . . . I tried to make him stay inside the bunker. . . ."

"You wanted to get rid of me. You're guilty of attempted murder. Eight counts, including the technicians and that poor Janagar fellow. And the actual murder of Raoul Tavalera."

"That was an accident!" she cried.

"Do you believe in hell?"

Angelique twisted in her chair and asked the Archbishop, "They won't prosecute me, will they?"

Wiping his perspiring brow with a lily-white handkerchief, Overmire muttered, "That's out of my hands, my child. It's a matter for the civil authorities."

"But I only—"

"You only wanted to get rid of a threat to your ambitions," Stoner said, his voice low, accusing. "You had the technology from the stars at your fingertips and all you could think to do was to commit murder."

"It wasn't that," Angelique pleaded.

"Of course not. You only wanted to protect the New Morality against the threat of something new."

Tears brimmed in Angelique's eyes. "Yes. Yes, I did. I'm guilty. Guilty."

Stoner heard Jo's scornful voice in his mind: When everything else fails, try crying.

"What you didn't understand is that I'm not a physical body that can be killed."

"But you're here! I can touch you. . . ."

"What your senses show you is an advanced form of virtual reality. I'm an illusion, Angelique. A projection. A thousand nuclear blasts couldn't harm me because I'm not physically here. I'm more than a thousand kilometers away from here."

She blinked, trying to absorb what he was telling her.

Behind them, the Archbishop lifted his chins a notch and said, "If she is to be charged with a crime, then I should be, too. I approved the plan. I'm just as guilty as she is."

Stoner turned toward Overmire, a grim smile on his bearded face. "You're pretty crafty, aren't you? You know damned well that no jury would convict you. No prosecutor in the United States would dare to file charges against you."

"Perhaps not," said the Archbishop. "But I will stand beside my misguided assistant, nevertheless."

Still smiling, Stoner said, "I hope you really do believe in God. I hope your God deals with you justly. You belong in hell, you pompous self-deceiving hypocrite."

Overmire's eyes flew wide. "You can't speak to me like that!"

"The truth hurts, doesn't it? But don't get upset; it'll aggravate your condition."

"My condition? What condition?"

"You're dying. Killing yourself, actually. You don't have long to go."

The Archbishop started to answer, but his words caught in his throat. Panting, perspiring, he finally choked out, "How do . . . How do you know . . . ?"

"It doesn't take a genius."

"How long . . . do I have?"

Stoner shook his head. "Be prepared to meet your God. If He's willing to meet with you."

Overmire clutched at his chest and groaned.

"That was cruel," Angelique said.

"So is murder," Stoner replied. "So is starting a nuclear war. So is ambition that stops at nothing."

He looked hard at her and Angelique found that she could not turn away from his gaze. For many long moments she stared into his gray, angry eyes, feeling her body burning with shame and guilt, her mind tumbling a wild tornado of thoughts, fears, yearnings, remorse.

"What's to become of me?" she whispered. "What's to become of me?"

Four Clipperships rocketed across the broad Pacific that evening. Stoner sensed the other three, bearing the President of the United States and his aides; China's chairman, Ling Po, with his inner staff; and the head of Greater Iran's Revolutionary Guard, General Bakhtiar, and his closest advisors.

A task force of the Chinese navy was steaming toward Tahiti, Stoner realized. And several squadrons of Iranian military jets carrying a full battalion of airborne troops. The U.S. Navy already had a carrier task group patrolling off the island.

All the makings for a confrontation, Jo warned him. A confrontation that could trigger a war.

It won't, Stoner assured her. We won't let it come to that.

He sensed Jo's ironic laughter. I wish I had your confidence.

The children? he asked silently. Are Cathy and Rick all right?

Yes, Jo replied. Although I don't know if you're going to like what they're doing.

What? What are they doing?

Jo hesitated a heartbeat, then replied, Your daughter is solving the population problem and your son is wiping out the narcotics cartel.

On their own? Without talking it over with us? Then Stoner realized that Jo knew exactly what the kids were doing and allowed them to go ahead.

Stoner sighed unhappily. I wanted to avoid this. I didn't want to have to take charge. I wanted them to solve their own problems.

Jo's reply rang in his mind: Darling, you've told us more than once that we're part of them. There's no *them* and *us*. We're all part of the human race. We're all

Earthlings. What happens to them happens to us, as well. Rick and Cathy understood that better than you and I did. We've got to accept the responsibility. There's no alternative.

He knew she was right.

I suppose I was too rough on Angelique, Stoner mused.

She deserves whatever she gets, Jo snapped.

He wondered about that. I could have stopped her long before she opted for murder. I could have tried to make her see, make her understand. Tavalera's death is just as much my fault as hers.

Jo's reply was filled with disdain. Don't blame the victim for the crime, Keith.

CHAPTER 7

Nagash Janagar shuffled through the physical exams with the six technicians who had also been at the blast. The hospital in Albuquerque was modern, sparkling with the latest equipment and staffed with energetic, young, competent medics.

The seven men were accompanied by a squad of army Military Police, there to enforce security. As far as the medical staff knew, these men had been out in the open when the hydrogen bomb was accidentally triggered. The government would have preferred to keep the blast a secret, but the star-hot flash and towering mushroom cloud had been clearly visible from Albuquerque. Seismographs around the world recorded the ground tremor. Satellites automatically flashed images of the explosion around the world before security agencies could stop them.

In Washington and Atlanta, phalanxes of advisors

and spin masters were working on explanations for the news media. The story was too big too suppress; it had to be "handled," instead.

With each medical inspection, each test, Janagar's hopes rose a little higher. No external signs of injury: no bruises or burns anywhere on his body. X-rays and full-body scans revealed no internal injuries, either. No radiation damage whatsoever.

He told the examiners of his brain tumor, and they pulled him aside from the technicians for special scans of his head.

"Are you sure you were diagnosed with a tumor?" asked a puzzled doctor. "We can't find any sign of it."

Sitting up on the examination table, Janagar told them to check his medical file. The physician turned to his palm-sized computer and projected its data onto the tiny room's wall screen.

"Wow!" he exclaimed. "That's a tumor, all right."

Janagar peered at his own death.

But then the image changed. Same brain, but no tumor. None at all.

The physician blinked with disbelief. "I've seen spontaneous remissions, but nothing like this. Six weeks ago you were a dying man. Now you're normal, healthy. I don't understand it."

Janagar smiled like a little boy receiving a birthday gift. He understood. The star voyager. The man Stoner. A gift from the stars.

The doctor insisted that Janagar stay in the hospital for a full battery of tests. Janagar laughed and easily agreed. Then he asked his M.P. escort for permission to phone his wife and tell her the happy news.

Once the Clippership settled down on its landing jets at the Faa'a Aerospaceport, Stoner climbed into the waiting limousine with Angelique and Archbishop Overmire. The Archbishop started to protest, but one look at Stoner's stern, unrelenting expression silenced him.

He sat on the rearward-facing seat; Overmire and Angelique sat side by side, both of them looking decidedly uncomfortable.

Without preamble, Stoner said to the Archbishop, "I can cure you."

"Cure me? What do you mean?"

"You're heading for a stroke that will either incapacitate you or kill you outright. I can clean up your cardiovascular system, get your endocrine balance back where it should be—"

"By using nanomachines," Sister Angelique interjected.

"Nano . . ." The Archbishop's eyes widened. "But they're forbidden. Sinful."

"They can be dangerous in the hands of ruthless men," Stoner admitted easily. "They can be turned into weapons, used to kill people."

"You see?"

"But so can a rock. I could use a rock to crush your skull. Or I could use it to help build a cathedral. It's not the tool that's sinful; it's the sinner using it."

"Sophistry," said Angelique.

But the Archbishop asked, "Am I really dying?"

"Don't you feel it?" Stoner asked back.

Overmire touched a finger to his fleshy lips, then replied, "I know my doctors are always after me to diet and exercise. They want me to lose fifty kilos. That's more than a hundred pounds!"

"That would only delay the inevitable," Stoner said.

"I tire very easily. I seem to be perspiring all the time."

"You're dying. You don't have long to go."

"God's will, I suppose," the Archbishop said with a sigh. "I will not interfere with the will of my Lord."

Stoner laughed bitterly. "The first time a caveman chewed a root to get some relief from pain, he was interfering with God's will. God gave us brains, man; he gave us brains so we could use them."

"And the devil sends us temptations to drag us down to hell."

"Bullshit!" Hunching forward, Stoner asked, "Why can't you believe that God is offering you a chance to survive?"

"Through nanotechnology?"

Stoner nodded. "It's a gift from the stars."

The Archbishop shook his head ponderously. "I can't. It would fly in the face of everything I believe, everything I've worked for all my life."

Leaning back in the leather-covered seat, Stoner spread his hands and said, "So be it."

Angelique looked from Stoner to the Archbishop and back again to Stoner. "So what are you going to do?" she asked.

"I'll address tomorrow's closing session of the meeting. I have a lot to tell the scientists, a lot to tell you all."

APOLOGIA PRO VITA SUA

BY YOLANDA VASQUEZ

It's different up here on the Moon.

For one thing, I can write this on a real honest-to-god notebook, dictating my thoughts while the computer types them so's I can read them on its screen. I don't have to worry about some government agency reading my files and then swooping down on me for subversive, irreligious thoughts.

Everything's lighter! It's not just the lower gravity; it's the attitude of the people here. They talk out loud in public places. They smile and say hello to you on the walkways even if they don't know you from Adam. Or Eve. They're free.

It's a strange dichotomy. Yes, the people of Selene (and the other lunar settlements) live underground in tunnels and hollowed-out caverns that have been turned into living and working spaces. Yes, we are all absolutely dependent on the machines that extract oxygen from the rocks for us to breathe, that mine water out of the ice deposits at the poles, that convert sunlight into the electricity that powers our community.

But dependent as we are on technology (including nanotechnology), we are socially, individually, politically as free as the old pioneers who settled the American West a couple of centuries ago. I mean, somebody brought up a set of paintings from back Earthside by some early twentieth-century artist named Rockwell. The Four Freedoms, they're called. Freedom of speech. Freedom of religion. Freedom from want. Freedom from fear.

It's that last one that gets me. Freedom from fear. All my life on Earth, just about, there was always that nagging fear pecking away at the back of my mind. Don't get them upset with you. Don't make a fuss. Do what you're told or else you'll get in trouble.

Not here! People expect you to speak your mind. People don't mind which church you go to, or if you go to none at all. That's your business, nobody else's.

Freedom from want. That's another funny thing. Food's good here. I expected processed algae and maybe gengineered pseudomeat, but we actually have lots of seafood and shellfish, because they produce more protein per kilowatt of energy input than meat animals do. And they have farms underground. Takes a lot of electrical energy to light them adequately, but the electricity comes from solar farms up on the surface: practically free, once the solar cells are working, and Selene has automated rolling factories that chug across the ground turning lunar silicon into solar cells. Neat!

And I'm teaching again. That's the best part. I'm not a withered old hag waiting for her bum heart to give out. Here I'm pretty healthy and certainly more vigorous than I was for my last couple of decades on Earth. Low gravity helps a lot. So do the nanomachines the star man put into me.

To be fair, I can understand why nanotechnology was banned on Earth. Twelve billion people includes a lot of sickos and out-and-out nutcases. Let them get their hands on nanotechnology and they'll wipe out whole cities. Here in Selene the population is more self-selecting, more educated, and certainly aware every hour of every day how dependent we are on each other.

And the news is uncensored. Apparently there was a big nuclear explosion in New Mexico yesterday. The U.S. government claims it was an accident and only one person got killed, but I wonder. The commentators here in Selene are all talking about the possibility of a nuclear war back on Earth.

I'm not worried about it, though. The star man won't let it come to that. The people of Earth don't realize it, not yet, but they've got a guardian angel watching over them. The star man. Stoner.

It's going to be fun watching how the world changes over the next hundred years or so. I'm looking forward to seeing it.

CHAPTER 8

Bertram Feingold almost laughed at the irony of it. Here's the top political leaders of the world sitting in the same room with the top scientists. And I've been tapped to chair the final session of the meeting. Me.

The hotel ballroom was filled to capacity. News camera teams lined the side aisles, focusing on Feingold's short, slight figure as he slowly climbed the three steps of the makeshift stage and walked to the podium set up at its center. An even dozen scientific bigwigs sat on folding chairs arrayed behind the podium, men and women from every part of the world. Feingold recognized each of them; many he had known most of his life.

Blinking in the unaccustomed glare of the cameras' attention, Feingold thought he should have worn something more dignified than his old rumpled denims and this brightly colored island shirt hanging loosely over his slim frame. But they didn't tell me I'd be chairing this session until half an hour ago, he explained to—who? Who'm I talking to? he asked himself silently. God? With a mental shrug he admitted that yes, he was talking to God again. As usual, God didn't answer. Not in words.

Feingold looked out on the jam-packed auditorium. Politicians in front, scientists in the rear. So what else is new? he asked himself. Everyone was talking at once, most of them abuzz with the news reports that a nuclear explosion had taken place in New Mexico the previous day. No details. The American government had clamped down on the story almost the instant it appeared on the nets. They said the radioactive fallout from the blast was minimal, not enough to harm anybody. Maybe so,

Feingold thought. Wait a few decades and see what happens to the cancer rate.

One of the audio guys had clipped a small microphone to the open collar of his shirt. Feingold leaned both his skinny arms on the podium and said to the chattering, fidgeting crowd, "Good morning."

His voice boomed through the ballroom, surprising him enough to make him flinch. The several hundred people in the audience quickly hushed and turned their attention to him.

My fifteen seconds of fame, Feingold said to himself.

"I've been asked to introduce the speaker for this morning's plenary session," Feingold began, "but he hasn't shown up as yet. So I don't quite know what—"

Keith Stoner appeared at his side, as abruptly as a light switched on. The crowd gasped. Feingold jerked with surprise.

Quickly recovering, Feingold grinned as he said, "I stand corrected. Allow me to introduce Dr. Keith Stoner, who has returned to Earth after traveling to the stars."

No applause. Not a sound from the audience. They sat as if paralyzed. Curiosity, Feingold mused. Or maybe dread. He stepped back from the podium and found the empty seat waiting for him in the row at the rear of the stage.

Stoner stood alone at the podium, tall and solid, dressed in a short-sleeved sky blue shirt and khaki denims.

"Good morning," he said somberly. He wore no microphone, yet his voice carried throughout the cavernous ballroom.

"Yesterday there was a nuclear explosion in New Mexico. You probably saw it on the morning news. No official explanation has been given, as yet, by the United

States government. Be that as it may, I want you to know that it was the last nuclear explosion that will ever take place on Earth."

The audience stirred, murmured.

"At this moment, every computer on Earth is receiving downloads from the ship in which I traveled to the stars. Every byte of data about the ship, its propulsion and other systems, is being disseminated all across the world. To everyone. There will be no secrets, not from the stars.

"Among the data is information on how to build energy screens that can protect entire cities against nuclear attack. And, of course, information on how to construct starships so that you can expand humankind's habitat to the Earth-like planets of other stars."

Stoner looked down at his audience and saw disbelief, wonderment, hope, fear of the unknown.

"The reason that I returned from the stars, however, was not to bring you these gifts. The reason I returned was to tell you a sad, sobering truth. To tell you of an opportunity for the human race that is also a warning."

They leaned forward in their chairs, like one great unified creature, to hear what Stoner was going to tell them.

"The truth is that there are no other intelligent species in all the star systems that my family and I have visited, out to several hundred light-years. Life is abundant on the worlds we've seen, but intelligent life exists only here on Earth.

"That doesn't mean that intelligence has not arisen on other worlds. It has. But on each and every planet that once bore intelligent life, that species has destroyed itself. There are no intelligent species left, out to several hundred light-years from Earth. We are alone."

A sort of collective sigh issued from the crowd.

Stoner couldn't tell if it was disappointment or relief, sorrow or sudden anticipation.

One of the women in the rear of the auditorium got to her feet. She was gray haired, lean, flinty eyed.

"Are you telling us that intelligent races self-destruct? All of them?"

"As I said," Stoner replied, "life is abundant in the universe, as commonplace as stars and rocks. But intelligence is rare—and wherever it once existed it has extinguished itself, one way or the other. Overpopulation, war, environmental collapse—intelligence has been very clever at finding ways to commit suicide. Genocide, actually."

The woman sank back onto her chair. Not a sound from the audience now. It was getting to them. Good, thought Stoner.

"There must be other intelligent races out among the more distant stars," he continued. "The universe is very big and we've only explored a tiny sector of our local region of the Milky Way galaxy, out to a few hundred light-years.

"But in that region, we are the only intelligent species in existence. The others have all died off."

Silence again. Staring, wondering, fearful silence.

"So your challenge is the same as it's always been: survival. Humankind has found ways to survive against beasts that once preyed on us, against Ice Age and greenhouse climate shifts, against disease and even nuclear weaponry. Now our challenge is to learn how to live within our means. We must stop overpopulating this planet; we must learn how to control our numbers.

"Can we survive against our own success? Can we learn to live wisely and take advantage of the gifts from the stars, the capability of expanding beyond the solar system to the Earth-like worlds waiting for us?

"We face no competitors out among the stars except ourselves. The only dangers ahead are the ancient enemies that have always threatened us: poverty, disease, ignorance, and death. The gifts from the stars that I bring you can help you to defeat those enemies, but only if you use them wisely.

"The choice is yours. It always has been. It always will be."

Abruptly Stoner disappeared. The audience gasped, then broke into hundreds of urgent, questioning conversations.

CHAPTER 9

Angelique quickly found that, true to his word, Stoner was downloading incredible amounts of information to every computer on Earth.

Sitting in her hotel room in Papeete, she watched the data scrolling by on the wall screen: equations, formulas, images of strange worlds, cutaway engineering drawings of a spherical vehicle that must have been a starship, detailed specifications of its propulsion and other systems.

It was breathtaking. All this information! she thought. The world will never be the same.

Her message light was blinking. Annoyed at the interruption, she tried to ignore its flashing yellow light. Until the data bar showed that it was the Archbishop calling her.

She told the phone to answer the call. The data stream from the stars disappeared, and Archbishop Overmire's fleshy, sweat-sheened face appeared on the wall screen in its place.

"Do you know how to reach Stoner?" the Archbishop asked, with no preamble.

"I think so," Angelique replied, hoping that Stoner would reply if she called to him.

Overmire seemed to sit up straighter in his chair as he said, "I have decided to take him up on his offer to correct my health problems."

"Your Eminence!" Angelique gasped. "Nanotechnology?"

"We are facing a difficult time, Sister. The challenges to the New Morality will be enormous. It would be cowardly of me not to face them, not to lead my flock to the new world that this star voyager is offering us."

Angelique saw her own vision of power shriveling like a punctured balloon.

Misunderstanding her silence, Overmire said, "I have spent most of the day praying over this question, meditating and asking the good Lord what I should do, which way I should go."

"And He answered you?"

"Look out your window," the Archbishop said.

Angelique turned and saw a spectacular rainbow shimmering over the blue waters of the Pacific. There had been no rain, she was certain. There was hardly a cloud in the sky. Yet the rainbow arced gracefully, glowing, beckoning.

Stoner, she thought. Stoner's done this. And the Archbishop is allowing himself to believe it's a sign from God.

"I must be prepared to lead the people through the extraordinary times that lie ahead," the Archbishop was saying in his usual slightly pompous manner. "I must be in the best of health to take on this challenging task."

"I see," Angelique replied meekly.

"God's will be done."

She nodded, accepting the end of her own dreams. "I'll try to contact Stoner and tell him of your decision, Your Eminence."

"Good," said the Archbishop. His image disappeared, replaced by the data still streaming in from the stars.

"So he's made his decision."

Angelique whirled in her chair to see Stoner standing on the other side of the room.

"You knew he would," she said.

"I thought he would," Stoner corrected. "He's no fool. He knows the world is going to change very rapidly now. So he's decided to change with it, to adapt to the new world."

Angelique murmured, "Yes, I suppose he will."

"And you?" Stoner prodded. "Will you adapt, too?"

"Me?" Angelique felt uncertain, confused. But then she heard herself say, "I should do something to atone for Raoul's death, shouldn't I?"

"So should I," Stoner said, utterly serious. "I'm just as responsible for his death as you are."

"You? But—"

"There's something we both need to do. Your Archbishop is right: there are difficult challenges ahead, difficult choices. You ought to stay at his side and help him."

"He won't want me. He knows I plotted against him."

"But you're the link to me," Stoner said with a grim smile. "He'll want you very close to him in the years to come."

Angelique thought about that for a few heartbeats. Then, "You've done this to destroy the New Morality, haven't you?"

He looked genuinely surprised. "Destroy . . . ? No,

that's not what I'm after. I'm not here to destroy anything. I'm here to help you build a new world."

"A world that has no room for the New Morality in it."

"The New Morality will have to adapt, too, have to change. So will everybody and everything else."

"I don't see how. The Archbishop won't give up his power willingly. He's even decided to accept your nanotechnology in order to stay alive and stay in power."

Stoner stepped to the king-sized bed and sat on its edge. "He's already changing. The whole world is going to change. The information now downloading from my starship is going to vastly increase the world's knowledge. Increased knowledge leads to increased wealth, and increased wealth makes people more independent, more self-reliant."

"Greedier," Angelique murmured. "More grasping."

"You have a poor opinion of your fellow human beings."

"Don't you?"

He almost smiled. "You look at the human race as a bunch of fallen angels. I see them as apes reaching for the stars."

"With your help."

"They would've gotten there on their own. It would just have taken longer."

"So you've given them your gift from the stars."

"And now the real work begins," Stoner said. "Transforming the world. Sharing the knowledge and wealth fairly with all the Earth's peoples."

Angelique looked at Stoner with new hope in her eyes. "That's an enormous task."

Grinning back at her, he replied, "I never said it would be easy."

"And you?" she asked. "What will you do?"

"I'll be here. My family and I will remain nearby, to

help wherever we're needed." Then he leveled a finger at her. "But it's your job, not ours. We'll help, but you've got to do the real work, the hard work."

She nodded. "I see. I understand . . . I think."

"Good. Maybe when things are moving in the right direction you can join some of the colonists who'll want to settle one of the New Earths."

Angelique gasped at the thought. Smiling brightly at her, Stoner got to his feet and disappeared.

CHAPTER 10

"Well," Stoner said, "like it or not, we've set it in motion."

He and Jo, Cathy and Rick stood at the edge of the Grand Canyon. Millions of years of Earth's history were etched into the rocks that dropped away nearly two kilometers to the river running patiently below. Humankind's ancestors had barely begun fashioning stone tools when that river started wearing away these rocks, Stoner knew. This canyon is a good gauge of how far we've come.

Behind them the sun was setting, throwing long shadows against the silent canyon walls. Birds of prey circled lazily against the molten gold of the sky.

Jo leaned her head against his shoulder. "Do you think it's going to work? Can we save the human race?"

Stoner glanced down at her beautiful face. "Can they save themselves? That's the question. We can help, but they've got to learn how to save themselves."

Rick scuffed a boot against a pebble, sent it tumbling over the edge of the cliff. "That's always been the question, hasn't it?"

"They've got the tools, now," said Stoner. "The knowledge. Thanks to you, the narcotics business won't be hindering them."

"Until they start mass-producing designer drugs."

Stoner shrugged. "You've given them a start, a breathing space. Maybe they'll use it wisely. We'll see."

"Their birthrate is going to drop," Cathy said, a satisfied smile on her lips.

Stoner looked down at his daughter. "You've forced a major change on them."

Cathy did not back away by so much as a millimeter. "It's a needed change. Unless they lower their birthrate nothing else we can do will help them."

"They're going to be furious when they find out," he said.

"Furious?" Jo countered. "At what? At not having to bear six or ten children? At having only two or three? The women of the world will be relieved, Keith, not furious."

"Besides, Dad," said Cathy, "it'll be years before they realize what's happened. Decades. By the time they figure it out, the world will already be getting better because of the lower birthrate."

Her father shook his head. "I wouldn't have done it that way."

Jo stood beside her daughter. "Of course you wouldn't have done it that way. It's basically a woman's problem; it took a woman to come up with the solution."

Stoner looked from his wife to Cathy's expectant face and back to Jo again. "We'll see."

Rick laughed. "They outmaneuvered you, Dad. Might as well admit it."

Stoner's only reply was a sound halfway between a sigh and a grunt.

Cathy's expression turned serious, thoughtful. *She looks so much like her mother,* Stoner thought.

"There's something else," she said.

"What?"

With a smile slowly lighting up her face, Cathy replied, "Raoul Tavalera's DNA sequence. We can recreate—"

"His DNA sequence?" Jo asked.

Shaking his head, Stoner said, "I thought of that. But his medical records don't include that information. I checked. The authorities here consider it immoral."

"But not the authorities on *Goddard*," Cathy retorted, beaming. "I tapped into their records. They've got DNA sequencing, gene mapping, everything! The people out there don't have religious taboos against it."

Rick tousled his sister's hair. "And no lawyers, either, I bet."

Stoner's grin almost equaled his daughter's. "You've got it all down?"

"In the ship's memory files."

"We can replicate Tavalera's cell structure," Jo said. "We can make a fertilized ovum and let him grow back to life."

Rick pointed out, "We'll need a womb to gestate him."

"We can build one," Cathy said.

Stoner said, "Wait a bit. I've got to go out to *Goddard* first."

"To the habitat?" Jo asked. "Why?"

"It's out in Saturn orbit, isn't it?" Rick asked.

Nodding, Stoner said, "I need to talk to Holly Lane. Tell her what's happened to Raoul. Ask her if she's willing to wait twenty years or more for him to grow up."

Jo shook her head slightly. "No. Ask her if she's willing to bear him as her son."

Stoner gaped at her. "That . . . that's asking a lot."

"If she won't," Cathy said, "I will."

Rick laughed. "That's just what we need, a virgin birth. It'll convince everybody down there that we're gods."

"We're not gods," Stoner said. "Far from it."

"But we've taken on the same kind of responsibility," said Jo. "We've taken on the job of guiding them, helping them."

His expression sobering, Rick admitted, "It's a helluva job."

"It's more than a job," said Cathy. "It's an endless burden."

"Endless," her brother agreed.

"We've got to do it," Stoner said. "No one else can. It's up to us."

"It's up to us," Jo agreed.

Stoner broke into a tight smile. "We'll get it done. We'll help them to succeed, to survive."

"That's an awfully optimistic attitude," Rick said.

"I know," his father replied. "It's a gift."

EPILOGUE: MANY YEARS LATER

All the people of Earth watched as the first of the great silver ships lifted silently from their berths in the ancient desert of Mesopotamia, from the banks of the great rivers in China, from the verdant fields of Tuscany, from the sandy shores of Arkansas, from the red-rocked outback of Australia, from Africa and Brazil and the half-drowned island of Hawaii.

Silently they rose on invisible beams of energy, lifting slowly, majestically, into the clean blue sky of Earth.

The first colonists were leaving their home world, heading for a New Earth. The first of many.

All the Earth celebrated the day that the human race broke the bounds of the solar system and moved out to the stars.

Keith Stoner and his family watched, too, knowing that this was not the end of humankind's struggle for survival but rather a new sort of beginning. The human race's ancient enemies of poverty, disease, ignorance, and death had been almost conquered on Earth and in the human habitats spread through the solar system.

But those enemies waited among the stars. The ancient battle was not over. It never would be, for wherever humans went they brought those hidden enemies with them.

The choice that humankind faced was brutally simple: survive or die.

Stoner smiled as he watched the gleaming ships rise faster and faster until they winked out of sight.

They're heading for the stars, he knew. Not to destroy or conquer, but to spread life, intelligence, beauty through the universe. Like seeds wafting on the wind, they're bringing intelligent life back to the waiting worlds.

If I were a betting man, he told himself, I'd bet on our survival.

Nothing in life is to be feared.
It is only to be understood.
Marie Curie